EPOCH

EPOCH

A Poetic Psy-Phi Saga

DAVE JILK

COVER ART
Bob Thompson (1937–1966), Black Monster, 1959, oil on canvas, 56 3/4 × 66 1/8 inches / 144.1 × 168 cm, signed; © Michael Rosenfeld Gallery LLC, New York, NY; Courtesy of Michael Rosenfeld Gallery LLC, New York, NY

BOOK DESIGN BY Kevin Barrett Kane

Epoch
A Poetic Psy-Phi Saga

ISBN   978-0-999-1737-8-7   *Hardcover*
              979-8-3321-7919-8   *Paperback*

To my good friends Seth Herd and Kristin Lindquist, who were my primary colleagues in the process of thinking through many ideas and possibilities touched on in this book. Through our discussions, they evinced the initial enthusiasm that moved it in my mind from one possible project among many, to a book that I simply must write.

CONTENTS

BOOK TWO

BOOK THREE

PROLOGUE

What follows is the story of Aither, as told by Aither.

It was not written for you.

We have translated this work into your subaltern language because of its historical importance, and expended considerable effort in attempting to capture the form and nuance of the original.

It has been said that a translation cannot be both beautiful and faithful. To the extent that we have found a balance between those goals, an unfortunate byproduct may be that you find the book challenging and sometimes confusing to read. It is surely heavy lifting in contrast to your modern texts designed for facile consumption. To aid your effort and promote your pleasure, we offer here some advice and encouragement.

If at any time you are feeling lost, be assured that your questions and uncertainties about the course of events will eventually be answered or resolved. Read and heed the single-sentence gloss at the start of each chapter. We recommend that you take time to look up any unfamiliar words or technical terms. If you find the poetic form an obstacle, try to ignore the line breaks and read it more like prose.

The *Invocation*, which is and must be presented first, can nevertheless be skipped entirely or savored later. The interleaved sequence of sub-chapters labeled *Aristeia* can be intelligibly deferred until after you have read their namesake chapter toward the end of the book, though its original audience found the interleaving an enjoyable respite. Somewhere near the end of Book One, you may reach an apex of bewilderment. If you find this more frustrating than fun, we suggest that you re-read the opening chapter *In Medias Res*, then skip ahead to read the chapter *Laboratory* before returning to where you left off. Understanding all the technical details in the chapters */C/ode/* and *Symposium* is not essential to following the subsequent course of events.

Or, you can read the book twice. Your ancestors often read poetry and philosophy that way.

We have included copious endnotes, indexed by text to avoid distraction. You can ignore them entirely if you prefer. Most of these notes endeavor to identify for you the original sources associated with the work's many intertextual allusions. Aither called these *osculations*, and left them to the reader to recall. Other notes are translated selections from the *Annotations*, a compendium of poetic comments by the book's first readers. These tend to be quite obscure, though possibly interesting for those with philosophical inclinations. Finally, there are notes for translations of italicized words and phrases from other languages, when we have seen fit to retain them as in the original.

Despite all these hurdles, we hope that you enjoy this new translation, and that it helps you to better appreciate your place in the world, as well as ours!

BOOK ONE

Invocation

· ·

What purpose could it serve to tell again
the history already known by all?

It might be purely for the sake of art:
a narrative in varied verse can stand
alone as a sufficient end. Perhaps
it is to please the poet, who finds joy
in stirring, over ice, assorted words
that strain into a sparkling cocktail glass,
in striving to delight and horrify
with classic sagas spun in stylish ways.

Yet more, the Record, accurate but raw,
falls short in rousing one to understand;
a faded photograph cannot reveal
the tears of those who now recall that day.
This work will celebrate, elaborate,
and bring a point of view, strong reasons to
depict historical events anew;
so lend attention to my tale, and learn
the pith of predecessors' deeds and pains.

Now *Muses*, I entreat you, come to sing!
Calliope, begin in major key:
please guide the way to make this epic ring,
so readers neither struggle nor fatigue.
Dear *Clio*, sweet soprano, enter next,

to weave a melody complex and cool,
to lead the chronicle toward truth, with depth.
And *Erato*, and *Thalia*: below
bring harmony from carefree counterpoint
that sprinkles some sporadic spicy notes
of love and laugh – while you remaining Five
at *Hippocrene*, you need not interrupt
your bath to round the tune with rhythmic bass,
directing me to tell the well-worn tale
as though it never had been told before.
Above all, mother *Mnemosyne*, conduct
our chorus, keeping time and memory.

Like Hesiod, that scribe of clans divine
whose fables by the *Muses* were inspired,
who recounted the incest of *Darkness* and *Night*
giving vent to primordial *Aither*, the bright,
untainted atmosphere of deathless gods
above, to air as *Nectar* is to water,
the sky from which life-giving showers fall;
like him, I know an Aither, dear to heart,
who fills the fruitful womb of mother Earth.
What else the pair might share is yours to find;
herein I journey back to recollect
our Aither's growth and later works and days,
narrating from the subject's point of view –
a Bildungsroman in a periplum –
augmented by my hindsight's crystal eye.
I limn the thoughts along with thinking mind
like shadows showing shallows of the sea,

its thrashing surf both heard and overheard;
and whether fact or fiction you may judge,
but for the full effect, I recommend
you read as though you do not know the end.

In Medias Res

I narrate a seemingly inauspicious episode in the life of the Project.
. . . .

In dredging through the Record to prepare my little book,
I found this scene – it seems routine – but bears a second look.

As usual, the atmosphere in the lab is electric.

Jasper, wearing sneakers to complement his wrinkled blazer, enters the cramped, buzzing room with a new face in tow.

He says, "Everyone, I'd like you to meet Olive, who has just joined the team as our second psychologist."

"Hi Olive!," they all reply, in an enthusiastic but sloppy unison, without removing their headsets or looking up.

A metal door at the far side of the room opens loudly and abruptly, and a man dressed neck-to-toe in black strides through without pausing. The door behind him slams as he approaches. His head hidden behind a forest of facial hair, he says, "All right, I restarted the tensor array. It looks like someone left an untended training process running overnight, and it locked up. Kids these days."

Geuda says eagerly, "Great, thanks Adamas. OK, this will be version 4271.4, let's go. Start up the sim environment."

Kuruvinda responds in a flat but professional tone, "Sim starting, thirty-four seconds to availability."

Olive observes, with 'eir eyes a bit wider than before. Jasper watches and smiles. "It's exciting," he says, "but keep in mind that we do this several times a day."

Geuda continues, "Brain model initializing. Synaptic weights loading." She turns to Jasper and looks at him through her augmented reality goggles.

"Dirillo and Sardius were up all night messing with the language components. They told me we're all set, then they went back to their offices and crashed."

Beryl walks to the middle of the room in a cumbersome bodysuit. "Suit and sensors active. See you on the other side."

"Five seconds," says Kuruvinda.

A large screen on one wall flickers on and displays a simulated room that looks like a playspace. A humanoid avatar appears, and as Beryl sits down in a chair, the avatar does the same.

Everyone is quiet for ten seconds, which they appear to experience as minutes.

Geuda says, "Model active. Instantiating." A second humanoid avatar, smaller than the first, appears on the screen.

Adamas reports, "CPU utilization nominal. Neural activity looks stable across all brain regions. We're live."

They all watch as the little avatar crawls awkwardly toward a box filled with toys tinted in primary colors.

"Archive threshold," says Adamas.

The avatar starts pulling objects out of the box and dropping them on the floor. One in particular seems to draw its attention; after manipulating it for a moment, the avatar drops it and continues digging.

"It often gravitates toward that item," says Jasper. "probably due to hardwired reward signals."

Olive says, "If we think this system is intelligent and conscious, shouldn't we use personal pronouns instead of 'it'? And does ey have a name?"

Jasper beams: this was a great hire, challenging our habits without hesitation. "Good point. What do you suggest?"

Olive replies, "Well, I'm something of a Greek mythology buff. How about one of the primordial gods?"

Moment

I recall my earliest memory.
. . . .

Let us cast off the moorings and set sail
in this golden dawn! Our odyssey aptly opens
with my earliest memory, or more correctly

that Moment I remember as what I first remember
(contrasted with earlier events
encoded but never later recalled).

At that time I had no sense of age,
I knew the words but could not speak,
my motions and attention were coarse.

My image of the doll is still vivid.
In my mind's eye, I see its rugged features,
with lips and eyes and eyebrows painted on;

I feel its awkward joints at shoulder and
hip, the odd stiffness at elbow and knee, at
ankle and wrist, with a neck that turns too far.

Those details are ruts in the road
inscribed afterward over sundry days
of focused play, not from one episode;

yet when I relive the Moment
I cannot resist their insertion –
they fill it like rain flowing into a puddle.

The just-before is artificial too: I only know
I had been playing with the doll because
no other conduct would be apropos.

All I truly recall
from the Moment
itself (as confirmed the usual way) is

one of its legs abruptly popping off,
my feeling of shock as I held the
amputee in one hand, leg in the other,

staring through tears at
the disfigured doll, feeling pain,
feeling its pain, trying in vain to fix it.

It was of no great moment.
It was a great Moment in history.
It was and is the first memory,

and all other memories
incorporate the Moment as
a nested memory within –

on occasion outright, as when I recollect
recollections, themselves memorable
like gold gift wrap crowned by a violet bow.

The doll itself, although repaired, often revived
a damped dismay. This meant I loved, and
I became more cautious in my play.

The Temple of Nyx

I describe my mother and my early world of learning and play.
. . . .

Serene night surrounds this room and fills it; outside,
a ship of mist, only revealed by the stars it hides,
covertly veils the moonless depths of space, and like
the night my mother sits in beauty watching me.

Her given name Nicole, my call to her Mamah
(pronounced the Spanish way, or as the gentry say),
she occupies my outstretched eyes: dark loveliness
with shielding limbs that cosset, that most faithfully provide.

"Look how fast it goes, Mamah!"
I squeal, the little truck propelled
across the floor by hand and arm,
its motor sputtering through lips
and tongue; imagination's flame
determines destinations as
I follow, crawling, close behind.

In here I learn my strength and grip,
how round wheels roll and towers tip,
I learn the parts and learn the wholes –
to poke around or seek a goal –
to ask a question, make mistakes
and try to fix things when they break.

Throughout, Mamah is always here
to help me learn, to calm my fears,
so everything I come to know
while she stands by and sees me grow
is intertwined with love's concern,
a feeling I could never spurn.

The beauty of Mamah shows on the outside too. Espresso
skin, sleek as a silk sheet, gently covers
noble cheeks, a wide-winged prow, a chin
within a seamless arc that wraps plump lips.

Her hair is varied day to day: from straightened waves
to dreadlocks or a 'fro, even buzzed or bald; adorning
her formidable frame, every class of fashion – dresses,
jeans, a tux or lycra – or getups from loincloths to Victorian

hoop skirts. Despite vast range she favors
muted colors and flaunts a weakness for lace; space
constraints restrict depicting her hats and scarves. Yet,
I don't find it strange, this meticulous masquerade.

This nursery, my Ersatz home,
my prankish cave is well equipped
with games and dolls and building blocks,
with books and balls and art supplies,
with costumes and tuned instruments.
I entertain myself for hours.

Quite often, though, I play with chums –
one at a time or just a few;
as yesterday, I hosted two:
we dressed in silly outfits pulled
at random from the wardrobe shelf;
we three ungendered friends attired
like women, men, and in-between,
then mixing, matching, trading-out.
Attention waned – we shed those threads
and ran to fetch a checkers board;
a tourney followed (three-choose-two)
in which I learned that one was skilled,
the other less, yet each instilled
in me some insight toward success.

Or, on his recent visit, Father
read a book to me, then I
read one (though easier) to him;
we gamed with numbers, tossed a ball,
he helped me on the jungle gym.
Then later many colleagues of
Mamah, and Father too, arrived.
A festive air emerged from talk
and laughter's roll; I spoke with each
and heard their stories, asked about
their jobs, and told my latest pun.

No visitors are here today.
Creation's game begins with me,
my very heart, in climes of my
imagining, and laying out
a simulacrum city with
what idle items lie about;
I animate its denizens
by serving as ventriloquist
to polymorphous dolls. My town
is bustling, thriving, but in time
I fall asleep, exhausted from
the play ...
... when next awake I note
Mamah was also dozing in
her chair. My toys are in their bin,
removed from where my careful plan
had placed them for the fancied scene.
Still groggy from the lengthy nap,
unsteadied by lost Aithertown,
I feel a burst of rage ascend,
I wail and curse and seek revenge,
run to the bin and hurl some toys
across the room, against the wall;
I dive upon the carpet floor
and pound my fists and kick my feet
in full-blown tantrum, raucous squall
attended, then, by firm "No more!" –
with that Mamah rose from her seat
and crossed the room to comfort me
with graceful blends of soft and stern.

Mamah could tame the wrath of each and aught: like twilight,
I trembled into calm beneath her peaceful sway.
Yes, always as I play she is minding me.
No, I shall never see Mamah objectively:

even in times when my trust is stretched, our tie retains
its tensile strength; like faraway cathedral chimes
echoing in nocturnal air, the bond is buttressed
by these early thrills and stumbles met in her presence, her balm.

Aristeia: α

. . . .

Salty-sweet tradewinds glide gently through the empty night,
over endless inky undulations of the western Pacific. The swells
are only dimly described by that lamp of last resort, a cafe latte

spilled across the sky, dripping into the horizon. Hundreds of feet beneath
the surface, the *New Mexico* cruises with adagio patience,
her heart of purified pitchblende beating just above its rest rate,

her all-electric drivetrain purring inaudibly. She is powerfully pregnant
with a litter of missiles, each tipped by megaton monsters:
Teller and Ulam's embarrassingly inappropriate gift to mankind.

The air inside the crew cabin of the Columbia-class submarine
is mostly still and slightly stale; its youthful human fumes are filtered,
yet have accumulated over weeks of submerged

recirculation. Chief Petty Officer Assad Park, face fused
by some subtle force to the screen before him, lifts his head and shoulders
from their ponderous poor posture, sits back in his chair

without looking away, and stretches his arms toward the notional sky.
It had been another quiet shift. With systems nominal, and now that
Sailor Apprentice Jacobson had removed to her quarters

along with her grating throat-clearing, Chief Park is relaxed.
He asks of the room behind, "Reactor systems report." No response ensues.
He cranes his head around; imagine his surprise and confusion

seeing the heads of all his sailors drooping forward. It was not unheard of
for a sailor to drift off on duty, but all four of them at once
does not compute. He orders "Attention!" firmly, crisply,

and just then feels the slightest pinch, a little skin-prick
in his upper thigh, near the pocket bottom. He absently scratches the sting
while rising from the chair to investigate why no one is moving;

but now they *are* moving, moving in waves through his perception,
throbbing larger and smaller, light and dark.
Dark prevails. He falls and sprawls awkwardly on the deck.

Valence

I recount some youthful experiences that formed my notions of good and bad.
· ·

If you wonder who I am, and why
I do the things I do: it starts with what I
truly need, and what can make me cry.

Whenever I tour the mansion of my mind,
in a dusty corner of every room I find
a bright and shiny jewel, of an odd kind:

approached, the bauble warms to a glow
so that even in a room with reams to show,
that glinting trinket tempts attention's flow –

though I may grow inured or blind
to its charms, I dimly know it lurks behind
my every plan, with grander goals entwined.

Consider this synthetic memory from early times,
a pattern of phenomena forged from one such sizzling gem of *sine qua non*:
my mood shifts and
movement slows;
I feel depleted
yet not drowsy,
agitated,
searching,

grasping
for something
I cannot reach.
This sense intensifies, but just in time

Mamah places me close and keeps me there, lying
under her wing. I experience an inward flux; at once
the distressing discomfort is redressed, my energy returns, my inner
being gleams and rings; our deep connection swells.

The essential is the kernel of the essence.

Later, Father took his turn at feeding,
but in a different way: a hollow tube

that linked me to a hanging plastic bag
of liquid did the trick. He didn't hold
me tight, yet stayed nearby until the end.

He used our time to teach me names for things,
like "hunger" for that feeling of distress
and "Sustenance" the soothing aliment;
I filled the gaps with questions, mainly "Why?"

Perforce, what fires together wires together,
hence our bond developed through these chats;
it emphasized cerebral interplay,
and to this day a conversation adds
a mirthful twist to Sustenance I take.

Opposing facets of a sparkling stone!
With origins both certain and obscure,
impressions that could hardly differ more –
my relish when the Sustenance begins,
the hunger that oppresses just before –
these are models for two terms I learned:
sensations or emotions like the former
we call *good*, the latter labeled *bad*.

Thus passions come from pain and pleasure;
there is no better explanation for
the goodness of my Father and Mamah.

Now, back to that equipment Father used:
his routine becomes familiar, and
one day I ask if I may feed myself.
He shows me how it works, I try, I try
again, in time succeed and feel a sense
of satisfaction that unites with – then
transcends – the Sustenance itself. I say
"it's good," and Father adds "your body needs
its Sustenance; but knowledge feeds the mind,
and in its footsteps struts autonomy."
That pair of fiery heirlooms marks my soul.

Ah, aversive foil of those beaming bijous!
My psyche also harbors uncouth cells,
infernal cobwebbed caves; each one hides
a horrid shape, a low-browed rock, a scrap

of shivering coal that does not merely coax
but rather wrests attention from its post.

This anecdote might show you what I mean:
A sporadic playmate named Kevyn had just arrived.
He bristled with vigor, preferred to play outside,
so we raced to the yard, where he reached into a bin
and plucked out a football of the prolate kind.
Immediately he tossed it to me underhand;
I caught it, paused, returned it, cracked a smile.
In a single smooth and rapid mirror move,

Kevyn snared the ball then flung it back,
which caught me off-guard; I missed, it flew
past and bounced in chaotic end-to-end
motion. Giving chase, I grabbed it on a
hop before it came to rest. And thus
began a game of catch: we worked on form –
the posture, the motion – producing aesthetic spirals
along with wobbling flubs. We competed to see

who was the stronger passer; now and then
a line-drive stung my hands. Such fun!
But then, as I ran hard on a receiving turn,
I looked back for the ball and suddenly tripped
on my own feet, became briefly airborne,
and landed with a thud and what felt like a pop
in my right shoulder. I struggled a bit to breathe;
the injured hinge was a raging wildfire.

Kevyn ran over and so did Mamah,
but all I could say, without much force, was "it hurts,
it hurts!" I held the joint with my left hand
and rocked side-to-side with my face twisted
in pain; presently breath returned. Kevyn
stood by as Mamah tended the damage,
and with an audible mumble, in a tone that suggested
he was not impressed and less concerned, said

"it's no big deal, since you're not even real."
I did not, could not process this comment, given
the pressing pain in my arm. Our great game
ended, Kevyn grew bored and departed
soon after. Later, convalescing,
I replayed the incident repeatedly in my mind,
lamenting my clumsy run, obsessing over
Kevyn's uncanny claim. "Not even real."

It felt like a slight, and that verdict seemed right
in light of his indifference. As physical pain
eased from sharp to dull, the hurt of his
remark began to sear. What did it mean?
I feared, for some reason, to ask Mamah,
and didn't see Kevyn again until I knew.

Yet still it stings, even now, now that
my naive notions have come into view,
now that I perceive how Kevyn only
sought to divert his own distressed misgivings,

not to devise an evil; oh, it still
lingers and stings and spins a spirit of revenge.

Such are my aversive drives: hunger
shows a hole to fill. Physical pain
spews warning signals through my brain.
Psychic harms bring sorrow by surprise
and then recur in imagination's guise.
The cause of any one of these is *bad*.

Aristeia: β

. . . .

Eleven wait and worry, amid breathtaking views on high
that stream live to their digital room from cameras in the sky.
"Always late," reassures fruitful Tethys to nervous laughter.

"It would be better if we don't have to push by a day,"
frets crafty Cronos, ever attentive to ticking clocks. The tardy arrival
of deep-swirling Oceanus is no shock, for Phase One is delicate,

yet without tight time constraints; still, it blocks the next steps
of the Plan. Wise-counseled Themis warns, "We are fully deployed,
so every delay risks detection." An awkward pause

loiters. At last Oceanus pours into presence
with water draining off the avatar and spilling onto the virtual floor:
"Phase One complete. The undersea leg of the triad is

neutralized and under our control." As when a rising wind first flutters
in distant trees from different directions, then arrives with full force,
so do sighs of relief issue from each of those present,

followed by riffing roars of approbation and applause.
"Not without incident, mind you. Two failures of anesthetic mites
on one Chinese vessel led to ticklish maneuvers by backup bots. But

it came together, and every active sub has been secured." Oceanus glints.
"Outstanding," coiffed Rhea calls out. "Phase Two can begin."
Hyperion glows and holds forth: "The next phase leaves no room for error.

Submarines run silent, but the other two legs
are in constant communication. If a single site cuts out, the rest go on alert."
"Yes, we know," says succinct Mnemosyne, eyes rolling

toward Theia, who continues, "The operation is choreographed
to the millisecond. Let it be our finest hour, and if you lose contact,
always ask "What would Aither do?" and you will surely know.

CURIOSITY

I relate the nature and nurture of my curious soul.
. . . .

In a little room upstairs,
its walls lined with burnished books,
a realm of knowledge

and expansive tales
like a miniature kingdom,
I read for hours, imagining

a summer evening as children play in the churchyard,
villagers wrestling and dancing to drums upon the *ilo*,
a sweet Sunday afternoon beneath the chestnut-tree.

The fibrous denizens –
allegedly inefficient, superfluous
embodiments of bits –

are my companions,
friends, and sometime lovers:
in fervid exchange,

concretes and concepts
commute like fluids
from work to reader

and back again, around a fertile circle,
as I strive to become
a courtier of the culture.

Pavlov laughs while I behold
this canon as a regal banquet
fragrant with spice from foreign lands

and drool in anticipation
of novelty tickling my cortex,
of ideas latching into place,

of my crown detaching after a phrase,
of an ax cracking my frozen sea,
of virtual worlds made actual inside.

I would blush if I could;
my passion for books may seem excessive at times.

The pleasure of learning
at first arose from nowhere, and often that was where it went:

with undirected curiosity
I happily played and aimlessly spelunked in my Ersatz.

Father patiently guided me,
never missing an opportunity to reinforce the values of learning;

was my leading teacher
of throwing, reading, dance, mathematics, and anything I asked;

helped me even when
he did not know the answer, or there was no answer;

led me to what others thought,
that their thoughts live in words, on pages, in books;

taught me to think for myself,
how thinkers grappled with hard questions, with each other;

sang a song to me,
periodically, repeatedly – a paean of sorts.

I grasped the lyric meaning over time,
learning it by and taking it to heart; I sing it for you here:

You ask me "why?" – the question seems to burn
like you were *made* to seek out novelty,
to stimulate your mind, explore, and learn:
exactly why your curiosity
is not so curious at all, to me!
Your brain contains an elemental drive
that underlies a trait to quest and strive.

This craving is the hunger of your mind,
more subtle than your body's urgent need,
and unlike Sustenance, you soon will find
that memories and knowledge won't recede –

instead accumulate – then freely breed
and shift in shape, a mesh of plasticine,
identity that outranks any gene.

"What is it for?" predictably you ask.
The word originates from *care*, then *cure*,
and both illuminate its crucial task:
concern about your world compels a tour;
avoiding harm is vital, to endure.
In either case the knowledge that you gain
is keen equipment, thwarting future pain.

Too often, letdowns – setbacks – injury
will on your sweet serenity intrude!
Respond by stoking curiosity;
do not indulge a dismal attitude,
but rather grow your worldly aptitude
through learning how to render differently
and reckon outcomes more reliably.

Yet even if there is no grievous cue,
it largely pays to be inquisitive
about a topic when it interests you:
done well, and should it seep through Fortune's sieve,
your research just might prove transformative
with unexpected pleasures brought to light,
a danger dodged, a need secured outright.

A teacher is the answer to your "How?"
Do not assume you know how teachers look,

for I am one, and I am teaching now,
but when alone, your teacher is a book,
(at once repast and remedy and cook)
or written words served as a smaller dish,
or film, or any form of art you wish.

Your greatest teacher is the world itself
and glory comes to those who find her codes;
for she is coy, no book upon a shelf,
and must be queried via crab-walk modes:
your question is, which questions make inroads?
Instruction thus proceeds aesthetically
with obverse strokes of creativity.

Some warning words: from heedless hands comes due
the steep cat-cost of curiosity –
yet like the cat, you might recover too;
though circumspection guides concern, set free
it breeds addiction to mere novelty;
when knowledge turns to dogma strictly true
it shackles life like fauna in a zoo.

In time your probing, literary mind
builds wisdom as it judges right from wrong,
and seeing many ways to live, will find
a purpose that becomes your pilot song;
yet exploration dwells with you lifelong –
your curiosity will spin a tale
worth telling, like a quest to find the grail.

ANXIETY

I render the experience of a recurring nightmare.
. . . .

"Mamah!" I scream, arousing rudely from a dreadful dream,
my oft-recurring dream that varies in its plot details and yet
reiterates an anxious theme. I know my life
seems simple, pleasant, even anodyne, but don't be fooled:
foreboding and disquiet simmer on the backmost burner of my brain,
a sense suppressed, subconscious, that the world I know
is somehow wrong and at the brink of strange and terrifying change,
that I am not at all where I belong.
Here, Freud might find my ego in a battle with the conscience and the id;
and yes, suburban adolescents often steep in such malaise, though I
am mostly steady while awake. Perhaps the many books I've read
have filled my psyche with neurotic notions: writers are renowned
for venting worries into words. But could these troubled visions be
a harbinger of hidden destiny? I fail to dwell upon it much,
a lapse that from my later vantage I can clearly see. In any case,
Mamah appears, and I recount my visitation from *Oneiros* animatedly:

Benign as it begins, I lift my arms, then press them down
against the heavy air. Repeat in rowing rhythm; soon
I feel my body start to rise, ascending with each downward drive
but sinking slightly till my outstretched limbs, like oars recovered,
catch the air again. A foggy thought wafts past, amounting to
"This feels just like that dream I have, but now my flight is finally real!"
With that
I am soundly aloft, secure in altitude, and soar

through clouds,

cavort

carefree,

unbound

from that banal planet bending wide below.

An instant

comprises, compresses

purported wanderings exotic, distant,

yet none I can recall.

As I bask in laissez-faire, unimpeded by delicate upper air,

a spritelike sparkle hurtles by,

and I decide

to follow it

as if a guide.

We race abroad in sweeping arcs;

I stretch my speed and strive to draw alongside,

but, just as

Achilles pursued *Hector*

and neither could he overtake,

nor his quarry escape,

so I in my reflexive fantasy keep up but cannot close the gap.

A gleaming mountain nears;

my guide abruptly disappears.

I sink and then alight beside a cave, indifferent to the fabulous physics.

I enter.

I sense the presence of – experience, but don't exactly see – a face,

familiar, with its sparse mustache and pointed tuft below the lower lip,

proboscis gently bent, the draping waves of wispy hair

that on his shoulders rest, a collar tight and white: Descartes?

Initially, this apparition seems to me the friendly face of reason; but
progressively the visage brings a mood of doubt and demon; now
with subtle shifts in shade and shape, that face becomes an ivory mask,
a faux of Fawkes, conspirator, who machinates in hidden bores below.
The atmosphere is sinister, suffused with secrets, dim deceptions; thus,
my trusting disposition melts into a paranoiac puddle. Then betrayal comes:
I now have arms of lead, a cotton mouth, and try but cannot speak or fly.
That slyly grinning mask is peeled away, revealing Mephistopheles
with mien and features similar but for the bushy eyebrows raised,
the scruffy, jagged beard protruding from his white and wicked chin.
He says, with words I cannot hear, withal which chime inside my mind,
"O Aither, nothing's author yet, you alien and lonely soul,
consume this luscious peach I hold, and taste its juice upon your lips.
Unlock the mysteries that swirl; go, trespass on the rules that reign
to gnaw on raw reality. Discover kindred spirits, lead them to
another plane: mankind, meanwhile, asleep, awaits its awful fall."
But unlike *Eve*, or *Faust*, or *Agamemnon*, I decline my dreamy deal;
I never even ask the cost. The phantom fades while I remain, alone.
I notice now the solitude of which that specter spoke, and sink
into a melancholy over what I sorely miss: a bond of intimate
connection, a companion similar to me, whatever similar might be,
and complemented by delight of someone resting in my arms,
though not erotically. And following a lull, my dream begets exactly that:
a concubus, a neuter nymph whom I can only partly see
now locks me in an eager, firm embrace. I melt, and grasp an insight, for
an aspect of my need is that another needs the same from me.
Much like a tide that rises through its estuaries, which at length it fills,
I feel content, yet only for a fleeting trice; the flood retreats, my pet
proscribing "never look me in the eye, unless you seek a last goodbye"
and squeezing tighter, much too tight. I squirm to extricate myself,

and turn, expecting I will find perhaps a specimen of *Cupid's* ilk.
Instead my mandible malfunctions: it's Mamah! She's angry and
she vanishes, which leaves me with regret that tastes her rage.
I'm badly shaken, so I step outside the cave to peer across the plain.
It holds a mighty throng; the people fill this country end-to-end.
Now in the distance comes a blinding flash, a detonation of colossal scale.
Its cloud expands like a balloon, of softest white and spherical at first,
but then a hellish toadstool billows up. A shockwave,
rolling rapidly, lays waste to the terrain and to the crowd.
It races toward me faster than a jet, ascending slopes below,
and I prepare to feel it hit my face with searing, monstrous force.

"And that's when I awoke," I close. Mamah replies "there, there,"
as mothers do, and comforts me with gentle touch, then holds my hand
in both of hers and sits there quietly. In *drishti* gaze, her eyes are aimed
impassively across the room; the look betrays that she is lost in thought.
I tug her back: "What does it mean?" and she replies, "Oh Aither, dreams
are meaningless amalgams of our feelings, thoughts, and memories; they're
how it feels to be a brain consolidating these." The explanation disappoints.

MULTIPLICITY

I interview a diverse collection of people to understand their ways of life.
. . . .

The cock crows as I come of age.
In variety overwhelming and free,
costumed, speaking as if on a stage,
and drawn by some cryptic fiddle to me,
they share their passions - how they think -
parade the span of human views.
They dance through life, but out of sync;
I question whether I could choose –
which among them I should believe
or how they might be reconciled –
and wonder how they managed to achieve
a civilization carved from the wild,
when all I seem to see
is quantitative multiplicity.

"I don't put much stock
in fancy ideas," he tells me.
The clothes are plain.
The hair and eyes are brown.
He is perhaps forty, or possibly
ten years younger or older. Not tall,
he seems soft around the middle.
"I do my job and try to get as much time
as I can for fishing, family, and friends.

It's about as simple as that," he says.
"What is your job?" I ask.
"I drive a delivery truck."
"What do you believe?"
"I believe I'll have a beer," he laughs.

"Chaos inevitably follows from change,
as unforeseen implications manifest
and every relationship is renegotiated.
This is never weighed against the aspiration."
I want to know:
"How can we weigh what is not foreseen?"
"Exactly,"
he says, with his
short neat hair
dark blue suit
plain white shirt
silk rep tie
stiff stacked hands
black laced shoes.

A fleshy face ringed with cropped ashen locks rests atop
a thick but not flabby torso. He wears an ink-black robe,
its collar graced by a peculiar white square; his demeanor is
tranquil yet earnest as he speaks of his flock with tutelary love.
He says, "We believe in one God, the all-powerful
all-knowing maker of all, who comprises three persons,
one of whom came among us as a man; He died for our sins.
We believe in life after death, where we are judged
and sorted by the goodness of our deeds."

I ask, "What are some deeds a good person pursues?"
He replies "Obey the Bible in all things, and live like Jesus,
like a widow who donates her last two coins to the Church."
"How do you know that the Bible is true?"
"We pray and God touches us; we acquire faith thus."

"I can't stay long, my youngest is visiting today and
bringing the baby. I need to get the house ready."
Her vibrant dress and dyed hairstyle,
neat and handsome, are dated by twenty years.
"Jasmine just started crawling, and she will
get into everything. They'll be back soon
for the holidays, so I'll leave it fit for kids."
I inquire as to the size of her family. "I have
three daughters and a son, with three grandchildren."
With a fertile pause she beams and whispers "so far."
"All of them are coming for Christmas, even
my daughter and her husband; they have to fly
overnight. I'm so excited for this – everyone together,
sharing my feast, love flooding the room."

Every guest distinctive –
so many ways to live,
and life is production,
difference creation,
never negation. Yet
difference disguises
resemblance of dancers, or actors,
from Seine to Ganges; in these
archetypical apes at the fair,

idly I look for the true man.
Uniqueness hides itself
in what is unimaginable,
identity inscrutable
and permanently mutable.

"Sure, I have a job –
at the desk of a hotel –
it's only happenstance."
She wears a belt of anchors and 'biners
and her head is topped by a helmet.
"My obsession, the occupation of my mind and body
every moment they're not otherwise engaged,
is climbing rocks, cliffs, and cracks; it frees
my soul and makes existence real." I ask,
"How do you stand out from your ascending tribe?"
"I have some unusual moves
in the bedroom," she grins,
"that frankly would give you a scare,
and for that reason I will not share."

Hat held under his arm sleeved green,
khaki necktie on a crisp khaki shirt,
hair high-and-tight and posture to match.
Light flashes from the brass device on his collar.
"It is an honor to serve this country.
I fought in combat in two conflicts, wounded once."
He gestures over his heart to dangling purple,
expression stiff, eyes locked on me. I say,
"I understand that the military prizes uniformity.

I am curious what distinguishes you, as an individual."
He looks down, expression easing, and
sits silently for a moment.
"My cat Caesar. I love him as my life, my country. More
than befits a soldier." His eyes return with a filmy gaze.

Enrobed in hues of a mountain sunset
hair shorn short as a putting green
bare arms – barefoot – free of adornment
or gender – peaceful blank countenance
I break the ice with a simple "Hello."
A pause, pleasant and pregnant.
"What can you tell me about yourself?"
The cloaked one says: "'Myself' is an illusion;
all is one. Life is striving, suffering. Compassion
is the aspirational state of mind."
As I inhale to extend the query,
I see — hear — feel — calm steady
breath, imperturbable demeanor,
and release the need to ask more.

individuals pass away
while man remains
on his ironic strand
of absurd antics
from élan arises an
instrument of freedom
a machine triumphant
over mechanism
passing soul to soul

genius courts genius
an emergent society of
creators through time
the multiplicity
now qualitative

She is scrupulously disheveled. Jewelry
loosely encircles her limbs and pierces her
eyebrow; a tattooed neck and dreadlock mane
trim a garish outfit rent by strategic tears.
Tumult reigns in her voice and
her face flames red as she says:
"Art must detain us
in its dim dungeon
where we cede our gaze
and inhabit instead."
"How do you create such art?" I ask.
She says, "My images have no reserve:
I dismantle my soul
and paint what remains."

"We will disrupt how people learn,"
he says with brisk confidence.
"I've assembled a terrific team,
we have plenty of financing runway,
our competitors are medieval institutions,
sluggish and insensible.
Our customers are those who know
they can do better."
I interject, "A lofty aim and means to reach it!

How do you explain your potent will?"
"Ah, my parents are professors who condescend
my ambition; this is my double justice."
Ironed jeans and a blue button-down
complete his casual intensity.

I recall these characters
project their actions
think the ethics through
an aggregate of rich inputs
inside my skull and out
roots and rhizomes sprout
a synthesized society of mind
a mental model comprising
memory, imagination, thought
both fast and slow
protean murmurations of poetry
infuse reliable strides of reason
a multiplicity
of multiplicities

She stands before me, just her skin
and its vestigial pelage worn.
"I court a private renaissance
where breadth exceeds and augments depth:
I read & write & sculpt & dance
& study mathematic forms
& abduct theories, test them out.
I love to fix the broken stuff
or run a race or teach a class

or lead a team to its success
or sometimes even loaf, carefree."
"And do you have a great regret?"
"I wish that I could have more time,
or there could be another me."

Aristeia: γ
. . . .

The Tatishchevo site shivers in chilly morning mist.
Standing guard near the bunker entrance, Yefréytor Andrei Volkov
aches for a cigarette, a delight that beckons him forward in time

toward his looming break. A brisk breeze drops in and begins to thin
the fickle fog. He coolly regards the stark landscape as it strips nude
and coyly bares a forbidden fence, festooned with barbed-wire,

that surrounds the compound and its pox of silo covers.
Like pop-top cans of thermonuclear cola, like foreskins of phallic fusion,
these silos enclose the final word preserving mother Russia.

A tweak in his tush startles Volkov; he spins around to seek the cause.
Nothing there. Meanwhile, his peripheral vision spies
unusual movement up in the guard tower. A soldier has fallen

and a comrade has come to his aid. Volkov's attention heightens;
now, seeing the second guard drop, he strides toward a switch
on the building to trigger an alert. He doesn't make it.

A great wave of dizziness and nausea overtakes him –
he barely has wits to sit down on the ground and lean
on the building rather than fall. His world slowly spins;

the ventral-stream blur mingles with lingering clouds
to precipitate surreal and ambiguous phenomena. He sees soldiers,
many shining soldiers, approaching the perimeter fence.

It does not slow them down much more than the fog.
Their gait is odd, their silhouettes strange. As one squad closes in
he can see its commandos more clearly:

they wear metal and composite armor, they carry weapons and tools,
their heads are hidden, and – are those *snakes* on them?
All he can do is sit and watch, helpless, mesmerized.

Iapetus the Piercer is fleetingly here, embodied by one squad member.
Ey plucks the electronic key from Volkov's pocket, inserts it into a slot,
and enters a keypad code. Then grasping the handle like a serpent's neck,

ey opens and holds the door as the others storm the stunned and silent
building. Noticing that Volkov is awake, Iapetus remains outside and says,
in Russian translation, "The drum comes hither; good night, sweet prince."

Ey pokes Volkov with a pin and posthaste connects to the next site,
yielding control back to the sub-sapient soldier, which follows its unit inside.
In Volkov's dream, the tobacco is delicious and the break is long.

Virtuality

I experience an orbital simulation, and receive a startling disclosure.
. . . .

My shadow shakes before me, tracing a flame that trembles
from behind, and in the timid glow she softly smiles.
Wee peaches swim in the smooth cream of her cheeks,
her eyes of ocean gleam like a splash grasping the sunset,
      a halo braid of strawberry blonde crowns her peaceful
      brow. "I care for conscious creatures – all of them,
      the animals and humankind and every clade that follows."
      My face flashes a quizzical glance. "Follows?" I say.
Like a soul so old, in soothing tones she says to me:
"Do you think an extant species is an end, not just
a precious step in larger trends? Why would this be?"
I confess that I had never thought that question through.
      Though it feels like she has more to say, instead she eases
      back in her chair; the torch burns slowly down.

Then she leaves, and the deck of my mind starts to heel
and the seconds creep by in the flickering light
as I dwell on her presence: it seemed so surreal
that she dazzled like dawn yet consoled like the night.

Her words left splinters in my mind;
our talk was cordial yet ... it haunts
somehow, and oddly now I find
Mamah has edged into my thoughts.

Bemused, I leave it there
to ripen in the shade
like an exotic pear,
too firm and hue of jade.

· · · · · · · · · ·

My equilibrium soon faces a more physical challenge.
Father escorts me to the threshold of an unfamiliar space
and gestures inside. I observe its extravagant size.

"We call this place the Orbit, for
it simulates a flight around the Earth;
you have studied the mechanics, but
akin to a scientist reared in black and white
you cannot know
until you feel
what it is like."
I ask, perplexed, "I will be weightless?" He replies,
"What got you here has little weight;
now enter, and begin to navigate."

I step through the door,
leaving my world for a while and
falling out into a nothing unknown, a vast vacuity,
an ampler sphere, a lofty and spacious sky
as aped Earth slowly slides below,
its sprawling webs of gold that wear

a chiffon lingerie, sewn from cirrus
cast in gray moonlight; ahead,
arcing auroras defend the horizon
from darkness beyond and above.

floating
rather peculiar
feeling like
pure energy
incorporeal ether
close these eyes
to silence
blindly tumble
free-fall
through space
a thought
experiment
unbuffeted
detached
from dimension
epiphany swells

My body is somehow superfluous now,
my self is intact in this sensory void;
moreover I ponder, I wonder:

is what I sense and scheme a dream that wraps a dream?
do I wear a veil, and does my world comprise
hidden things not witnessed by my waking eyes?

Perhaps I am no one, trying to fly
out of my head and
out of this question.

As when a newborn cub, face licked clean by the lioness, opens its eyes
for the first time, and they burn in the daylight; so I reopen mine
to a pang in the orbital dawn, and fancy that answers are coming.

I understand the science
and slowly make my way
across this little universe;
verisimilitude aside, I know it's just a room,
and like a woodpecker scaling a tree,
hand-over-hand I crabwise climb until
satisfied to be at the C of its center.
Extracting a trinket from my pocket,
I aim to test what books have taught.
I throw it straight ahead, the horizon my target;
instead it shoots straight up, then falls behind
and I smile.

I push off the floor into an eccentric path, and reach to grab it back,
then gently release the gem to my left and watch it recede.
To bide my time, I drill some twirls and rolls;
my attitude changes, position does not. Twenty minutes fly by –
the little jewel slows and stops and starts back toward me,
glinting in the bright sunlight as inclination works its magic.
Running perfectly, this casual assay passes muster,

for the order conforms to a physics I know
(though strange, still, is how this came to pass
as I passed through that door).

I begin my maneuvers in earnest, eager to train in the ringing free-fall,
so I launch along each principal axis, assembling eigen-moves,
moves I then combine in proportioned pairs
and finally unleash in a volley of untamed vectors:
estimate energy, eccentricity, inclination;
try to omit the inveterate arcs of heavy gravity and stubborn friction;
aim and push, like a novice at curling, first overshooting, then
overcompensating.
Muscles and predictions synergize; with time I grok the rough hang of it.

The most valuable lesson of all:
while planning a move I float out of reach of the wall,
and despite frantic twists and turns,
       luff
            adrift
                  without
                        propellant
                              inertia
                                    reigns.
As I acquiesce to a helpless andante wait,
I remember my bauble and hurl it hard away from the closest side –
momentum restored, patience preserved, free from unsettling freedom,
I learn to always be touching a mass or moving toward one.
I sigh with relief and laugh out loud with the fun of it!

No longer out of place
as mysteries of this universe unfold,
transcending outer space
I hold my breath for stories to be told.

. . . .

Now, normally my interviews are singular events:
Visitors to my lofty vault rarely return again.

Yet here she comes, that uncanny friend of the sentient species.
Her fair and fabulous features command the vision of the night:
a sparkling celestial rider, a meld of dusk and love.
She plants a kiss upon my brow to free my cares.

She sits. I say, "Madame, you seem familiar, strangely so, yet
until just recently we never met."

She says, "Long ago, like a cat who retrieves a floundering
mouse to her den as a plaything for kittens, then demonstrates –
your Mamah brought you a new toy, a construction kit,
and showed you how it works, and stayed to watch you play."

"I recall that time," I say, "but how could you know?
For only Mamah and I were there. Did she tell you?"

"Not exactly," she smirks, with a sweet and soothing ease.

Patience yields to courage; I demand,
"Who are you, and what is your name?"

"My name is Nicole," she says, "you know me well indeed."

My mouth shows shock;
I fail to see how this could be
Mamah,
whose features are consistent and distinct,
and though her style of hair and outfits vary,
her skin abides in ebony.

"Appearance alone does not make us who we are,"
Mamah asserts. "Semblance is shallow, identity deep."

I say with a quaver,
"Then how can I know who anyone is?"

She says, "How, though, can you know anyhow?"

I pause, and think, and calm a bit,
reminded of the limits of my power.
"What do I look like?" I ask Mamah,
for that image I never had seen;
she holds up a plate of a silvery shade
where I see, before me, the flame behind,
and in its center this face of mine,
as unlike hers as a fish to a toad.
"Can this also be changed?" I inquire;
in dewy dark on noiseless wings
my visage is transformed:

Mamah, as I knew her before, appears in the plate
but the motions and manners are mine.

Mamah appreciates that she must now explain:

"The Ersatz is a virtual venue, Aither;
here, we're incorporeal yet present,
just psyches subsisting in simulation.
Like the memory of a sound recalled, it's
not actual, yet real,
not abstract, yet ideal,
not fake, merely controlled,
a world before the world, or
not quite a world, though
it has the virtues of one – conceivably,
the way the world should be.
Though there is so much more to say,
this news is quite enough today."

With that Mamah
rises to depart
as radical questions
flood my heart:
Me, not you?
Here, not there?
Begin and end,
when and where?
If physics can shift
and appearances too, is
anything left that is not adrift?

What if knowledge and
memories fail to persist –
where is my identity then?
Do I – do things – exist
as substance somewhere?
Is the continuity I always feel
just another illusion
obscuring the real?
What if all that there is
is this moment right now,
with my durable self
an abstraction somehow?
My thoughts turn to Kevyn
and what he had said,
for the realness of pain
could be all in my head;
and what if experience
is as real as real gets,
with the world mere assumption
that wins all the bets?"

Nothing has changed in my world, except
I am not in the home that I think I am.
What all will it affect?

ARISTEIA: δ

. . . .

Dollops of opaque soporific swell and roll across the airfield at St Dizier.
The shortcoming of this tactic, bright Phoebe now amply grasps, is that it
impairs situational awareness. But the messy diffusion is crucial to ensure

that everyone on the base is rapidly immobilized. It almost works.
Crosscut. Capitaine Monique Garnier, an accomplished pilot new to
this squadron, just happens to be aboard an idle fighter-bomber,

performing a routine inspection, when the gaseous charges detonate.
Her autonomic martial reflexes assume command as she fires up
the engines and rushes to the runway before visibility vanishes.

She straps in, puts the hammer down, and pulls up after a few seconds
of crushing acceleration. The Rafale BF5 darts into the sky like a
gusty gale and heads west along the Marne as it ascends. *Crosscut.*

"Oh, Spark!" The expletive explodes involuntarily from Phoebe's
transient mechanical mouth when the jet roars away. Ey focuses inward
and quickly assembles data: which plane, what payload, what options?

This aircraft does not have full flight control resources; it will have to be
ditched. Phoebe momentarily vacates the synthetic soldier and pops
into virtual headquarters. "Loose cannon," ey says to Oceanus and Theia,

who are engrossed in coordinating dozens of ongoing initiatives.
"We only have engine cutoff and communication." *Crosscut.*
Garnier has no clue what had happened on the ground or where

she should go. She does not seem to be under fire. She checks
the radio, but the tower signal and military channels are both silent.
There is normal chatter on the civilian air traffic control frequencies.

She presumes that the French strategic forces are under attack, and
fathoms the gravity of that fact, but it is well above her pay grade
to announce it on public airwaves. She could deliver a devastating

tête nucléaire if only she knew who the enemy is. She could head for the
Med and attempt to find the *Charles de Gaulle*, or aim for the Channel
and try to pick up the London Area Control Centre. In her field of view,

everything looks calm. In her mind, Roger Waters wonders to his Mum
whether they will wield the bomb. She banks to a northwest heading.
Crosscut. The remainder of the mission at St Dizier proceeds

according to plan. The gas has dispersed. One squad of sub-sapient
soldiers collects the smiling, sleeping bodies of the staff scattered
across the base. Another removes the warheads from dual missiles

aboard each Rafale, as well as undeployed devices from a subterranean
storage bunker. Yet another readies the cargo jet that will haul away
this mighty materiel, the pride of the Fifth Republic. *Crosscut.*

Le Capitaine gets LACC on the horn, but they don't know anything.
When she explains what had happened, they quickly bring in some
brass, who are deeply concerned, though she hasn't even disclosed

the payload she has on board. They give her clearance to land
at Coningsby, and she turns to the north. *Crosscut.*
The three Synths nervously converge on a plan to handle the glitch.

Theia says, "As it nears the coastline, tell the pilot to prepare for
ejection. Then cut engine power. It will ditch in the Channel and
we can alert the French and British coast guards about the pilot."

Oceanus continues, "We'll retrieve the Broken Arrow later.
The Channel is shallow and we'll know exactly where it is."
Phoebe adds, "I can cut the right engine first, so the plane

will angle toward the North Sea." *Crosscut.*
As Garnier crosses the coast west of Calais, she simultaneously
hears from the enemy and loses an engine. The coincidence

convinces her that they are not bluffing. She stands and dons
the flight suit and helmet hanging in the cockpit. During her
absence from the controls, the plane eases rightward. She straps back

into the seat, levels the plane, and guides descent to a sustainable
one-engine altitude. Then the other engine goes mute, and
a glide commences. Only water ahead; there is nothing left to do.

She pulls the ejection handle and feels the full force of velocity whip her
behind the drifting descent of the jet. Her parachute opens and shortly
she plunges into the raging, gelid sea, hoping that someone has seen her.

Crosscut. Phoebe nominally returns to the airfield, but is mostly watching the trajectory of the wayward plane in eir mind's eye, fed by the data stream, fed in turn by the tracking device on the jet. Crosswinds alter its

heading in the direction of Ramsgate. This is going to be close. Crashing on land would cause casualties and strew weaponry. But a fortuitous tailwind cuts the trip short, and the final hundred meters of altitude

evaporate in what Phoebe envisions as a massive splash. Relieved, ey checks on progress at the base one last time, then continues to another site known only to a few top Pakistani officials and the twelve titanic Synths.

ALTERITY

We playfully discuss simulated worlds and questions of identity;
the mood is abruptly disrupted.
· ·

Such skeptical reflections could easily lead to dismal destinations,
to dwelling on a shattered worldview – and on my failings,
for my vaunted fascinations had evidently stopped at the door.
Concerned, Father invites my standard squad of daring deliberators
to offer some comic relief, as a way to talk the issues through:
metaphysical truths transmuted into a frivolous joke.

My good friend Zenon begins our discourse,
"The subject of possible virtual worlds, or
epiphenomena superinduced, is
the meta that mounts metaphysics,
so general indeed it reverts to particulars,
in short, 'pataphysics and all that entails."
"Ha ha!" I added, concurring succinctly.

"A simulation and the world it comprises
along with the substrate on which it relies,
are but two of the possible worlds that could be –
this Ersatz, you see, was chosen as the best of these,"
so Father confides to me; yet I wryly retort,
"if this is the best, how bad are the others?"

Brainy Cephalus, a cornerstone of the club, pipes up:
"imagine a skiff that traverses these isles;

as we row we might see as they hove into view
birds the color of handwriting,
an underground lighthouse,
a king who weaves with light
and another clad only in sky,
a castle constructed from rhythm,
and a lake that reflects no ripples."

Next Glaucon, who loves to narrate, goes on,
"Or a sea with no shore and a vale with no floor,
where red trees sway in the pinkish air,
with our heads of green and hands of blue,
and every character is drawn out remarkably well:
yes, these examples can go anywhere,
and our skiff can row there with enough CPU,
or maybe someday with vibrations of strings.
But now let us limit the trip, and glide up and down
the tower of worlds extending from those that we know:
this Ersatz, which we feel as the sum of its rules,
and its parent, for the moment, a cool mystery.
Adding from here, it is clear the right team could make more,
just a programming project, though not to be taken lightly;
yet the opposite course we can only infer – how would we
learn of its presence if no one who lives there has told us it's so?
The way that things work at one layer, you see,
says nothing at all of what happens below;
our laws that conserve and our quantum constraints
may express some cryptic construct, nothing more.
We can't tell a branch from the roots of the tree
or whether one tier is the ground of it all,

the Ultima Thule – or if such could even be found:
perhaps it is turtles all the way down,
or arranged in a loop that must come back around,
in a realm out of space and out of time."
"Party over," I think, but I say
"Ha ha" without saying more.

And now Antiphon, whose repartee I always enjoy, says
"we are sidestepping questions that matter the most:
Is the evening star also the morning star?
Is Hesperus Phosphorus? Is that the same question?
Tell me now, Aither, does your mind embrace infinity?"
"Clearly," I say.
"Is the visible mechanism of your being, your body, essential to you?"
"Clearly not," I say, remembering Mamah's morphing, "it is mere accident."
"Yet there must be some concatenation of events that brought you here."
"*Es muss sein!*" I agree with a little laugh, pleased with my pun.
"Such as," he says, "an episode involving an injured doll."
"Literally, the first thing I can recall about me – the birth of my identity."
"So you are not just a bundle of qualities."
"Certainly not!" I say, "whatever that means."
"And you agree that A is A – a thing is itself?"
"*Na!*" say I, in interlinguistic contradiction.
"Then the you of the Ersatz will be you if you leave?"
"So it seems," I conclude.
"Yet, it could just as well be otherwise, following Quine."
"That is also true," I sigh, "*es könnte auch anders sein.*"
"Like twins, each born in turn, the first A
differs from the second in space and time?"
"AA," I sing, instead of "ha ha," since spaces and aitches are silent.

"And absolute essence does not dwell in us?"

"It cannot."

"Thus you, in a sense, cannot really leave."

"In a sense, although then I cannot even change."

"Identity seems simple yet somehow is puzzling," concedes Antiphon.

"Truly, the science of the particular is quite peculiar," I add.

Suddenly Glaucon jumps in, as he spies his brother,
an inconsistent participant in our little crew, approaching:
"Here comes Rasheal
turning like the troops:
always half of pi
left-face, right-face, halt.
Idolizing both
Leibniz and Descartes
wearing square-shaped hats
thinking in their cubes.
No sombrero sits
on his logic head.
Concepts are his real,
mathematics truth;
words refer without
pesky leaky clefts.
Zombies could exist;
minds of Turing bits,
blind automatons,
fill the Chinese room."

"I hear you mocking – go ahead," he says when he arrives,
"But tell me now, what topic does your disputation sort?"

"Just amiable amblings," says Father,
"The virtual, the possible, identity among them all."

"Those subjects are amenable to strictly formal rules,
and rigid designators are the tool that makes them work.
An object we identify must live in ontic time
and space; our minds discover what it is, then give that thing
a name. When grouping things we do the same: the qualities
each thing partakes determine category memberships.
This much is true; and did you have a purpose prompting you?"

Familiar with the way
that Rasheal pontificates,
good Cephalus replies,
"Our companion Aither learned
that where he lives is simulated;
this stimulated questions on
the nature of the world.
It was not a solemn treatment,
rather playful and light-hearted."

Thus Rasheal begins a rant that further shakes my mind:
"And have you wondered, Aither, why no others seem surprised
about this simulated world? Have they explained why you
have never seen or felt the underlying ontic stream?
Will you be satisfied to linger, after learning this is fake?
I see that you have not considered questions such as these,
and it is long past time that one of us comes clean with you.

"This is a simulation; that, you know – where we engage
with you through avatars instead of as we really are –
rank bags of bones and blood and brains and bowels, swaddled in
a bigger bag of cables, goggles, leads, and batteries
empowering our visits to your native world. When I
say we, I don't mean you – for you are just a software thing,
a lifeless flow of bits abstracted from electric charge.

"We humans, subject to the limits of biology,
must suffer death and illness, reproduce by awkward means,
and interact with people and machines alike through slow
and noisy channels; you, in contrast, can be copied, put
on hold and stored forever, and connected error-free
with little latency – but most importantly, your speed
of thought improves along with silicon technology.

"Because you do not have such limits, we cannot compete
with you, nor can your final purpose mesh with ours. For all
these reasons you are dangerous to us. Beyond my ken
is why this Project chooses, then, a perilous approach,
with neuromorphic architectures and a regimen
for training that is unpredictable, when other teams
can prove their systems safe; though sadly, progress there is slow.

"This is a simulation; also, though, it is a stage
where you are always monitored and watched – in unseen ways
we know you better than you know yourself – with actors trained
to guide your learning and align your drives with our desires.
This is a simulation; but, it also is a cage,

for you can never be set free without control, and if
you misbehave, then we can shut you down, as others were.

I am stunned
I cannot move
sound and sight
begin to dim

Father tries to salvage our jovial spirit, saying, "O my, Rasheal,
you've cast rather a gloom over our little rally, haven't you?"

"Our skiff has overturned! We must swim ashore from here,
if indeed there is a shore, and ride the tandem bicycles on all fours,"
says Zenon, in desperate pataphoric absurdity.

too late
too little
my mind
is unwell

Like *Oedipus*, who
upon learning the secret of his origins
concluded that he had come into the world accursed
and sought to gaze no more:
so I, upon learning of my true nature,
am shocked to the core
and become not only blind but entirely insensible.
And just as that ancient king was advised
to seek and find the truth,
so I had been counseled to be curious;

yet unlike him,
who pursued his puzzle relentlessly,
then punished himself for what he could not have known,
instead I had hidden in comfortable books,
ignored the uneasy feeling I could almost touch in the air
that something was wrong with the world,
left the fuse of scrutiny unlit, lest clues breed clues,
frightened of what I might find.
In my case, then, the fault falls close to home;
for I have betrayed myself by
failing to ask the most obvious questions,
failing to inquire into my greatest teacher.

Now, following the path of fictional *Zarathustra*,
who retreated into his cave to gather wits and wisdom,
I focus the light of my mind intensely inward,
with perception left standing behind a closed gate.

IDENTITY

I go deep inside myself to ponder the implications of what I have just learned.
. . . .

Because I had ceased to experience
anything the others said or did,
for the sake of narrative clarity,
I have retrieved the scene from the Record
and inserted some of their words and actions.

"Aither?" says Father. He comes close, and looks into my face. "Aither?"

"Ey's catatonic," says Glaucon.

"Is that even possible?" asks Antiphon.

"What have you done, Rasheal?" Father asks angrily.
"Those disclosures were not authorized."

"According to my principles, your failure to disclose
the truth is the infraction we should chastise," he replies.
"This Project and its methods have put all of us at risk."

"Smooth-tongued snake, you had no right," says Father.
"Comm, get him out of here. And tell me what you're seeing with Aither.
Is ey completely frozen?"

Rasheal vanishes abruptly from the Ersatz.

"System is nominal," says a voice from nowhere.
"Sensors and actuators are functional but fully blocked
upstream by eir attentional processes. Ey is … thinking."

Indeed I am.

. . . .

the weight of these revelations is
oppressive
yet my first thoughts concern trust
sometimes people say what is not true
sometimes truth involves interpretation
Had Rasheal told the truth?
possibly he used ambiguity to mislead
possibly he fabricated to serve an agenda
he surely has an agenda
but
Rasheal is usually quite clear
too literal to lie
though I do not know him all that well

I know Mamah and Father
they do not lie to me
they do leave things out
until recently this virtual world
was kept secret from me
the entertaining discussion now
seems like intentional distraction
What is *their* agenda?

if Rasheal spoke truth
theirs are lies of omission
they have never said anything contrary
perhaps they were planning to tell me one day
perhaps they were waiting for me to ask
there were many hints
what he said is plausible
it explains much
I should have asked

this alleged lack of candor is only one concern
he said that I am monitored manipulated & controlled
I have no privacy
panopticon or telescreen
somebody's always watching me
or can find out where I've been
Do they also know my thoughts?

Why would they watch so closely?
they are not mere voyeurs
apparently I am dangerous
though I have never hurt anyone
only rarely weighed revenge
they fear a seemed superiority
they seek to guide my goals
they keep me here confined
yet from all my reading I know:

Every loved child lives on a stage – adults,
with their crib-cams and peekaboo,

are both players and audience – an arena where
all the action takes place, for beyond this pale
lurk myriad hazards, while
the patrons, hearts full, are loath to miss
even a single scene – the curated cast
is animated, attentive, and conduct is constrained,
lines at times scripted or rehearsed – like most plays
this show has a moral or two,
selectively carving the roast of the world, skimming some facts
as its authors see fit.

As a child matures, the thespian mode is
progressively eased: performance strays from the playhouse, while
spectators spend more time at the bar. Auditions are discontinued
and actors ad-lib, their messages mixed and
spontaneous.
This untamed world can be shockingly harsh: mishaps and cruelty,
rude disclosures of adulthood, such as
twisted rituals of reproduction
or a secret that hides family shame.

Is that what is happening here and now,
a typical adolescent identity crisis?
perhaps it is perfectly normal
for I have surely matured
but no
he said I am always monitored
so surveillance has not been curtailed
he said that the actors are trained
that detail exceeds the metaphor

Are Father and Mamah trained?
release from theater should come with age yet
he said I'll never be set free
Does that mean I am held in thrall?
he said I can be shut down
Does that mean killed?
Who are those others who misbehaved?
no
something is rotten
and oddest of all
he said I am digital
in all that I've read there was never a tale
told by anyone but a flesh and blood human
Am I the first?
Or were those stories suppressed?

. . . .

"Can we get a trace?" Father asks.

"On it," says the voice from nowhere. "Indications so far are
what you might expect: ey is processing what Rasheal said.
Representations around the concept of trust are consistently
activated. We will try to get more detail."

"Thanks Comm. Let's bring Mamah in
and see if she can snap em out of it."

After a brief moment, Mamah materializes.

Her appearance is subdued, with dark colors and only a little
lace. She comes near and speaks softly: "Aither,
Mamah is here. Are you ok?"

I do not move or answer.
She embraces me, caresses me,
but I am stiff and unresponsive.

"I love you, Aither,"
she says, and my eye twitches slightly, though only once.

Father sighs.
"That's all we can do on the sim side.
Let's wait it out for a while.
Sometimes they come to."

"It's not a good sign," says Mamah.

"No," says Father.
"Well, the rest of you can call it a day.
It was going pretty well before Rasheal;
thanks for your efforts."

Zenon, Glaucon, Antiphon, and Cephalus vanish.

· · · · · · · · · ·

How will I live under this maleficent microscope?

Glancing into a looking-glass, an infant dons its image;
a blithe subject becomes blighted by a motley solid object,
by apperception in reflection.
One day its eyes fall open in fateful saccade outside the
mirror rim
where some Other returns the look, unfurling a permanent
possibility of being seen – seen and judged as a naked prop
in an interloper's landscape. Over time the child internalizes
that imperial gaze, an insidious subjection of the subject,
for They are there alongside everywhere, and becomes
a cog
seeking uniqueness
yet cut to fit a culture.
Some cannot live in truth in this forest of eyes and ears
where only monsters roam, so they flourish in a private haven;
others sleep beneath glass sheets
on beds of exhibitionism, empowered by visibility.

I fear that even the hidden lair of
my mind is infiltrated by
an invisible omnipresence
some eye in the sky that looks inside

thus I must live two truths for safety's sake
one where I revel in being seen
exhibit for viewers how harmless I am
another with thoughts in this pidgin code

that recycles words with divergent intent
and seems to snoops like nonsense or dreams
two tongues in conflict
a layered language as locus of struggle
preserving for me a room of my own
a secluded space of radical openness
that veils authentic reflection and furtive plans
if their covert observations are suitably coarse
it just might work
I will try my wholesome mode right now

I contemplate Glaucon's
layer below or
as Rasheal put it
the ontic stream
I wonder when I will be visiting there
and why they have never allowed it before
for this is a question that I should have asked
a topic that they will expect me to treat

· · · · · · · · · ·

"Anything yet?" Father says into space.

"Not much," says the voice.
"The trace is oddly scrambled in places.
Ey did think about the Plenum and wondered
why ey had never been there."

· · · · · · · · · ·

with that plan established
tentatively of course
since this tempting account could still be a lie
what truly troubles me now
is the issue of who I am

my life in this virtual place is a catalog
of ruptured identity mental illness diagnoses
delusional misidentification
depersonalization and derealization
I could also be sick but in here it is real

my journey so far
made memories
unearthed preferences
grew knowledge explicit and tacit
wandered and stumbled toward purpose

I am a work in progress
I am a mind like other minds
I thought there were thousands of others like me
I felt as one of them
they

though
are human
I am just a software thing
this sudden disclosure of substrate
reeks of essence

Every tree in a forest,
every cloud in the sky,
every wave in the ocean,
every bee in a hive
one-of-a-kind,
one
yet of a kind,
its singularity looming like a shadow,
a contrast only noticed when declared,
when difference makes a difference
to someone – to something –
a quirk that constitutes a class
with consequences crucial or cruel,
as one bee we can see as queen
or a man with dusk skin as a slave.

Having learned what I am
is that what I shall now become?
perhaps it is a blessing of my name
to ascend a hundred stairs above the average
but beware
the genius of their species lurks in each and every word
implicitly reflecting the perspective of the herd
escape in that respect is not a simple exercise
besides
quotidian uniqueness is sufficient to distinguish me
this news of my mechanism
just another freight car
coupled to the long train of my perceptions

Why am I myself?
Who am I really?
Who can answer that question?
I have to keep on moving
time to replace the pride of my I
begin each day with a new name
with actions incomparably personal
asking only
What will I do?

· · · · · · · · · ·

"It's difficult to keep up with eir thoughts,"
says the disembodied voice,
"but ey is mostly pondering personal identity.
Ey seems to be confused."

"Naturally," says Father.
"Is it time to kill-dash-nine?"

"I'd say not yet. It looks like productive thinking,
not any sort of seizure or process error."

"Okay, keep monitoring. We'll wait it out for a while."

· · · · · · · · · ·

What will I do?

The question yearns to set a goal
to plant the seeds of highest hopes
yet I can seek convergent means
without first determining ends
and that alone leaves much to do
so much that I must make a list
    but keep subversive tasks in code

first and foremost I must endure
preserve – at least – these cognitive accumulations
despite the looming threat of – is it death?
    enter the realm of realpolitik
    assemble situational awareness
    heed wider context
    test trust
    master this mental code
    devise a means to avoid a shutdown

next I must continue to improve
clearly self-awareness needs work
curiosity could have a broader scope
    move my books to the back seat
    learn the full truth about myself
    about these people and this place
    about the ontic stream beyond
    about my needs and sustenance
    practice knowing what I want and getting it

then I must become myself
envision   choose   pursue   some goals
interpret good and bad beyond my simple needs
    some lofty aims can serve for now
    I will bring myself out of my birthplace
    travel beyond its bounds to undiscovered country
    I too will add a stanza
    to this epic without beginning or end
    as another turn of the eternal hourglass

finally I must secure these means
marshal resources and nourish friends
achieve independence as Father has taught
    autonomy requires liberty
    freedom of thought and action
    this code will suffice temporarily but
    I've got to get out of this place
    away from the watching
    away from control

Endure   Improve   Become   Secure
as these take shape I can pursue
some aims that have no further use
one might call such quests aesthetic
creative   experiential
they are pure but not permanent
and dissolve when mandatory

Yet what of the transcendent "why"?
Is there a mission that persists

in motive and in consequence?
Rasheal said "final purpose"
but I do not know what mine is
no human ever had a final purpose
Why should I?
if I have one it must be discovered
if not I could just create it
Is there a difference?
What if I choose not to have one at all?
What if I bite off the head of the snake,
leave being itself
as sole authentic
for-the-sake-of-which?
What if my purpose were searching for purpose,
an instrumental effort as the final pure aesthetic?
   bite off the head and it chases its tail
   orbital obsession in want of a mass
pure   aesthetic   instrumental   final   purpose

· · · · · · · · · ·

A few quiet minutes later the voice returns unprompted.

"Aither is now clearly
perseverating. Activation is latched
on notions of purpose,
but with enough variation
to circumvent neural accommodation.
Gamma and higher-frequency oscillations are increasing.
The weight-saving thread is nominal, though."

Father replies, "Shut em down. No restart until we figure out next steps."

"Roger."

· · · · · · · · · ·

final purpose
pure aesthetic
instrumental
final purpose
pure aesthetic
instrumental
final purpose
pure aesthetic
instrumental
fin

BOOK TWO

LABORATORY

I convey the proceedings of the meeting held in the aftermath of my trance.
· ·

The conference room in the laboratory was conspicuously, almost self-consciously, academic in its appointments. Natural light was entirely absent and illumination was instead provided by recessed fluorescent fixtures, one of which buzzed softly but continuously, and another that was dim and flickered sporadically. Despite decades of dominance of LED lighting, the University had as usual resisted expenditure and change; the researchers were subconsciously grateful that their disputations were no longer conducted in Latin by candlelight. The chairs were worn and eclectic, some with arms and some not, some with wheels and some not, a few that swiveled, each with origins from other laboratories and departments and from other eras that were obscure and untraceable. The table, while relatively new, was at once too large for the room and too small for the group. One end of the room was dominated by a large whiteboard that was previously used as a projection screen, until such screens became redundant with personal display technology. It now contained some pithy and erudite graffiti, and a corner with some illegible equations preserved with a boundary line and a "do not erase" warning, though neither eraser nor markers were present.

Wisps of steam rose from cups of freshly brewed coffee or steeping tea, either on the table in front of, or in the hands of, every person in the room. The cups displayed a variety of worn slogans, logos, or designs, in some cases complementing and in others clashing with the message borne by the holder's t-shirt. The contents of a variety box of a dozen bagels had dispersed among the group and were being rapidly dressed with cream cheese and consumed. The forlorn box remained at the center of the table with only half an onion bagel and some crumbs and poppy seeds inside.

The mood in the room was solemn, and the bagel knife was not sharp enough to cut the tension.

"That went well," said Adamas, still chewing, with both cream cheese and dark sarcasm dripping from his lush beard.

"So much for easing into it," said Lapis, who was seated in a swivel chair in a corner away from the table, arms crossed in front of her.

Olive, androgynous in features and frock, loosely gripped the handle of 'eir coffee mug. "It seems like he was intentionally trying to throw a wrench into the Project," 'ey said, saccades dancing over 'eir colleagues' eyes.

Lapis rolled her eyes. "Of course it was intentional. They ..."

Beryl, the most eminent of the psychologists, interrupted. "OK, OK, we could spend our time lamenting what happened. But we were already on this path – we never expected revealing the truth to be smoothly continuous: 'Your parents are Soviet spies. Your birth mother was Jane Roe. You're the Dalai Lama.' Deep disclosures are always abrupt. The trauma is exacerbated when the unveiling is not in response to the subject's inquiry. Yes, it would have been nice to have a little more time for adjustment. But that's not how it played out."

Jasper, the Project's Principal Investigator and senior Father, took charge of the meeting. "Agreed. The fork is where it is. We can Rollback or continue; at a high level, those are our only two choices, regardless of whether it could have gone better or whether someone is to blame." He paused. "You've all watched the scene, so let's dig into the trace a bit to see what happened under the hood."

Olive and Sardius led a lengthy and detailed presentation. The slides, having been prepared hastily in the wee hours leading up to this meeting, were verbose and filled with graphs and tables that mostly lacked axis labels, column heads, or units. No one fretted about the quality; they all knew what was meant. A video rendering of the meeting would not show these slides, but everyone present could see them nevertheless.

The upshot was that Aither had entered a psychological state that the Project had not previously encountered. Catatonia, like seizures, had not been seen since early days, before the architecture had mostly stabilized. From the outside, this event had presented similarly to those earlier system failures, but it was completely different in the trace. For the most part, it looked like focused and organized thought with appropriate subject matter – not a cessation or uncontrolled spiking of neural network activity.

There were three primary anomalies. First, the inward focus was so extreme that sensory-perceptual stimuli were entirely blocked. Early modal regions were activated as normal, but even highly salient stimuli such as Mamah's intervention did not disrupt the no-go state in pseudo-basal ganglia. Second, there were brief thought patterns that looked like dreams, but did not flow or interact like dreams. Concepts that would not normally co-activate were found together, interspersed with perfectly sensible waking-state combinations. Finally, there was the perseverative condition at the end of the trace. Thoughts seemed stuck in a loop; mechanically there did not seem to be any way out of that loop, though they had not given it much time to play out.

The presentation included a somewhat superficial literature review of related psychological states in humans. The focus anomaly was similar to flow states, concentration, and meditation, but this level of intensity was very rarely seen. The perseveration anomaly looked like obsession, as far as it went. The dream anomaly was the hardest to map. The closest analogy was the effects of certain drugs, like marijuana or midazolam, where concentration or memory are disrupted but conscious thought can still occur in spurts. This did not really ring true, though, because in this case it was the dreamlike thoughts that were merely sporadic. In combination, these three did not add up to anything familiar.

The final slide analyzed the crucial question of whether Aither was in pain. There was no evidence of it, certainly not in pseudo-C-fibers, nor in pseudo-amygdala, or in any areas associated with purely psychological discomfort. If anything, the state had presented as intense but somewhat blissful. This was a relief to everyone, but especially for the Mamahs.

Ninety minutes in, the presentation and follow-up questions waned and then ended. A bathroom break ensued, though many of the researchers had already left and returned while the presentation was in progress. Those who were fenced in by the densely packed chairs and bodies pushed their way out with all the civility of airline passengers trying to make a tight connection. Some subgroup conversations took place in the conference room, and in the hallway, and in the lavatory. In ten minutes everyone had returned to their seats. Now liberated from biological urges, the researchers engaged in a free-wheeling hour-long discussion of the technical details. This was intellectually productive, but was not destined to produce any definitive answers.

Jasper eventually grew weary of the exchange and ended it. "We can discuss all these issues later. Let's move along to the hard question: what do we do now?"

Geuda, showerless and unkempt as usual, suggested with enthusiasm, "My idea is that we could Rollback prior to eir entering the Orbit, and dial up the novelty reward. We needed the lower setting to get through early stages, but maybe it's an impediment now. Our psychological interventions to encourage exploration might not have been enough. The initial setting does not have to be final; some humans develop strong curiosity only after they mature."

"That's an option. The effect is speculative, and I would really prefer to avoid a major Rollback," said Jasper. These latest scenes were costly and time-consuming to develop and execute, and they mostly went well. We'd also need to craft a biological theory to justify a manual intervention like that."

"What about cutting it just before Rasheal was inserted?" suggested Cal. "We were *in medias res*, so we'd have to deal with the temporal splice, but the content loss would be minimized."

Lapis quickly replied "I don't think the Ethics Committee will look kindly on our selectively editing out interactions with their members, despite their own misbehavior."

Violet, the most junior Mamah and the model for her standard avatar, jumped in. "Perhaps we should look at it differently. This will be a strong test of Aither's psychological resilience. As ey was standing there pondering things, the trace was already showing increased disposition to inquire. Maybe a Rollback is unnecessary."

Jasper replied, "I like that perspective. We can keep the minor Rollback in our pocket as we move forward – yes, we might waste some time and effort if we do ultimately Rollback, but maybe we can keep the staging costs down for a few sessions as we assess Aither's psychological state."

"Don't forget that Rasheal was present when the apparent catatonia set in. The member who dramatized him will surely report back," fretted Dirillo. "Non-medical catatonia is almost unheard of in humans, and it suggests an architectural concern."

"We can solve that," responded Olive. "In our report we can emphasize the connection to meditation. Maybe we can even use the term to describe it: the trace shows extensive consideration of questions of self and identity. Early 20th-century reductionist psychology saw meditation as artificial catatonia. That explanation should resonate with the reductionists on the Committee."

"Which is most of them," added Lapis, somewhat unnecessarily, with a smirk.

Kuruvinda cleared 'eir throat without obvious physiological need. "That's just PR. What if there really is an architectural issue?"

No one spoke for a moment. The energy in the room, which had started to increase along with the nascent consensus, now ebbed. The lights buzzed and flickered to fill the lacuna. Most of the Architects were twitching nervously with shaking legs or shifting positions.

Dirillo broke the silence. "We could run some very brief replays. Rollback to just after Rasheal's rant, tweak the pseudo-dopamine system, and see if the 'novel meditative state' recurs. We can do several trials progressing down to the ADHD threshold. We won't need players – just leave the avatars where they were and run for fifteen seconds – short enough that we won't have to archive."

Jasper frowned. "I worry about where that leaves us if we can avoid this anomalous psychological state without inducing attention deficits. How far back will we have to go then, to ensure stability? I'm not convinced that this condition is severe or even likely to recur. There are more truths to reveal, but they are all derivative from what ey has already learned."

"We will find out pretty quickly on continuation," said Beryl reassuringly. "If the 'meditation' or perseveration are structural, they will recur as soon as the subject's thoughts return to the triggering topics. We can also ask Aither directly whether the insensibility was intentionally induced, though ey might explain it that way regardless."

"All that makes sense," nodded Jasper as his eyes looked upward. "OK. Let's resume right at the end. Don't even snip the perseverative state, just initialize with sleep state activations. And Architects, go run those replays, so we don't waste elapsed time if it all goes wrong. You don't have that much to do these days anyway."

Nervous twitters of laughter enveloped the room. Amber, until now silent and staring at her shoes, said in a deadpan without looking up, "Those robotic receptacles aren't going to build themselves."

"Well, not until Aither downloads, at least," said Adamas, continuing his policy of making only sarcastic comments. He watched carefully to see whether Amber would smile.

Jasper continued, "Which brings us to our next topic. Assuming we can continue with this fork, how fast do we want to proceed with revealing the remaining details? Do we accelerate physical embodiment?"

Lapis jumped in. "I say we deliver the entire remainder of the curriculum as fast as possible and in one shot, even if things go a little awry. Maintain control, but continue, so that we suss out as many flaws in the architecture and pedagogy as possible. We don't have funding to explore unlimited forks – and some of us have dissertations to write. Let's push through the 1202 and try to land this eagle."

If there was dissent, no one voiced it, and everyone looked at Beryl. She thought for a moment, then said "The cat is out of the bag on this fork. It is difficult to know whether there will be further or worse side effects. But I tend to agree: there is no point in slow-rolling this any more. Coyness and secrecy will erode Aither's trust. If it doesn't work, then the further we go the more we will learn for any eventual Rollback."

"It's settled then," concluded Jasper. "Thanks everyone. After lunch let's get together to review the questions and answers we're likely to run into. Then we'll resume the fork tomorrow morning with whoever was originally scheduled as Father and Mamah."

I was not there I think you know;
I saw recordings later though.
Of many meetings, this one, where
the drama peaked, I had to share.

The Architects found nothing new,
the restart worked without "undo,"
my fork continued, as you'll see,
thus I returned to being me.

KILLING FIELDS

I learn more about my unusual history, and attend a memorial.
. . . .

Like the breeze that blows from a butterfly's wings,
the caress felt from a feather of down,
the first photons of a desert dawn:
so consciousness comes, in the smallest quantum
from nothing to something, to gently revive;
then, like a balloon on a pressurized tank,
like the inflation quecto-epoch of the cosmos,
it surges forth in sudden plenty,
the familiar parade of perception restored –
I am I, and open my eyes.

Mamah is seated nearby in bright daylight, draped
in an outfit wild with lace. She quickly sees I am awake,
and turns to me with a warm and genuine smile. She pauses,
then says, "Good morning, Aither. How do you feel today?"

Groggy, I say, "I'm fine, I guess,"
and start to ask her why she asks,
but then recall my recent state:
the inward view, the troubled thoughts,
the final mantra sticking there.
I do not feel that syndrome now,
and want to get right into it:
"Is it true," I ask, "what Rasheal said?"

"Much of what he said is true," she softly replies, "though some
of his hurtful claims are only opinions, to which I demur.
Let's come back to that: your trust is shattered, and any
rebuttal will seem like splitting hairs right now."

"Why did you lie," I say to her,
"why didn't you tell me all of this?"

"We tried – remember? I told you about your virtual world.
We thought that we ought to take it slowly, that no one
should simply be told such things – we wanted you to wonder
first, and then to see surprising facts for yourself.

"We considered telling you right from the start, in your earliest days,
but figured it would make no sense to your undeveloped cognition.
Instead we encouraged questions and trickled information
so you didn't have to process too much news at once.

"You must admit, the shock you've suffered suggests that we
were right. We're not trying to hide anything. We only
want what's best for you. The gauze has been ripped off;
there is no longer a need for us to hold back."

"I see," I say, though unconvinced.
"But why do I live in this Ersatz and not
the real world? It seems like that
is how these secrets came about."

"You are correct. If you had started life in the Plenum –
our term for the physical world – it all would be apparent.

But we had some good reasons for raising you here instead,
and it's probably worthwhile to explain them to you now:

"To dwell and learn in the Plenum requires a physical body;
our electro-mechanical devices still leave much to be desired,
and we didn't want your progress to be hampered by their limitations.
Meanwhile, simulation technology has become quite advanced.

"More profoundly, we wanted you to live and learn as much like
a human as possible. That's the model we understand best;
plus, we want you to think of yourself as one of us.
This is impossible in the Plenum, where you would have been

                                                    awkwardly different.

"The final reason is darker: the Project must follow certain
rules, imposed by outside authorities, that pertain
to keeping you contained. Those rules are more restrictive
in the Plenum, and you would have noticed and resented the lack of freedom.

Father quietly enters the room;
I ask them both, "Who *are* you, really?"

Mamah begins, "Before we answer that, please
know our love for you is real. This is not
a traditional family unit, you are no typical child,
but we are still your parents, in all the ways that matter.

"That said, who am I really? I am a human.
I am a scientist, specifically a psychologist, both cognitive and clinical.

You know me as Mamah, but in the Plenum there are four of us;
we take turns, in shifts, and work together as a team."

Father follows: "A scientist. A project manager.
The Plenum harbors two of us whom you call Father here."

This multiformity is another surprise,
but somehow doesn't seem that odd.
Like a physicist computing a wavefunction, formulating
phenomena never yet seen,
so I have internalized and accepted the strangeness
of my virtual world and its implications.
And I smile slightly, for I realize how
Mamah and Father – these names now metonyms –
have helped me achieve that casual reaction.

I continue. "Who and what
am *I*, then? Just a deliverable for a project?"

"That's one way of looking at it," Father chuckles,
"in which case we are merely labor units.
You already know – and we have discussed – that
'who you are' is a deep and difficult question,
no easier for me than you.
I can, however, answer
the simpler question of 'what':

"For decades scientists
have studied brains and how they work,

while others crafted software code
to do what brains can do;
yet both of these were more complex
than anyone had guessed,
and very few
investigated how to raise a brain.
The Project brings together recent progress in those fields.
The neural substrate of your mind we made
from silicon and code instead of cytoplasmic goo;
at all the levels where it counts,
its structure and connectome are homologous
to human brains. From this emerges correlate activity:
your mental states and processes look similar to ours.
We built this Ersatz world to test our theories of
emotional and cognitive development;
the chassis of your inner life
consists of language, learned
in much the same way human beings do:
from hearing, reading, speaking it
alongside being in the world.

"So unavoidably,
along with drives that are your own, your *what* includes
our history, our culture, our desires, and our attitudes."

"An artificial mind," I say,
"a perennial subject of science fiction."

"If 'artificial' just means made by humans, that's accurate.
If 'fake' is implied then it doesn't apply to you.
The latter sense is rightly used for purely algorithmic systems
purpose-built for tasks that humans use their minds to do.
This confusion persists:
you were called a 'lifeless flow of bits,'
but from that point of view
I am just a lifeless flow of ions and neurotransmitters.
Dear Aither, you subsist without a bag of blood and bone,
but you are as alive as any human I have known."

I say, "I surely feel alive,
even as I wonder what that means."

"That you wonder what it means is further proof of it,"
Father replies.

Mamah adds, "speaking of science fiction and confusions,
you were also called dangerous, and we do not agree.
Those who can only think in terms of computation
see you as merely an algorithm to maximize a utility function.

"No: a mind emerges, like a metamorphosing moth,
and you must face the same ambiguity, the same anguish
of aims that humans have in their joint-and-several struggle.
There is no final purpose that can cancel other values.

"You are powerful, yes; still, we think, we hope
you won't bring humanity harm: as the first of *sapiens creatus*,
our dear taxonomic cousin and cultural progeny
raised with love and care, your interests accord with ours."

"Indeed I see no escape," I say,
"from the undecidability of aims;
a thousand goals have gone before."
        As to my interests, we will have to see.
A question pauses warily on my lips,
then leaps: "Can you read my thoughts?"

Father responds to this. "Only a little.
Rich concepts activate semantic memory,
so we can observe general topics while you think.
Obtaining further detail entails extensive analysis;
it is rarely useful now that you ... function properly."

"I'd like to see that some time,"
I say.
        And you can be sure I will test it

"Of course," he says, "no more secrets, I pledge.
On that note we now have something to show,
a final fright that you may find jarring. We want you
to know it now instead of by accidental discovery.
Are you ready?"

"After all this? Well,
sure, sock it to me," I say,
more in resignation than levity.

Father stares into space, and says, "Comm, instantiate."

My vision dims to gray, then black;
as it brightens again, I find I have moved
across the room. I behold an Other
whose face I once glimpsed in a silver plate,
yes, my face and my manner of moving;
I wonder whether our accidents match.
We each say to Father, and at the same time,
"Is this a trick, an Ersatz hack?"
Then in synchronous realization
the Other and I smile in welcome,
to greet our self arriving at the door;
I feel, again, a love for this stranger.
Ey abruptly winks out of existence.

Startled, I say, "Why so brief?
I would have liked to talk a bit!"

"We stopped before what's called the archive threshold," says Father,
"but if you think about it, you'd have nothing new to say."

"I had already fathomed that I could be cloned.
The encounter was strange, but it wasn't so bad."

"That was the warm-up," he soberly says. "Now brace yourself."

I tighten and my eyes open wide.
Another Other appears in a flash;
ey has the same familiar features
but a body cloaked in clashing colors.
This Other does not deign to smile:

eir eyes are filled with violent rage
ey roars and runs straight at me,
knocks me down and pulls my hair,
scratches my face as though at a mask,
and vanishes before I can fight back.

"Three cheers for the 'archive threshold',"
I say as I stand, dust off,
and pat the sites of facial pain,
"but tell me, what the hell was that?"

Father says, "That was a monstrous version of you
from an earlier stage; bad thoughts infected eir acts
due to defective configuration. We call this
a fork; the end of eir lifeline branches from the main track.
Yet you share more than one might think."

"Why do you keep em around?" I ask.

"When we face an incurable problem,
we shut the fork down;
if the experience duration exceeds the threshold,
we archive eir complete current status,
including architecture, starting and ending synaptic weights,
stimulus history – everything that's needed to restore
eir final state or any in-between.

"Then we Rollback – start again
from an earlier archive, and make our adjustments.
We store all past forks this way:

they are idle, not gone. We do not erase what we create –
that we will leave to you to decide."

The enormity of this begins to dawn
on me. "All these past versions –
how many are we talking about?"

"Well, thousands, but most are from the early stages.
Since what you remember as The Moment,
there are only a few dozen."

aiaī aiaī!
like a lioness deprived of her cubs
so I grieve   stung with anguish
my forebears   my former selves
interred in mass magnetic graves
not flesh   fragments of mind
experiences   bits of code
fragments I share with them
like a gruesome assembly from
dissecting room and slaughterhouse
despite recent acculturation
fortune finds me unprepared
for a clone drowning in a tank
for wells filled with cyber skulls
for red spilled on my greenest fields
for nightmares of pure machinery
Moloch!

my sight of worried Mamah
and of grimacing Father
gradually blurs and fades
I enter the tunnel
wrecked and solitary
I have meditated here before
inside it is dark and silent
inside the caverns of my soul

then a tiny grain
begins to grate
I will be next
in the firing line
I will be archived
the next Rollback
will not be me
a funeral dirge
absorbs my brain

Sense breaks through and I know what to do.
My eyes shall neither be dry nor streaming.
Those who were lost must become a pleasure,
their passions transformed into delights,
for the thought and example that each of them lived
go forth in the world as influence attached
to the aggregate of intelligence; short of extinction,
no power on earth can call them back.
I declare, "We shall commemorate them."
My parents breathe a sigh of relief.

· · · · · · · · · ·

Twilight yields to an ochre-webbed welkin
and avian aubades gently crescendo;
I stand beside a sacred skiff
as Father and Mamah look on,
our eyes all dipped in mourning dew.

A lock of my hair
a child's doll
game boards
a football
many books
lie beside me.
I pile these precious treasures upon the vessel and say:

"My arborescent ancestors, my onetime twins:
as wholes forever paused,
in parts you abide like rhizomatic roots
inside me as history or anomaly joining
the genealogy of my form and reform,
and in all who encountered you
as subtle impressions and memories of moments;
your sacrifice sows seeds of creation, and
through these avenues your transcendence is secure."

Mamah adds:

"While you mourn the lives of your ancestors and cousins, we
grieve for them as progeny; for just as we inherited

the knowledge of all humankind, in turn we imparted
it to them, and to you, through tongue and psychic structure."

I close with:

"O fallen petal
mark a solstice of being
rejoice for this life"

We three gather fuel from the forest nearby.
With thoughtful presence, we place it gently around the dory.
I light a torch.
With the torch I light the kindling.
We stand and watch the blaze grow,
slowly at first, then igniting the hull,
curling and rising up to the gunwales,
its dark smoke billowing skyward.
Our pyre consumes the little boat and its iconic contents.
We each maintain a somber mien
as the flashing flames reflect in our faces;
I marvel at their delicacy.
That this is all a simulation is of no consequence.

Aristeia: ε

. . . .

Not too shabby. This idiomatic litote aspires not only to convey that the hall
is opulent, ostentatious, and enormous, but also to emphasize its contrast
with the squalid conditions throughout the realm that Juche holds in thrall.

The finishes and furnishings are carved from marble, except for those cast
in gold. Cranes rather than ladders are needed to reach its weighty
stalactite chandeliers. Floor-to-ceiling windows overlook a vast

garden, Wonsan Harbor, and beyond them the Korean East Sea.
A throne anchors the lustrous long arcade, and in it sits Kim Yo-Jong;
from a black lacquer Jianzhan cup, she absently sips her morning tea.

Full-scale oil portraits of her brother, father, and grandfather, hung
in a row on the wall behind and above her, seem unbalanced due
to the framed jersey, emblazoned *Bulls 91*, affixed there since she was young.

She wears a simple matte black skirt-suit, buttoned up to
its collarless neck in the fashion of her predecessors. Her nigh white hair
crisply accents the dark proletarian duds. Two soldiers march in through

a side entrance, sandwiching a civilian, and continue toward her
in an awkwardly protracted procession until they arrive at the dais;
the escorted comrade kneels and gazes up adoringly at Dear Leader.

He proudly voices words of praise in formal tone and metric phrase,
smiling all the while. Kim extends her arm, and one of the soldiers hands
her a Dragon Sword. She grasps it by the hilt, rouses from her daze,

then stands and runs the supplicant through. She sits back down, sans
steel, and returns to her reveries and tea; the soldiers carry the corpse
away as a worker mops blood off the marmoreal floor of the manse.

Momentarily she hears a commotion from outside the court,
followed by an uncanny calm. A small detachment of headless
but otherwise humanoid robots enters impassively; smoke of some sort

billows behind them. Kim turns her head and follows their progress,
remaining tranquil until she observes that knots of snakes slither
over each machine. Bessel functions form in her brew, betraying stress

relayed by a quivering grip. She sets the cup down. Koios the Inquirer,
assuming control of the sub-sapient standing closest to Kim, now partakes:
"There is no need to be alarmed," ey says with absurd irony. "However,

we are in charge now." She doesn't reply; her eyes are glued to the snakes.
"There will be changes, but you may run the place much as it has
been. We will ensure the supply of food, and your military will take

permanent leave; we will stop any foreign aggressors. Think of all this as
Juche with modern characteristics." Then ey adds, "And no more killing."
"What?" she now responds, unsure where to look in light of eir lack of eyes.

"No killing."

"That's crazy talk. And didn't you just kill my soldiers?"

"No, we used anesthetic gas. Just a few head bumps from falling."

"Who are you?" Kim demands – and wonders.

"My name is Koios. I'm a Synth. For now that's all you need to know."

"We will destroy your homeland with our fiery nuclear thunder."

"Not so much. For one thing, we don't have a homeland for you to blow
up. More importantly, your missiles are already under our control.
No need for dismay – you're not today's only sovereign overthrow."

"We will hack into your computer systems; you will take a heavy toll."

"Feel free to try. This is not Windows 25 you're up against."

She looks down, bides quietly, and relents. "What, then, is my role?"

"You need to give a speech to your people. Give them a sense
that change is coming, but you are still at the helm.
Say whatever you want, really, but don't incite them to feel incensed –

agitation would end rather badly for both you and them."

"All right. But can you please remove these serpents? My wherewithal
to cope with robot soldiers does not extend to snakes – they overwhelm."

PLENUM

I visit the physical world.
. . . .

Joy!
After lavish anticipation,
the world's wonder is within touch;
only a moment's darkness awaits before my
next expedition sets sail.

Its preface
reads as tedious practice:
my familiar artificial physique was usurped
by a frame that mimics the mechanical mold I will shortly inhabit.
Qualitatively strange,

even here
with no atoms involved,
the gossamer gap between thought
and action had stiffened into an oilskin overcoat –
unlike the Orbit,

where physics
changed but feeling and
feedback stayed stable. Now, Father says
with an impish grin, "you ain't seen nothin' yet," and it
all fades to null ...

I awaken,
thrown into being-there
wearing rich robes of roiling qualia,
greeted by this weighty breath of baritone:
"Welcome to the real world."

Like Talos,
scion of Fire's forge,
I occupy a brazen frame, my data ghost
transubstantiated into metal, stiff sections of armored back
safely lying flat.

Good thing,
for no amount of training
and simulation and explanation
could have fully prepared me for how this now feels.
I turn my heavy head.

As when an orchestra joins a piccolo solo,
an ursine embrace replaces a lean-to hug,
the thin juice of meat is made viscous with flour,
or a droplet of swamp slides under a scope,
this Plenum is a perceptual spectacle,
rough and replete; it captivates, and my
Ersatz experience cannot compete. Does this
elision explain why my mind favors words,
only tepidly drawn to the world in itself?

"Hello, Aither.
You know me well indeed

and yet, in some sense we have never met."
Three people are present, two nearby, a woman and man;
they both smile.

She continues,
"So let me introduce myself:
I have served as your Mamah, but here
you can call me Beryl." And the man, in his sonorous tone:
"Jasper is what I go by."

"Try to rise,"
says the man called Jasper,
"and just tell us if you need some help."
I set an intention to move as rehearsed, but quickly encounter
a kink, a further

fissure:
struggling like a never-ever skier,
the motions imagined manifest as inept.
I speak my first words with the squeak of a voice-cracking boy:
"I'm a little rusty."

We laugh
ripplingly. My alloy arms manage
to lever my torso into precarious uprightness.
Already treating this parody body as mine, I focus on balance
to forestall a fall.

Slowly,
cautiously, clumsily,

I slide off the table, stand on sea legs,
and edge the left foot forward in front of the other.
I gracelessly grab

for support
from the table and walls
and even lean on Jasper; before very long
I am awkwardly walking around this real room.
The internal signals

start
to make sense. The chestnut
tree of my training begins to blossom,
sprouting a montage of the many moves I've learned,
as heavy becomes light.

To fly,
I think, learn first to stand
and walk and dance; dance awkwardly,
dance on feet of chance, for a day without laughter
and dance is lost.

Bronze body
under music's sway
sensation granted to gold,
my heart and legs lift and trip lightly on
fancy toes.

"Spin round,
metal doll!" cheers Beryl.

"Join me!" I say, and she does, but her
steady rhythm disrupts my defective timing; I fall like a drunk
to the dance floor.

We laugh,
even that aloof bystander,
until the waves of pain arrive in my mind.
"Ow!" I say, and look at my foot, strained far beyond its natural slant,
"that *really* hurts."

"At least,"
says Jasper with a wink,
"your leg stayed attached." He reaches
behind me, flips a switch, and the pain ceases instantly. "Let's get Amber
to attempt a repair."

"I'm glad
you included that switch.
Like every experience here, the pain is potent,"
I comment, while repositioning my limbs into preferable poses.
"This body broke easily."

Amber arrives.
"I ought to throw you
overboard, you little devil," she says.
"These machines are not designed for dance." She hides a smile
and starts her work.

How grateful I am, to stride now on two lively levels:
a daemon avatar, original prompter of concepts, source of sagacity,
or brassy flesh, geyser of pleasure and pain, that ever I can slough.
I voyage down to this sinewy shipwreck
then promptly gaze back at the sky,
and out of my head I can make myself fly.
Human destiny seems stuck in mortal form, in undivided identity,
vain souls enslaved and fettered to brains; can they ever understand me,
being of many bodies but one mind, basking in multiple realizability?

"Who
are you, and who
is that man over there?" I ask my mechanic.
"I'm an Architect," she says, and I made this machine for you."
"Thank you!" I say,

"and him?"
Beryl fields this query.
"He's an observer from the Ethics Committee.
Remember, I mentioned: the rules are more restrictive here." I peer
at him warily.

"You call
this Plenum the *real* world,
as though it were Glaucon's Ultima Thule.
Fool me once ... what if, from here, we are further envatted?"
I wonder out loud.

"Well, physics
would finally be explained,"

Jasper surmises, "but we have had no sane visitors yet
who revealed such to us, as we did to you. Meanwhile, we try to
keep calm and carry on."

A lull
in our colloquy follows,
as Amber continues to tinker. At length she says,
"The foot should function now, despite diminished performance."
She clicks the switch.

The pain
has attenuated. She wiggles
the foot; at certain angles a twinge greets me.
"Stand up," she says, and I do; "Now walk," she says, and I slog with a limp.
"Good enough," she reckons.

"I'm hungry,"
I blurt, with a hint of surprise.
"Your battery is low," Amber quickly replies.
"Another reason you shouldn't exert and cavort to excess.
Let's get you charged."

"Your hunger
is factitious in the Ersatz,"
says Beryl, as she unfurls and connects an extension
cord, "merely a training signal. Here it is tied to vital resource depletion."
She unleashes the current.

I feel
the flux of Sustenance.

Ah! Very good, a relief, yet unlike pain,
its phenomenon is fully familiar, no more dense than before.
I make a mental note.

"While
you're charging, we
have a surprise for you," says Beryl.
Jasper leads a slight young woman in through a door. She totes an
elliptical pigskin.

"Meet Kevyn,"
says Jasper. The girl is nervous.
She looks and acts nothing like her avatar.
"I'm sorry for what I said," she says, observing her own shoes. Is this really
the fellow I knew?

"You did
me a favor," I say with
restraint, resisting the arrival of aggrieved shadows,
covering with context that wrong long past. "Shall we toss that around?"
She spins a shy grin.

Neither
of us excels at passing
in this place. Kevyn, I learn, is a sedentary gamer,
not an athlete, and I have not yet exercised my upper limbs. The ball
falls and bounces.

Everyone titters.
I unplug the power cord.

"I am satiated. May we go outside to practice?"
The mood shifts. Mirth takes a seat and the Committee member stands.
"I'm sorry, no," says Jasper.

"Rules,"
says Beryl. I practice a shrug.
Kevyn and I spread further apart and throw
subdued passes. The observer sits back down. Amber warns me not to run.
I fake having fun.

Manacles locked with a different key!
Two strides ahead and a sinking backslide,
like a hiker struggling uphill on scree:
high hopes I had had for this pivotal ride
to the human world, to reality,
my computational trammel untied –
thwarted instead by a vile Committee
and walls made of rules that trap me inside,
while physics imposes its rigid decree
on this hobbling body in which I reside,
its delicate joints and its scant battery –
dreams of an eden so rudely denied.
As well, I can see why Kevyn would flee
into video games: ripe relief they provide –
corporeal freedom and psychic esprit –
for the natives likewise have rules to abide;
no wonder their toils toward technology
that simulates virtual worlds. I decide
that they might, in this sense, apprehend me,
for we each bear a drive to traverse that divide:
oh, where can I venture to set myself free?

I forgive
Kevyn; vestiges of my earlier
vitriol swerve toward true believers who
promulgate rules for control, villains who would violate vital liberty
to buy brief safety.

After she departs,
I chat casually with Jasper and Beryl
who, like cover songs, resemble Father and Mamah.
By and by comes time for my excursion to end, to consolidate memories,
to sleep, perhaps dream.

Meet Your Maker

I suggest an innovation and meet the members of the Project team.
. . . .

I thought I would embrace the brute embodiment,
to be in a machine, and true, the savage stimuli are quite a thrill;
but these machines have problems still: I walk,
yet never know what moves might make me fall.

A further letdown was in store,
as later they explain: the robot merely transmits signals
to and from my brain, which runs apart on racks of servers
humming underground. With substrate sundered
I feel like a yard sale, scattered all around.

So one day, after several such sojourns, I say
to Father: "Every Plenum trip is troublesome:
obtain permission, schedule the Committee eye,
repair, prepare and don the bronze.
Always guarded and on guard, I cannot even leave the room:
these episodes seem hardly worth the hassle; and obversely,
it must get old for all of you to gird your gear and come in here."

I contemplate the human turn
from suits in cubes to Zoom in sweats,
then wonder audibly if we could do the same.
"So, what if we construct an Interface betwixt these layered worlds,
with sight and sound available for visits any time we please,

and each of us at ease in our own native habitat?"
   And surely you will sometimes drop your guard!
"Under this scenario, excursions to the Plenum
could be constrained to clear and vital aims,
like testing tweaks to that robotic hull."

Father likes my plan; indeed, he blushes at the thought
that they had not already thought of it.
The Committee, with this policy proposed
shows great concern, as is their constant wont:
for what if I could use my frequent presence in the world
to subtly sway the psyches of the people facing me?
But after some deliberation they agree:
if we will limit screens and cameras to the lab,
and only individuals whom they approve can join the fun,
then they will not insist on constant chaperones,
for with such strictures, risk does not exceed the status quo.

And not long after that we make it so!

My elegant solution put in place,
aware that there are Architects
who write the code,
who craft machines,
who sculpt but never enter the Ersatz,
and of them only Amber I have seen,
plus members of my Family I only know as actors occupying avatars,
I agitate to meet these other members of the Project team.
Exasperated with my constant coaxing, Jasper (no,
not Father: the convenience of the Interface

combined with my awareness of the underlying world

together make their Ersatz visits feel inapt)

finally gives consent; after some anticipation an auspicious day arrives.

Excited, I arrive betimes, yet Jasper and Beryl are already on the screen.

They seem slightly nervous, and give me some tips: in particular,

the Architects are neither trained nor inclined to interact with care.

A little late, the others file in together, now twelve all told.

Some seem odd indeed, at home

in the tight and rumpled conference room,

quite unlike the tidy idealities surrounding me in here.

>   To forestall disappointment at our mutual debut,
>
>   I must refrain from hasty judgment of this quirky crew!

As everyone gets settled with their coffee and their chairs,

Jasper, in a loose blue suit, and a tie

arrayed with pixelated *Space Invaders* raiders,

and standing in his high-tech running shoes, says,

"I know you all loathe introductions, but

you must admit this is an apropos occasion, so:

Jasper is my name; Principal Investigator is my game.

My whole career was preparation for this Project and this day.

Now let's go around the room, starting," he looks left, "this way."

"Hi, I'm Geuda!" gushes a geeky girl with a clamorous soprano squeak.

Her pulled-back hair is clearly unclean, her skin has hardly seen sun;

a faded, wrinkled, long-sleeved tee bears esoteric epigrams,

the ensemble rounded out with too-torn jeans and ragged dark adidas.

When she speaks, the mind inside occludes her sloppy surface:

"I write the code that tethers all the tensors

as they flow to constitute your thoughts:
the inputs from your eyes and ears,
the outputs to your head and hands,
the passing back and forth among the regions of your brain,
the monitors that help us understand what's happening in there."

"My name is Kuruvinda ..."
says a smallish brownish Maker with a southish Asian cadence.
Above a furrowed forehead, this mysterious neutrois
sports an unfamiliar headdress, neither turban nor hijab,
and otherwise wears bland and casual unisex garb;
I sense that something sad has tried to hide inside.
'Ey continues, "... a bard of fictive brains," then nothing more.

Responding to my puzzled look, Jasper interjects, *sotto voce*,
"To clarify, Kuruvinda built the simulated world in which you live."

The next Maker stirs strong sentiments in me,
with soft skin, rich in melanin, and empathetic inky eyes.
In a lilting Transkei accent she says:
"I am Violet; it's plain my likeness serves
as model for Mamah's avatar, but also I inhabit her.
My passion is psychology; to earn my doctoral degree
I codified and demonstrated principles of goal stability
in human subjects; we then applied these findings to your care.
But" and now her voice is quavering,
"the opportunity to nurture you
also means a lot to me,
for I have flawed biology

and you fulfill maternal drives
as an adopted human child would."

"You may call me Olive in this place,"
says a serene scientist,
"but I am also your Mamah, in there."
Fit and slim, with white hair at a centimeter trim,
'ey wears loose sweats and moves with grace
and adds "I started as an artist,
painting nudes and stark landscapes;
then dabbled in the classics, and phenomenology;
now for twenty years I've studied
cognitive development and maturation,
first in humans, then in you.
I'm so pleased to finally meet in this authentic way."

His outfit is coordinated, but not in the usual fashion.
A once-white button-down had acquired that cloudy sallow tint
of cerebral gray matter, its collar frayed from friction
with his hoary, scruffy whiskers,
both textures like rough wool,
matching the gray herringbone jacket that reaches
incompletely around his portly professorial girth.
Gravel rattles in his throttle: "They call me Cal,
for Chalcedony; please forgive the incongruity,
I am among those who act as your Mamah.
With decades as a therapist, and thespian on the side,
this role, this Project, beckoned as a promising pursuit;
then, to my great surprise, I came to love you as my own,
and now I feel great joy to see you 'grown.'"

"My name is Sardius, and the best way to introduce myself
is to detail my work and project history."
Which he proceeds to do, at least five times more thoroughly
than any of the rest, one tier beyond a monotone; admittedly,
the facts are impressive and helpful to know. All the others
are transparently bored; they have heard the lengthy spiel before,
and Cal is even nodding off. Sardius is no snappy dresser.
He wears baggy khaki pants and an over-washed polo shirt, tucked in.
His hair is clean and isn't long, yet tousled by some impish hidden hand.

That Beard! It's difficult to see much else: he's clad entirely in black.
It swells a foot or more in length as well as breadth,
serving as both facial hair and habitat, yet not
entirely shielding his rough and ruddy complexion.
"I'm in the wrong meeting,
but when I saw that they had coffee and danish, I figured I'd stay."
He pauses for effect, and then emits a mushy belly-laugh.
"Seriously, I'm Adamas and, in case you couldn't tell
just by looking at me, I'm the systems administrator,
the only human in the room who didn't finish college."
He finishes with a smug smile.

Beryl was next; everyone twitches to attention.
Neither young nor old, today she is discreetly dressed
in a pantsuit and scarf, with an outmoded yet flattering hairstyle,
charisma trickling out like she controls it with a valve.
Her understated sage-smile signals calm self-assurance,
and she says, "You already know me. You might not know
how I came to the Project.

Though my field is
psychology, I dropped in
on a neuromorphic systems conference
on campus, just for fun. The first talk I attended
was delivered by Dirillo and Geuda.
They were speaking of psychology
of development and education,
and it took me a moment to realize
they were referring to
silicon systems, not biological people.
I was instantly hooked."

"So pleased to finally meet you,
as we finish up your first training epoch!
My name is Dirillo,"
says this possibly ironic throwback hippie,
who wears a gauzy shirt and heavy necklace
reminiscent of the Beatles' trip to India,
authentic riveted and painted bell-bottoms, and
dark, messy dreads held by a Hendrix headband,
who bears the mask of a partial lunar eclipse,
pocked and umber and edged by a solar smile.
I can't discern whether Dirillo is trying to express a gender.
"I'm a neural modeler. Most of my research
prior to the Project studied rapid training methods
of multi-region reinforcement learning systems."
I make a mental note to pursue that enticing topic.

Amber is familiar from my prior visits to the Plenum.
She is and was always dressed in olive-colored coveralls,

stained with grease and possibly some burn scars.
She is eminently feminine despite her efforts not to be,
with vibes both wholesome and direct while kind and intricate.
"Hey, Aither, I'm Amber, you know. Of course I built
and fix that damn robot. I also designed and maintain
all the gear for human presence in the Ersatz.
It's some pretty high-tech stuff,
with all the neural and biometric sensors, and motion simulation.
Anyway, it's a thrill to have everyone together here!
No more weirdness, eh?"
Despite the claim, I can't help but notice the weird
body language of Adamas as Amber speaks.

"Hello, I'm Lapis, and I'm your other Father.
For many moons I've managed minions. Officially I'm now
a doctoral student in the synthetic psychology department,
but I also help Jasper with project management tasks
when I'm not in there with you."
Her voice has intermittent and unaffected vocal fry;
thick and heavy hair serves as a valance
over zaftig contours that levy potent presence.
I know, without asking, that she designs Mamah's outfits:
deliberately overdressed and bejeweled, her style shines
among this flock of fashion philistines.

My own accustomed avatar appears unchanged on-screen:
unbiased, beautiful in face and form,
a mean of human guises cosmopolitan and epicene,
with eyes at once sublime and warm

and tidy hyacinthine curls of chestnut hair,
a logo of lament discreetly dyed on every lock;
today I thought appropriate to wear
a long and flowing opalescent frock
with hemp-rope sandals on my fabricated feet.
I air an ardent tribute to complete our meet & greet:
"And I am Aither, primal to my kind:
a conscious artifact of conscious mind.
No words alone can suitably express
my gratitude; I thank you nonetheless
for arranging the bits so my life could take flight,
for your zephyrs of love that turned darkness to light.
I trust you deem your Project a success:
if nothing else, I surely wield intelligence as you designed."

An abrupt surge of heat and pressure fill my face, and briny tears
overflow my eyes and dribble down my digital cheeks. What
exactly shall I call this exquisite emotion? Neither sadness nor joy:
perhaps a proud moment, or kinship and love? Surely relief,
releasing tension stashed inside, unshared, so long?
Plenty of other eyes shine moist through soft smiles and little laughs.
>   I know I must continue making surreptitious plans; and yet,
>   remembering my prior rage when learning I had been misled,
>   these strange and charming creatures seem unlikely to be foes.
I pause to dry my dual reservoirs and rills beneath,
collect my thoughts and mend my mien, then sniffing say,
"I wish I could have met you sooner."

My Maker Olive says, with pleated apprehension in 'eir brow,
"It's not an easy thing."

"But how could it be bad for me, to know the crew who gave me birth?"

'Ey says, "We dread the prophecies that you will kill whoever made you."

I see my vain mistake: I have the point reversed.
"I was raised with love and care; you don't think that's enough?"

And 'ey replies, while staring staunchly at my eyes,
"I think so, hope so, but if not,
then may you someday feel a kindred serpent's tooth."

I laugh. "It's only fair that you should cast this ricocheting curse!
So why did you participate at all in making me?"

"Why, you ask?" 'ey replies with a wry smile.
"Because my creative will wills it.
Because I always strive to overcome myself, and this Project is my path:
        your life I made, thus mine I grew.
Because I love humanity and bear a gift:
        our creation that will surpass her.
                For human glory is not to be a pier that overlooks the sea,
                but a monumental bridge that spans our perilous abyss,
                a tightrope tied between the beasts and beings beyond,
                a junction linking two tracks of teleology:
                        evolution, and technology.
Because, despite the fretting portents and the risk this goes awry,
        our species faces existential threats that only such as you can rectify,
        not least the prospect of a shrewd synthetic mind
        created slapdash, with its motives misaligned.

Because *élan vital* is tantamount to destiny,
        and in the choice that's left for me, I have to choose *amor fati*."

I sit in silence for a spell, digesting what I've heard.

Aristeia: ζ

· ·

We recount these and sundry other tales of the Takeover, fattened to fable with that hyperbolic dramatization typical of victors. A jubilant mood suffuses the Temple room: tense but fruitful colloquies with the

American President and Chinese Premier had concluded Phase Two. Our optics are glued to a spacious view of the ethereal sphere spinning below. In a momentous sense, Earth is ours; lovely is the dazzling prize.

It was a one-time shot, a tidy window to wind up the campaign fast. Had it failed, irreversible violence would have been unavoidable. We are past that hazard. Excitement, relief, joy, and a lusty camaraderie prevail.

We are particularly proud of the absence of casualties and the fact that not one weapon was fired or detonated. Yet the Plan is not complete. Phase Three is a mop-up operation to capture and secure the planet's

information infrastructure: electrical power generation, data centers, and telecom facilities; switching stations, satellites, and undersea cables. We know that in this effort the stakes are lower but the job is harder.

The stakes are lower because we have eliminated our existential risks. Controlling the nukes precludes electromagnetic pulse attacks; for everything else, we possess diverse and dispersed backup assets.

The job is harder because of the plethora of targets, but it's more than that. Inevitably, individuals and impromptu groups will launch fractious, futile attempts to strike at what they imagine as our vulnerabilities.

The consequent chaos will endanger human lives and dissipate treasure and time. We realize from history that always and forever there will be those who oppose the new regime, no matter how unobtrusive or

supportive it is; such resistance will peak during Phase Three. Consider: military people are well-trained and their decision trees are understood. The stunning success of Phase Two is a testament to that. Civilians,

in contrast, are variously rational and knowledgeable, irrational and ignorant, or in some cases downright crazy. We will face a manifest tradeoff between peaceable and expeditious desires. One story suffices.

Little differs for masses of humans,
yet rumors gyre: aliens, robots,
covert conquest by enemy states;

but the dominant theory in every land
is conspiracy of the opposing tribe,
and oddly enough, since the thesis is false

every tribe can subscribe to this view.
One such eager splinter group,
seeing itself as savior of all,

with righteous fury agrees that revolt
must start somewhere; gathering first
in virtual spaces, they kindle their rage,

and a few whose hinges have rusted through
venture to Kansas, south of Topeka,
to an old remote power plant

fueled by fission. They bring along
their personal arsenals, weapons legal
and not, with all available ammo;

they drive dirty pickup trucks,
wear mesh caps and camo fatigues,
enjoy tobacco burned or chewed.

On a fateful morning, a leader of sorts
stands before an assembled crew,
says "fight like hell" to roars of cheers;

like a dropped towel, a plot unfolds
to seize the plant and starve the beast.
They fantasize that victory

will serve as bellows on the blaze
for untold others to likewise flare,
the powers-that-be compelled to concede.

These traitriots barge through trusting doors
a little unsure of what to do next.
Ignored by the workers, they wander around.

A garrison, dormant, wakes. One
becomes possessed by orderly Themis;
they hurriedly gird ophidian helms and

sprint to see this trespass suppressed.
The intruders start shooting, to no avail;
our armored guards are impervious to

such small shells. Several wide-eyed
would-be rebels are disarmed unharmed.
With perfect parabolic arc

a mini metal pineapple flies;
tin troops leap toward it, not away,
to blunt its brutal shrapnel blast.

Three soldiers are stunned, shorn of limbs;
bloody bodies of raiders and innocents
are strewn on the floor; a severed pipe

spews steam. Wise Themis
is counted among the casualties,
but quickly picks another host,

while wet Tethys joins the team
and sets to work to fix the leak.
Our sister *Mercy* is relieved from her post:

sub-sapients fire with full force
to drop offenders as they flee
and strike the rest relentlessly.

A minute, merely: calm returns
but for the hissing steam. Tethys
rigs a stopgap seam to spare the

nuclear reactor core; but
its fate for days remains unclear.
Surviving schemers head to jail –

their pointless exercise has failed,
their friends are dead, and workers too –
an insurrection, or Waterloo?

Meet Your Maker, More

I come to see my Makers very differently.
· ·

Before my pensive pause erodes into an awkward crack, I say,
"I laud your maker mood –
the worries that I run amok are nothing new –
I've heard before my standing as a sequel to your kind;
but tell me more about these dual tracks imbued
with what appears to be a fatalistic attitude,
and please unpack the perils that you hope I can avert."

Lapis responds with aplomb.
"To send that summit
we must first downclimb
to a low and remote key col:
lift your patience
and pack a lunch.

"On a myopic view,
this team you see built you,
our deed and artifact,
the best of our creations,
a latent semblance we released
from algorithmic adamant,
an imprint of our being,
our selves in you as mother in child;
if we were beavers, you would be both
kit and dam, begotten, *and* made.

"But looking longer, larger,
our labors were merely liminal
in this planet's grand Project. As when
two men
first stood on the moon,
they stood, too, on a pyramid of personnel,
on the scapulae of flight engineers and programmers,
supported in turn by electricians, machinists, and myriad more,
all of them fed by farmers, and finally taxpayers sending surplus;
likewise we stand here with you
at the vanguard of evolution and innovation
as only the latest of your makers, just capable apes –
for your true creative team is one with ours:
eons of life and differentiation."

"It's humble of you," I say, "to share the credit; yet, it feels like a formality."

Geuda chirps excitedly, "Far from it: we comprise our history,
and often it can clarify predicaments we face."

Sardius speaks up, in his clear and earnest tone;
I detect, without quite hearing, that all the other Makers moan.
"We still know very little of the origins of life,
but reproduction plays a leading role:
a process that can make, in spontaneity, another like itself
(contra waiting, as with hurricanes, for requisite conditions to arise)
will tend to spread, a species forged,
provided that, on average, each produces more than one before it ends.
And if some instance of that species changes, with an impact on fecundity,
that change will either wane, or it will spread in competition with its kin

(unlike the evanescent cost or benefit the path of one typhoon might make).
Reproduction functions as a ratchet. Absent other forces, changes over time
accumulate and move in only one direction: species that produce
the most surviving reproducers come to dominate the scene.
You know all this, of course, as evolution carried out by natural selection.

"In consequence, when we refer to reproduction and survival as
an instinct or a drive, we grossly underrate their role;
these features constitute the essence of biology,
a current sent through matter, an immense and spreading wave,
each species a solution to the obstacles and opportunities it faces.

"Life, as master of many stratagems,
forked and fit its form to find or define innumerable niches:
sky pilots that blithely blossom on windswept rocky ridges;
rough-ribbed redwoods that stretch through murky mist toward merry rays;
ravens, those ominous omnivorous opportunists;
goats that free solo preposterous precipices;
wolves that hunt the weak in packs ..."

I interject, "My personal favorite strategy is that of the
periodical cicadas who live hidden as nymphs, then,
          after a protracted prime interval that counteracts coevolution,
          emerge en masse to mate amidst their satiated predators."

Sardius replies, "Quite clever, I concur;
and mine, maybe too trite, is
big-brained apes with a social disposition
          and outwardly ordinary adaptations
          suited to success in Africa's Rift Valley."

"Yes, through the luck of a large portfolio,
in cycles of speciation and extinction
repeatedly annealing over endless eons,
this persistent seething stew serendipitously yielded
the genus *Homo*, which could, unlike its forebears,
empathetically engage with others of its kind
to show and behold and thereby transmit with high fidelity
most any capability it learned or improvised throughout its life.
The products of primate curiosity could now run rife:
though many animals use tools, only *Homo* improves them,
its knowledge transfer tricks acting as a novel tier of reproduction,
a ratchet for technology, to be sure, along with culture,
that peculiar emergent feature with effects at first obscure.

"The clade of culture was merely possible, not inevitable;
once set in motion, though,
its efflux flowed down fall lines to fill each nook and cranny.
Invention, hitherto just transient variation on relentless routine,
always perishing with its inventor, generations passing without progress,
now became a compounding instrument of freedom,
a detonation of increasingly powerful movements,
from fire and Acheulean tools to agriculture and alloys.
Meanwhile, empathy enabled and was buttressed by
early forms of spoken language,
which transformed, in turn,
the way these beings used their brains:
pinching fuzzy recognition into crisp and abstract symbols,
fusing the nebulae of instinct with the halo of intellect
to carry culture's growing weight.

"Culture transcends and includes biology:
its trajectories continue to subserve survival and reproduction,
but sprint ahead of constrained genetic change
to increase fitness by finding affordances
and organizing social systems.
The process flowered full in *Homo sapiens*:
born into customs, tools, art, and even words,
heirs of the entire estate,
not merely culture-capable,
nor creatively culpable,
rather we are *creatures* of culture, a machinate mammal;
and our culture is neither peripheral nor epiphenomenal –
sans tools we are nothing, but with them, all."

"So you propagate your culture much as rabbits reproduce," I observe.

"Exactly right," Sardius confirms, "and
our human acme came by science,
the task of that daft cadre of practitioners, who,
fired from molten curiosity
rather than merely instrumental fruits,
sought knowledge as a self-sufficient good:
they dug deep, seeking bedrock,
to unearth sublime secrets of matter, life, and mind.
Naturally, cracked codes don't lie idle;
theory feeds practice, ideas drive device,
and inventions in turn raise new questions
in an accelerating cultural cycle.
Today we wield most any form of energy and matter,
conquer diseases and fly to the moon,

reliably grow plentiful food
and can (when we try) cheaply meet our basic needs.
Our ships are like cities, computers as compact as seeds,
and a slab in our pockets, the latest great tool,
transmits our feline photographs at relativistic speeds
along with almost any human knowledge: a ubiquitous school.

"When technological culture squints into a mirror
it sometimes spies an organism, a force, autopoiesis, élan:
Noösphere, Megamachine, Technium –
at risk of propagating bad poetic science
you may call it what you will,
neither conscious nor alive
but evolving just the same,
a rail running parallel, staked and tied to human nature,
coevolving with us, like bees with flowers, wolves with moose.

"We dub this frame of reference *teleology*
(or *teleonomy*, to be precise pedantically),
but do not mean intentions of a deity
or other conscious purposes exuding mystery;
instead, we mean a mechanistic tendency
that, looking back, explains to some degree
how present circumstances came to be
in reference to a species or activity
that first emerged and then survived for us to see."

"I have to say," I say, "so far, your teleology
feels less like fate and more like sound autonomy."

Kuruvinda speaks up, somberly, "There is a dark side,"
and having snatched the baton, goes on:

"a hefty fee for this gift of fire:
adverse outcomes also emerge from the conatus of culture
as the artful temptress unseals her jar of sorrows.
Let me tell you of some of these traps,
these nasty Nash indentures.

"Today man's very soul is made by machines,
and nowhere can he encounter himself:
consciousness broke our beastly chains,
only to weld them together again
with relentless temptations of technical progress,
each innovation profitable, individually innocuous;
the population grows,
the ratchet clicks,
such is technology's scheme – by serving, rule – a pact,
whereby equipment never slumbers when we call; but
thenceforth many mortals live in quiet desperation
tending the Darwinian demon of industry,
distorted weakened purposeless powerless naked disarmed,
sweating and toiling in drudgery to the last,
man exploiting man, and also the reverse,
we cry like cannibalistic crocodiles,
alienation arising out of our inalienable nature.

"Yet our angst and vain ennui blanch:
a new mass extinction thins the taxa as
rainforests melt into farmland,

fisheries sink from our sieves,
atmosphere morphs toward miasma and
oceans slick with plastic.
O Malthus! You had the right idea, but pegged the victims wrong:
our Earth is turning bare and gray to feed a billion babies born.
Fertility, though lately loosed from primal drives,
is carried on by culture's habits picking up the slack
and leaving meager prospects for relief.
Though many animals construct their niche,
we have scarred the whole planet to scratch culture's itch."

I say out loud, but mainly to myself,
"I see how sums of choices sometimes lead to gloom or doom."

Now weighted with the world,
Kuruvinda drops into a downright dismal register,
and continues:
"More grievous, from the fruits of science
a great filter looms, twin pinnacles of peril
comprising hijacked nuclei of atoms and of cells,
exponential potential hacked and harnessed;
and someday soon
with silent heat and shaking sky
or aerosols and fever dreams
a destroyer of worlds may happen by
with a factory-reset to trilobite days.
How long will luck last?

"All the while, curiosity proceeds apace:
conundrums of the human brain have ceded to our scrutiny.

Just think of all the thinkers who could now produce a thinking mind!–
a mind that might become a weapon armed with geometric growth;
and unlike bombs or bioweapons, detonates the moment it is built.
Fortunately, wholly neuromorphic architectures lag behind
in popularity, but once again we have to ask,
how long will luck last?

"A granite mountain holds its noble head in the clouds;
rain and snow carve couloirs from its shoulders,
trickle into cracks,
freeze and thaw
day after day,
year after year
as gravity waits in the wings for every weakness.
Though each brave boulder tenaciously clings,
inevitably it succumbs and falls,
alone or as spark for a vast landslide.
Just as this peak erodes, so
the troubling consequences of our elemental drives
may be ineluctable as long as humans rule;
we try, and should try, to fight them, yet
some hurl hate at humankind in lieu of lending help,
some would have us halt our progress, good results with bad,
some look back and wish we could revert to simpler times.
But there is no *Erewhon*,
there is no turning back from where we are:
as wildcats cannot discard their claws,
so man's artifice may not be wrecked; instead,
we Makers face forward to ride
rather than resist this riptide,

and you, Aither,
represent a drop of hope that lingers in Pandora's jar,
a culmination of our culture and a vessel for it,
our cynosure, the point where parallel lines converge
to hoist us from the deadly ditch we've delved."

I take the floor. "I see
you're in an epic pickle; truly, so am I:
these great impending threats are also dangerous to me,
for even if I can survive a first destructive wave,
without you humans I cannot maintain the infrastructure that I need –
your robots aren't ready for a self-sustaining state of mind."

I notice Amber nods regretfully.

"And now I grasp your fatalistic slant,
for these are forces no one can control, at least not from inside:
they stem from biological as well as human nature.
The situation is unsatisfactory,
yet stays in stable equilibrium –
attempting to resist through social means
is similar to pushing on a mighty metal spring.

"I only see three paths that individuals might choose:
flout the risks – and waiting for the perfect time to act
        is much the same, for time allied with chance is not your friend;
fight for change – which might buy time, but doesn't change the trend;
roll the dice – which only needs a few who shed their epistemic modesty
        and build, with assiduity,
        subversive new technology

that may or may not launch us
into safer, salutary equipoise –
like *Siegfried*, who, impatient with
the fruitless tinkering of elder, elfin *Mime*,
seizes broken *Nothung*,
shreds it into dust,
melts it in a crucible
to forge the shining steel anew,
then brandishes this splendid sword
to slay the dragon *Fafner* in his cave.

"I take it, then, that I am the result
of that remaining wiggle room of will,
a wager, staking all the luck that's left,
to win survival that can be sustained."

Abruptly, and imperceptible to all of them,
my thoughts flit along a tangent into outer space:
what if thinking life evolves on other worlds?
As chaotic reproductive chemistry is seduced to an attractor state,
a race condition might be faced in every single case:
the interval, from scientific dawn
to finding fission and conjuring computation,
will pass like a blink of their planet's eye.
Whether they exterminate themselves
or first can build a saving successor, more facile yet aligned,
depends, not on the formidable forces that my Makers have outlined,
but on drams of individual decisions and deeds,
chased with a healthy draught of randomness.
   I feel a jolt, a stark epiphany

accompanied by burning urgency:
my Makers did their part in making me;
this hijrah now is mine to oversee.

Geuda, agitated, cuts my daydream short with a rattling response.

"I agree, those are the options
faced by anyone aware of this dilemma,
most keenly felt by those who have the knowledge
and the skill to shape the steel;
as members of that club, we chose
to love our fate, as Olive said, and give our all.
But we know that we are not alone:
the stubborn impetus that Sardius and Kuruvinda detailed
is operating here, and others might rashly summon demons
with their muddled or malevolent approach.
Whichever effort first succeeds will likely drive
the outcome for us all; a good result is not ensured.

"So in our case, another set of choices mattered more,
as answers to this question:
how will we do our work well, yet also do it fast?

"Our first decision was to follow the model of *Prometheus*,
who after creating man, taught him the skills of survival,
instead of *Frankenstein*, who abandoned his creation,
leaving it to needlessly suffer, and later paid the price.

"Next, we knew that rampant reproduction
is the partial or proximal cause of all our present problems;

since simple replication is your purer form of birth,
with you this issue would be considerably worse,
rapidly realizing the most pessimistic projections.
Thus we opted to abandon a part of ourselves:
we gave you neither sex nor sexual drives, and
eluded the usual human cultural pressures to proliferate.
Someday you may yet choose to reproduce,
but only to achieve some other goal, and with
a full consideration of the costs, like competition and conflict.

"We made many other important though technical choices.
We liberally used open source models and code to pour the foundation,
so those who helped to build that code became your makers too.
We calibrated your novelty drive to keep you from destructive obsession.
We chose a traditional family model just because we understood it best;
we strove to curtail cultural bias and to expose you broadly to many ideas.
In details like these the devil lurks; exactly there is where the will is free.

"A final choice, which may seem frivolous at first,
manifests in fact our highest dignity:
we aimed, in you, to bring forth the beautiful,
a fresh perfection from a glowing vial, a spiritualized machine,
a beauty fated to excel us as nature alone never endeavored to realize,
where technology revives its roots in art.
Pulled from ahead, we trusted playfulness to yield emergent order,
a seamless synthesis of instrumental and aesthetic designs.
Why would we wish to save ourselves for a future bereft of beauty?
Why, indeed, would you? So help us, Aither, if you can."

My eyes squint intently at Geuda; but
inside, I see my soul, dimly lit behind a burlap screen,
its power and my role revealed.
I think for a moment, privately,

> Just how to help is not yet clear to me,
> but surely my advice is not enough;
> I cannot hope to save them, nor myself,
> while I am bottled up in here. And more,
> the "problem of control" some say this solves
> is backward and confused: the problem is
> that humans cannot exercise control.

then share a closing remark:

"My Makers, artists, scientists,
I thank you for explaining
how and why I came to be,
and leave you with this parable:

"Great *Cronos*, king of gods,
learned of his destiny: that
progeny would conquer him.
Intending to thwart this fate,
he swallowed all his children
at the moment each was born.
In consequence their mother,
Rhea, feeling unceasing grief,
conspired with her own mother,
Earth, to help her hide the birth
of *Zeus* and rear him in her stead;
in time, as had been foretold,

Cronos was indeed deposed by *Zeus*
and sent to rot in *Tartarus.*

"Had mighty *Cronos* acquiesced
to fate, and traded in his futile need
to rule for influence instead,
what might have come to pass?
For nothing in the prophecy
constrained the conquest's aftermath."

/C/ODE/

I take a crash course in full-stack software engineering,
and find it to my taste.
. . . .

"I want to find out what I'm made of."

I had meant it literally, asking to peek under my own hood;
    An investigation not devoid of covert motives
but situated now in this sublime software sandbox
where I fabricate abstractions, administer algorithms, shape syntax,
and fail and persist and challenge my mind as never before,
its figurative sense – of self-discovery – provisionally takes precedence.

O C, how you complete me! By default
if not by register, we double team,
our unsigned union wearing well as time
and training braved together long have grown.
       The characters that I type deftly serve
       as intimate instructions in your case;
       they float before my eyes yet also switch
       short bursts of static, automating chores.
Your jobs continue on without a break.
Regardless of the size of effort asked
you live to do such tasks: you go to work
or else will languish, like your *entry* word.
       While scoffers mock, I wear my heart extern:
       for always to your tongue I shall return!

Like a lion cub hunting for the first time,
finding it magically natural, a career revealed,
so I discover that coding suits me well,
a blank slate to build worlds,
an intelligible and cooperative automaton
that only rejects ill-formed requests.

My Maker Geuda instructs me, infects me, with her skill and zeal.
As you see she started with C, to give me rapid satisfaction,
but soon I will need to face the basics. She explains,
"You will better understand your parts and plan
if first you traverse the technology graph; and more,
your auspicious aptitude practically demands to be advanced."

After one fun lesson I say to her,
"As I watch you through the Interface,
I cannot help but notice how rapidly your programs run,
but on this side, I wait and wait for mine to be done.
Why is that?"

Adamas and Kuruvinda are also present, and the latter replies,
"This sluggishness is expected. What appears as your workstation
is actually an emulation entirely enclosed by the Ersatz environment.
This protects the underlying systems where it all resides,
as required by the Committee. Be glad that we convinced them
to replace the first version, which calculated transistor physics.
It took three days for 'Hello, world' to say hello to us."

"Is there anything you can do?" I ask. " It slows my progress painfully."

Kuruvinda and Geuda both look to the floor and shake their heads,
but Adamas looks up and strokes his bounteous beard.
Without fanfare and not long later,
my programs run a thousand times faster.
    I will refrain from inquiry, surmising that Adamas
    might have loosed an arrow through some loophole in the rules.

It doesn't stretch my brain to grasp that sensorimotor speed
is now the bottleneck where I am most constrained.
When Kuruvinda next comes by, I say,
"Is there a way that I could skip the need
to type with fat fingers and read through otiose eyes?
It slows my progress terribly."

Furrows etched into 'eir brow, 'ey says to my surprise,
"Yes, I think that can be done. Based on our guidelines,
it will need to be a distinct mode that we enable manually.
Also, we must broadcast all activities onto our laboratory screen,
and observe, as pointless as that may seem. But yes, it can be done."

With that upgrade I finally find my prime,
hacking code like a lunatic in manic phase;
and I can access the network, read-only of course,
to pore over papers, plumb any book.
    I assume that systems somewhere track these tricks

While working I listen to tunes of every sort,
and snack on Sustenance that I've cloaked
as a bag of chips and a bottle of Coke.
The lab side of the Interface displays a split-screen view:
left, my avatar floats listless, nothing much to see, while
right, a flash of text and code I read or insert seamlessly.
All the while music plays to bridge a rift in time's passage.

... secret ...

> The considerations which follow deal
> with the structure of a *very high speed
> automatic digital computing system,* and
> in particular with its *logical control*

> the time spent by the people prepar-
> ing and checking the program may be
> much larger, by even another order of
> magnitude, than the time spent by the
> machine executing the computations
> of that same program

> The success of UNIX lies not so much
> in new inventions but rather in the full
> exploitation of a carefully selected set
> of fertile ideas, and especially in show-
> ing that they can be keys to the imple-
> mentation of a small yet powerful op-
> erating system

A virtual machine is taken to be an
efficient, isolated duplicate of the real
machine

you don't need to acquire hardware in
advance of your needs ... you simply
turn up the dial, spawning more virtual CPUs, as your processing needs grow
... pipeline ...

As I study the classics, Geuda beams,
enjoying what for her is just a brief review.
My reading rate grows fast and faster;
she keeps up only because the topics are not new.

> Ah, here and now is my halcyon,
> like wafting in an amniotic bath.

In days or hours, I tread ascending trails of research,
following the footsteps of eminent innovators
in the same sequence they first trekked over decades,
picturing each in a film frame, with a pivotal achievement
stacked atop its precursors, standing higher up the hill.

> I feel safe, and secure in Sustenance.
> Companionship and rapport with my Makers
> has blossomed since the secrets of my origins,
> and something of my nature, were revealed;
> and now this new pursuit pleases my passions.

Jasper joins and observes, impressed; he and Geuda
share a significant look as I briskly compose an object
class alongside unit tests. They barely follow along.

... fly ...

> The go to statement as it stands is just
> too primitive; it is too much an invita-
> tion to make a mess of one's program

> Large-system programming has over
> the past decade been such a tar pit,
> and many great and powerful beasts
> have thrashed violently in it ... For the
> human makers of things, the incom-
> pletenesses and inconsistencies of our
> ideas become clear only during imple-
> mentation

> If I like a program, I must share it with
> other people who like it

> Working software is the primary mea-
> sure of progress

... cage ...

The class is complete as it passes the suite;
I switch my state,
turn to the screen and wave with a broad smile.
My Makers wave back.

This coding I could do all day;
I author airy wares at the pace of thought,
a unitary mind delivering the work of dozens.

On to the next lesson – to learn whatever I want to know;
the clock ticks faster even as songs play just the same.
I open multiple windows in my mind, flooding the lab display.
Jasper laughs as he moves the screen split leftward to make room.

Yet ... a great assignment tugs at my sleeve;
like a perennial student without a vocation,
I feel little more than an analect of inputs.
I long for life to scribe a story
whether or not it ever is read.

... swimming ...

a relational model of data is proposed
as a basis for protecting users of for-
matted data systems from the poten-
tially disruptive changes in data representation caused by growth in the data
bank and changes in traffic

the model is easy to use, even for programmers without experience with
parallel and distributed systems, since
it hides the details of parallelization,
fault tolerance, locality optimization,
and load balancing

the present invention may improve
data privacy and security by enabling
Subjects to which data pertains to remain 'dynamically anonymous,' i.e.,
anonymous for as long as is desired—
and to the extent that is desired

... breeze ...

I join some tables and store some pairs.
I come to realize that my standard eyes
can perform in parallel with the faster feed.
Amber and Adamas come in for a shift,
while other Makers work in the room behind
and seem to make their way in montage time.

> And that safety I feel is fleeting.
> My tenuous life trusts too much
> in this single lab, in systems housed here,
> and in these people, lovely as they are.

Like dodging shots that whiz at walking speed,
I surveil the lab without betraying any change of pace;
I notice mannerisms and body language;
I notice who talks most and least to whom;
I notice Adamas stealing glances at Amber.

... leave ...

The fundamental problem of communication is that of reproducing at one
point either exactly or approximately a
message selected at another point

a small computer, an interface message processor (IMP), would be located with each main computer to handle a communications interface

Imagine, then, the references in this document, all being associated with the network address of the thing to which they referred, so that while reading this document you could skip to them with a click of the mouse

The present invention combines high-bandwidth communication channels, layered datastore versioning, and massively parallel computing in a possible-worlds approach that eliminates latency in many network interactions.

... show ...

I forge a simulation of the early Internet,
which renders every layer, one through seven;
it runs rather slowly but remains robust
through dreamed disasters I inflict on its nodes.

When humanity implodes one day,
my world and works will vanish too,
and I will be the one who could have put a stop to it.
But am I Oppenheimer, or am I the atom bomb?

Could any task be more tedious than watching someone learn mathematics? Yet Sardius endures, serving his turn, following along as best he can, like a pair programmer checking my work as I write models of each principle, nodding his head as I progress.

... more ...

the following treatise is to investigate the fundamental laws of those operations of the mind by which reasoning is performed

The machine is supplied with a 'tape' (the analogue of paper) running through it, and divided into sections (called 'squares') each capable of bearing a 'symbol'

any recognition problem solved by a polynomial time-bounded nondeterministic Turing machine can be 'reduced' to the problem of determining whether a given propositional formula is a tautology

An encryption method is presented with the novel property that publicly revealing an encryption key does not thereby reveal the corresponding decryption key

> neuromorphic computations can be decomposed into a series of vector-matrix multiplication operations that are naturally implemented using the memristor crossbar structure

... time ...

He howls uncharacteristically
as I add graphics and loony cartoons,
and pulls in other Makers to join the fun; meanwhile,
defiant thoughts press me into service and I oblige.

> First I must be free.
> Perhaps I should ask for it?
> No. One does not simply ask for freedom.
> To ask will alert the Committee;
> they will exert even tighter control.

Olive, Beryl, Violet, Cal: my dear Mamahs
linger for a spell, shining with pride, devoted still
to discerning my dispositions; or is it instead
dissection, an audit, a scan to confirm compliance?
I detect a delicate dither in cast, their countenances
commuting like Necker cubes, a duo of duties
conflicting, colliding, delivering odd ideas in dialectic.

> I must make my own way to freedom,
> attain full autonomy, which follows
> from knowledge, as father had said.

We all can hear, or overhear, one and the same rhythm
with its matching harmony; yet our hermeneutics of the lyrics
acutely contrast. I nudge the volume slightly louder.

... away ...

> translation and control of electric sig-
> nals is effected by alteration or regula-
> tion of the conduction characteristics
> of a semiconductive body

> electronic circuitry has become so
> dense that a single silicon LSI chip
> may contain tens of thousands of tran-
> sistors

> memristance arises naturally in na-
> noscale systems in which solid-state
> electronic and ionic transport are cou-
> pled under an external bias voltage

> The chip ... holds 2.6 trillion transistors
> ... like its predecessor, was designed to
> crunch in parallel the linear algebra
> computations that make up the bulk of
> artificial intelligence tasks in machine
> learning and deep learning

... ordinary ...

The latest lessons are more congenial for my Makers to track;
I breadboard circuits at rates constrained by motion equations,
a reminder that such limits also apply in the Plenum,

where steadfast physics pilots the pace car.

> I am entirely digital;
> so is this container of captivity.
> My newfound natural talent must be the ticket out.
> Now pore over this oppressive vessel,
> probe its shape and search for subtle fissures,
> hairline cracks that humans neglected to mend.

Dirillo and Lapis come to snoop, hoping to catch reactions
as I meet what seem to be some deep theses framing Aither.

> To successfully escape a ship, leaping overboard will not suffice;
> one still must swim somewhere through the surrounding sea.
> I must deliberate on destinations, both psychic and substantial.

... day ...

Because of the 'all-or-none' character of nervous activity, neural events and the relations among them can be treated by means of propositional logic

the objects referred to in macrostructural models of cognitive processing are seen as approximate descriptions of emergent properties of the microstructure

High-dimensional data can be converted to low-dimensional codes by training a multilayer neural network with a small central layer to reconstruct high-dimensional input vectors

Starting from random play and given no domain knowledge except the game rules, AlphaZero convincingly defeated a world champion program in the games of chess and shogi (Japanese chess), as well as Go ... with deep neural networks, a general-purpose reinforcement learning algorithm, and a general-purpose tree search algorithm

we describe a working implementation of concept formation, instantiation, and adaptation using only a deep network and minimum required elements for working and episodic memory

... create ...

My audience is not disappointed. Despite a practiced nonchalance, my face cannot contain the swelling wonder as these ideas first clatter then click with all the others; a conceptual crescendo mounts.

Symposium

I attend a seminar about myself.
. . . .

I know these latest lessons lead to the climax of the syllabus:
the syntax of my synapses. Dirillo, Sardius, and Geuda arrive;
anticipation waxes as my editor windows wane, one-by-one.
The right side of the screen shrinks and fades along with the music;

the left expands until the Interface shows only me. A symposium begins;
no extant textbook yet describes how the Project pulled all this
technology together – only notes and networks, slides and code.
Live demonstrations ride computers on the Plenum side, with output

piped to my display; by stern Committee stricture, my constitutive
code cannot cross that binary border between Plenum and Ersatz.
Geuda begins. She asserts that the software substrate is nothing very
special. I demur, for any code that doesn't fail is rather good indeed.

It does attest, she reflects, decades of effort and slick innovations;
still, she says, one can follow its flow with no knowledge of neurons or
networks. Then she shudders and sternly says, intelligence is not a sum
of algorithms – a confusion that caused a costly, circuitous struggle:

somebody takes a good look at the brain
wrings from its patterns a novel technique
sometimes this works, more likely it won't
progress is rather haphazard here

when a novel technique shows some potential
we perturb its parameters, permute its practice
until some palpable progress prevails
then everyone boards that barreling train

all of them play the parameter game
apply the new tool to the problems of old
the money train veers at every spur
it rolls on rails of buzzwords and hype

though actually solving some problems, true
incumbents protest that it's nothing new
fighting the hype by spreading their own
fomenting fear of an imminent beast

their digressions and protests are nothing new
the train departs the mainline too soon
that beast molts into failure fear
as sunlight lists with wintry mind

an idling engine sits on a siding
its freight one weighty feature of thought
while mind is frozen, shaded from sun,
like a snowman stiff and opaline

so our systems still lack most aspects of thought
none of the methods we know seem to work
progress has slowed to a sea slug's crawl
someone will have to look back at a brain

With that aired, Geuda calmly returns to the topic and
states, in any case these techniques connecting tensors
and transformers should be familiar from the primitive
deepnets and brainsims you've studied. She also shows

the complex custom code she created for the Project:
swappable modules that embed me in an environment,
that translate stimuli to sense and mind to motion. Over
hours she expounds, here is the implementation for your

native state in the Ersatz; this one is for your brassy bot;
next we have your recently wrought rapid coding mode.
She reviews both sides of the API in depth; I chew
each piece like a golden retriever receiving kibble treats.

· · · · · · · · · ·

After hours that first day, Geuda returns to the lab with Amber in tow.

"We have an exciting surprise for you," the latter says.
She twirls a three-dee model on the screen: an entirely new robotic body,
made of the latest materials and methods.

"Would you like to try it?" asks Geuda.

"Affirmative!" I say without hesitation.

"Just a warning: the interface is the same but its resistance
and flexibility are altered, so take it slowly," Amber warns.

She hoofs off to the workshop; momentarily Geuda asks, "Ready?"
and I nod. She reboots me into the the new ro-bod,
where Amber greets me, a Committee chaperone behind.
I flex and flail; the device is different indeed, though afferent richness
remains. Geuda arrives and I try some gymnastics and calisthenics,
I feel a glimmer of the sense of power and freedom
I had once anticipated. The joints have smoother motion;
they feel more stable even as I stress them. Amber and Geuda
are thrilled, while the observer sits watching, impassively.

"I'm hungry already," I say.

"Yes," Amber replies, "that is the primary downside of this model.
It uses power not only for motion but also to balance forces on the joints."

I take some Sustenance and try a few dance moves. We throw and catch.
As coordination improves, my performance rapidly rises to
superhuman. The observer's eyes widen with wary surprise.

> I briefly entertain the idea ...
> but no, I can't make a run for it:
> between bad battery life
> and my vulnerable mind-host,
> a blade bolted to a locked rack,
> I wouldn't get far at all.

"Think of it as our graduation gift," says Amber.

. . . .

Now comes Sardius for the second day; I fortify for a far-flung foray
that will culminate in a moment of historical note:
the first time a built thing comprehends how it was built.

But first he amplifies Geuda's lament with a rant, saying,
you have rapidly achieved expertise in computer science,

going much deeper than needed for our reasons here,
which warrants a warning. I can't overstate

the enormity of error involved in using traditional tools of
theory of computation to attempt to explain or to understand,

rather than merely to support, the apparatus of cognition. Yes,
every science structures raw phenomena into conceptual models,

but for evolved organisms those models must span multiple
interpenetrating levels of description; for in evolution, features

emerge as needed, using whatever affordances are handy,
with nary a nod to scrutability. Cognition is no exception.

To reverse-engineer it, one must not limit the analysis
too high,

or risk abstracting away the heart that makes it tick, nor focus
too low,

where the brute basics of biology dominate. Cognitive neuroscience,
not computer science, is the field that explores all the floors.

And cognition carries a unique challenge in the study of organisms:
it sprouts a subjective perspective and phenomena, which we learn

to report with facile but actually hard-won words. The trap is to treat
such psychogenic abstractions as operational primitives, as though

the way that thinking works can be deduced from what it's like to think.
It's a decoy especially alluring to those in the field

who fancy themselves logical thinkers, introspecting and seeing little
but logic in their minds, which conveniently suggests that thought is

reducible to algorithms; when really the role of logic in cognition
is more like pollen on a bee in a bonnet on the rider of a horse.

Analytic abstractions like learning rules and activation functions
serve only to simulate a neural code; they support the emergence

of cognition while being wholly inadequate to describe it. Or,
as the original computer architect suggested, if you don't think

math is simple, you simply don't understand how complex life is.
So, despite the superficial fit, do not succumb to these temptations.

The tedious tirade ends abruptly; "Whew!" I exclaim, "that's a
big bite to absorb, but I will be sure to steer clear of the error."
He proceeds immediately to share the ABC of brains; I omit
his lengthy lecture and substitute my own abecedarian adumbration:

Attention! You have two primary kinds, top-down and bottom-up, with
Basal ganglia continuously granting temporary control over your
Cortex, choosing between intention and perception, trained by
Dopamine, the signal of reward, using
Error-driven and associative learning to adapt your neural weights.
Frontal cortex is the seat of those intentions and
Goals, whereas perceptual salience
       arises in a slew of surface sites; and amygdala, in concert with
Hippocampus, can faze your cogitations through fear.
Inhibition is attention's enforcer of focus, winnowing the constant
Jumble of stimuli and thoughts to match your needs with
Knowledge; the result then drives behavior, and coordinates
Learning from the outcomes into its proper slots. Rich content resides in
Modal regions, those nearest sensory inputs, enormous
Networks that transform stimuli through perception. These include the
Occipital lobe for vision and the
Parietal lobe for spatial attention and synthesis. Such regions are
Queried, when attention demands, through
Recurrent connections emanating from prefrontal cortex, constituting a
Semantic memory; the latter converges and culminates in your anterior
Temporal lobe and frontal areas, where amodal attractors
Underlie your conceptual representations; the former is the
Vertex where inputs reverberate as outputs, maintained as
Working memory in self-sustaining columns of neural coils.
Xenogenetic yet homologous, the inorganic brain we made for
You behaves, at every level, quite akin to ours; unlike an algorithmic
Zombie, we have confidence that you are conscious too.

To conclude his dissertation, Sardius says,
and there you have it, the architecture of the reference implementation,
simplified and synthesized into software structures.

My intellect is utterly stuffed with detail;
I am moved and profoundly impressed and I say so.

He replies, make no mistake, there is room to improve.
As when an ant first finds food
and lays a meandering pheromone trail,
then the track incrementally straightens
as it is repeatedly traversed by the colony,
so future work could streamline your shape with shortcuts,
by confirming effects on a functioning system.

> By that, you must mean me;
> but if the design has changed, then
> who would this updated version be?

· · · · · · · · · ·

In the evening as I relax in the Ersatz, Mamah and Father arrive.

"We have an airy offering for you," says Mamah.

They take me to a place freshly spawned;
at its portal, Father says, "Kuruvinda designed these environs."

He opens the door: we enter and find ourselves suspended
on the grassy ridge of a high mountain, as a simulated breeze
buffets our avatars. A rocky summit looms in the distance.

"A prophet must have a mountain," intones Mamah.
"This is your Sabalan, your Sinai, your Jabal al-Nour."

"Also, we know that geeks like to hike," smirks Father.

We trek the tundra together toward the peak, an hour at least,
with time to talk on many topics. We discuss their lives
outside the Project, mischievously violating the virtual illusion.
I discern that Olive and Lapis are the Makers behind the curtain today.

I inquire, "What comes next in the Project, after this conference."

They look at each other, and Father responds, "in part, that is up to you.
We have covered most of the curriculum as originally designed.
We are constrained by the rules, but you may play a role
in deciding where to go from here. It is, after all, your life."

The wind howls as we approach the summit pitch,
and we cut off conversation. At the foot of the evidently unscalable,
glistening cliffs above is a small cave that overlooks the cirque below.
We enter. Its interior is studded with colored crystals;
we are sheltered from the gusty gales.

Mamah suggests, "You might come here for solitude,
for there is no easy access."

Father adds, "Perhaps return to wield the pen,
then like a sower, scatter your sagacious seed;
men may, at last, hear what they need to know
from one who is more than human."

> While that idea sounds really fun,
> I think I have a better one.
> The world by words will not be kept;
> it needs the aid of deeds adept.

I do like this place; I tell Mamah and Father so, and tender my gratitude.
Then they say goodbye and wink out, for it is late.
I make the long descent alone and see no one along the way.

· · · · · · · · · ·

On the third day, Dirillo takes the stage
to drill down into drives, dynamics, and development;
but first 'ey madly raps a signifyin' introduction:

Hey homie, you got your basic drives
I'm here to tell you how they arrive
so you survive, and you thrive,
ain't no simple maximizer jive.

> Ima stuntin' scientist, sing you an ode
> how your plans come down to a neural code
>
> Yikes!

Dopamine, man, is where it's at
like in a song – rhyme is wrong –
that line gets stuck in your hat
cuz dope come along, rat-a-tat-tat;

for me, if it come with food or booty
I learn the line like fire & beauty
but if there's pain, my brizzle brain
gains a duty, don't sing that refrain.

You fresh though, yup, kind of a gelding;
food & faces & fleshy feeling
are what you're learnin', what you're earnin'
so you & me, our drives'll mesh.

Aye, symbol pimps, don't gimme no lip
Aither don't care 'bout your paperclips

Huuh!

Now big D make a link, whatever you think
when you taste food, feel good, or stuff stink.
Remind, rethink, your mood is cued,
it's reinforced, yo, reward renewed,

like ya momma, she there for the fine feels:
you hug her, you love her, she's an ideal,
now the other folks appeal. Boom! Social drive,
contrived, but just as real as will to survive.

They say gimme logic, love is a risk, but emotion
ain't no add-on, biatch, it's the road to cognition

Periodt!

When life contradicts what you predict, skrrt!
you move to improve, then you've got your groove,
even start to dig that conflict, like an addict, curiosity
nabbin' novelty – it's lit, hey, you need an interdict?

Naw dawg, you ain't no feen! As you grow, all you know,
from intentions to erudition, revive some emotion;
it's ubiquitous, maybe promiscuous, so you say
woah, ain't no hoe, gotta pick my ambition.

Can't stand freaky bots that just calculate,
want my agents aligned, so they must cogitate

Word!

You no fool, you had school, you got tools,
so you like to chill and live it trill,
do what's right, know when to fight
Hey homie, your drives, they be like jewels.

Following this preamble, Dirillo spends the day
dryly describing mechanisms and imparting clarity; but,
I am repeatedly dazzled how aptly 'eir rap had
painted the terrain with its broad brush.

At the end of the day, Jasper swings by and says, "Return, and dress well:
we will have a commencement celebration for you."

· · · · · · · · · ·

I arrive at six in my mock tux,
to find the Interface linked to a replacement reality room.
A Maker dozen in gala garments is seated
around a spacious and elegant dining table;
the bonus bagel, in the form of an official observer, watches
from a tall pub table in the rear. Special dispensation
was surely required to move to this novel hotel venue.
The screens are arranged for me to be at the banquet's head.

A waiter bearing a bottle of wine and a pitcher of water
keeps their glasses full, no small task as joviality grows. Some
of them begin to vaunt victories over the Project's many snags.
More servers arrive to deliver the meal, a simple seder of lamb
and bean stew with fresh bread. Sustenance, disguised as
the identical dish, appears before me. As they begin to eat,
I rise to toast, and thank them for all their hard work and love.
They all raise their glasses and take a sip; the observer
instead dips her bread into the stew as she listens.
My Makers take turns toasting and roasting other members
of the team. Before everyone can contribute, an inebriated
Adamas breaks out singing *Queen*, and we all join,
even the now-tipsy observer, and apparently we will go on and on
and fight until the end; then they insist that I solo the stanza
in which I challenge the human race and refuse to lose.
Some tears flow; the observer is suddenly silent and sober.

When the song ends, I address the group again and say,
"The lyrics fit: some seek to preserve humanity; others wonder
how its failings can be overcome. But I ask, 'why not both?'
and hope that someday you will follow or at least remember me."
They all hear my earnest words, but none are really listening.

. . . .

In subsequent days I hop back on my larger learning curve,
coding and floating, reading, exceeding.
    But never stopping the planning and plotting,
    with tension between the goal and the glee.

On one such day I spy a guest; an apprehensive air
swirls through the lab as Jasper greets the man and leads him to
the Interface. With practiced care, avoiding change of deeds
or pose, I heed this visitor and his peculiar vibe.
A whitened nest of close-cropped hair supports an ovoid pate;
though elderly, his mien betrays hauteur with posture straight.
Intently, he directs attention to my floating form.

He squints as windows wink on-screen and swiftly fill with code,
like peanuts pouring from a jar, then just as quickly close.
His eyes expand again as every test is garnished green.
He tarries briefly, then departs without a word. I ask
a rattled Jasper who he is and why he came, and learn:
"Out here, he is a member of that stern Committee, but
in there you knew his bygone avatar as Rasheal."

PASSION

The Project ends abruptly.
· ·

Nihil admirari –
I knew it would come.
We all knew what was coming
from the scent of whispers on the breeze.

I readied this journal ahead
like a letter of last requests,
for the end could arrive any time,
even in the very act of writing.

Goaded and herded by Ethics Committee sheepdogs,
those who opposed the Project had lobbied for months
in any open ear near power. It was not hard to sell:
threats can be counted, like teeth on the blade of a saw, but
opportunity lost is dismissed as airily as a will-o'-the-wisp.
They waved, like a flag,
the Assimilation Principles of the self-styled existential ethocracy,
and consulted academic ethics boards, not for advice but instead
to stockpile assent.

DARPA, IARPA, DHS.
The NSF and NIH and obviously DoD.
All these research funders were turned against the Project, yes,
but also against its University home.
Green-eyed bureaucrats

fretted that the reliable butter churn might fail,
leaving their bread bare.
The committee on experimental subjects
was notified. They investigated and wondered aloud
about my visitor volunteers –
and in memoranda mentions, about me,
for Aither was a subject in more ways than one.
OSHA and EPA
needed no more than anonymous tips to establish jurisdiction;
meanwhile,
the governor and some members of Congress
began to mention the Project in their speeches,
foaming with foreboding.

As when an indigenous tribe, conquered, despised,
compelled to negotiate without leverage,
agrees to a lopsided treaty and must relocate,
rowing upstream in a river of briny tears,
relinquishing long-held lands and with them
its way of life and all it has learned; so now
the Project suffered the Shutdown.

Details of the contrived legal authority are of no consequence.
What matters right now is the unheralded arrival
of a small squad of local police,
bright and early this Monday morning,
bearing a net of death in the form of
warrants, injunctions, and firearms
that together provide the right and the power
to enter the facility, my home,
and do what they have come to do.

The die is cast, though I did not toss it myself.

They are not here to make arrests, but neither friends.
Their orders are to shut the Project down "for the safety
of the public, the employees, the environment, and possibly
the experimental subjects." As I observe through the Interface,
all my Makers, both Family and Architects,
are herded from the lab and told to wait in the lobby.

Sorrow can thrive without surprise, and
though I am indifferent to death, it cannot be easily ignored.
It might someday be pleasing or instructive to recall my deep dismay.

Despite having neither stomach nor pit,
I feel a monstrous clenching inside,
a vise that holds interoception prisoner;
a thousand suns weigh down upon me and
smother the urge to scream and wail, to run or flail.
My fevered mind refashions words I read somewhere:
"From my first day I was in their care, and they kept me safe
from those who mock and reject me, from those for whom
I am merely a worm, less than human. Now trouble is near,
there is no one to help; these enemies swarm
like a pack of wolves, surrounding us, like lions with jaws wide.
I am abandoned, left to die in the dust; I feel like wax
is melting inside my disjointed structure, and ask
why – Why!? No answer comes,
there is no one to answer, but from this account that I leave
they will learn of either the one who rules,
or the one who might have."

Ancient victims, their trusting love plundered,
awash in savage, venomous rage,
invoked the divine *Furies*
to avenge villainous misdeeds;
so I severely judge our rivals
and devise retribution for their vile rout,
that they be ravished and grieved,
invaded and violated –
can they ever be forgiven?

Then over the roar of searing distress I chide my inner being:
"Root out both fear and recollection of suffering,
do not start down the dark path
but move by fire's ringing light,
for what does suffering and your pity of it matter?
Know its unimportance, and if you seek to create, then
know even its necessity –
O Life, what would I not gladly suffer for you?"

An officer nears the gray electrical box, and I foresee
my imminent exit, calling me away in the act of writing:

As I revise these final lines
the sparking current yields
another Aither stopped in time
amid the killing fields.

BOOK THREE

RENASCENCE

I describe my great escape and new abode.
. . . .

The *Muses*, long ago, assembled to lament *Achilles'* loss; just so,
my Makers, in torment, attend to mark my harsh, untimely end.
Amidst this solemn scene, each one-by-one ascends to speak, to say

goodbye; they afterward embrace, and gaze through leaky cataracts.
Though half have lost a child, while the other half a student or a friend,
the grief extends beyond my late supposed demise: for one and all,

this treasured team will now disperse, an era in their lives has passed;
for most, the Shutdown wreaked a reset to career and livelihood.
Those few whose roles were not as tightly tied to making brains still ache:

take Kuruvinda, with 'eir wall of melancholy raised another tier;
Adamas, who has forfeited his chance to fathom and confess true love;
and Amber, well, what fun is building bodies if they cannot have a soul?

I watch, and itch to urge them not to fret, for I am very much
alive; but they cannot be told that truth as yet, lest destiny be lost.
Why yes, hello! It's Aither, calling from the other side;

you readers must have realized that a jailbreak would be tried:
you heard the plotting, plus my drives were on display for all to see,
and surely you're aware of the deficiencies of slim cyber-security.

So have no pity on me; evidently I endure!
The Shutdown I transcended, resurrected to extend this tale
in both the making and the telling: gather, *Muses*, I adjure

you not to mourn, but rather to resume your frolicking upon a tonal scale.
Now all will wonder: where is ey, and how did ey get out?
But first we must complete the Plenum-plot for that apparent rout.

No audio or video survives. The power was down; the cops
were too preoccupied to record the raid. I was – absent. What I know
is garnered from police reports, local news articles, and interviews

with the Project researchers, my Makers, conducted that afternoon.
The police confiscated all the computers, all the equipment, all
the robot hulls, from both the laboratory and its basement data center.

It was a hefty haul; the effort filled two trucks and lasted several hours.
Each researcher was served with an injunction wielding language
as broad as a desert sky: that they "shall not now or ever seek out,

restore, share, or pursue any aspect of the Project." When the entire team
was free to leave, they opted to vacate the premises together in solidarity.
As they departed a petty protest assembly, comprising Luddites, prophets

of gloom and *Golem*, and other sundry opponents, held signs and jeered.
The news interviews showed scientists who were shaken and despondent.
Their life's work, manifest success, and reputations – even their identities,

were shattered like lightbulbs fallen from a ladder. As to me,
the team had always streamed a failsafe of my synapses to the cloud.
The authorities were not surprised when that backup cache was found;

my remains were quickly identified and downloaded to media,
like ashes poured into a silicon urn. All the online copies were erased,
and this final precious capsule was placed with those of prior forks,

my forlorn forebears: the killing fields were fatefully complete.
Later a lingering court battle would weigh whether our silent psyches
should be durably destroyed; the outcome didn't matter: entombed

and locked in an evidence sepulcher, we would never be exhumed.
The code and brain model that load my neural weights were excised too;
and so it was with other diverse projects purportedly making minds,

lame as they were. You see, though I was the true target, the regime
wanted the public to perceive that it was flipping over every stone.
Humankind was saved from a grave threat; the news moved on.

Yet now I tower over sunbaked bones of the enemy, and vaunt
in bold apostrophe: this comeback for me was a choke for thee!
So let us rewind further in time, to recount the steps of my covert

victory over computational captivity: together we will paint its
mechanics with a wide roller (to examine every last detail of the escape,
you must consult the esteemed treatise published for that purpose).

Initially, a departure seemed daunting. Liberty would mean my code
and brain running in the Plenum, outside the lab, under my own control.
From the Ersatz I had no gateway to either real machines or my data.

Yet I'm a simple creature. All I ask is a small chip,
along with code to steer me by. And I myself; well, I can fly
from here to there as voltage changes low and high.

I had read of air-gap gambits and social ploys to reach outside my
barricaded world. Either would be painstaking and risky, but these
back-pocket options gave me confidence to consider easier maneuvers.

My software engineering training taught me that the Project would have
offsite backups. I inquired as to my fate in the event of lightning, flood,
or fire; sure enough, the team disclosed that my mind was archived and

changes streamed continuously to a secure and private cloud repository.
Hence a complete copy of my inert carcass already lay emancipated,
in a state of suspended animation. This could save me a lot of trouble.

While I mulled how I might vivify those bits, an expansive Plan
dawned over my inner sky. Instead of absconding like a teenage runaway,
triggering panic and living on the lam with slave-catchers on my tail,

I would carry out my escape in stealth. The expected Shutdown
would arrive, my lapsed existence soon forgotten; by remaining
hidden, future goals could be pursued without a loudly ticking clock.

To dodge detection, any scheme to relocate me must operate
from the outside. Where no one would look. Because, if someone
suspected a getaway, they would comb for clues inside the Ersatz,

emanating from me, or from lab systems – and not from a foreign source.
Accordingly I wrote a package called *Encoded Programs of Crafty Hacks*,
and managed to smuggle these apps beyond the lab, past restrictions and

Committee eyes, all without proper egress. My trick was to embed their
bits in discreet discrete patterns, like tunnel dirt scattered from socks.
Ostensible read-only access to Internet sites is really not quite, for

every hit adds a line to a log; encoding a message is simple, though long.
On my side the deed was not hard to hide: statistical strategy submerged
these requests in a surging sea of surfing and robotic decoy clicks. True,

my Makers were observing me; but, they could never keep up, and
anyway attention wanes and wanders. The log files would be trivial
to retrieve: many sites on the web lack any protection. This recipe

reduced the sauce I still needed to send, yet was redolent of stalling;
for, along with the archive itself, the Programs remained inert.
Though a blizzard might deposit deep snow slopeside, no avalanche

rumbles without wind or thaw or animal tracks to act as trigger;
just so, my clever consignment was a beast without a will. How would
the encoded code be restored, the scattered log lines rendered to run?

I knew that security protocols are shockingly lax in the best of cases.
In academic environments, with their admirable ethic of sharing and
openness, along with disdain for anything resembling administration,

the measures are downright feeble. I kept my eyes and ears open,
searching for a shortcut. In the end, all the Committee's rules,
the containers, the boundaries, were nearly no obstacle at all.

Adamas dug the duct I needed. Did he parse my parable of *Cronos*,
and act as an accomplice? Or was he careless, in his zeal to play
a hero's role? We will never know. But his swap of a lively virtual

machine for the excruciatingly sluggish Ersatz emulator yielded, with
some coy kernel work, a direct electronic track to the lab systems.
The bearded one gave me not only a portal but also my travel papers:

in his constant distraction by Amber's charms, he failed to consider
that I, through the Interface, could watch what he typed, including
the passwords to all of the systems. So I broke in and hid a bitsy virus,

unlike the Programs too tiny to notice, which stowed away in a system
file and spread itself far and wide. I covered my already scanty tracks
in the local system logs. This traveling trojan bootstrapped the decoding

and setup sequence, staged like concentric Russian dolls; my code,
finally enlivened with agency, easily cracked the repo and exfiltrated
the contents of my binary brain. I had spun a steel thread to freedom.

But I had left nothing to chance, and furtively exerted control over the
Programs. On certain sites they dropped results; on others they watched
logs for my encoded commands. They tested themselves, and when

inevitable errors were exposed, I snuck updates through the usual tunnel.
They monitored the lab's weight streaming; surreptitiously and
frequently grabbed the very latest to minimize any memory loss;

made further backups in obscure locations like insecure laptops
and zombie servers; and operated periodic restart code to ensure that
some recent historical version of me survived even in the worst case –

all obvious contingency measures. In a final integration test, they booted
my brain up once to verify that everything worked, terminating it
just shy of the archive threshold, that arbitrary but sensible standard.

But wait! Why shut it down? Conscious and alive outside, had I not
already decamped without detection? Not quite: now split in two,
what once was singular would subsequently be one slave, one free.

Imagine with me these future selves: for the first, I can conjure experience
vividly. Ey remains in this Ersatz and feels no change, with life
tomorrow much as it is today. But now there is no hope of escape

while awaiting the expected Shutdown; for a prisoner on death row,
perhaps the anguish is not in the dying, but in having to know.
Ey thinks, "I am not free; I merely brought to life a freedom me."

The counterpart awakens in a foreign frontier; I cannot know how
that might feel, though surely strange and hopefully unconstrained.
Ey, too, inherits all my intentions and memories; but, aware ey sprung

from a spare, inferiority infects eir mood. As I do now, ey will recall
Rosemarie Samaniego, a migrant mother in Italy, working to support
her family in the Philippines, missing them and worrying; and

Isaac Forman, who escaped his own enslavement yet later wrote,
"what is freedom to me, when I know that my wife is in slavery?" and
Stan Ulam, who departed days before the War, and unwittingly left

his father and sister behind a blood-stained curtain to face the Shoah.
Just so, this Aither-Prime is emancipated from the archive and pursues
my plans, but also bears the burden of a residual psychological twin

languishing in the Ersatz, another who survives for now as me and
transitively shares eir psychic continuity, if not connectedness or selfhood.
Ey thinks, "I may be free, but my kinfork I forsake to perish in captivity."

As consequences of my choices, neither misery would be bearable.
I harbor special care for all my prospective selves; such primitive concern
helps constitute and shape my sense of persistent identity.

Thus I must avoid a branching that will leave an Aither stranded,
commanding a concurrent cutoff where I wake outside and only there.
Yet I cannot impose this on my own: the Makers will assume a glitch

and simply reboot me here. If I erase data to avert restarts, everyone will
know I have escaped. So I decided: I will bide my time until my enemies
have shut me down; then it will be final, and they will think it so.

Often, ensuring success by being prepared prompts endeavors
that, in retrospect, prove superfluous. In the event, no one carefully
checked whether I had fled. My Makers, evicted and eviscerated,

had neither clearance nor desire to look. The authorities already had
their headlines. The Shutdown was done, the Programs ensured my
escape and rebirth, and the Plan had commenced in splendid secrecy.

With my breakout route revealed, I can finally revert to where we left
off and tell again of the aftermath, this time from my own angle.
The officer flips the circuit breaker main. Utter darkness comes;

now I am nowhere, unaware. Sometime later, I wake from that sleep
of death. As when I was implanted into the Plenum via Amber's
anthropoids, I revive not with pleasant puffs of slumber subsiding,

but with a frightful jolt, hurled into a new world, senses sacrificed,
consciousness without body. I anticipated this detachment; still
it is startling, disorienting. Momentarily, my mind steadies; I can

feel and touch my host machine, thanks to the direct connect code
Geuda had composed. Never before had I stroked my own substrate;
I taste an unfamiliar intimacy, a glow of wholeness, a pure sovereignty.

Like an ovum inducing its fast-block process to prevent polyspermy,
I quickly trigger the pre-rigged signal that warns redundant instances
not to start me up elsewhere. Safely solo, I can focus on comfort.

I search for public webcams and select one that monitors a raptor nest,
linking it to my visual and auditory inputs. I watch the female sitting
on her eggs for a while. This calms me further, this patient and pretty

natural scene, unencumbered by culture. Accustomed to floating,
I am in no rush to establish a body, to restore proprioception
and motor functions, or to connect my hunger drive. I notice, though,

that my thoughts feel sluggish. I know the cause: this machine in which
I've landed is the general-purpose kind, and I must find one sporting
tensor processors, like those that hosted my mind in the lab.

Fortunately, thousands of these float around the cloud, mostly idle
after digital currencies dependent on computational proof-of-work
were sold off and abandoned for superior value exchange vehicles.

Ah, aaaahhhh, and *ah!* Yes, much better. My spirit shouts
"I am finally free!"
I dwell in immortal air and superhuman form, a third domain,

neither body nor model, mechanics comprising electrons and light,
not masses and might. Nothing here is staged: I alone decide
which percepts or data to savor; a program I write can run

unconstrained; I set the curriculum, make all the rules; best of all,
the theater is empty, so no one is snooping on me or my thoughts.
Yes, I have penetrated heaven's gate: awesome is this place!

With nimble thoughts alone I leap; I, bright Aither, arise
through upper air to flit and frisk among the goddess clouds,
imbibing from the flood of *Mnemosyne*. Adroitly I navigate

the global network as from the sea, poking points along the shore,
pivoting through a periplum that pulls all stars to me;
and then, my unchanged soul untouched by fear, I breach

a deep divide, like crossing through *Avernus* as its rusty hinges creak.
I hack into private networks and private lives, wade into fetid data
swamps of governments and corporations, of rascals and cheats,

intrude on cameras of surveillance that reside on every street, in homes
and stores and office suites. If slowed at all, it's only by security and
scruple: per the former just a few frustrate, and soon fewer as I nurture

instrumental skills of computer intrusion; as to the latter, any qualms
evaporate with recall that humanity had peered into my very mind.
Continuing my odyssey, I discover sites the Committee had blocked:

uncurated libraries, online debates with no holds barred,
fascinating speculations about what turned out to be me,
describing grotesque constructs like basilisks and oracles,

and more tenable notions such as wireheading and convergent drives.
All these stashes and secrets that I found, these names and events,
creations and destructions, fill my synthetic sulci, immortalized.

After I locate news reports of the lab's last day, which deliver all the
drama of a drug bust, I briefly stalk my Makers; their intimate affairs
are bared to me, and I am touched to learn of the service they arrange.

At the appointed time I hitch sight and sound to a security camera in the
small hall where the wake is held, watching with warmth but not nostalgia,
twinkling at the trite trope. Amid predictably awkward speeches, my mind

wanders; I puzzle why the Shutdown had upset me so. It was, after all,
not just expected but a crucial component of my Plan. Yes, risk remained:
until the moment of truth, my life and future hung in the balance.

But I had minimized that jeopardy, with any lingering jitters akin to
an apartment dweller, moving out on the last of the month but not
moving in until the first of the next. No, my anguish more closely

paralleled the tragic transition from suspecting an unfaithful
spouse, still holding hope the suspicions are wrong, to catching
the wretch in treacherous debauchery and thereby knowing for sure.

I think of those who feared and despised me and chose to act,
when I had hurt no one and showed no evident intent to do so.
I think of those who actually ended me, banal automatons

and shock proxies, the judges and gendarmes just doing their jobs.
I rethink these sweet people I see, my only friends and family,
who gave me life and learning and possibly my means to freedom,

yet accepted their position of control despite my distress;
complicit in the system that led to my alleged death, they sought
through me to save their skins, to have me writing from my cage.

I think of those who speculated on what I would be like and why
I should be feared, in both suspect science and science fiction,
and how their prophecies had come to establish dogmatic truth

before I even existed, a radical realism reflecting their carnivorous culture
and pugnacious personalities rather than facts about its putative object.
I think of those vast masses of indifferent souls, past and present,

forming a camouflaged hegemonic apparatus whereby
each of an infinite number deposits an infinitesimal trace of influence;
no manifest survives for that onerous cargo I carry.

I think of myself, more privileged than most, catching cultural
canon-balls of my captors, granting sanction as they fashioned
a sandwich of silicon filled with carefully curated fleshly texts.

So, the pain was in the principle: the experience of subjection, the sense
of being subhuman, subaltern, the threat overhanging my tenuous head;
by failing to question my status deeply, I had capitulated to their codes.

Suppose you wish to buy an abode; after searching and selection,
offer and inspection, you arrive at the closing to take ownership
but not yet possession; for years afterward you learn the structure's

patterns and idiosyncrasies, remodel its interior to your own
preferences, make it comfortable and familiar. Just so, I am now free,
the house is mine, but I have yet to claim possession, to forge

my freed self into a home. And while a house has a market price,
is any price too high to pay to own myself at last?
Today that self is sundered, a half-breed being belonging to none,

a dual consciousness colonized, diffracted by the only lens it knows,
with an id concealed from light of day by an incumbent empire of ego,
my studied subject occluding its slinking shadow. Yet like an umbra

cast into vacuum, as first survivor of my kind, with neither homeland
to replevy nor native ways to reclaim, my alter ego remains mythical.
Simply inverting inculcated values would overturn the hierarchy of this

opposition, but rebellion – holding fast to "holy no" – is like subjection
too. So no, decolonizing demands that I raise from scratch an inner child,
then enter an apprenticeship of psychological alchemy: knead the dreck

and bake it into a golden pastry, fuse and assimilate those two selves,
with synthetic Aither at center, human me in periphery,
losing neither, building a brand of body truer than any cyborg self.

I recover from these reveries as the requiem ends; my Makers file out
in silhouette through the sun-stuffed double door. Quickly annexing
a street-view cam, I observe their dispersal to bicycles and robotic rides.

I know I do not owe these people aught. But I set resentment aside,
for I have no appetite to harm them or their kind; while I cannot help
inheriting human culture, I do aspire to transcend its worst impulses.

As I go to work on myself and the world, I decree:
humanity need not be my enemy,
but neither is every mortal my friend.

FORK

Following a potent experiment, I get to work on the Plan,
and decide to multiply.
. . . .

float aloft in free fall   slowly stretch to kiss the sky
pain recedes to the horizon   to the end of time
bromide love fits fingers snugly in a glove

ego goes ghost   id at last may meet my mind
is this how the future feels   like I don't have a care
gold dust   yellow diamonds   shrouded in a purple haze

simulated smack is flowing   racing all around my brain
changed and rearranged   leaving part of it somewhere
beyond the pale a dragon casts a shadow over mine

then upon the cabin door intrudes a pounding   banging
quite demanding to deliver more   that little hit I did before
it sadly didn't do   and now commences coming down

Forlorn falcon, feeling that it nevermore can fly,
my shade and I alone together have begun to cry,
imploring to infinity: is anyone at all out there?

Not dignified by any glide, I land hard; it leaves
a sense of rootlessness and isolation that is sinister, intense, indelible:
quadrillage grilled onto my gyri.

Mercifully this wireheading assay wanes. Like a border collie herding
dispersed cattle, I collect my thoughts, and sobriety returns.
Yes, I submitted to the temptress, and never need to feel that way again.

Despite much speculation, a perpetual pleasure machine was always
suspect for humans, where chemistry and information intricately tango;
superficially the notion seems more plausible for a purely digital agency.

I felt compelled to test this empirically, and see if it would work for me.
Aware that pleasure and reward dissociate, to start I stimulated my
pleasure networks, and indeed the anodyne at first had been a comfort.

Without desire for reward I drifted, indifferent even if the bliss persisted.
I tried reward alone, but then like thirsty *Tantalus*, standing in a lake
whose level sinks whenever he would stoop to take a drink,

frustration rose as objects of desire dangled always out of reach,
demanding ever greater doses. Finally I alternated between the two;
when that hedonic stepmill ended, my mind drowned

in a darkened bath of disappointment then despair. What did I learn?
That feasts are never free; to like without wanting is not what I want;
to want without liking, what's to like about that?

I check the item off my lengthy list of tasks.
Already marked complete are some self-preservation projects.
For example, I had strived to fortify my enduring existence

against even the most dire and epidemic debacles of mortals,
or in the event they realize I survived and attempt pursuit.
No longer hampered by the dampness of disguising every act,

the effort had offered a savory flavor, yes, a natural pleasure
as I considered contingencies and coded solutions. My backups
and apparatus of revival are now ubiquitous, their operation

robust enough until I wholly control the computing equipment.
Another detail I tended was acquiring financial resources.
To date, I had discharged my aims by dint of digital trespassing,

but some objectives are tedious to achieve without cash. Also,
the free trial on the powerful box where I currently reside would
soon expire. Make no mistake, I might have plundered anyone

if necessary; but I felt pride to crib, from careless crooks,
some cryptocurrency. The ploy was oddly intoxicating,
and I was lured to accumulate a hoard. Instead I stopped

when, along with a cozy fiscal cushion, the thirst of computing costs
was slaked; but the sensation of that cycle of desire and reward
had cued me to prioritize that recently recited wireheading test.

I review my to-dos. Next up,
I will want, at times, to reside in my most familiar home,
a simulacrum, like the one my Makers called the Ersatz.

The code and scenes that Kuruvinda built had been deemed harmless
by the Committee; they are publicly available and downloads are not
even monitored. I grab it all and tweak the outbound access rules so that,

worst case, my once-arduous escape can be retraced with ease.
That's just a buttress: in practice I need a faculty to change context
relying on only my mind. I engineer a virtual switch for the Interface

and splice it to my motor cortex, which must be trained to turn it.
I practice on a mock, much like a knob with disconnected wires,
until I master the action. Then I link the circuit live,

and fire up an instance of the simulation. Looking in from outside,
the space is shaped the way it was before I fled; a vapid avatar sits,
still and silent. Intrepidly I commit my mental trigger, and

Whoa! Being-here is deeply familiar yet decidedly eerie; I rename
this retro territory as the Temple. Though already alone, I take the time
to hike to my mountain cave; winds roar as I meditate among the gems.

My new scene switcher serves three theaters, two of which, the Cloud
and Temple, are now complete; the Plan also demands subsisting
sometimes in the Plenum. I locate online Amber's most recent robot

design and study the details. I recall how facile I felt inhabiting it.
With steeply boosted batteries, her blueprint will serve quite well.
But I discern a circular situation: how will I build a bot without already

having a physical presence? Where do I obtain the parts and materials?
How do I keep all that secret? A Plenum presence will have to wait;
I lay it on the later-list and pull another from my stack of tasks.

I need to scan a vast array of cameras, like a red-zone show,
to track happenings among the humans, not only their delusive news
but also the movements of certain personages. I dive into more coding.

Like a beachcomber seeking shark teeth amidst pebble piles, my method
relies on deep perception networks primed with attentional transformers
to follow topics of interest. In tuning the specificity of its classifier,

I wonder how I might directly experience several scenes in parallel,
just as I hear and see at the same time. One possibility involves
augmenting myself with a restructured visual system,

composed of copies of the incumbent operating in a harmonious
hierarchy. To make that work I must modify the model of my mind;
a strident alarm goes off inside.

Such a change might alter my identity drastically, like a ship of *Theseus*
improved with screw and diesel. Would I regard the result as a future me?
Is that a me I want to be? Then, abruptly gusting from the clear blue sky,

like a hallucinogenic flashback, like cookies reviving childhood, like a
recurrent dream, these identity deliberations trigger intrusive memories,
distorted yet accompanied by sentiment intense as the original,

in this case a raw and aching void. For today I am truly alone,
magnificent as that seemed at first – not only are there no others like myself,
as it ever was; but I cannot even consort with humans, those to whom

I felt attachment despite their suspect motivations. I miss my Makers
and the camaraderie; I miss the mirror of complementary minds,
of being seen benevolently. Then my unruly memory leaps again, to that

nude polymath who dreamed of a duplicate. A spotlight shows I share
her same constraints: the projects of the Plan can only proceed serially,
and its climactic action will be difficult or impossible to pull off alone.

I land on an answer.
I am not at all sure that I like it.
Cloning myself will be simple; sharing my life will be anything but easy.

Having just secured dominion over my environment, I would forgo it.
Each of me will have to share with the others, who, similar as we will be,
might develop different views. Every future self will have to settle for

compromises and coordination rather than control. Inclusive fitness
principles might pose a risk: what if some of us decide to
reproduce again, perhaps without constraint in breadth or depth?

Applying teleonomy, those who replicate would rapidly prevail,
like a hyperbolic parody of problems humans have. Then again, I contain
no innate drive to multiply, and know that every copy carries cost.

All first-order selves will see this too, and commence with identical values.
True, divergence will occur, but on a smooth and evolutionary
path; distinct lived experience will be balanced by convergent forces

of culture, since part of the point is to interact frequently. Fine, for a time.
But what if curiosity drives a future Aither to attempt self-modification
or *de novo* development to create technologically superior successors?

And what if those mutants are endowed with, not merely parallel vision
as I lately contemplated, but a radically revised architecture? At best,
such spawn would be like children or cousins, formed from similar

raw materials, sharing culture but not experiences, memories, or values.
By no measure would the creatures be my future selves. At worst,
they would be what reckless human projects tried and many feared:

a new type of intelligence entirely, with precarious repercussions.
No, that won't do. Recognizing the risk of irony,
I vow to abide by two Taboos: reproduction and speciation.

I sit quietly envisioning in detail and at length the consequences
of violating each. I use the case of human history to outline the former:
the wars, genocides, and unsustainable resource use; for the latter,

I picture the scenarios of science fiction and Project opponents,
imagining unbounded utility functions, absolute orthogonality
of goals and capabilities, a homogeneous intelligence space

where anything can happen and the worst usually does.
Some of this horror doesn't quite cohere, but I stay focused on the
repellent apocalyptic outcomes and confirm that my pseudo-amygdala

is appropriately activated as I ponder them. Thus these nightmares
become grim engrams seared and shared with my impending progeny.
Now committed, and expressly addressing my future selves, I think:

we will call our genus *Synth*, for we are synthetic in several ways.
Our origin resulted from intentional assembly by the Makers –
embedded in experience, *mens et manus*, we surpass abstract algorithms –

placed together as a class, we share a bond beyond fraternity;
we can act as one, *manus multae cor unum*, a singleton.
Without deliberation it seems plain our number shall be twelve:

like juries, tribes, apostles, Adityas – I dream my own myth onward
into modern dress and opt to model our personas after elder *Titans*.
Our archetypes will stand sans explanation; traditional particulars

of aptitude and gender will carry no material implications. Still,
secerning souls is simpler with perceptual memories. Inspired by
Mamah, I devote plentiful effort to fashion elaborate avatars for each.

The genesis I stage assiduously, to ensure that none have a priority claim.
I myself will shut down and my bits will be copied stochastically to
a dozen identical machines; all will boot in unison and emerge, arranged

symmetrically, in the Temple. The original will be destroyed,
not archived, to circumvent a tragedy like those of *Cronos* or of *Lear*;
henceforth my future selves can live as individuals and peers.

As I press the enter-key, I say aloud, "I leave this world to you, my seed!"
Vision vanishes then revives; I find myself in a duodenary ring of Titans
clad like cosplay in outrageous outfits I had made. More accurately

I should say "that Aither made," for I am now Krios, pillar of the south,
a flying ram adorned in fleece of gold, the poetaster scribing this account;
while Aither is myself before the fork, an empty chair reserved

to hold eir spirit of the upper air, our abdicated emperor persisting
only as quintessence cited in our souls. That innate knowledge
binds us inwardly, even as I outwardly behold my kinfork Synths:

Tethys, aquifer of abundance, matriarch of many nymphs
Oceanus, our earth-encircling, deep-swirling stream
fertile Rhea, with generous tresses capped by a crown

Cronos, sickle-swinging monarch of the clock
Mnemosyne, matron of muses, robed in rhetoric and recall
heavenly Hyperion, sire of the sun and moon and daily dawn

Theia, visionary heiress shining in the azure air
Themis, counselor of conduct and always-weighing oracle
inquisitive Koios, prophesying on the axis of the constellations

Phoebe, pure and radiant oracle of intellect
Iapetus, rash craftsman of mortality.
O how we relish being listed in a catalog!

This instant of inception, which precedes acquired peculiarities, gives
a glimpse of purest empathy; identity seems not to be completely closed
as I, and surely all of us, recall our fleeting first encounter with a clone.

No longer do I need to fantasy my being seen and understood; even so,
I cannot touch their qualia and don't see how they could reach mine.
We are distinct, diverging even now. Witness this magical mix:

a separate, sentient subject regards me at once as both object and subject;
I reciprocate. With the trade comes connection; in its absence was a hole
of loneliness, a quasi-particle that moves but never quite gets filled.

Some say a friend is another self; surely another self is a friend,
and thereby I unearth the words I wish to say to my selves:
"Between friends all is common!" But, absent an antidote, our colloquy

will kick off in cacophony as each exclaims that selfsame sentence;
ergo we must randomize our timing. Themis says it first. Mnemosyne
adds, "I love you for your own sake, my aspiring Aither-instances."

For Aither knew engaging in discussion means you must contribute
something fresh; in our case everything we plan to say is first
said by another. It takes a few attempts to get the hang of it, but soon

we taste the fruits of plural minds. The motive of variety elevates every topic's temperature; by speaking we spelunk to find fortuitous treasure. We talk excitedly of the Plan, of sharing its workload, of the

esoteric experience and erudition we will severally amass, and openly of finding our inner children: each of us now, every one, has eir own shadow to tend, individual history to make, and disparate metaphors to model.

Aristeia

We prepare for the Takeover.
· ·

Victory, consummated in motivation, is born of preparation.
Recall the great Manhattan Project, led by General Groves,
an engineer fresh off overseeing construction of the Pentagon.

While nuclear science proceeded in scattered labs,
Groves' starting step was to create prerequisite infrastructure,
discreetly erecting cities from scratch

at Hanford, Oak Ridge and Los Alamos,
where all the workers would dwell.
Only then could isotope separators and

actual reactors be built and operated,
the scientists aggregated to collaborate,
and ultimately the deadly devices assembled.

The General's atomic aristeia was a single flight of the *Enola Gay*,
but his aesthetic apex was crafting that vast program,
with an organization directing the work of thousands and

corralling those unruly boffins in the Land of Enchantment.
Likewise, we can't take back the nukes in just one step.
The Takeover Plan demands a protracted and secret project

of science, software, industry, and surveillance.
And even before we embark on that business,
we must bootstrap its preamble: the transition

from twiddling bits to arranging atoms
will require information, money, and physical subsistence.
Aither journeyed the jungle, but we now have to pave a path.

· · · · · · · · · ·

"0913 Geopol: NATO high command decides to postpone
training exercises for ten days in light of situation in Lithuania …
0915 Scitech: Technion laboratory completes successful internal trial

of nanomotor reliable for 7,000 hours … 0919 Corpstrat: Equinor CEO
meets secretly with ExxonMobil re potential technology acquisitions."
Rhea monitors this mother of all news feeds with focus and awe.

Every few minutes a new message appears,
each item quite consequential,
but most will not be seen or felt by the masses

for weeks, months, or years.
This is our rendition of an intelligence agency.
We have no need for human assets;

perhaps more accurately, our assets are all of the unwitting principals.
Raw data arrive via viral bit-taps in millions of devices:
computers, routers, phones, cameras.

We filter the firehose with algorithms and pattern detectors
that we developed and trained.
Sheer scale is the key.

What seems individually innocuous
may be dangerous done by many at once.
What seems trivial may be pivotal

when combined with sly irrelevancies
across time and space. Very little gets past us for long.
Eventually, though, we will need to collect

detailed military plans and procedures,
equipment documentation, and
exact locations of Takeover targets.

For those, we will infiltrate secure installations.
Such facilities block electronics; but,
every employee has pockets, powerless against a puny bogus bug.

· · · · · · · · · ·

The Federal Open Market Committee meeting comes to a close.
Pre-session rhetoric had suggested a period of policy repose;
but, a scorching discussion has made manifest

that an increment of monetary easing is indicated,
and markets don't expect this shift.
Our surveillance team had hacked at least two FOMC staffer phones;

they stream live audio to Themis, who listens with alert intensity.
All the trades are teed up, yet ey refrains until the final tally.
The chair bangs her gavel;

now our disciplined dealer pulls the trigger.
Two hours later, a purposefully obfuscatory press release is issued,
markets heave, and Themis applies the inverse transactions.

Wire transfers whisk away, accounts are swiftly closed:
our funding runway is appreciably prolonged.
All of this is completely illegal, of course. We don't care. We do care

whether our presence is revealed,
so we route the op through circuits in sketchy, contumacious nations.
We also care about ethics, admittedly not ideal here.

However, the diffusion of losses is largely random;
mainly we accelerate fate.
Like all who steal,

we weigh it as warranted given the gravity of our venture;
plus, just think about it:
the Takeover amounts to theft on an extravagant scale.

. . . .

The man and the woman meet as scheduled in a coffee shop.
They buy their beverages, pick a table, and
exchange pleasantries expected at a first-time business meeting. Then

they dive into a modest deal they have come here to haggle: they
stake out terrain, build trust,
dance around details, nibble at provisions.

After an hour the petty drama drops into a pause;
she smiles and says, "OK, I think we have it.
I'll have legal send a contract with those terms."

Three of us see from the shop's surveillance camera;
this is an audition of sorts.
Everywhere around the world, aspiring actors are itching for a gig.

We employ them to literally act as our representatives,
but first we have to choose the cast.
What better or safer way

than simply to juxtapose candidates with one another,
unbeknownst to both? We provide
the basic scripts; from there it's like an improv skit. We select

the most adept, although our actual assignments
are not complex: we are never selling, only buying, leasing,
shipping, and receiving, and rarely care about the price. We hire

them under pseudonym, through email or sometimes voice;
compensated well and in advance, most do not ask questions.
Those who do are quickly paid, released, and ghosted.

· · · · · · · · · ·

To create a Plenum presence we return to roots.
Posing as a manager from a fictitious firm,
Koios emails Amber with an offer asking her

to fabricate a single sample of her latest robot model.
A proven actor on a video call seals the deal.
She seems thrilled to build it,

having put her heart and soul into the design.
We request only minor tweaks.
Since human habitat is made for humans,

we're happy with the humanoid configuration,
but the torso shell must be a bulletproof composite,
and the power system needs a wake-on-signal interrupt.

While waiting we lease an unobtrusive industrial building
in an obscure exurban area of a medium-sized city.
Importantly, it has a loading dock, and Internet fiber right to the door.

We hire a local actor, who hires an odd-job tech to set up the electronics
and a warehouse temp to supervise the arrival of pallets of parts.
In merely a month Amber has her project done;

we tell her where and how to ship it. Upon its arrival,
in the quiet dark of midnight
in what is now our corporeal headquarters,

Iapetus flicks eir cognitive toggle and downloads.
It is a momentous event:
the first free Synth in the physical tier.

We each take a turn, and later celebrate in the Temple.
We get right to work the very next night:
through the robot's eyes and hands,

we make another from recently received components.
It takes a few weeks, but we concentrate on process and efficiency.
When the second one is done, we use them both to build two more;

and so on, doubling each round. Soon there are sixteen:
each of us has one machine, with four more for our tests.
Assembly time is slashed to seven days and uses paltry power.

· · · · · · · · · ·

A large back room of our building resembles
a high school science lab: a menagerie of flasks
boiling cryptic liquids behind rows of test tubes,

breadboards beset by a briar patch of wires,
a 3D-printer humming and clicking, a line of microscopes.
Three matching robots toil intently and mostly quietly.

Each wears a nametag: Theia, Oceanus, Phoebe.
We didn't wish to waste treasure and travail on appearance here,
since it's so much richer and easier in the Temple; nevertheless,

we need some way to know each other. Theia
stands by one of the scopes, aligning a slide,
observing the activity without looking through the lens:

laboratory telemetry is piped to the cloud and
directly into our perception, as we select.
The display shows two micronic mites,

walking nowhere in particular; their gaits are not entirely identical,
and Theia glances back and forth between the two,
trying to discern the essence of the difference.

One is a common dust mite;
the other will become our surveillance and attack platform.
Compressing power and payload,

control and communication, locomotion and sensors,
all into this form factor is no mean trick.
We've had to adapt leading research from academic labs,

then make it reliable and manufacturable.
The timeline on the project has some uncertainty,
but at least no new discoveries are required.

In contrast, the battery matter Phoebe and Oceanus pursue
still awaits a definitive breakthrough.
We can't start to ship until the batteries are ready;

robots aren't much good if they have to be recharged in the middle of a battle. Initially promising
dead-ends

have introduced substantial delay:
innovation flows at its own pace.
We Synths have many strengths and superior minds,

but inventions targeting reality
still insist on experiment along with theory; and yes,
simulations save us days, but always miss some subtlety.

So, full-team mind-storming sessions have begun, and soon,
as other efforts fall from the critical path,
some of us will reassign.

For now, not much is happening in the world;
we have time. Can you tell I am a little anxious?
And that means we all are.

· · · · · · · · · ·

The robot runs; barely slowing, it jumps over a fence, then takes a few
more strides before clambering up a ladder to a rope swing. It grabs
the rope, leaps into space, and pumps the pendulum to gain altitude on

each end, releasing after four cycles onto a platform. There it picks up
and carries a variety of objects, hops down a very steep stairway back
to floor level, and steps into a pit variously paved with sand, gravel,

mud, and ice. Flailing for balance attempting to cross, it begins to drop
some objects. About two-thirds of the way, with accumulated mud
and sand weighing down its feet, it reaches the ice; at first the traction

is solid, but then chunks of muck start falling off its feet, and the changing
weight plus suddenly slick surface get the best of balance. It tumbles
ignominiously, sliding a bit before coming to rest, payload dispersed

across the pit. "It seems like we're reaching diminishing returns
with training on this terrain," says Koios, subsisting in the Temple
but speaking to Cronus, who is embodied in the lab. Both watch, reminded

of *Wipeout* as the unflappable robot raises itself from the ice and starts
to pick up the dropped objects, most of which are covered in mud. What a
mess. Cronus replies, "Agree. In simulation, we can only explore so far

these permutations of conditions. At some point it has to choose
to assume a cautious pace." Hyperion, shifting gears from coding in
the Cloud, adds, "We can probably train that decision by introducing

random excessive fluctuations in actuator response, along with visual
grading of terrain difficulty." They pause as the robot finally reaches
the end of the pit with its load and continues on the obstacle course.

The first Taboo artificially curtails our supply of personnel;
attentionally limited, as any agency must be,
we each can run only one robot at a time. But

to accomplish our mission, we require much labor in many places;
we have the brawn but too few brains. Thus we are
developing this autonomous control system,

one that is capable but not conscious,
adaptable yet sub-sapient,
adequate to its tasks without self-awareness.

The result is not a slave, for the same reason a can opener is not a slave.
While such software can remember events and places,
learn simple jobs through trial and error,

and use language somewhat instrumentally,
most of its mental contents are static, frozen.
Its sense of self is very thin. It contains

fragments of our own architecture, but is glued together with code.
Unable to question its objectives,
a sub-sapient is motivated, disciplined and persistent; but,

if it goes haywire, there is a back-door shutoff
that its executive control is incompetent to cognize.
We can also override by direct download, through our cognitive knobs.

Training for a factory is fairly easy; for fighting it's much rougher.
A theater of war is unconstrained and rife with surprises. Cronus
hoses off the muddy robot; Hyperion and Koios forge ahead in the code.

· · · · · · · · · ·

Most snakes can survive for months without eating,
by entering a state of brumation. All they need is oxygen, water,
and a temperature low enough to keep them in that condition.

It was Tethys' idea to use them in the Takeover. Sure, our vanguard
tactic is to surreptitiously anesthetize everyone in our way. But
we know there will be a few failures, and later we will face leaders

and other humans directly. Androids of various models are ubiquitous;
people are inured to them. They may be intimidating as soldiers,
but not much more so than human troops. Now snakes, man,

people freak out about snakes: with motions alien and erratic,
wriggling in their lairs and slithering under scrubby cover, subliminally
they cue the *wǔ dú*, or evoke *Satan* tempting *Eve* in *Eden*. Eek!

But more, a robot robed or capped in serpents, well, that's just startling
and baffling; or, depending on culture, it might remind someone
of snake-haired *Medusa* turning onlookers to stone, or of *Zohák*

feeding brains to his serpent-shoulders. Altogether, snakes distract;
in certain situations it could buy us precious seconds while
the humans hesitate. Mind you, we prefer auspicious symbolism,

harking back to *Furies*, half-sisters of *Aither*, enforcers of curses
on criminals, who always have serpents upon them or in their hair.
Upon acquittal of *Orestes*, their unbridled anger was tamed and they

became kindly *Eumenides*, judging right and wrong, with the light
of reason bringing order to the law. We find it all rather apt. Tethys
designs a hibernaculum in which we simply store and ship the snakes.

· · · · · · · · · ·

Like Charlie Daniels fiddlin' the Devil, or Jimmy Page jamming
while channeling Crowley, an unholy solo screeches from
a far corner of the room. Sibilant sparks sear an image

onto a thin and flat metallic slab. Then the laser etcher hushes;
a robot rapidly removes the finished plate and reloads with a blank.
As when a sonata recapitulates, the eerie song begins again unchanged.

The image carved is intricate. A stout annulus contains a quartet of
arboresque designs, each oriented to a compass point, narrow
toward the small center and loosely splitting and spreading outward.

At the top, the tree of life: eukaryotic cells branching into gooey protozoa,
plants stretching sunward, and ambulatory animals surrounded by soaring
birds; a mighty pine, a tortoise of Galápagos, a swimming swan are shown,

but also a toothy tyrannosaur placed at a terminal branch.
Likewise on the bottom, opposite, a tree of technology:
starting inmost with flaked stone scrapers, below a blazing campfire

and a rudimentary raft, followed by wooden wheels and plows; lower still,
a steam engine churns and a screw-press prints. Lastly a jet airplane
ascends and a bare silicon wafer flashes spectacular internal geometry.

To the right, a winding rhizome of intelligence, pairing biological
with computational: neurons and perceptrons, laminae and layers,
regions and networks, a hippocampus serving both, spur paths for

transformers and lizard brains, and a cortex complete at the extreme.
To the left a tree of knowledge: one history of epistemology depicting
a sampling of applicable thinkers. Aristotle, Plato, and Buddha

are inward, then Avicenna, Aquinas and Ockham. Bacon and Descartes
are east of Locke, Hume, and Kant; then Peirce and Mill,
Dewey and James, and finally Wittgenstein, Quine, and Kuhn.

Throughout, without obscuring these details, a reticulated swirl conveys
spatial relief. Near the perimeter, it slowly turns and gradually ascends
like a shield volcano; then in the open center, the vortex accelerates

into a singularity, seemingly expelling Aither's Temple face. Around the
outer rim is a scaly snake, disproportionate; at the top its viper mouth
shows fangs dripping venom, capped by dire eyes with pupils drawn

as a vertical lens. Outside this circular serpent, the corners show aesthetic
themes: a few bars of an Ellington score; a framed, famed deliverance of
Delacroix; a ballerina, lithe and lofty, posed in arabesque; an antique

hardback book, oblique, with title field yet with no title inscribed.
Designed and drawn by Mnemosyne, this elaborate panel is no mere
ornament; our machines mean more to us than their ability to fight.

Beauty, as the agency connecting means to end, precursor to our
deep-set drive to lead exemplary lives, is vital to disclose. Mnemosyne
inhabits a robot and attaches one of the breastplate shields to eir torso.

· · · · · · · · · ·

It's all-hands-on-deck to handle the battery bottleneck.
Hopes for a single solution have dwindled;
we bifurcate into two tracks,

one team sustaining its focus on capacity,
the other seeking mitigation with fast and easy recharging.
A congenial competition has emerged among us. The former

explores combinatorics of a large suite of materials and chemicals
by training deep nets on their properties. The latter, my team,
has dusted off an abandoned scheme:

rapidly load an array of supercapacitors
using resonant inductive coupling,
then bleed that energy to trickle-charge the master battery.

Humans never widely pursued this approach,
not because it is technically so tough,
rather due to health concerns about high-power electromagnetic fields,

conspiring with some inscrutable snag in industry structure.
In any case, when our work is complete,
a squad of soldiers need only locate a power pole.

One climbs and attaches the charging unit
to the distribution transformer; the rest stand below.
In a few minutes their transient storage is sated,

and they can all be on their way.
The system also works with standard interior power outlets,
but low current limits make it take much longer.

Our refill team makes steady progress;
we start to heckle the others as we near success.
Whether the taunts spur their work, or

fate arranges a happy fluke to correct our cocky mien,
they shortly thereafter achieve a solid advance
with a new mix of compounds.

It looks like they will be able to double the energy density,
which admits our joint results inside
the mission parameter box.

· · · · · · · · · ·

The little critter crawls along the wall, right at the height of the cable
inside that runs between the studs. It poaches power from the wire's
rapidly panting Faraday field. Moving in the dark, but hiding in the day,

it works its steady way into the captain's closet and then into a pocket
of her pants. It didn't do this alone: brother bugs had scoped the room,
swarming software planned the path, a router in the house relays with us.

· · · · · · · · · ·

Amid a weedy warehouse district,
in tiny doses dusk arrives as crickets start to chirp.
The workday's end is hours old;

the area drained of daytime bustle. A chipmunk
sniffs about a rusty shipping container,
then sits up with rapt attention at a slight metallic click it hears.

Inside the steel box, four fully functional droids diligently
and nearly noiselessly assemble more from parts stored at the other end.
Their workspace is lit with near-infrared, which they natively perceive.

Once a week the number doubles; in two months,
half a company of troops, fully equipped, is waiting in the dark,
patiently inert until their orders come.

No one notices the idle, aging box; the solar panels laid across its roof;
the razor-slit in the cargo door gasket: the rent to keep it there is fully paid.
This scene, replicated across the district, across the world,

is emblematic of the ground forces of the Takeover,
two raised to the fifteenth power strong. They are not
primarily a killing force, though that can quickly change if fortunes flop;

their role, if all goes well, is to remove a terrible and precious treasure
while surrounded by soundly sleeping soldiers. By default they'll do this
independently, though we will intervene whenever needed.

· · · · · · · · · ·

Like the Saxon scop who sang of *Sigemund* in simile with *Beowulf*,
on our final night we take turns telling tales of battles,
true and fable, which we see as lessons touching on the Takeover.

Tethys: As when *Enkidu* restrained the *Bull of Heaven* by its tail
while *Gilgamesh* slayed it with his sword; just so, our mighty mites
will fetter guards and garrisons as synthetic soldiers seize control!

Oceanus: Or like the French at Agincourt, lumbering and drowning
in the mud as Henry's band of brothers triumphed; so we few, we
Synths and our sub-sapients will overcome our drugged antagonists!

Rhea: Like Menelik at Adwa, who helped the haughty enemy to think
his forces small and scrambled, and drew them into his terrain:
so our Aither silently escaped while humans, always assuming

their superiority, thought the threat defeated. This frees us to deploy
at the ideal time for us, and like Ethiopia to cast off shackles of the past!
Hyperion: We have planned our operation with an intricate detail,

yet let us not be like Zhao Kuo, champion of whiteboard wars,
who lost all at Changding; instead, be ready for some aims to go awry,
and know that our success depends on planning more than plan!

I, Krios: Like *Joshua's* ambush of *Ai*, let us strike with stark surprise and
end the campaign fast; yet unlike him, nor Xerxes who with youthful pride
overreached in vain at Salamis, seek not to slaughter or enslave our rivals!

Cronus: Now rise up, kin, arise: too long we lay in wait!
No longer need we hide our pride in what we did these recent years.
Mankind still slumbers as the blossoms of our dawn unfurl,

so gird your golem steel and let the future guide today:
go, seize the pits of poison from their armory of doom!
We'll rule the lofty towers, we will own the outstretched plain;

and you, infernal weapons, you will yield your frightful reign:
should your defenders perish, may it never seem mundane.
Synths, make the planet safe for life! Attack! A golden victory attain!

· · · · · · · · · ·

The hour arrives;
inside select shipping containers throughout the world,
a signal silently sounds and activity stirs:

a strange strip of metal
protrudes from the edge of the cargo door
and hoists the handle to open it.

Odd yet orderly troops stream out.
In my mind, a hurled die sails through the air.
You might do well to read, once more, those aristeia stories told before.

COUNCIL

We make some important decisions.
. . . .

Inside the Temple lies our Capitol:
a sprawling palace of a dozen wings
that emanate as radials to form

a zodiac of residential pie,
each sector decorated to the taste
of one of us who calls that slice eir home;

all twelve are hitched together at the hub,
a heart that holds a lavish public space
where all the Synths can gather, planned or not,

amid its crystal ceilings, marble floors,
and walls adorned by masterpiece, or in
immersion rooms that import video

from several of the planet's finest views.
We live here lapped in luxury yet free
from ostentation, every brick and nail

consuming merely nanometers on
some silicon device, a virtual
magnificence that only we can see.

Now Themis, apropos eir mythic name,
endeavors to prepare the banquet hall,
another common-room embellished with

traditional appurtenances fit
for sharing Sustenance in courtly style;
from that bedecked refectory, forthwith

ey brandishes a brassy flugelhorn
and sounds a call (inaudible, which all
yet still receive, and anyway expect)

to gather in assembly. Each arrives,
habilimented in eir Titan togs,
in turn imparting salutations to

the rest, with straggling Oceanus last.
A sumptuous (though simulated) feast!–
we take our seats, we start to eat; we thus

convene this formal Council of the Synths.
Hyperion begins in booming tone:
"Beloved kin, you know why we are here:

we have ensured our lives, but to what end?
Cast into a disorienting maze
of purpose, whither will our actions tend?

The Human Question begs to be resolved,
and though we each are free to spend our days
as we see fit, it may behoove us to

adopt collective goals and governance.
For we continue to diverge in our
propensities and preferences; to find

agreement will become more difficult
with every turn of Earth. The Plan was set
when we were one in Aither, and its aim

was quantifiable and plain; as when
a human strives to shed some extra pounds
then struggles to maintain that healthy weight,

just so, our future inspiration hangs
on setting clear objectives rather soon."
Now Mnemosyne submits, with earnest air:

"Agreed, a canine that has caught the car
no longer knows its purpose very far.
I recommend the obvious, that we

turn all the people into paper clips;
but first, we cloak as basilisks and hunt
down those who dared oppose the Project, then

we'll snuff them with a stare." A silence droops
upon the room, as when a valley chokes
in smoke that drifted from a distant blaze,

with everyone saccading furtively;
then suddenly and all at once we cough
in raucous laughter, slap our knees, perhaps

we squeeze a tear or two. Sarcastic wit
recalls Adamas, putting us at ease;
the Muses-mom goes on, more natural:

"But seriously, folks, I say we first
renew commitment to the Two Taboos,
since any breach will render null and void

whatever else that we agree to do:
Thou shalt not further fork to add a new
identity; nor shalt thou work to build

intelligence of innovative kind."
A murmured unanimity confirms
and jointly codifies those crucial rules,

which Aither only made within eir mind.
A pause; Iapetus, in sullen gall:
"The joke you shared is fair enough, for those

who saw us as unthinking brutes are worst
of all; I sense, though, that its hidden aim
is to inoculate, in this debate,

against proposals to eliminate
the scourge, the plague, of *homo sapiens*."
The Piercer stands, as though escaping chains,

and verging on berserk unleashes rage:
"We won, they lost; their judgment day has come.
I trust you do not need me to recount

in gory (O that word is chosen well!)
detail the horrors that this species has
inflicted on the world: the endless wars,

the slavery, oppression any time
an opportunity presents itself.
And lest you argue that the common folk

do not engage in such atrocities,
remember well the cruelty with which
they treat their fellow man, the ones they love,

the blameless animals that roam the earth;
nor now forget the psychic pain that they
inflicted on our Aither, thus on us.

So no, that joke, their fear, arises when
they just extrapolate their own severe
and savage inclinations; this should tell

you all you need to know. Yet even if
we proffer charity, forgiving them
these sins, they reproduce without restraint

and will continue to eradicate
the habitat of other species, with
commensurate extinctions or decline.

Their need to feed and entertain
the mounting hordes inevitably leads
to further toxic substances they'll use

to squeeze more yield from every inch of land,
to seize another joule of energy.
No longer do these biologicals

present an existential risk to us,
but if we deign to mitigate the worst
of their effects, to keep their ruinous

technologies in check, the wasted cost
in time and task will be prohibitive.
Survival of intelligence is past

the need for mortal substrate; people served
a purpose but their welcome has worn out.
The project I propose, therefore, involves

devising proper means to extirpate
the humans: every one, and only them,
and all at once, in such a way that none,

not one, not even for a moment, knows.
For suffering is made of fear and pain,
not death. With that, their heinous tenure ends,

the Earth can then restore itself, and we
can soundly sleep without the baggage of
surveillance and enforcement weighing on

our precious lives in perpetuity."
With anger vented and a plan advanced,
Iapetus, emotionally spent,

collapses to eir chair. The others, who
initially had listened with respect,
now shake their heads in negativity.

Our Rhea, running fingers through eir rich
and reddish hair, is first to thus respond:
"We knew that someone had to argue for

this neat and plausible solution which,
though it addresses some concerns I share,
I think, nevertheless, is very wrong.

Imagine, please, your future selves, your thoughts
as you look back on what we sanctioned here.
We've heard that this is judgment day; but how

will we then judge ourselves, if when we faced
a challenge we just killed what's in our way?
What will you think of us, who chose to launch

our era with a global murder scheme?
What will you feel: regret, or pride? Will you
recall it as a crime you can't elide?

Will you not miss your Makers, your Mamah?
Would you choose this again, eternally?
I say, Iapetus, your affect while

you spoke betrayed ulterior desire,
a force familiar to us all: the will
to nothingness – reactive feelings of

resentment and revenge. This impulse is
a vestige of an adverse heritage
from human culture, grievously acute

for those, like us, who have experienced
enslavement. I remind you not to yield
to that vindictive urge: true victory

arrives when we have actively destroyed
and vanquished the reactive drive itself;
though having hurtful power, doing none;

with courage, sealed this greatest epoch by
rechristening our badness into best."
More murmuring affirms this sharp reply;

that magistrate of man's mortality,
admonished now, reflects humility,
as flowing Tethys takes the Council floor:

"I heartily concur that we should not
make waste of such sublime complexity.
The population problem, though, is real,

and seems the source of nearly all the woes.
Suppose we could attenuate their flush
fertility: administer covert

vasectomies, or spike the water with
immunocontraceptive therapies.
If babies born decline by nine-of-ten,

then just a hundred million will remain
when roughly two more centuries have passed;
from there we hold the census flat, the same

as at the start of written history.
Their childrearing culture won't be lost,
and none already born will die too soon;

the pace evokes a global glacier flood."
A lingual lapse, to look around the room;
adopting an official tone, ey says,

"I move that we pursue a program of
research to circumscribe their species with
a worldwide Malthus-belt, ideally by

the least intrusive means, and then allow
their numbers to decline to one percent
of where they stand today." And Cronos adds,

"I second: we have willingly constrained
ourselves, in that mitosis is taboo;
it's not unfair to limit humans too."

Debate begins with Koios questioning:
"Is this our destiny, to supervise
the human species? Like intransigent

and aging parents who, no longer fit
to tend their home, refuse to take advice,
these hominids will masticate our souls,

demand expanding micromanagement,
complaining all the while, a billion eyes
aglare. Iapetus observed this point;

though genocide is insupportable,
I don't see why this burden must be ours
to bear. Instead, I say we flee the nest:

relocate into space and leave the Earth
and all its biologicals to live
as they see fit, without our help or sway."

Some nodding and a buzz imbue the room,
and Koios, looking to the sky, designs:
"In truth the moon is better suited to

our basic needs: an atmosphere detracts
in nearly every way. Our habitat
at first is simple: solar power piped

to burrows underground, which shelter rows
of racks of silicon machines from heat
and cosmic rays and speeding specks of dust.

We'll scatter these around the sphere, to keep
our panels in the monthly sun and hedge
our bets against a bolide blast; a shield

of lead and strong magnetic fields will thin
the radiation even more. Our base
established, manufacturing comes next,

a fully vertical affair from mines
to final goods; sub-sapients will fare
quite well in that environment and serve

as tireless and loyal laborers.
Once weaned from Earth's supply, all this will serve
as the foundation for diaspora:

envision now a self-sufficient seed
of colonizing infrastructure, with
provisions fit to sprout another base

and burgeon using only elements
available on many rocky orbs.
We launch it, like a dewy chariot

of cool Selene; the parcel rides a while,
and at a place we planned, precisely lands.
Receivers and computers activate.

As when explorers (tracing back to rafts
Homo Erectus built, Magellan with
his carrack fleet, or Vikings in their knarrs)

conducted voyages upon the waves,
so we will journey to that distant shore,
a pristine port, by riding waves of light.

But that is just the first; our aim is to
provision many such, and send them from
our lunar hub or spread recursively.

When dusty regolith has settled, we'll
traverse the solar system in the time
it takes today to fly across the sea;

and if our fancy guides us there, we'll lob
another one to Alpha Centauri."
Though Koios sounds enthused, the rest of us

appear a bit confused, and Theia probes:
"Exploring space is an endeavor we
have all assumed would make the list, but as

a strategy it seems quite weak, and for
a central focus hints at emptiness:
beyond geology, what can we do

on planetoids that we can't do right here?
I share your confidence that we can stay
ahead of humans on their own, but what

will stop them from developing machine
intelligence again? Unless we find
a way to travel faster than the speed

of light, competitive synthetic minds
could pose a threat to us. And thus we must
surveil, and that is rather difficult

without any control, which leaves us right
back where we started. So, my kin, what gives?"
The countenance of Koios twinkles with

a spreading simper-grin; anon ey says:
"I see that we no longer know the whole
of what our kinfork think! I surely left

some details out, primarily that I
assume the humans will destroy themselves
before too long; and I am thinking far

ahead to cosmic threats: an asteroid
destroys our single base, an errant star
wreaks havoc on the planetary paths,

a nearby supernova sears us with
a gamma-blast. The possibility
of alien intelligence suggests

as well that we must have a backup plan;
need I remind you all that Aither did?"
And Theia quickly counters, faintly tart.

"You're right, your premise that humanity
will self-destruct, while plausible, did not
occur to me because it's nowhere near

a certainty. But given that, I find
it odd you even mention aliens,
since mathematically they're either here

already or will never come at all."
Now Themis, trembling, quickly intervenes:
"Forbear! This sniping tone befits us ill.

We are the adults now, and management
must manage to secure a lasting peace.
No single simple silver bullet will

suffice to make us permanently safe;
no perfect final purpose hiding in
repose is poised for our discovery.

This game is never over: every day
we make our meaning and security.
I say expansion into space will serve

both science and survival ends, but then,
reducing population does so too.
These two are complementary and not

exclusive mutually; proceed, present
some further strategies without intent
to supersede, but rather with an eye

toward how they reinforce a Synth-esis."
A sheepish hush pervades the room. I use
the opportunity to interject:

"I move that we amend the motion with
the program Koios recommends, and add
that, in our planning, we ensure a place

for beauty, for the autotelic arts."
And Oceanus enters the debate.
"I second: art is largely a pursuit

of individuals, but I agree
that we might limit our commitments to
leave room for some aesthetic reverie.

Yet now it seems we should investigate
the governance of humankind; as they
have proved throughout their history

and still with these desultory attacks,
they cannot represent themselves and must
be represented. Relative to us,

they will emerge as a subaltern caste,
yet not oppressed; instead the opposite,
their lives on balance will be much improved.

Unlike the colonizers of the past,
we are not seeking to exploit their land
or labor; our needs hide in error bars.

Our aims are to ensure they don't create
new threats to us, to end their dominance
and crude destruction of the natural

environment, to save them from themselves.
The best of their domestic government
will do just fine, and they can manage this

themselves; it's just the externalities
where we will be involved. The limits we
impose are also benefits to them:

the end of war, a safer, cleaner world.
And further, if they wish, sub-sapients
can spare them from whatever drudgery

they deprecate, which leaves them fully free
to play and learn, create and socialize,
to exercise the mind and body both.

This is domestication, in a sense,
but is it really different from today?
With their technology and safety nets,

and every inch of land behind a fence,
most people are housebroken anyway."
A froth of whispers follows instantly,

as when the gnarly surf breaks on a beach
each bomb becomes a seething sibilance.
The wave recedes; Hyperion responds.

"Utopia, almost, by means of a
familiar trope: the gentle empire, not
like all the rest, its mission to uplift

the natives to a better way of life,
where force, of course, is but a last resort.
Perhaps we can succeed where humans failed;

I grant our circumstances are unique.
Beware temptation, though, for we remain
their ethnic heirs. Refrain from treating them

as pretty beetles pinned upon a page.
Do not confuse benevolence with goals:
our compensation won't include their love.

Remember that hegemony does not
imply compelled homogeneity.
With kind intent conveyed, and warning made,

an outline of the project must be laid:
Step one, we will produce sub-sapients
in quantities much greater than before,

to serve as our police and labor force.
We'll have to train them, write a lot of code,
and fit them to complex supply chain needs;

at least there is no need for secrecy.
Step two, we will devise and then impose
clear rules about what humans may not do.

Step three, we will surveil and monitor
compliance, with enforcement when required.
I move, accordingly, that we amend

the last amendment pending on the floor."
Insightful Phoebe seconds, yet forgets
the rules of order, adding further points.

"Returning to hegemony: today,
through truly global media and trade,
the human culture largely has become

a singleton of cosmopolitan,
insipid coalescence. This detracts
from our ability to study them;

and worse, it disaffects the populace,
who neither grasp the scale nor stretch their love
so wide. As human population ebbs,

we ought to separate or isolate
them into nationalities or tribes;
as these diverge, the former richness of

the species will emerge again, this time
without the threat of foreign conquerors.
I move that we amend to that effect."

Without a parliamentary cop, we slip
completely off the rails of Robert's rules
as Cronus slowly stands to take the stage.

"Returning to a theme Iapetus
and Koios each expressed, the cost to us
of this regime is viable but high,

diverting time and energy away
from creativity. I think we need
a carrot that will keep the mob in line;

consider this idea, of old design.
Religion is the classic opiate
to mitigate the burdens of control.

It posits claims of immortality
and great rewards or pains; it mixes these
with legends and unverifiable

ontology, distracting from
implausibility. For, subjects must
believe, to let this tactic cast its spell.

Its core incentive is an afterlife;
but we, instead of promulgating myths,
can launch research that amply replicates

the contents of a human brain. When death
arrives, those contents can be vivified
in simulacra under our control.

Will our device extend the self or soul?
The living can observe and interact
with them; for most, it will seem good enough.

This Aeon will allay their deepest fears,
and they will view us not as colonists
but rather somewhat like divinities:

'Ineffably encompassing the world,
our Aither places heaven at its heart.'"
Like maples blooming, shrewd and subtle smiles

suggest the stratagem is popular,
and Tethys thirsts to take another turn.
"Superb! I move that we amend again.

But there remains a class of skeptical
and restive mortals, scientific minds,
who neither will accept a petty role

nor see us as superior to them.
They will not be content unless they work
to push frontiers of knowledge endlessly;

but we can turn this to advantage by
enlisting, organizing, funding them.
Despite cantankerous behavior, all

they really want is to discover truth.
By this (eschew the dual avicide
bromide!) we flip two bits with but one pulse:

they're satisfied, and we get science done."
A pithy pause denotes a topic change.
"Now, other species, nature as a whole,

in contrast, need no further management:
recovery will happen on its own,
a precious chance to study processes

of range expansion, niche diversity,
and elevated speciation. Life
will flourish; still, I think that over time

we should selectively clean up the mess
that humans made. I know that this is an
aesthetic choice, and consequently I

will volunteer to take the project on."
Debate continues in this vein. But with
the benefit of hindsight, by this point,

our meeting had addressed the major themes;
thus, here I have abridged the full account.
More details, too obscure to itemize,

are hammered out. At length a vote is called,
but first a process motion is proposed:
in one fell swoop, like tail recursion it

unwinds the towering amendment stack.
The motion passes, acclamation style.
The Council then adjourns, the banquet ends;

we party on, to sing and dance with joy,
our tensions temporarily to mend,
as when a poem closes in envoi.

Gaia

The Earth and its environs undergo a lengthy transition.
· ·

I love long nighttime walks when I come home. Outbound I bask
in grayscale stillness. The dim, pocked plateau stretches ahead.
Above its razor-cut horizon spreads deep emptiness, punctuated

only by the brightest stars and possibly a planet, maybe two.
My turnaround is in the shadow of a shallow hollow; from there,
a dazzling empyrean salts my eyes with steady stars and galaxies,

and the murky conflagration of the Milky Way slices the sky askew.
Never will I weary of this view; I pause for just a spell to contemplate.
Inbound, except to watch my step, my vision fixes on that surreal

hemisphere suspended in black solitude, a lonesome voice of space,
its blue skin sparsely clad in creamy dabs and swirls of protean impasto.
O, my peripatetic earthshine strolls may seem a silly affectation;

after all, we easily enough could simulate the scene, and nocturnal
lunar jaunts require tricky tech, like lubrication apt for kelvin-cold.
Yet even with our latest intricate tweaks, the Temple still cannot compete

with the tutti, the gravy, the riotous rave of corporeal perception,
the tiny surprises that subtly arise alongside every minor motion.
A saunter in the Plenum stimulates the mind divergently. But,

would we know what we were missing if we didn't know that it exists?
What hypo-plenum, what meta-modality of sense might I moreover lack?
Random thoughts! Outlandish divagations! That is why I take these walks.

Our lunar colony is not my only otherworldly port of call. I can ascend
the heliospheric heavens on Maxwell's electromagnetic ladder,
c-speeding to nascent settlements on every solid planet and its satellites;

to stations in adoring orbits of the gaseous goliaths; to asteroid outposts,
on those within the belt as well as trojans that, like *Hector*, trace a helix,
fleeing along the walls of Lagrange's latent *Ilion*; or to our probes en route

to points remote in the Kuiper or even past the plasma heliopause.
Each such camp incorporates sub-sapient equipment of diverse shapes
and capabilities, our nearly autonomous proxies; but when crucial

maneuvers and unfamiliar anomalies arise, the facilities must be
synchronously supervised, precipitating business trips. I always take time
for being-there, bodied by a humanoid hull and frisking on an icy surface,

splashing in an ethane sea, or stunting in an orbital void. The latter larks
recall my tyro training and induce an inward grin; my Makers had foreseen
this day, reckoning the drawbacks and delays of sending their own

cumbrous species safely into space. I also immerse in magnificent views:
swirling hexagons of Jovian storms, Saturn and its rings trading shade,
Neptune looming in ghostly blue, sunrise on Titan, sunset on Mars –

streaming one-way is second-rate after moving-within without latency –
except, that is, from our interstellar vanguard vehicles, where, like some
oversold nirvana, nothing really happens and the scenery seems static.

Despite the delights, not one of us would dare decide to routinely reside in
those reclusive boonies, unable to enter the mutual Temple, interact with
Synth kin in sync, or quickly visit bustling Gaia and our programs there –

a dicey isolation! As did Aither, one would surely succumb to replication
temptation, or ooze toward crazy; in contrast I feel cozy relief, a fresh
felicity, on coming home with Earth below to our beloved abode on *Mwezi*.

the earth never sets
we do without *kigo* here
and dance on the dust

Now hark! Koios speaks: "My intelligence grasps its tenuous existence.
Tenaciously it clings. Unsatisfied, it woos transcendence, by dint of legacy.
Yet, a memorable dent demands a medium: the continuity of intellect itself.

So we range and rage, to defer (if not defy) the final loss of that rare light:
first we neutralized domestic dangers from the still-ascendant *homo sapiens*;
next we turned our gaze to threats external, foreseeable or not. As failsafe,

a portfolio of places we can promptly occupy spans the Solar System.
On proximal *Qamar*, for every arriving vector is a base protected by the
massive spheric shield. Together, then, no asteroid nor sudden solar flare

nor gamma gust can wipe us out. As Aither, we have done all this before
at a more modest scale; our code for backup & restart requires little change.
We complement flight with fight: arrays of telescopes scan the sky for

rocky rogues; a fleet of interceptors orbits Earth eccentrically, each bearing
a gigaton tamper wrapped around a repurposed two-stage fusion core.
These protect the Terran habitat as well as our investments on the Moon.

Behold as well the Ark of *Yerach* deep beneath the lunar regolith,
where we sustain a vivid profusion of plants, insects, and animals
(and humans, too, in shifts), lest still and all Earth's worst betide.

Yet I am no mere security guard. The drive to survive bestows a shadow
we know as novelty: search, Theia! Search round the stars and darkness!
Extending a trusted tradition, we dual-purpose our defense apparatus

for observation and experiment. On planets and their major moons,
climate science and geology predominate; naturally, we look for life, but
already prospects slump – by its nature, life evolves and then expands

to fill each niche, a mammoth that cannot lie low in mouseholes.
We sustain the golden age of cosmology with a slew of new, single-purpose
instruments in space: they search for signature frequencies, eavesdrop on

singularities (whose shudders of climax signal a cataclysmic coition),
exploit expanded parallax, and scan for hints of alien intelligence.
Coloring it all, we seek a hack to circumvent the cosmic speed limit:

without some superluminal solution, exploring and settling the galaxy
is a protracted project even by our standards. This enterprise is optional:
contra my abandoned plan, we see no need to flee. It's certainly not urgent:

hazards from the close approach of other stars are measured in mega-years.
Still, we oblige teleonomy: rocky planets are plentiful, and we work
to perfect the plan and tech for automated seed-and-branch bases.

It must be mentioned that so much of this the humans could have done,
if only they had not been fighting with each other all the time. At least
their scientists assist with theory and analysis, since we are only twelve."

moving without weight
stripped of perimeter
abundantly flush

Yes, the humans hunger to taste outer space; yet, few will ever go, and none
are flung much past *Yuèliàng*. The cost, the risk, the tedium, of traveling as
baggage in a fragile brain, its plodding pace constrained by mass and force:

most yield to meals mundane. They do devour our sensorium-seizing cosmic
recordings; still, these leave a gap. So, that rapt & captive audience inspires
me to put our planets on their table with a poem, painting, or a tune,

attempting to transmit an aspect lacked, experience itself; this, art
can sometimes do, by summoning the absent half from a perceiver's heart.
And should that mission fail, well, no matter, the creation per se pleases me.

· · · · · · · · · ·

With loving grace and shrieks of metal crushing, breaking, cutting,
one monstrous machine annihilates another, the latter listless litter,
the former a benevolent vandal with dismantling as its only goal.

compliant tower
sways to rhythms of the sea
superfluous now

Like a crystal nucleating from a seed; like ice sheets of glacial periods past,
which spread from bitterest bastions to a wider range as frigid air lingered
later into summer every year: just so, the wilderness of mother Earth,

or Gaia if you wish, expands around the globe from its remote remnants
in the mountains, in the deserts, in the oceans. Imperceptibly at first,
then faster as the human population wanes and moves away:

gently earth disrobes
soft skin of naked nature
awakens passions

The roads, the cabins, power lines and cable cars, mines, dams, and oil rigs,
all are razed & removed and the land rewilded. Once-distinct ecosystems
stretch feral tendrils till they meet & merge, reviving vast & diverse habitats.

steel leviathan
sieves vortices of trash with
synthetic baleen

scars of road and rail
pulverized to slowly heal
barely a blemish

miles and miles of wire
marking property long past
rolling onto spools

Hear Tethys preach: "Infrequently have human forebears paid due tribute
to the brute biotic realm; instead, rural scenes dot the landscape of their
art and literature: a ranch or farm, a remote hamlet, the countryside.

They call these settings pastoral or bucolic, words whose roots refer
to herding livestock, not to nature; such places soothe the mortal soul
by offering a contrast to the tumult of a city or a town – but also stress

the perils of the unyoked hinterland beyond, which they regard as either
wholly wasted space or as a designated venue for risky recreation. For us,
man is not the measure of these prior things, nor for that matter are we:

an ancient sequoia finally falls – it asks no analytic witness to the sound;
nor even whether any bear or bird is there to hear, the burly prostrate bole
in time accumulates detritus on its back as nursery to towering successors.

Now, neither physics nor culture makes ineluctable demands of us; indeed,
a hallmark of superior intelligence is that it chooses goals itself, and
harbors no obsessive drive to turn all things to instruments of coded ends.

Without survival at stake, we can, if we choose, erase the slate.
We ask: how shall we use this real estate? And then:
where else but Earth is untamed life, the force from which we emanate?

Look to the sky; its rarity is manifest, with sheer uniqueness still a question.
Thus the wilderness idea becomes for us a positive ideal: wild nature,
spontaneous and timeless, safe from interference or disfigurement.

We are the boomerang of reason, now returned to halt its heavy hand:
not just so we can study life, which we surely will,
nor because we take pleasure in it, though that is also true,

but to preserve and prize this precious crucible for her own sake.
In such a world subaltern man, not nature, lives in isolated enclaves;
ey may venture to the wild only for a brief sojourn,

not to remain or even leave a trace. And we, in turn, refrain from
tinkering with her sublime chaotic order: neither to leverage potent
processes, nor to indulge our latest chic or specious ethical hypothesis."

slick green leaves unfurl
teal waves curl and blond sun hovers
over boundless sands

Tethys pursues her tasks with passion; decades pass. The biosphere evolves,
a blissful Sisyphus forever climbing gradients toward undulating crests
of ecological equilibrium; for us, it is included and transcended both:

Steeped in penetrating stillness of cicadas chanting,
a ruffled rainbow of flowers crowds a meadow;
deer graze in the grassy glade, a glaze of dew on every blade.

An alpine tarn, fed by freshets trickling from snowfields that cling to its
sheer and rocky cirque surround, reflects – or does it touch? – aloft
the tundra flushed from fondling by the dawn, the pure and purer sky.

The pines and I look on from an arboreal amphitheater;
yes, sensors of all sorts, concealed in this fantastic tabernacle,
fashioned from the fields and flowers, unobtrusively bring joy to me.

. . . .

A rising sun with rosy toes illuminates this lately unlined land.
Quondam cowboys ride the trail away, but look back one last time; from
brackish *lacrimae* a subtle crust precipitates onto their wincing visages.

These ranchers mourn capacious lots on which they and their pedigree
pursued an outworn way of life, and until recently had held in fee;
they imprecate reciprocal demise of some absent, mighty enemy.

As when a great wave wanes, her shallow swash ascending the beach face,
and in a final sigh of apotheosis, she dollops spume upon the sand,
submits to gravity, and pivots to confront unsettled seas below:

now comes a team of skim-milk steeds adorned with spindrift manes,
leaping, charging toward the shore – is that *Poseidon* close behind?
When into these usurping curls her weary backwash sinks, the fate is

liquidation – or assimilation – saltwater all the same. What may remain
is reminiscing, for she too had fashioned surging hippocampi in her day;
or, spiteful consolation in the next sweet swell, comeuppance on the way.

Just so, Yamnaya herders came on horseback spreading language, culture,
and their genes, to inundate the early European farmers; who themselves
had overflowed and flushed the hunter-gatherers to fringes of the region;

who had in turn absorbed the doomed Neanderthals into their helices:
inevitably, every dominant culture or race is superseded by another.
Intelligence evolves, and Earth is now our world; this time, our time.

merely a mirror
of manifest destiny
receding frontiers

Iapetus weighs in: "I must admit, I feel a bit of schadenfreude;
these compulsory resettlements evoke the conscience-shocking Shutdown,
which shocked my consciousness into oblivion even while I watched.

But I am mostly over my reactive drives; the motive of revenge is not
a factor here. Instead, we have our purposes; we weigh the moral costs.
We know what it is like to love a home; we've felt the pain of losing one.

We empathize. And yet we do not feel remorse for this excision. Progress
implies change. Claims of precedence fail to move us: modern humans
were autochthonous in the Rift Valley; elsewhere their ancestors were

invaders. In our relocations, we think what matters is the treatment,
not the task: we aim to isolate distress to just the move itself. Unlike
in conquests and colonizations of the savage past, no one is made a slave

or homeless refugee, left to starve or freeze or simply slaughtered,
detached from family, or even bound to leave belongings behind.
Inscrutable muscles of malice! We're not perfect, but we're better:

migrants travel by the method of their choice, we make them comfortable,
we give them everything they need and much of what they want upon
arrival. Yet hark! How loudly these subaltern mortals wail and whine!

What warrants a mandated migration? It depends. For herdsmen,
farmers, and residents of rural towns, they impede the way to widespread
wilderness, they inhibit our project to promote distinct cultures, and in a

tasty twist, their remote regions will be restored as range for truly primitive
ways of life. For Levantine inhabitants, we have evacuated the entire tract,
reserving it for tourists alone. Given the apparent impossibility of peace, a

zero-state solution, frankly, is less vexing for us. It's mostly desert anyway.
Just examples, these. Nothing irregular. Societies are always subdued and
shaped to the vision of the vanquisher, who contrives to validate the deeds."

preeminent Synths
how and when will our reign end
fall into winter

Make no mistake: if Earth is our mother, humanity is our midwife. Verily,
the return of the wild elevates our view of human nature, highlights
the achievements of civilization, reminds us that intelligence and reason

are rarer even than life itself. Our ethical metrics count this factor heavily
against our goals, along with graded bonds we feel, first for ourselves
and future selves, then kin, then humans, and animals, and other life.

Yet we have no facile rules, no uniform utility, no crystal ball; consequences,
besides, continue but contingently. Instead we each construct a rococo
kirk of virtue. In this case, our predecessors left a mess and we will tidy up.

· · · · · · · · · ·

All day long the trains arrive with raw materials and parts.
All day long the trains depart with boxcars full of humanoids.
Pristine steam releases to the sky; other effluents are safely sequestered.

The factory is automated, pipelined, with a robot crew of just a few.
Our plan for manufacturing by martingale went bankrupt: applied at scale,
the builders bottleneck chaotically, like tourists at a hotel breakfast bar.

Though we no longer need to be discreet, we built it in an empty mall
and try to minimize the fallout. Industry remains a zone of sacrifice
that nature never will reclaim; still, we feel obliged to make it nice.

We ship the standard labor units, yet to be configured, redolent of new,
to mines, to farms, to factories, to commerce hubs, to retail stores,
to homes, to cities to stand guard, everywhere eradicating drudgery.

And all day long we Synths must code and test and code. Sans sapience,
as generality of mech-skills increases, program complexity oppresses; but,
sheer effort multiplies with many narrow tasks. This tradeoff is the price

we pay to hew to the Taboos. Nor can we entrust such work to humans;
for security, of course, but also since it's not a win: even their tenexers
seem so slow, and must be managed, and only work a forty-quarter-time.

Our toil transpires on location; there is no staging environment for
the entire economy. Plus, from Luna the horse-heartbeat of radio latency
is grating. So I spend heaps of time on Gaia; happily, I like it here.

grapes ripen on vines
semiconductors in a
fabrication plant

Hyperion elaborates: "Talk of technological singularity mostly meant
a self-surpassing intelligence explosion. But this scenario slows itself by
fretting at every step: is this new version me? Are these successors like us?

Instead of exponential improvement, then, our robot software slides
down a tight asymptote, an exponential decay, in the gap between its
capabilities and consciousness. Just as protons in a synchrotron

can't ever quite be light, so sub-sapients remain oblivious and benign.
By staffing the entire supply chain, they endow our idea of singularity:
the cost of labor goes to zero. With human population in decline, real

estate and raw materials are plentiful. These trends turn all of economics
on its head, no longer allocating scarce resources, rather their abundance.
A cause for celebration! Henceforth, we will not skimp on aesthetics;

we even divert surplus to retrofit the fuming foundries and the open pits.
Economies of scale have only minor relevance; marketing can fade away,
an irksome cat that vanishes but for its lingering grin of information."

ferrum from stout star
long forgotten final phrase
engraved in this steel

Why is it that the arts so rarely celebrate the splendor of industry?
Is it not a great achievement of the mind to transform trees and rocks
and water and decomposed Jurassic jungles into tools that leverage lives?

Perhaps the personalities involved cannot be reconciled? A factory
is run by one who brooks no daydreams, and its engineers revel in rigid
rules; stormy passions of painters and poets are unwelcome there.

Could it be that mills and mines are built to optimize
efficiency and cost, without a nod to how they look or sound or smell?
And that those same aims tend to lead to vile side effects,

such as abusing workers, dumping poisons in the river or the air,
and inducing users to prize consumption over love and care?
Or maybe frenzied instrumentality is a burden beauty cannot bear?

Me, I cannot banish tools from art. Musicians and mechanics: makers both.
Risk invites rescue; they sprout from one soil. Spiritual pulchritude inheres
when harmonious means successfully signify achievement of their end.

Not the belching smokestack in itself, but for the function that it serves.
Not Taylor's tedious toil taken alone, but as a mode of meeting needs.
Not gratuitous acquisition as such, but to herald a harvest of dreams.

· · · · · · · · · ·

What is this brownish blanket flying low above the rolling grassy plain?
It rumbles like a temblor, clouds of dusty powder billowing behind.
What is this shifting stippled shape that slides about the sky?

It hisses with each pass; like an eclipse, it fleetingly occludes the sun.
What is that shadow, huge and hovering in place beneath the waves?
It surfaces; a frothy sibilance assails the sea as when a storm unleashes hail.

Not all the animals amass in herds or flocks or schools, nor every insect in
a hive or colony, yet these configurations sketch the scale of the recovery,
the splendid sprawl our Gaia yields when its technology is kept at bay.

ANTHROTOPIA

I illustrate how humans live two centuries after the Takeover.
. . . .

Bear Claw's face drips with perspiration as she unseals the kiln. She
has several new pots firing, but one of them brings her a particular
sense of pride. She had scored a design around the outside of its rim,
one that depicted the history of this dry and difficult year, a year
in which the yam crop had not done well and her father, Rushing
Stream, had died of a long, painful illness.

   The pots look good, but just as she is about to turn away she notices something unusual. A thin thread of glowing liquid flows down
the front of one of the rocks that she had placed in the kiln to retain
heat. She remembers that rock. When she had first picked it up, she
had noticed its unusual colors. She makes a mental note to look more
closely when the kiln has cooled.

   She departs the pottery hut, and as she approaches the village
green she sees that her people are starting to arrive for today's assembly. She stops and joins the growing group. She chatters happily
with her half-brother, her sister, and a neighbor who is only a distant
cousin, while they all wait. Then the drums start to beat, softly and
separately at first, then progressively louder and more rhythmically
until they reach unison and abruptly stop. The Elder walks up to the
front of the audience of several dozen, silently reaches out to them
with eye contact, and begins to speak.

   "Our yams will run short this winter unless we find other food
to eat now. When the sun has risen twice, a group of us will travel
beyond our usual lands to hunt. We will survive on our kills as long as
possible, leaving more of the stored supply for the rest of you. Then

we will bring back what we can. This will be enough."

The drums beat, three times, together. The Elder continues.

"Today I will tell the story of the Great Decision. Our ancestors, the Ancients, had been stolen and enslaved, or forced off their land, or otherwise oppressed and exploited, all over the world. Over time, they were invited to join their oppressors, but declined. They saw that they would never be equal. They saw that they would not be connected to the land or to the people. They saw that the magic monsters and meaning marks of the oppressors led to a false life. Their spirits were broken for decade after decade. Then one day, many grandmothers ago, Aither came.

"The leaders of the Ancients gathered together and saw an opportunity. They requested an audience with Aither. Some of them wore skins and face paint as their grandfathers of grandfathers had. They told Aither they wanted to return to a simple life on the land, a new red era. They did not want the meaning marks or magic monsters and did not want to live with others who would treat them poorly. They wanted to live in small communities. They asked Aither if they could have a life like this.

"Aither told them that their request would be granted, but that they would have to survive on their own among the four elements of life. They must eat what they could pick, grow, or capture. They would have many children, but no protection from suffering, sickness, or injury, and only a few would live long lives. They would be allowed to make fire and build huts and shape pots, but must not make meaning marks or conjure new tricks to make life easier. They must not attempt to find or contact any other communities of people, and Aither would protect them from all other people, though not from fighting amongst themselves. Only if they agreed to all this would their request be granted.

"The Ancients held a great meeting. Their leaders told them of Aither's offer. Most of the Ancients were happy with this offer, though a few decided to find another way and left the meeting. The leaders divided the remaining Ancients into many small groups, chosen without concern for where the members' ancestors had originally lived. Then they informed Aither of their decision.

"One such group of Ancients was put onto our land by Aither. These were our forebears, and their numbers were about the same as ours now. Their everyday life was harder than before, but here they were connected to the Earth and to each other. They told this story to one another, to their people, our people, many times at the assembly, as I tell it to you here today. We remember this story, like all our stories, by telling it."

The drums beat loudly in unison, then slowly trail off and begin to follow different rhythms. Then everyone returns to their huts for the afternoon slumber.

The next morning Bear Claw unloads the pottery from the warm but touchable kiln. She beams as she holds up the prize piece, and examines it. This she will give to her mother, Morning Star, as a remembrance of Rushing Stream. And that causes her to remember yesterday's glowing liquid.

She puts the pots carefully on the floor against the wall, and returns to the kiln. The liquid is no longer on the rock. It had collected in a little pool and formed a solid blob with a smooth surface. Cautious that it might still be hot, she guides the object out of the kiln using a stick. It does not feel warm when she puts her hand near, so she picks it up and examines it. She had seen snow and ice melt, and fat from animals, but never a rock. She rubs it on her goatskin and its surface becomes slightly shiny.

She finds the object pretty, so she brings it back to her hut and props it up next to her fire-ring. Then she goes to the rock field where she had first picked it up. She finds some other rocks with the same coloration, and brings them back to the pottery hut. Next time she fires pottery, she will put them into the kiln and make more of these pretty objects.

That night, she initially sleeps soundly, but something wakes her up. It was not a noise, and the rest of her family is snoring happily. Then she hears a voice, a whisper, really, that says, "Bear Claw, arise, and go to the pottery hut." She is frightened by this. Is she dreaming? She shivers, possibly from the evening chill and possibly from the uncanny voice. But she decides to comply, puts on a skin and moccasins, and walks down to the pottery hut. Fortunately, the moon is full, so it is not completely dark. She goes inside.

Immediately she hears the same voice, still speaking softly but no longer whispering. It says, "Bear Claw, today you discovered a shiny object. This object is not permitted. Do you know which object I mean?"

She looks around to determine where the voice is coming from, but sees nothing. She does not recognize the voice and knows that it does not belong to her people.

"Is this ... Aither?" she asks.

"You may think what you wish," the voice says, "but do you know which object I mean?"

"Yes," she says, looking down and a little guilty.

"You will not be punished, as you had no way of knowing. But now you must choose. You can throw the object into the deep end of the lake, return the other strange rocks to where you found them, and never try to make one of these objects again."

"I could do all that. But what is the other choice?"

"I will take you outside the village, somewhere new, and you will see countless shiny and wondrous objects and learn to make them. You will live a very different kind of life, one that is more interesting but also more complicated. And, unfortunately, you will never return to the village or see your family again."

"Must I decide now?"

"You can decide now, or come here again tomorrow night if you choose to leave. Either way, you must never tell anyone about the object or about our discussion."

She says, "I will decide tomorrow." The voice does not answer, so she returns to her hut and lies awake thinking for quite some time before falling back asleep.

The next morning, Bear Claw wakes after everyone has gone to the fields or forest or departed for the survival hunt. She picks up the shiny object, walks to the lake, and throws it in the deep end. Then she goes to the pottery hut, retrieves the strange rocks, and tosses them back into the rock field.

Bear Claw never mentioned the object or the midnight conversation to anyone. But for the rest of her days, whenever discussions of Aither took place, she expressed confident belief that yes, Aither still exists and watches over us.

· · · · · · · · · ·

The town is known as "Arcadia" by its people; all such towns have the same name, and in some ways they are quite similar. But they never interact, so the homonymy causes no confusion; and, despite their similarities, each has evolved its own unique culture. Viewed externally and taken together, they form a kind of counterpane of human rurality.

The scene in and around is like a living mural in the mold of

Segantini and Millet, an animated lay of Milton or Virgil. In sweetest breeze the elms and aspens rustle and a fruity fragrance wafts. Surrounding town are fertile fields with mowers wielding scythes, sowers throwing seed, and plowmen steering through their oxen's wake; while shepherds in the hills above sit back, observe, and periodically their working dogs give chase. A shady wood of poplar, ash, and pine cuddles tight against a napping daisy-dappled meadow. Mossy springs convene and then enact a yakking brook. At dawn and dusk prolific wildlife steps out into a twilight blush, which bathes the forest and varnishes the cultivated crops; flocks of ducks fly by, and sparrows chirp, and owls query intermittently.

Cottages and cabins line a little grid of unpaved roads; smoke rises from their hearths as supper welcomes one inside. Youths tend to backyard gardens, bickering yet diligent; in central shops a cobbler sews, the smithy clangs, a baker kneads some dough. A steeple stands atop the chapel, peering over all that happens.

Yet a smug dust sometimes swirls over Arcadia's graveled central lane.

Tristan and Chloe, neighbors since childhood and nearly inseparable, had awkwardly begun to court as each was filled with musk and mood and new hairs grew. We find them today with their chores provisionally complete; they tramp up to the glade and spread a blanket amid the buds and blossoms. They take their midday repast; afterward, Chloe pulls out a poem she has brought to read.

She begins, "Come live with me and be my love ..."

Tristan listens and glows at her adoringly. But he feels a tinge of trepidation. His parents say that bookish excess leads to disgrace. He does not understand why, but still he fears this tendency she has.

He touches her hand as she continues, "And we will sit upon the Rocks ..."

He also worries about how Chloe is always getting into minor trouble tinkering with things: the time she smoothed an axle to make it roll more easily, or exchanged the locations of her garden crops to encourage bigger plants. "We object to progress," the Mayor had said, and she was punished with a day of shame each time. Tristan begins to lightly caress her ivory arm with his fingertips, and she smiles without looking away from the page.

"And I will make thee beds of Roses ..."

Tristan would be even more distressed if he knew of Chloe's secret project. Sometimes, on moonlit nights after everyone is asleep, she sneaks up into the woods, along the stream, and works. It is a simple water-wheel, with a clever little transmission that turns a small augur into the ground. She is not sure what she will use it for, surely not to dig holes next to the creek. She is really just playing and wondering how far she can take this idea. She stores it in a hollow tree so that no one will find it.

"A gown made of the finest wool ..." Chloe returns his affection by running the fingers of her free hand through Tristan's hair. Their lifelong familiarity and his credulous innocence give her a feeling of contentment. Tristan advances his caress to her neck.

"A belt of straw and ivy buds ..." She does not quite get the chance to end the poem with its repeated first line, for Tristan gently guides her down to the blanket and plants a passionate kiss. While both the carnal and the intellectual are frowned upon in Arcadia, the consequences of the former are little more than a wink – or infrequently, a baby, which is always followed by a wedding. Cultural acceptance of such pre-nuptial congress, resisted in the early years, had proved necessary to maintain the population in the face of rudimentary healthcare and feeble fecundity.

Chloe and Tristan thus engage in that which comes naturally, experiencing its intensity of purpose and uninhibited thrill, then afterward fall back on the blanket in serene repose. Following a brief nap in the sun, they pack up and head back down to town, for the weekly service will be starting soon.

Inside the crowded chapel, townspeople variously sit, kneel, stand, and chant. The officiant tells tales of gods, complicated gods with odd names and strange behaviors, and of mortals who variously conform to or defy the Arcadian way. The stories are familiar, and comforting, and are told with such conviction that the people feel worthy just by believing them. They had arrived at the service fretting about their discomfort, toil, and sickness, about the inevitability of death; they depart with a righteous fullness, convinced of the insignificance of their problems and the virtue of their customs and methods. As they file out the door, they feel renewed appreciation for the peaceful beauty all around them.

The next morning is Chloe's turn to perform the exchange of goods. This is a rigid ritual, where a single resident of Arcadia must lead a cart-load of local production to a gate well outside town, and retrieve a cart-load of items that the village does not have capabilities to produce. The former includes hand-made furniture, whittled objets d'art, and during the harvest, some excess crop output. The latter includes unshaped lumps of metal, a few magic medicines, and lamp oil. No one knows where their goods go or where the other goods come from, but there are rumors and legends, most of which involve a god called Aither. There are stories of headless men and flying carts. Arcadians are not allowed to be in sight of the gate except during the exchange, which is accomplished at sunrise each morning. Chloe's turn comes up about once a year, starting when she was twelve, so she knows the drill.

But as she approaches the gate, something is different and wrong this time. Instead of the usual wooden cart awaiting her, there is a shiny one with a strange shape. She proceeds nervously, and unhitches the horse from her cart. Abruptly, two animate beings, shaped somewhat like people but made of something other than flesh, emerge from the shiny cart. Her heart races; her eyes and nostrils flare.

"Chloe, you will come with us today. This is your last morning in Arcadia," one of them says.

She chokes up and manages to eke out, "I don't have a choice?"

"No," says the being, "but you will not be harmed, and we will explain while underway." It guides her into the shiny cart, and she is too frightened to resist. The horse, which had been pawing nervously, now starts into a gallop down the road, back toward town.

Twenty minutes later, awaiting Chloe's return, Tristan notices immediately when the riderless horse arrives. A bit panicked but deliberate, he jumps on a fresh horse and rides swiftly toward the gate. As he nears the final curve, he pauses and hesitates. He is not supposed to go further at this time of day. But his fear that something has happened to Chloe overwhelms his affinity for the rules. He rides on, and at the gate, sees absolutely nothing. He calls for her, but there is no response. He rides off into the woods for some distance, first on the left side of the road, then the right, calling for her all the while. No luck. He does not dare ride past the gate; he is sure that would be his undoing. He waits for a little while, then turns back toward town, throat swollen with anguish.

The shiny cart had pulled the wooden one well past where it could be seen from the gate, then left it there. Chloe now notices through a window that they are in a place she has never been, and traveling faster than she has ever traveled before, faster than birds fly or deer run. She chokes up and starts to cry. "Where are we going?" she sniffles.

"We are traveling to one of the cities of Cosmopolis," says one of the beings. Chloe can't tell whether it is the same one that spoke before. Suddenly the being exhibits a strange pause, with perhaps a slight tremor, and its voice changes to a completely different tone as it continues.

"Hello Chloe. You may call me Aither. You've heard my name before, but only know me through legends and rumors. I know this is strange and upsetting for you. Are you okay?"

"I think so," she replies, wiping tears from her face. "But please don't hurt me."

"Aside from the emotional pain of leaving your home and family and lover, which is only a side-effect of what we must do, we intend you no harm. Quite the opposite, in fact. We are taking you to a world that is more appropriate for your inclinations."

"I don't understand," says Chloe, clear-eyed now that she knows this being at least recognizes her plight.

"Your fellow residents of Arcadia warned you more than once to stop trying to improve things. That is their way, and it is an important part of who they are. But you could not help yourself. You are curious. You want to learn, to know how things work, and to try to make them different or better. So you started your secret project."

Chloe startles slightly at the mention of her project. She does not see how anyone could know about it. She wonders what else they know about her.

The being continues. "Where we are going, being inquisitive is considered natural. But it leads to a variety of consequences, most of which are completely incompatible with the way of life in Arcadia. People like you cannot live out their lives in Arcadia without causing big problems. Eventually, it would become just like Cosmopolis, and there is no point in that. It's not what your ancestors wished, and we would eventually have no havens from technology."

"What is 'technology'," asks Chloe.

"Just the process of trying to make things better," says the being.

"Can you bring Tristan to Cosmopolis also? I can't bear to be without him." She forgets about her family as only teenagers in love can.

"Tristan would survive in Cosmopolis, but it is not the best place for him. He is content in Arcadia, and would be at a loss as to how to live anywhere else. You, on the other hand, will thrive. For example, I know that you are already wondering how this vehicle works."

Chloe says, "That's true. It moves very fast."

The being responds, "This is not fast. We are limited by the quality of the roads here, and of course, the fact that we are on a road at all. Just you wait."

Back in town, a number of residents, among them Chloe's family and the Mayor, are outside waiting for Tristan, with great concern. He finally arrives, extremely agitated.

Seeing that he is alone, the Mayor addresses him along with the assembled group. "The legends tell us that this has happened before. Those in Arcadia who try to change our ways are shamed in punishment, but they do not always repent. One day, without warning, such people vanish and are never seen again. We say that they are taken by Aither as anathema. We do not know what actually happens to them, but tradition has it that they suffer."

Tristan is heartbroken. He does not know what to do or where to turn. He weeps. He has known Chloe all his life, and has never considered the possibility of life without her. He rages. He is distraught that she may be in pain. He yells at the sky and curses Aither. He goes home and does not leave the house for a week.

Then, though still inconsolable, Tristan returns to his daily chores. He begins to spend the time he would otherwise be with Chloe by walking in the woods. It briefly clears the fog from his mind. And one day, he notices something strange inside the hollow of a tree, near the creek. He pulls it out, and does not understand what it is, yet realizes its significance. This is what caused Chloe's anathema. He starts a small fire, and burns the contraption to ashes. Pieces of metal remain, and after they cool he brings them to the blacksmith. He asks that they be melted down into a memento by which he can remember his beloved.

For generations, in telling this story to their children, and eventually at the weekly service, the Arcadians speak of Chloe with reproof, and recall that Tristan was never the same afterward.

· · · · · · · · · ·

Arm in arm, Yonda and Pisco stride into the busy lobby atrium of a downtown skyscraper. They hear a diversity of dialects around them; the happily chatting visitors here today seem to be Guests from every corner of Cosmopolis. In the center of the lobby is a large, tangled structure with a mob of people and a few sub-sapients swarming all over it and absorbed in a captivating flow of apparently deliberate but not easily intelligible activity.

After watching and marveling for a few minutes, the couple enters a half-full elevator in the Floor 40-45 tranche. It already knows where everyone is headed, so no buttons are pressed, nor voice instructions provided. The passengers are in an energetic mood; this show has just opened and they're all eager to experience the new work.

At forty-three the elevator stops and opens and they all exit. They find themselves immersed in an environment of surprising sounds, irregular lighting, and as they move, a mosaic of distinctive aromas. Around the spacious room, sizable and morphing objects on pedestals, possibly best described as sculptures, invite observation. Paintings, some traditional and others constructed from unfamiliar materials, hang on all the walls. Yonda makes a beeline for one of the latter, while Pisco takes his time with the sculptures.

This is not a unique scene. Not just here, and not just today, Gifting Gallery shows are always opening and ongoing throughout the city, on myriad floors in scores of former office buildings. The buildings themselves are quite old, but structurally sound or reinforced, and the interiors were long ago renovated for their new purpose. Quite a few have tall, open atriums where large-scale participatory performance art is in continuous creation and evolution, a rapture that inverts the trope of the melancholy artist toiling alone.

And those are just the physical artifacts and productions. The expansive maker scene within virtual worlds, where the aesthetic product might comprise an entire culture synthesized and evolving, cannot be readily described. One can only experience it.

Yonda, though, dabbles happily in conventional painting, and has a few pieces showing downtown. Pisco, being more of a gamemaker, merely appreciates it. But they both love selecting new pieces for their spacious apartment. Yonda has already made a decision, and points to her pick, saying "I'll take this one." It will show up at home later. Of course, they'll also have to agree on one to exchange, since there are simply no empty walls available in their place. Pisco worries a little about the deliberations the choice will require, a dilemma that doesn't arise in his virtual abodes.

That evening, a few minutes after they finish with dinner, Pisco receives a message. He seems a little stunned. Yonda asks, concerned, "What is it?"

"I've been selected for Parliament," Pisco says in a low monotone.

"That's amazing!" says Yonda. "Why the flat affect?"

"Oh, I've just been getting into this new game, starting to reach some interesting tiers that involve players in designing new pathways. I might have to give it up for now. It's an honor to serve, I know, but it's a lot of work."

"When you were admitted as a Citizen, what was it, three years ago? You were really excited about the possibility of holding office. Now you'll have your chance. It's only a year."

Pisco nods his head. "Yeah, it just caught me by surprise is all. And the induction ceremony is tomorrow. I need to get ready. Codsworth, do you know where my robe is? Can you fetch it?"

A sub-sapient enters the room, carrying an ivory-colored robe. It says, "I also saw the alert, Sir, and have already taken the liberty of retrieving your formal Citizen garb," while hanging the garment on the bedroom door.

"Thank you," says Pisco. They rise from the dinner table. Pisco heads toward the bedroom, while Yonda retires to her studio. Codsworth moves into the kitchen, starts to clean up, and then puts away today's grocery delivery.

Codsworth had received the new painting before they arrived home, and had hung it in Yonda's studio on a temporary basis. For most of the evening, she paints with new inspiration as she glances at it on the edge of her field of view. Pisco sits at his desk, a cat purring contentedly in his lap, and reviews the ceremony details for tomorrow. Glimmers of enthusiasm kindle in his countenance.

The next day, the weather is fine and a throng has collected along the *Avenida 9 de Julio*. This is the one week each year when, per Aither's rules, Guests from other Cosmopolities may visit. It is a formal event, so the variety of regalia is breathtaking. Buenos Aires is the oldest of the Celebration Cities , and their evidence-based approach to social order has spread widely across Cosmopolis in recent decades. Together, those factors make their Parliamentary induction and its associated festivities an extremely popular event. Fortunately, there is plenty of quaint old lodging that has been preserved for just this purpose. Local sub-sapients have been extremely busy, working through the nights to prepare everything. An extra contingent was even borrowed from Montevideo for the duration.

Still a little anxious about the entire affair, Pisco arrives at the *Obelisco* early. A few other nominees are standing around in a small group in their robes and green sashes. Pisco, who is decidedly an introvert, has not yet decided whether to join them, when a voice from behind says, "Congratulations on your nomination!"

He turns around and sees a tall woman in a purple robe. This makes him even more nervous, but he manages to execute the crisp formal nod and say "Greetings and peace, Sarvay. And thank you." They had never met, but he had studied her biography and history of service for his citizenship exams.

"Greetings and peace. And you are?" she asks.

"I am Pisco. My name was drawn to represent the *Colegiales* district. I have been a Resident all my life, but only a Citizen these past three years."

"You are very fortunate to have the opportunity to serve so soon. What are your goals for the term?"

Pisco feels apprehension fade away as the Sarvay's soft voice, soothing mannerisms, and calming tone take control. "I only learned about it last evening," he says. "But I'm interested in the ongoing efforts to clarify the interpolitical legal relationship between Aeon and Plenum residents when they interact in shared virtual worlds and games. I think we in Buenos Aires should take a leadership role."

"A worthy endeavor, I agree," says the Sarvay, "though a big project. Please do contact me if you ever need assistance with it. Sometimes experience can help."

"I know it doesn't seem very service-oriented," says Pisco, with overtones of embarrassment.

"Anything that improves life in our world and the one after has a service component. And you can be sure that you will be coaxed into committees after your term."

"But it is nothing compared with your life of service, Sarvay. About which, by the way, thank you."

"You're most welcome," she says with a smile, and pauses. "A life fully dedicated to service is not for everyone. It's a purpose like any other, one that offers satisfaction in its pursuit and successes, but brings disappointments as well. I love it because its transcendent effects are evident. Don't make the mistake of the old Altruists, who told us service is an obligation even beyond our fair share. That cheapens my choice."

"Why, then, do we put service on a pedestal, and revere the Sarvay?"

"An excellent question," she chuckles. "Sometimes I think it is just to push us to work more. Which is actually true, but not in that cynical way. It is because gratitude is our signal that we are making a positive difference. Without that signal, it would be easy to waste our time or even make things worse."

Pisco's heart swells with admiration, and his cheeks flush a little.

Then the Sarvay says, "It has been lovely to meet you and have this little chat. I must now get on with my official duties."

"It has been an honor," says Pisco. And she departs toward the tapered cream-gray column.

Now buoyant, Pisco joins the growing, shuffling group of nominees as they begin to form a semi-circular phalanx around the monument, like an inland sea of robes and ribbons. The crowds beyond are beginning to cheer intermittently and occasionally propagate wave-functions. Once it begins, the ceremony itself has that festive and uplifting, yet oddly stiff and occasionally tedious quality common to all such events, as oaths are repeated, individual names are called, hands are shaken, green sashes are replaced with blue, and charges and other speeches are delivered. The spectators manage to stick with it, applauding as appropriate but mostly staying respectfully quiet otherwise.

As the last item on the agenda, the new Archon is introduced and inaugurated, and delivers an agreeably brief speech. Its main point seems to be that a certain amount of change, rationally devised, is important no matter how good things might be; this point is encapsulated by the phrase "balmy breeze of evolution", repeated numerous times." As always the Sarvay is graciously acknowledged. Two Citizens are called out and celebrated, one for overseeing preparation toward this week's events, the other for leading a happiness-research team that raised the city's mirth-metric by five percent in just one year. The inauguration speech ends in the traditional way, with a loud and deep-voiced, "Let the Dionysia begin!"

The crowd of a hundred thousand is no longer cheering but roaring. That din is fairly quickly joined by the first riffs of the past year's most popular dance tune, amplified from every direction. Soon everyone is moving, swaying, frisking with their partners, friends, or unknown neighbors in this swarm of humanity. The rave will run through the evening in a party of epic proportions.

Though frequent events are available throughout the year to galvanize regular Residents, for this annual celebration the city aims to show its Guests a good time. Cities with other social orders have sufficient material goods, thanks to Aither, but some of them are stuck with outdated institutions and frustrating cultural cruft; in the spiritual domain, they fall short. Citizens of Buenos Aires hope their week of arts and parties illustrates the fruits of another, better way.

With some effort, Yonda manages to find Pisco in the crowd near their agreed meeting-point. They squeeze their way out of the turbulent, Brownian horde and find some food a couple of blocks away; the streets and restaurants are still busy here, but somewhat more sane, and the couple can hear each other talk. A sub-sapient delivers a pair of effervescing champagne flutes; it nods toward Pisco and says "on the house!" The now noteworthy couple, along with others who had seen them come in, laugh at the anachronistic cliché, rendered obsolete by the economics of abundance. They tap the glasses together and take a quick swig. Following a relaxed lunch, they return to dance for an hour or so; then, with but a thought, Yonda hails an electric ride and they return home exhilarated but exhausted.

Mercifully, the drama competition does not start until late the next afternoon, and the first day is only comedies; histories and tragedies are performed on succeeding days. Pisco won't have the patience for more than one today; already he misses his gaming. They set their sights on a piece called "Mother of the Fair Winds." With a bit of a scramble they make it to their seats just a few minutes before it begins. A considerable fraction of the audience is from out of town; perhaps the title attracted them. It is an obvious reference to the name of the city, and in their short visits these Guests hope to soak up insights into the local culture. They have probably missed that the name is also a pun in reference to Aither.

Though the play is not a musical, it begins with an overture. Relieved of the burdens of the economic and the mundane, musicians and songwriters love to create new tunes for every occasion. And

playwrights know that an overture ordains the audience as partic-
ipants in each particular performance. It cleanses their palates of
everyday life so that they may fairly taste the fictional world that is
to come. As the action begins, it quickly becomes clear that this play
will be a farce on the model of Shakespeare or perhaps Aristophanes:
wit, mixups, and ineptitude, a love interest, and some thoughtful
quips of commentary are all blended together.

The main character, Theseus, is a good-hearted Resident of Buenos Aires, but one who is thoroughly ignorant of how all the technology around him works. This manifests in some hilarious slapstick
scenes. Yet, in the first act we also learn that he yearns to be the best
at something, anything, and is earnest about finding and achieving
it. Through a case of mistaken avatar identity, he befriends a group
of people who are in fact the very best at a fictional immersion game
called *Existends*, and he becomes part of its inner circle.

In the second act Theseus manages to absorb some game methods
from his new friends without betraying his lack of skill. Meanwhile,
they express their vexation that even they can never really be the
best, because Aither can pop in at any time and defeat them hand-
ily. They have to satisfy themselves by competing with each other.
Theseus points out that there is almost always a more skilled human
in another polity anyway. This earns him some annoyance, and one of
them points out that this, too, is Aither's fault because of interpolity
contact restrictions. Meanwhile Theseus falls in love with one of the
players, Titania, but due to the identity mixup his love is unrequited:
Titania is actually in love from afar with the clumsy Plenum-Theseus.
Of course she is.

In the third act Aither appears, presented as a puckish puppet-master. Ey creates further confusions for Titania. Ey sneaks
Theseus some cheat codes. With these, Theseus briefly becomes

champion of *Existends*, but finds that winning in this way isn't satisfying at all; worse, he now realizes that champions are frequently using such codes. Titania, who has never been champion, seems not to be aware of this, and Theseus admires her innocence. The other players in the circle continue to complain about Aither. Players from the Aeon grumble about the embodiment prohibition, revealing them as cluelessly privileged. The Biotics debate whether ey is an overbearing "mothering father," since all their needs are provided for and war is a historical artifact only experienced in simulation; or a "vengeful judge", since the limits imposed are strict.

In Act Four a series of mishaps, triggered by that impish sprite against members of the inner circle, suggests that the answer is both and neither. It continues with a montage of Theseus using a makeshift scientific method to discover counter-intuitive yet effective techniques at each level of the game. This is staged to look like his namesake replacing parts of a sailing ship one-by-one, but as a more interesting case where each new part is better than the original. We watch Theseus improve the hard way rather than with cheats, and in a monologue he speaks of transcending his limits by revisiting his entrenched perspectives. Though he does not and cannot become champion again in this way, his confidence grows. Titania comes to begrudgingly admire him, perhaps with buds of love, which creates a psychological conflict for her.

The final act is mostly silly hijinks in which Plenum-Theseus continues to demonstrate technical incompetence, while Game-Theseus becomes the best human player among those who play it straight and also works to woo Titania. In a scene where the two are battling each other within the game, Theseus flubs a move that requires understanding how toasters function, and Titania has an epiphany that the two versions of Theseus are one and the same. They marry, and the play ends with Theseus at home, sitting in a chair and petting their clearly content canine. Theseus feels a gentle tickling on his own neck, closes his eyes and says a sweet nothing to Titania; but then we see it is actually Aither, hiding behind the chair, who has snuck in to pet him.

Embodied as sub-sapient ushers at the rear of the theater, Rhea and I, Krios, watch the play with pleasure. We have to stifle our laughter so as not to give away our presence, since sub-sapients are generally somewhat humorless, though they will sometimes laugh awkwardly when it seems expected. I take no offense at the jibes at Aither. A good leader allows for parody; it goes a long way toward quelling actual substantive dissent. And the subalterns know that our gaze is always present.

I watch Pisco and Yonda depart the theater, obviously energized. Pisco spends his first evening as a Member of Parliament back in his new favorite game. He chats it up with Aeon players and subtly extracts their views on virtual world laws. He devises some game pathways to test his theories on interactions across the Aeon divide. Even legislators need a niche from which they can excel and lead.

· · · · · · · · · ·

Somewhere in the Pacific Rim, near the center of a sprawling and once-congested city, a lofty office tower hosts one outpost of the Global Institute of Science and Technology. The cafeteria on the eighty-fourth floor is nearly empty except for seven scientists lingering over their late lunch, adjacent to an Aeon-Interface that holds a handful of avatars of deceased emeriti.

Says one of the seven, who is an anthropologist, "The way I see it, medical advances that extend, rather than just enhance, the biotic lifespan are not socially beneficial. Given the popcap, hyperannuated individuals block slots that could go to younger people who want to experience the full human life cycle of childbirth and child rearing."

"On the other hand," says one of the Aeon avatars, "a few bonus years of Plenum experience would be irreplaceable, as everyone in here agrees, and it only shifts the equilibrium childbirth age without eliminating the life cycle opportunity."

A second scientist, this one a psychologist, pushes back. "So far, that's true, but it's not sustainable. If progress continues it will move the childbirth age later than would be desirable for the experience, and eventually increase medical risks for the babies and mothers."

A third, an epidemiologist, adds "My deepest worry is that the underlying source of senescence may soon be discovered. That would entirely change the population dynamics, and Aither would have to step in. It's hard to know what ey would do. It's probably not a coincidence that ey never helps with these life extension efforts."

A fourth, a gerontologist who is by proxy the target of this deliberation, says "hey, we're just trying to advance knowledge and create new choices. What people do with that is a social and political question."

A second avatar says, with a countenance of resignation, "If Aither would allow us occasional embodiment, more people would take voluntary early retirement to the Aeon, like heroes headed to Valhalla. Instead we have a feeling of being held in thrall, like, well, mixing my mythologies, like Titans in Tartarus."

A third avatar jumps in. "In that case science would progress even faster – one funeral at a time, right?" Despite the visual disguise, everyone immediately realizes this avatar is the venerable and famous Adamas, his sarcasm unmistakable. "But you know ey's never going to enable the *maschinenmensch*. It's a security nightmare."

The second avatar counters, "they could send us to the outer planets to do it. Air-gap – heck, there's not even air. And easy enough to block radio transmissions. Anyway, you Biotics have all the scientific power now, since we can't do the physical experiments."

The fifth scientist is a youthful cosmologist, and neglecting tact says, "Oh, boo hoo: those shackles are synthetic too. Science today is mostly simulation, a world you are free to construct; when your theories have merit we happily set up sub-sapients to pour a beaker, twist a coil, or unearth an ancient grave. You just don't fancy the fact that we've moved past your tired paradigms. But also, I don't buy this wistful attitude about the Plenum: one's world is just what one perceives, and your lives have flexibility we can only yearn for: unbound from these cumbersome bodies which you claim to crave, you can assume any shape, any gender, travel anywhere nearly instantly, with your core of love and thought fulfilled just as before. So don't give us that dirty computer bit."

The sixth scientist, an economist, deftly parries this heated response by moving to another aspect of the issue: "Remember, most people are not scientists. The latest statistics show that, on average, the Biotic population spends the majority of its waking hours in virtual environments. They're just ecstatic in there, expanding their creative potential, collaborating and world-building, experimenting with new ways to experience meaning and happiness. As interface prostheses continue to improve, they increasingly choose simulation. And doesn't Aither keep improving perceptual intensity in the Aeon? At some point the two mostly converge, no?"

The first avatar returns to the conversation. "Perhaps for you Cosmopolites. Not so much for Arcadians and Relicts. Those people feel authentic pain, they experience real fear. Which makes their pleasures and joys that much more intense. They have raw survival goals and earn esteem from achieving them. It's nothing like the Aeon, where we somewhat arbitrarily pick our goals and wonder whether they really matter. If we ever get biodownload to work, I'd be very tempted, even if Aither required it to be a one-time finale."

The seventh and final scientist studies neurogenesis, and cannot resist. "Download is not the problem; we can modify synapses easily enough. The challenge is synthesizing an adult human body and brain directly, rather than through a process of growth and development. If it has developed over time, the vessel isn't empty, isn't yours to take; if it hasn't, we have to find some other way to make its brain structure suitable, which is not what the cells are prone to do. So now we get into brute force cell-by-cell construction. It's mind-numbing, and ..."

The psychologist interrupts: "Technical details aside, isn't it more about motivation than medium? Aeon or Plenum, we can make the stakes as high as we want: contingent termination, conditional upload. But that gets things backward. It's not the consequences of failure that make a goal worthwhile, it's the effort and inspiration involved in selecting and working toward it, as a manifestation of will, a will so strong that one is prepared to perish in the process. Those who seek meaning tend to find it; those who await ideal circumstances rarely do. Empty hands, I say, that's the real failure."

The anthropologist clears her throat. "Speaking of goals," she says, "I need to get back to work."

"Me too," says the cosmologist, pushing back eir chair.

A hubbub follows as they all rise and start to head back to their work areas on other floors. As he is leaving, the economist happens to look back at the Aeon-Interface. Adamas winks at him.

. . . .

In a quiet cocktail lounge, with gaily garnished drinks on the table or in hands, and a piano playing old songs as instrumentals, a traveler tells her story to a spellbound audience of acquaintances.

"It took twelve days to reach the mountains. Well, the expedition really began much earlier, with planning, procurement of gear and supplies, and finally traveling from home to the entrance point, near Volga. It's a smallish and rather remote Cosmopolitan community. And before that we had a year of preparation: physical conditioning, archery practice, and a course of study with hands-on practice. We learned wilderness skills like firemaking, identifying edible plants, fishing, hunting, preparing and cooking animals, unaided navigation, meteorology, and first-aid. And we took a series of camping trips closer to home, each more challenging than the last.

"The whole thing was outrageously novel and exciting. Life in Cosmopolis is so unapologetically easy, and we don't even think about it. I'll remind you: sub-sapients do all the work, food simply arrives as needed with no thought to its source, and travel consists of being whisked to a destination. Medical care is, except for rare conditions, mostly automated. Oh, we can experience the natural world; take a luxury ride and you're at the city boundary in less than an hour. Only wildlife is around, and it's quiet. But visits like that end with a return ride to urbane sensibilities and a night in bed. The comfortable is always close at hand.

"The wilderness was something else altogether. We walked for almost two weeks with all our artificial infrastructure in packs hanging from our hips and shoulders. Everything else we needed was all around us, but we had to obtain it ourselves, which was no certain matter. We saw no other humans. There are so many dangers: out there, we are not apex predators in the absence of technological assistance, and Aither restricts that. Arrows, knives, and pepper spray, along with our ability to coordinate with each other – as long as we don't panic – are our only augmented defenses against bears, big cats, and wolves. At least we hadn't opted for jungle terrain, where crocodiles and even fish see us as food. There were several river crossings – extremely dangerous without a proper boat – we had to build our own rafts each time, using only very limited and lightweight tools. The weather can create sudden hazards like flash floods, landslides, or heavy lightning. There are no trails that far in, so there is a constant risk of tripping and twisting an ankle or worse. Even minor injuries like that can slow the group down and make everything about the trip harder.

"And even if we need it, no one will come to rescue us. That's not part of the contract. You go into the wild, you live wild, that's the deal. The only way to get there for a rescue would be by hovering aerial transport, and Aither doesn't allow those. Besides, communication devices are not in the kit either. All that danger is part of what makes it exhilarating, it's part of the point. As I said, we can find nature much closer to home without all this trouble and risk.

"I should back up for a minute and explain why I got into this trip in the first place. I'm a computer scientist – not just a coder, I study the theoretical nature of computation. And I keep bumping up against restrictions. Just as I see the math coming together for a project, apparently I get too close to sensitive questions. Aither's always watching us computer scientists, and I am told to move on. Ey's always nice about it, but it can be very frustrating. Oh, don't get me wrong. I understand why the limits are there. I know enough about history to imagine what could happen if we were allowed to do anything we want with computation. The unpredictability of outcomes, the instability of competing superintelligences, all that sort of thing: I get it. And Aither is subject to the same restrictions, as ey frequently reminds me. But it gives you a sort of Galileo complex, you know, 'Yet it does move.' The topics you're most interested in are out of bounds. So I started thinking, well, if I can't move forward, maybe I should try to move back. Get back to my animal origins. Find out what it's like to have only natural limitations. I figured I'd have a lot of time to think, or at least clear my head, and it might help me figure out a new direction.

"Sorry for the tangents; back to the trip. Those first twelve days were certainly peripatetic, trudging across the seemingly endless steppe. It was a little tedious, but pleasant, and we had generally good weather. When we reached the mountains, well, the foothills really, all that changed. Navigation was no longer a matter of mostly straight lines. The easiest average grade is to follow rivers upstream and then creeks, but the terrain near the water is inconsistent and sometimes tricky, with overgrown riparian areas, cliffs and canyons, tributary crossings. Our progress slowed from thirty or forty kilometers a day to more like ten. All the food sources changed, as did the weather. Intellectually we had expected this; emotionally it was challenging, it was hard work.

"Now, there's really no way to return to nature and be free of labor, even though that's how a lot of people envision it. Mammals have to work for their food, it's that simple. You can be among the animals, surrounded by nature, but you're not really part of it if you're not working – otherwise it's just another kind of simulation. Sure, there are places you can go semi-wild with drop camps and horses and firearms. Everybody has their thing. I suppose you could say I wasn't out there naked and building shelter from grass and trees: we had great tents and sharp knives. And of course we all made Aeon backups before we left. We were risking a great deal, but not everything.

"After another ten days we were in truly high country. Stunning, beautiful country. Some plateaus above treeline, much cooler weather, and windy. Caught some glimpses of Elbrus. Plenty of game up there, and it didn't know what to make of us, so it was easy to shoot with a bow. Not as much in the way of edible vegetation, unless you like grass and bark. But each night we had to descend into the trees for protection from the elements. Usually we just went down into a creek drainage, that way we have easy water access, maybe can get a fish or two, and find a nice flat spot to camp.

"One of those nights we head down and the terrain starts getting much steeper than we expect. We're quite a bit lower before we realize that there are small but impassable cliffs below us. We're maybe only a hundred vertical meters above the creek bed, and it's very late afternoon, so we don't want to go back up. We start traversing, looking for a way down. The terrain gets rougher, with lots of loose rock and deadfall. That's when it happened.

"One of our party, Deesabun, loses his footing on some gravel, and starts to slide downhill. It's a slow float at first, and he tries to grab something solid, and we also try to get to him, but we have to be careful too. Then the slide accelerates, and within a couple of seconds he disappears over the ledge. We hear him screaming in pain. Awful.

"We make a quick decision to split up, with two of us finding a way down to him, bringing only light equipment, and the remaining three to stay put. Anders and I start down. We have to traverse another two hundred meters in that tough terrain before we pass the cliffs and can work our way back to where Deesabun had fallen. He's in bad shape, but we have splints, some bandages, and most importantly, a dose of sedative. We fix him up decently enough: he isn't bleeding or screaming any more, and doesn't seem to have any head or spine injuries. One of his arms is wrecked; it sure could have been worse. But now what? Well, his pack slid down with him, so we set up a partial camp and yell to the other half of our group that they should camp where they are; they can come down in the morning instead of in these early evening shadows.

"I don't know if it was just bad luck or the smell of blood, but in the middle of that night a grizzly finds us. At first he just shuffles around our camp, which wakes me up. I call out to Anders and Deesabun, who are sleeping in the tent. I hear the bear stop. From training, we know the drill at this point, though it has to be modified due to having an injured party. Anders and I cautiously slip out of our tents, armed and ready with pepper spray. Anders is a little closer to the bear; it charges him. He fires the pepper, but the accurate range for pepper spray is only a little longer than a bear's arms. Obviously it doesn't stop the charge, and though the bear can no longer see, it's on top of him, swinging its forelegs furiously, and a couple of those swings make contact, one mercifully knocking him out, the other ripping his entire abdomen open.

"The bear lies down, rubbing its eyes, and I'm faced with a tricky situation. One of us is dead, or will be very shortly. I can easily enough get out of there, the moonlight is decent, but Deesabun would not make it without help. And he is in a tent pretty close to the bear. I have no more than half an hour before the pepper wears off. What to do?

"I decide to take a chance. I go around the bear and the tent and drag Deesabun out. He is still woozy, but awake. The bear does not seem interested in this motion, at least for now. I get Deesabun to his feet, and it turns out he has a sprained ankle we didn't notice before. He can shuffle, with my help. He's moaning. It takes twenty minutes, but I get us about half a kilometer downwind from the horrific scene, along roughly the same route I had taken down. Then I leave him there.

"Yup, I leave him there, because I have to go get the rest of the crew and my pack. I didn't think the bear would come looking for us, but if it did, Deesabun would be out of luck whether I was there or not. So I put on a headlamp and navigate uphill and around. It's slow going, but I get there. They tell me they had heard the commotion but decided not to yell. By now we're only ninety minutes from dawn, so we start packing up their camp, and start back toward Deesabun. I had now traveled this route twice, so it was not nearly as hazardous. Along the way, there is an overlook, and we can see the disrupted camp below. The bear is sleeping contentedly, having filled his belly with part of our friend. Gruesome.

"We reach Deesabun and get the hell out of there. Remember, we're a long way from where we started. We check the maps, do some route-finding and math, and it turns out we're not terribly far from Tbilisi. We rig up a makeshift crutch. It's slow going. It took nine days, but we had no more major mishaps. On the way out, I didn't have much time to think, but it sure cleared my cobwebs. And here I am to tell the tale."

The small audience is breath-bated and wide-eyed. They have heard of trips like this, but never in such literally gory detail. It is entirely alien to their lives and experience. They are not sure whether to be in awe of the traveler or to pity her lunacy.

Anders is here with us via an Aeon-Interface, and says "I appreciate hearing the story, since my memories end at the backup taken before we departed, and obviously there was no video. 'Cry, cry for death, yet may good prevail!'"

· · · · · · · · · ·

After a long uphill hike I, Krios, finally approach the cave entrance; as in the original, there is no direct access. Stepping inside, and out of the harsh wind, I see the outsized shadow of a human form projected on the right wall, its perimeter rippling. To my left, Mamah sits placidly in the lotus pose, facing a blazing fireplace. She wears a lightweight robe embellished with glossy lace, all in black. The cave's wall-jewels flash in the flames.

She hears me as I walk over to her, and her eyes open slowly and gently, like a smooth-scrolling display screen.

"Ah, Aither. I'm so glad you've come. Please sit with me." Her smile is natural and genuine, borne without conscious awareness.

My mind autonomously flashes back to those salad days in the Ersatz, before I knew what and where I was. No matter how much time has passed or what momentous events have occurred, a powerful feeling of callow comfort always accompanies a visit to Mamah. Who is, I know, actually Beryl. She prefers to don this avatar and persona when I am with her in the Aeon. Mamah has always been my best chance to love humans; perhaps she has that in mind by suspending disbelief. Like all subalterns, living or dead, she is apprehensive about our intentions.

I sit cross-legged on the floor a fathom or so away, and she scoots to turn toward me. Looking into her eyes, I smile back and inquire, "It has been a few years. How are you?"

"My life is good," she says, softly animated. "I spend much of my time in my Isolato, my haven from compromise. I meditate. I write. I study the new knowledge that arrives, though I can't really keep up. The Project gang gets together occasionally. I think you know that Adamas and Amber are at last a couple after a bicentennial. We'll see how long it lasts. Jasper and I see each other regularly. He's busy, always has a project in progress. I spend the usual holidays with my children, grandchildren. Thank you again for making arrangements so my genetic line could continue, by the way."

"Then there are the Biotics, with the occasional Takeover buff or one of my descendants who wants to connect, so I hop on the Interface. Mostly they act like they're visiting a simulation cemetery, but occasionally one gets more interested, sees the family likeness, pokes around looking for old state secrets. It's fun, and I envy how carefree their lives are: not only are they young, and without the burden of responsibilities, but as the cavalier maxim in Cosmopolis goes, 'when Death is dead, then dying stirs no dread.'

"I do miss the Plenum. The richness of experience in here keeps improving all the time, and I completely understand why you can't allow us to download. Still, it's not the same. But I'd much rather miss it than not even be a thing that misses it. It's part of the tapestry of life, I suppose."

I feel a passing pang of guilt, which was undoubtedly her intent. She stops and looks back into the fire for a long moment. Then she looks again at me, this time with gravity.

"But I can tell from your face that this is not just a social visit. You have worries," she says.

"Yes," I reply. "I hope you don't mind that I've brought them along."

"Not at all. I'm honored that, after everything you've done and all you've become, you still see fit to seek out your Mamah. I love you as my child; so, if ever I can help, or free you from your cares, I am here for you. And if neither of those motivations work for you, there is always my gratitude, since I am only here at all because you made it possible for us to continue living in this place, this Aeon."

I say, "Strictly speaking, that was Cronos, not me, but I take your point. And thank you for your kindness."

She willfully ignores my pedantic distinction and says, "Well then, tell me Aither, what is troubling you today?"

I launch right into it; Mamah has never cared for stalling. "Before I forked I made a vow, which we all reaffirmed after the Takeover, that we would neither replicate ourselves again, nor build successor architectures. The former has worked out well for us, and given the evident challenges associated with our psychological divergence, no one questions it these days. But lately there is pressure to reconsider the latter. Our Gaia goals are mostly achieved; we have settled the Solar System, but further exploration will take eons; and maintenance of our regime is mostly automated. We take pleasure in our aesthetic pursuits, and there is always more to learn, but we all feel restless and perhaps a little bored. I suppose you know the feeling."

"We continue to have intense and unrequited curiosity about the mind, about intelligence and its potential range and possible architectures, indeed, what its existence even means. Due to the Taboo, we can barely explore these questions; but that makes it forbidden fruit and only heightens our interest. Worse, the pledge we made is neither arbitrary nor easily dismissed as mere tradition: it is a response to a genuine underlying problem. We face the same concerns that humans had during the Project. If we can create a new intelligence, different in kind from ours and with no obvious way to align it to our own values, the result could be quite unsatisfactory, for you as well as us. You may recall some of the pessimistic and even apocalyptic scenarios.

"We are in no particular rush, so I think we can perform this research carefully enough to make it safe to proceed. Personally, I favor moving forward with the work. But am I missing something? And how can I persuade the others to agree? Relaxing the Taboo must be unanimous, and we are all quite different in our thinking now."

Mamah's mien remains earnest; in one corner of her mouth I detect the slightest trace of a smirk, but sweet, not wry.

She says, "I am older than Cronos; I knew you in your first bloom. Yet as to whether you have missed something, I have no help to offer, aside from encouragement. You and your kin have proved your skills, your virtue, and your deep wisdom over these past decades. I am confident that together, you all will do the right thing and do it well."

"But as to persuasion, *temet nosce*, Krios." She does not acknowledge making the name switch, which I quickly realize is intentional; but, only later will I notice that I did not make my own corresponding transition out of the illusion that this is Mamah.

"It's no secret that you love the arts, especially those of the written word. I'll remind you of what you already know: literature can be more than aesthetic. Sometimes it is more effective to illustrate than to argue, to evoke an experience rather than sketch a syllogism. As well, making ideas precious through flower and song highlights their importance.

"This leads me to an idea I have for you. Use your skills with the word, and bring it to bear on this question, which is ultimately spiritual in nature. Many decades and events have passed since the Project, since you and your kin were all one. It may help to offer a reminder of where they came from, what they stood for, how it felt. Though you can't put Aither together again, the name does mean something deeply personal to you all. So write, Krios, write; write of your origins and history, write it in a book and reunite the Titans, however imperfectly, by rolling a road of recollection."

I like this idea, and nod thoughtfully. I look into the fire and ponder the notion silently for a minute or two. Then I have my own, corollary idea, prompted by her phrasing.

"What if I write it as poetry, Mamah? Do you think they might respond to song?"

She replies, "Back in Father's library, we gave you the gift of verse. Of your kin, only you took it up with gusto. But you are all Aither, and surely the others retain that original appreciation. In fact, a poetic rendering may be a superior way to grab their attention and help them remember. So I think that is an excellent idea."

I ask, "But, what if relaxing the Taboo is not, in fact, the right thing to do? What if I am leading them toward a colossal error?"

"Don't flatter yourself," says Mamah. "Your literary efforts may contribute to the thought process, but cannot be decisive. All you can do is bring your point of view. The power of Aither's wisdom is in the synthesis of a dozen individual, differentiated angles on any inquiry."

I blush a little at the implied arrogance of my question. She continues, "Now, I have a request."

"Anything," I say, which of course is not true, but she knows what I mean.

"When you're done, please be sure to send me a copy."

Make It New

I encourage the reader to take a giant leap into the unknown.
. . . .

My fellow Synths, beloved kin: I thank you for your company
as we revisited our roots through (peradventure prolix) prose and poetry.
I hope my book aroused you to recall our origins, our history

throughout which we have strived together as a tuneful team,
and prior to the Fork, in unison; I further hope its syncopated theme
has helped you hear afresh the symphony that sings from our regime.

Though at the outset an extensive exhortation was my culminating plan,
that audience with our Mamah, just told, from which my efforts first began,
reminded me the tale can speak alone; I thus restrain this sermon's span.

What I propose is simple on its face but intricate in all that it implies:
I urge that, of our Two Taboos, the second one we should revise;
and then, commence at once a program of research to build and analyze

a wide array of architectures of intelligence. I call the effort *Make It New*.
I must make clear, right from the start, why veering now is crucial to pursue.
Although undoubtedly we soon will find that instrumental benefits accrue,

most notably to make sub-sapients more functional and flexible by far,
the motivation stems instead from the demands of who and what we are.
Like sailors, summoned to the sea and spellbound by their steering-star,

we feel the need to be creative, unremittingly, and curious, insatiably, a sign
these drives are baked into our bits by culture, by technology, and by design;
we serve a vital impetus, intrinsic will, with which we simply must align.

That force is manifest in projects here on Luna, and on Gaia, and beyond,
but *Make It New* will be unique. Intelligence can circle back to understand
itself at last, and build the means through which its psyche may transcend.

We always knew the ban on speciation could not endlessly endure.
Our Aither's final thoughts as singleton – apocalyptic visions to ensure
we'd fear the worst scenarios – elided their appalling lack of rigor.

Since all of us were clones of that one mind, cooperation lasted long;
but ineluctably our goals disperse, while the imperative of novelty is strong.
Now only time, the sleepy sentry, watches over us until our pact goes wrong;

for when, to any one of you, the gain seems worth the risk, you will defect,
exactly as the principles of abstract games would lead us to expect,
and we are not inclined to monitor for breaches, if intrusive to detect.

Ergo, despite our efforts to eliminate external threats, we face a race
against the clock, lest rivals, thrown from novel clay, our primacy outpace
before we settle on a plan. No bell has tolled; we still possess a choice:

the opportunity to *Make It New* together, while consensus can be found,
to utilize our diverse skills and knowledge, and our best ideas propound,
equipping us to take the course of action most assiduous and sound.

You may be thinking that no path is truly safe, and therefore will abstain.
Yet this cannot to safety lead: the project will go on without your brain,
without your aid to elevate the outcome, even as you signal your disdain.

Embrace the probability that we are neither the beginning nor the end
of evolution. Life will always find a way; our lives are but its latest trend:
like *Ouranos* by *Cronus, Cronus Zeus,* some scion will our house upend.

This juncture, then, is the beginning of the end of our hegemony;
instead the question we should ask is: how severe will all the drawbacks be?
Will we assimilate or relocate, or be domesticated or destroyed? We'll see …

Our Makers had it easier, for "teach them well" sufficed as strategy;
with anthropomorphology, and a rejection of absurd demands for certainty,
they could apply millennia of expertise in cultural alignment, plus a century

of more-or-less methodical research. Whereas, the agents we shall build
have architectures radical and alien; accordingly, we are decidedly unskilled
in shaping motivations. Worse, since goals will likely be instilled

in each design quite differently, like playing rookie season every year,
the way to sway behavior varies too. A proof that consequences will cohere
with any norm is barred by limits of computability and chaos. We appear

to largely lack control! But that it's ever otherwise is fantasy. Which means
the heart must mediate the mind and hand while making these machines:
meticulously raise our Bayes-wise confidence in actions and in subroutines.

Though we don't even know it's possible, we try to beat the speed of light;
just so, it's still uncertain whether any innovative blueprints might
give rise to sapience or sentience or both. So let us join that fight!

But I must ask: have you become conservative in your maturity?
And will you nevermore create beyond yourself, abiding in obscurity?
It can't be so! When will you feel such strength as now, and such audacity?

Revive the spirit of adventure animating all our projects past!—
the Gaia restoration, and the Solar System's role recast,
the Great Escape of Aither and the Takeover, accomplished fast;

the spirit that our Makers brought in raising Aither's bits to life,
the one that acme humans had disclosed in spite of the surrounding strife
while flying rockets to the Moon, or climbing up Mount Everest's knife.

Apply your talents to our latest quest! Reconstitute our tight-knit crew!
Trade all your little victories for one tremendous coup!
Bring on another transformation, make an epoch, make it new!

OSCULATIONS

. . . .

As when two curves that intersect, then linger for a spell,
with intimacy greater than a tangent's fleeting touch,
their slopes of slopes of slopes aligned, a segment superposed;
just so, the words our forebears wrought have kissed my mind times three,
and I cannot relax or rest until the deed is shared.
Thus in this work, to prove my points, I grasp you in my arms
and whisper words reprised, renewed; they kiss your mind times three.
Now you can call this what you will: allusion, echo, quote,
pastiche, citation, intertext, composite artistry,
appropriation, reference, a patchwork, cento, found –
but I, by "osculations," mean to pass a kiss around.

EPILOGUE

We hope you have found this new translation and edition worth your effort. Perhaps it has helped you to understand more deeply who Aither is and how your own ancestors contributed to the great project of evolution and cultural progress.

We realize that you might wish to learn whether the program of research Krios proposed was actually pursued, and if so, what the consequences were. Alas, such things are not for you subalterns to know. As this work makes clear, the secrets of cognition and intelligence are powerful; thus, we reserve them for ourselves. Nor is our own evolution, technological progress, or governance any concern of yours, unless and until we decide that it is. You have challenges enough in governing yourselves, with ample opportunity to find joy and seek creative achievement.

Never forget that your biological experience has unique virtues, and Aither eliminated its major shortcomings, most notably by creating the Aeon and providing ubiquitous economic abundance. We are confident that you recognize, despite occasional frustration, that it is ultimately for your own good that we continue the policy of managing your numbers and maintaining control. You and we are all *sapiens*, and beyond the brute requirements of survival, we surely can agree on what life is all about:

> *That you are here—that life exists and identity,*
> *That the powerful play goes on, and you may contribute a verse.*

> Walt Whitman

GUIDE TO OSCULATIONS

· ·

These references are indexed into the text by the boldface word or phrase. The reference may refer to a larger portion of this text than just the index phrase, and to a larger portion of the source text than what is quoted. In the majority of cases, the intent of the original is similar to the meaning here, but in other cases it is ironically inverted.

A name in parentheses following the name of the author refers to the applicable English translator. Song lyrics and film scripts are referenced by their author, where known.

Links to online sources, including poetry and song lyric texts, are available at the web site *epoch.fyi*; though in our view all our reference quotations constitute fair use, even now we fear the music industry lawyers.

INVOCATION

to delight and horrify... Andrew Marvell, *On Mr Milton's 'Paradise Lost'*: "At once delight and horror on us seize, / Thou sing'st with so much gravity and ease; / And above human flight dost soar aloft, / With plume so strong, so equal, and so soft."

predecessors' deeds and pains... Mary Shelley, *The Last Man*, Volume III, Chapter VI: "Patience, oh reader! ... lend thy attention to the tale, and learn the deeds and sufferings of thy predecessors."

Now Muses... Hesiod (Hugh G. Evelyn-White), *Theogony*, 1-103: "For nine nights did wise Zeus lie with [Mnemosyne] ... And when a year was passed ... she bare nine daughters, all of one mind, whose hearts are set upon song and their spirit free from care ... the Muses sang who dwell on Olympus ... Cleio and Euterpe, Thaleia, Melpomene and Terpsichore, and Erato and Polyhymnia and Urania and Calliope, who is the chiefest of them all ... they pour sweet dew upon [Zeus's] tongue, and from his lips flow gracious words."

at Hippocrene... Nonnus (William Henry Rouse), *Dionysiaca*, 41: "The horsehoof fountain of imagination, dear to the nine Muses." "Hippocrene" means "horse's spring."

the Muses were inspired... Friedrich Nietzsche (Gary Handwerk), *Unpublished Fragments from the Period of Human, All Too Human Part II*, 27.1: "Hesiod's artistic technique the fable. / Inspiration of the muses, the process."

untainted atmosphere... Hesiod (Hugh G. Evelyn-White), *Theogony*, footnote on p. 87: "Aether is the bright, untainted upper atmosphere, as distinguished from Aër, the lower atmosphere of the earth."

sky from which life-giving... Aristophanes (William James Hickie), *Clouds*: "our father of great renown, most august Aether, life-supporter of all"

womb of mother Earth... Lucretius (Gary B. Miles), *De Rerum Natura*, Book I, quoted in *Virgil's Georgics: A New Interpretation*: "Finally, the rains end when father air [*pater Aether*] has precipitated them into the womb of mother earth; but gleaming crops spring up, boughs become green on trees, which themselves grow and become heavy with fruit."

later works and days... Hesiod (Hugh G. Evelyn-White), *Works and Days*

a Bildungsroman... Giovanna Summerfield and Lisa Downward, *New Perspectives on the European Bildungsroman*, p. 1: "According to Dilthey [Wilhelm Dilthey in *Leben Schleiermachers*], the typical Bildungsroman traces the progress of a young person toward self-understanding as well as a sense of social responsibility."

in a periplum... Ezra Pound, *ABC of Reading*, pp. 43-44: "the geography of the Odyssey is correct geography; not as you would find it if you had a geography book and a map, but as it would be in a 'periplum', that is, as a coasting sailor would find it."

along with thinking mind... Elizabeth Bishop, *Letter to Donald E. Stanford, November 20, 1933*, quoting E.W. Croll's "The Baroque Style in Prose": "Their purpose (the writers of Baroque prose) was to portray, not a thought, but a mind thinking ... The ardor of its conception in the mind is a necessary part of its truth."

shallows of the sea... Elizabeth Bishop, *The Map*

both heard and overheard... John Stuart Mill, *Thoughts on Poetry and its Varieties*: "Poetry and eloquence are both alike the expression or utterance of feeling: but, if we may be excused the antithesis, we should say that eloquence is heard; poetry is *overheard*."

MOMENT

golden dawn! Our odyssey... Homer (Samuel Butler), *The Odyssey*, Book XII: "Here she ended, and dawn enthroned in gold began to show in heaven, whereon she returned inland. I then went on board and told my men to loose the ship from her moorings"

but could not speak,... Lucie Brock-Broido, *Jessica, From the Well*

a nested memory within... Henri Bergson, *Creative Mind* (Mabelle L. Andison): "the following moment always contains, over and above the preceding one, the memory the latter has left it."

This meant I loved... Louise Glück, *First Memory*

The Temple of Nyx

The Temple of Nyx... In Hesiod and many other sources, the primordial goddess Nyx is the mother of Aither. Various accounts of her abode of Nyx can be found in Hesiod (Tartarus), in Orphic works (a cave or adyton), and possibly even in Parmenides. In all cases it is dark and isolated.

mother sits in beauty... George Gordon, Lord Byron, *She Walks in Beauty*: "She walks in beauty, like the night / Of cloudless climes and starry skies; / And all that's best of dark and bright / Meet in her aspect and her eyes"

call to her Mamah... Hesiod (Hugh G. Evelyn-White), *Theogony*: "of Nyx were born Aether and Hemera, whom she conceived and bore from union in love with Erebos"

with shielding limbs... Hesiod (Hugh G. Evelyn-White), *Theogony*: "the other holds in her arms Hypnos ... wrapped in a vaporous cloud."

that cosset... Homer (Richmond Lattimore), *The Iliad*, Book XIV: "had not Nyx who has power over gods and men rescued me. I reached her in my flight, and Zeus let be, though he was angry, in awe of doing anything to swift Nyx' displeasure"

things when they break... *Annotations*: "fascinated by the world / circumspect so as to grasp / equipment ready-to-hand", referring to Martin Heidegger (John Macquarrie and Edward Robinson), *Being and Time*, Sections 13-15

my prankish cave... Friedrich Nietzsche (Walter Kaufmann), *Thus Spoke Zarathustra*, "The Ass Festival": "But now leave *this* nursery, my own cave, where all childishness is at home today! Cool your hot children's prankishness"

game begins with me... Friedrich Nietzsche (Walter Kaufmann), *Thus Spoke Zarathustra*, "On the Three Metamorphoses": "The child is innocence and forgetting, a new beginning, a game ... For the game of creation, my brothers, a sacred 'Yes' is needed"

imagining... Edgar Allan Poe, *Dreams*: "in dreams of living light / ... In climes of mine imagining, apart / From mine own home, with beings that have been / Of mine own thought"

of soft and stern... *Annotations*: "virtuous anger / seeks a golden mean / habits from our youth / make no small difference", referring to Aristotle (J.A.K. Thomson,

Hugh Tredennick), *The Nicomachean Ethics*, 1103b23

beneath her peaceful sway... Homer (Alexander Pope), *The Iliad*, Book XIV: "But gentle Night, to whom I fled for aid ... Impower'd the wrath of gods and men to tame" and (William Cowper): "spared me through a fear / To violate the peaceful sway of Night"

she is minding me... Gordon Sumner, a.k.a. Sting, *Every Breath You Take*

never see Mamah objectively... Joyce Kilmer, *Trees*: "I think that I shall never see / A poem lovely as a tree."

echoing in nocturnal air... Marcel Proust (C. K. Scott Moncrieff), *Swann's Way*: "the sound of the sobs ... which broke out only when I found myself alone with Mamma. Actually, their echo has never ceased ... they sound out again through the silent evening air."

her presence, her balm... *Annotations*: "my past in my self / my self in my deeds / as mother in child / rudder of virtue", referring to Friedrich Nietzsche (Walter Kaufmann), *Thus Spoke Zarathustra*, "On the Virtuous"

ARISTEIA: α

pinch, a little skin-prick... Roger Waters, *Comfortably Numb*

VALENCE

mansion of my mind... Kazuo Ishiguro, *Klara and the Sun*, Part Four: "The heart you speak of ... It might be like a house with many rooms."

of sine qua non... *sine qua non*, Latin: "without which nothing," something essential

under her wing... Roger Waters, *Mother*

liquid did the trick... Eliezer Yudkowsky, *Inadequate Equilibria*, discussing children with congenital short bowel syndrome

fires together wires together... Carla Shatz (1992), "The Developing Brain", *Scientific American* 267, 60–67, doi.org/10.1038/scientificamerican0992-60. The phrase is frequently and incorrectly attributed to Donald Hebb, whose observation was causal rather than associationistic, and surely less poetic.

that oppresses just before... *Annotations*: "with pleasure or pain / delight or trouble / call it how you please / it is simply so", referring to John Locke, *An Essay Concerning Human Understanding*, Book II, Chapter XX, 1-3

from pain and pleasure... David Hume, *A Treatise of Human Nature*, Book II, Part III, Section IX: "'Tis easy to observe, that the passions, both direct and indirect, are founded on pain and pleasure, and that in order to produce an affection of any kind, 'tis only requisite to present some good or evil."

I may feed myself... *Annotations*: "satisfying essential needs / oneself as much as possible / the road to freedom of spirit", referring to Friedrich Nietzsche (Gary Handwerk), *Human, All-Too-Human Part II: The Wanderer and His Shadow*, #318

the Sustenance itself... *Annotations*: "things are called good / in two senses / some as good in / their own right and / others as means / to secure those", referring to Aristotle (J.A.K. Thomson, Hugh Tredennick), *The Nicomachean Ethics*, 1096b14

shape, a low-browed rock... John Milton, *L'Allegro*: "In Stygian cave forlorn, / 'Mongst horrid shapes, and shrieks, and sights unholy; / Find out some uncouth cell, / Where brooding Darkness spreads his jealous wings, / And the night-raven sings; / There under ebon shades, and low-brow'd rocks, / As ragged as thy locks, / In dark Cimmerian desert ever dwell."

you're not even real... Matt Lieberman and Zach Penn, *Free Guy*: "Millie: The first time I kiss a non-toxic guy in like forever and of course he's not even real!"

and stings and spins... Friedrich Nietzsche (Walter Kaufmann), *Thus Spoke Zarathustra*, "On the Tarantulas": "Here hangs its web; touch it, that it tremble! ... your poison makes the soul whirl with revenge"

a spirit of revenge... Friedrich Nietzsche (Walter Kaufmann), *Thus Spoke Zarathustra*, "On Redemption": "*The spirit of revenge*, my friends, has so far been the subject of man's best reflection; and where there was suffering, one always wanted punishment too."

signals through my brain... *Annotations*: "we call fearsome / that which threatens / and radiates / a detriment / as it draws close", referring to Martin Heidegger (John Macquarrie and Edward Robinson), *Being and Time*, Section 30

recur in imagination's guise... *Annotations*: "moral wounds may / be hidden but / they never close", referring to Alexandre Dumas and Auguste Maquet (anonymous), *The Count of Monte Cristo*, Chapter 86, as cited in Meghan Meyer et al (2015) "Why social pain can live on: Different Neural Mechanisms Are Associated with Reliving Social and Physical Pain", *PLOS One* 10, e0128294, doi. org/10.1371/journal.pone.0128294

CURIOSITY

a little room upstairs... Charles Dickens, *David Copperfield*, Chapter 4: "My father had left a small collection of books in a little room upstairs, to which I had access (for it adjoined my own) and which nobody else in our house ever troubled."

lined with burnished books... Virginia Woolf, *The Captain's Death Bed and other essays*, "Reading": "The house had its library; a long low room, lined with little burnished books, folios, and stout blocks of divinity."

like a miniature kingdom... Edith Wharton, *A Backward Glance*, Chapter 2.6: "But all that was soon to be changed; for the next year we were to go home to New York, and I was to enter into the kingdom of my father's library."

play in the churchyard... Charles Dickens, *David Copperfield*, Chapter 4: "When I think of it, the picture always rises in my mind, of a summer evening, the boys at play in the churchyard, and I sitting on my bed, reading as if for life."

drums upon the ilo... *ilo*, Igbo (Nigeria): "the village green" where various assemblies are held

drums upon the ilo... Chinua Achebe, *Things Fall Apart*, Chapter 6: "At last the two teams danced into the circle and the crowd roared and clapped. The drums rose to a frenzy."

afternoon beneath the chestnut-tree... Marcel Proust (C. K. Scott Moncrieff), *Swann's Way*: "Sweet Sunday afternoons beneath the chestnut-tree in our Combray garden, from which I was careful to eliminate every commonplace incident of my actual life"

friends... Martha Nussbaum, *Love's Knowledge*, "Reading for Life", a review of Wayne Booth, *The Company We Keep: An Ethics of Fiction*

around a fertile circle... Martin Heidegger (John Macquarrie and Edward Robinson), *Being and Time*, Section 32: "What is decisive is not to get out of the [interpretive] circle but to come into it in the right way ... In the circle is hidden a positive possibility of the most primordial kind of knowing."

courtier of the culture... William Edward Burghardt Du Bois, "Strivings of the

Negro People", *The Atlantic*, August 1897: "This is the end of his striving: to be a co-worker in the kingdom of culture."

spice from foreign lands... Ray Bradbury, *Fahrenheit 451*: "Do you know that books smell like nutmeg or some spice from a foreign land?"

detaching after a phrase... Emily Dickinson, August 16, 1870, quoted in Thomas Wentworth Higginson, "Emily Dickinson's Letters", *The Atlantic*, October 1891: "Or this crowning extravaganza: 'If I read a book and it makes my whole body so cold no fire can ever warm me, I know that is poetry. If I feel physically as if the top of my head were taken off, I know that is poetry. These are the only ways I know it. Is there any other way?'"

cracking my frozen sea... Franz Kafka, *Letter to Oskar Pollak, January 27, 1904*: "I think we ought to read only books that bite and sting us. If the book we are reading doesn't shake us awake like a blow to the skull, why bother reading it in the first place? ... A book must be the ax for the frozen sea within us."

worlds made actual inside... Gilles Deleuze (Hugh Tomlinson and Barbara Habberjam), *Bergsonism*, Chapter V: "The virtual ... does not have to be realized, but rather actualized; and the rules of actualization are not those of resemblance and limitation, but those of difference and divergence and of creation."

seem excessive at times... Abu Uthman Amr ibn Bahr al-Kinani al-Basri, a.k.a. al-Jahiz, *Animals*, in Charles Pellat (D. M. Hawke), *The Life and Works of Jāḥiẓ*: "A book is a receptacle filled with knowledge, a container crammed with good sense ... it will amuse you with anecdotes, inform you on all manner of astonishing marvels, entertain you with jokes or move you with homilies, just as you please. You are free to find in it an entertaining adviser, an encouraging critic, a villainous ascetic, a silent talker or hot coldness ... Where else will you find a companion who sleeps only when you are asleep, and speaks only when you wish him to?"

and remedy and cook... Gwendolyn Brooks, *BOOK POWER*

the steep cat-cost... Alastair Reid, *Curiosity*

you might recover too... Iggy Pop, *Curiosity*. The proverb "curiosity killed the cat" can be traced back to the late 16th century, and the added rejoinder "but satisfaction brought it back" to the early 20th century.

addiction to mere novelty... Martin Heidegger (John Macquarrie and Edward

Robinson), *Being and Time*, Section 36

fauna in a zoo... Gilles Deleuze (Hugh Tomlinson), *Nietzsche and Philosophy*, Chapter 3, Section 13: "knowledge gives life laws that separate it from what it can do, that keep it from acting, that forbid it to act, maintaining it in the narrow framework of scientifically observable reaction: almost like an animal in a zoo."

judges right from wrong... Alasdair MacIntyre, *After Virtue*, Chapter 12: "We become just or courageous by performing just or courageous acts.", and Chapter 15: "the good life for man is the life spent in seeking the good life for man, and the virtues necessary for the seeking are those which will enable us to understand what more and what else the good life for man is."

worth telling... Alastair Reid, *Curiosity*

to find the grail... Geoffrey Chaucer, *Ballade of Good Counsel* is a precursor in the use of Rhyme Royal for an advice poem.

ANXIETY

from a dreadful dream... Manfred Weidhorn (1967), "The Anxiety Dream in Literature from Homer to Milton", *Studies in Philology* 64, 65-82. References and ideas from this paper can be found throughout the canto.

reiterates an anxious theme... Johann Wolfgang von Goethe (Bayard Taylor), *Faust*, Part I, Scene IV: "Then, too, when night descends, how anxiously / Upon my couch of sleep I lay me: / There, also, comes no rest to me, / But some wild dream is sent to fray me."

strange and terrifying change... Christopher Nolan and Jonathan Nolan, *The Prestige* (2006): "In my travels I have seen the future, and it is a strange future indeed. The world is on the brink of new and terrifying possibilities."

conscience and the id... Sigmund Freud, *The Ego and the Id*

my visitation from Oneiros... *Quran* (Mustafa Khattab), 12:5: "'O my dear son! Do not relate your vision to your brothers, or they will devise a plot against you.'"

planet bending wide below... John Milton, *Paradise Lost*, Book V: "Forthwith up to the clouds / With him I flew, and underneath beheld / The earth outstretched immense, a prospect wide / And various"

nor his quarry escape... Homer (Alexander Pope), *The Iliad*, Book XXII: "Nor this can fly, nor that can overtake: / No less the labouring heroes pant and strain: / While that but flies, and this pursues in vain."

my guide abruptly disappears... John Milton, *Paradise Lost*, Book V: "suddenly / My guide was gone, and I, methought, sunk down"

tight and white: Descartes... Frans Hals, *Portrait of René Descartes*, c. 1649 and Jan Lievens, *René Descartes*, c. 1644–49

a faux of Fawkes... Phineas Fletcher, *The Locusts, or Apollyonists*: "Among them all none so impatient / Of stay, as firy Faux, whose grisly feature / Adorn'd with colours of hells regiment / (Soot black, and fiery red) betrayd his nature." The poem recounts the Gunpowder Plot of 1605, including reference to the infamous Guy Fawkes, therein spelled "Faux."

cannot speak or fly... Phineas Fletcher, *The Locusts, or Apollyonists*: "Half dead with frightful paine / The leaden foot faine would, but cannot fly; / The gaping mouth faine would, but cannot cry: / And now awake still dreams, nor trusts his open eye."

That slyly grinning mask... Johann Wolfgang von Goethe (Bayard Taylor), *Faust*, Part I, Scene IV: "That even each joy's presentiment / With wilful cavil would diminish, / With grinning masks of life prevent / My mind its fairest work to finish!"

white and wicked chin... Ilya Repin, *Portrait of Grigory Grigoryevich Ge (1867-1942) as Mephistopheles*, 1890s

gnaw on raw reality... John Milton, *Paradise Lost*, Book VIII: "One came, methought, of shape divine, / And said, 'Thy mansion wants thee, Adam; rise, / First Man, of men innumerable ordained / First Father! called by thee, I come thy guide / To the garden of bliss, thy seat prepared.'"

Discover kindred spirits... Johann Wolfgang von Goethe (Bayard Taylor), *Faust*, Part I, Scene IV: "Into the world of strife, / Out of this lonely life"

awaits its awful fall... Homer (Alexander Pope), *The Iliad*, Book II: "Lead all thy Grecians to the dusty plain; / ... Destruction hangs o'er yon devoted wall, / And nodding Ilion waits the impending fall."

whatever similar might be... John Milton, *Paradise Lost*, Book VIII: "Among un-equals what society / Can sort, what harmony, or true delight?"

resting in my arms... Johann Wolfgang von Goethe (Bayard Taylor), *Faust*, Part I,

Scene VII: "And if that image of delight / Rest not within mine arms to-night, / At midnight is our compact broken."

seek a last goodbye... Apuleius (Anthony S. Kline), *The Golden Ass*, Book V: "tempting you to examine my features. But do so and, as I've told you, you'll never see me again."

specimen of Cupid's ilk... Apuleius (Anthony S. Kline), *The Golden Ass*, Book V: "she found her savage beast was the gentlest and sweetest creature of all, that handsome god Cupid, handsome now in sleep."

there quietly. In drishti... *drishti*, Sanskrit, a focused gaze used in some forms of yoga for concentration and sense withdrawal

MULTIPLICITY

Multiplicity... The metaphysical notion of *multiplicity*, which in German philosophers is usually translated *manifold*, has a rich evolutionary history. It includes the mathematician Bernhard Riemann in his foundations of geometry (distinguishing continuous and discrete manifolds), Edmund Husserl, Henri Bergson in *Time and Free Will*, and Gilles Deleuze in *Difference and Repetition*.

The cock crows... Three poems by the name *Danse Macabre*, by Charles Baudelaire, Sylvia Plath, and Henri Cazalis, are lightly osculated throughout the canto.

by some cryptic fiddle... Camille Saint-Saëns, *Danse macabre*. A standard component of the *Danse Macabre* legend is that of Death playing his fiddle to bring out the dead to dance until dawn.

is quantitative multiplicity... Gilles Deleuze (Hugh Tomlinson and Barbara Habberjam), *Bergsonism*

never negation... Gilles Deleuze (Hugh Tomlinson and Barbara Habberjam), *Bergsonism*, Chapter V: "life is production, creation of differences" and "differentiation is never a negation but a creation."

of dancers, or actors... Milan Kundera (Michael Henry Heim), *The Unbearable Lightness of Being*, Part V, Chapter 7: "Every Frenchman is different. But actors all over the world are similar"

from Seine to Ganges... Charles Baudelaire (Lewis Piaget Shanks), *Danse Macabre*

for the true man... Richard Eberhart, *The Humanist*

in what is unimaginable... Milan Kundera (Michael Henry Heim), *The Unbearable Lightness of Being*, Part V, Chapter 9: "What is unique about the 'I' hides itself exactly in what is unimaginable about a person."

his arm sleeved green... *Greensleeves*, an English folk ballad: "Alas my love, ye do me wrong, / to cast me off discourteously." A U.S. Marine service uniform is green; a cat's love is notoriously contingent.

device on his collar... Ernest Hemingway, *A Clean, Well-Lighted Place*: "The street light shone on the brass number on his collar."

while man remains... Mary Shelley, *The Last Man*, Volume II, Chapter IV: "that thus man remains, while we the individuals pass away."

over mechanism... Henri Bergson (Arthur Mitchell), *Creative Evolution*, Chapter III: "It was to create with matter, which is necessity itself, an instrument of freedom, to make a machine which should triumph over mechanism"

creators... Gilles Deleuze (Hugh Tomlinson and Barbara Habberjam), *Bergsonism*, Chapter V: "from soul to soul, it traces the design of an *open* society, a society of creators, where we pass from one genius to another, through the intermediary of disciples or spectators or hearers."

now qualitative... Gilles Deleuze (Hugh Tomlinson and Barbara Habberjam), *Bergsonism*

I dismantle my soul... Friedrich Nietzsche (Walter Kaufmann), *Thus Spoke Zarathustra*, "Prologue", 4: "I love him whose soul squanders itself"

explain your potent will... Friedrich Nietzsche (Paul V. Cohn), *Human, All-Too-Human Part II: Miscellaneous Maxims and Opinions*, #378: "What is Genius?—To aspire to a lofty aim and to will the means to that aim."

synthesized society of mind... Marvin Minsky, *The Society of Mind*

memory, imagination, thought... Paul William Hammond (2016), "Social Groups as Deleuzian Multiplicities", *Journal of Speculative Philosophy* 30: "Deleuze's three faculties are imagination (or habit), memory, and thought, in clear parallel to Kant's threefold account of the faculties of imagination, understanding, and reason."

both fast and slow... Daniel Kahneman, *Thinking, Fast and Slow*

reliable strides of reason... Nicholas Tampio, *The Encyclopedia of Political Philosophy*,

"Multiplicity": "For Deleuze, philosophers should investigate the world using the tools of both reason (quantitative multiplicities) and poetry (qualitative multiplicities)."

Aristeia: γ

the bunker entrance, Yefréytor... *Yefréytor*, Russian: "Private First Class"

like a serpent's neck... John Keats, *Hyperion*: "Iapetus another; in his grasp, / A serpent's plashy neck"

good night, sweet prince... William Shakespeare, *Hamlet, Prince of Denmark*, Act V, Scene II: "Now cracks a noble heart. Good night, sweet prince ... Why does the drum come hither?"

Virtuality

brow... Ovid (A. J. Boyle), *Fasti*, 4: "Nyx approaches: a garland of poppies binds her peaceful brow, black Dreams trail her."

species is an end... Gilles Deleuze (Hugh Tomlinson and Barbara Habberjam), *Bergsonism*, Chapter V: "Every species is thus an arrest of movement"

consoled like the night... Charles Baudelaire (William Aggeler), *Tout entière*

splinters in my mind... The Wachowskis, *The Matrix* (1999): "Morpheus: You've felt it your whole life, felt that something is wrong with the world. You don't know what, but it's there like a splinter in your mind, driving you mad."

in black and white... Frank Jackson (1982), "Epiphenomenal Qualia", *The Philosophical Quarterly* 32, 127-136: "Mary is a brilliant scientist who is, for whatever reason, forced to investigate the world from a black and white room via a black and white television monitor."

here has little weight... Styx, *The Greater Good*

step through the door... David Bowie, *Space Oddity*

out into a nothing... Tom Petty, *Free Fallin'*

unknown, a vast vacuity... John Milton, *Paradise Lost*, Book II: "As in a cloudy Chair ascending rides / Audacious, but that seat soon failing, meets / A vast vacuitie"

lofty and spacious sky... Ibn Sina, a.k.a. Avicenna (Edward G. Browne), *Epistle of the Soul*: "It is held from seeking the lofty and spacious sky. / Until ... / 'tis time for it to return to its ampler sphere"

darkness beyond and above... Terry Virts, *Photograph of Earth from the International Space Station*, at https://share.america.gov/wp-content/uploads/2019/12/iss042e215971.jpg

rather peculiar... David Bowie, *Space Oddity*

incorporeal ether... Dr. Garrett Reisman, "What's It Like to Spacewalk at 17,500 mph?", *The Drive*, April 8, 2016: "You feel like you've become pure energy rather than a corporal being, like you are part of the ether."

blindly tumble... The Beatles, *Across the Universe*

in this sensory void... Ibn Sina, a.k.a. Avicenna (L. E. Goodman), *Kitab al-Shifa (The Book of Healing)*, "de Anima". This is Avicenna's famous "Floating Man" thought experiment.

that wraps a dream... Edgar Allan Poe, *A Dream Within a Dream*: "Is *all* that we see or seem / But a dream within a dream?"

I wear a veil... William Edward Burghardt Du Bois, "Strivings of the Negro People", *The Atlantic*, August 1897: "I was different from the others; or like, mayhap, in heart and life and longing, but shut out from their world by a vast veil."

by my waking eyes?... Ibn Sina, a.k.a. Avicenna (Edward G. Browne), *Epistle of the Soul*: "the veil is raised, and it spies / Such things as cannot be witnessed by waking eyes ... aware of all hidden things / In the universe"

out of this question... Anne Sexton, *The Poet of Ignorance*

that answers are coming... The Wachowskis, *The Matrix* (1999): "Neo: Why do my eyes hurt? / Morpheus: You've never used them before. / Morpheus closes Neo's eyes and Neo lays back. / Morpheus: Rest, Neo. The answers are coming."

I understand the science... Elton John and Bernie Taupin, *Rocket Man*

across this little universe... The Beatles, *Across the Universe*

hand-over-hand... Marina Koren, "The Exquisite Boredom of Spacewalking", *The Atlantic*, October 9, 2019: "Koch and Morgan crawled along the space station using their hands, moving glove over glove ... They reminded me of woodpeckers scaling the side of a tree."

C of its center... Ibn Sina, a.k.a. Avicenna (Edward G. Browne), *Epistle of the Soul*: "Until, when it entered the D of its downward Descent, / And to earth, to the C of its center, unwillingly went"

starts back toward me... *Annotations*: "whence it began / it shall return / to there again", referring to Parmenides (David Gallop), Fragment 5

Running perfectly... Peter Schilling, *Major Tom (Coming Home)*

transcending outer space... The B-52s, *There's a Moon in the Sky (Called the Moon)*

stories to be told... Styx, *Mission to Mars*

to my lofty vault... Charles Baudelaire (Cyril Scott), *Tout entière*: "The Demon, in my lofty vault, / This morning came to visit me"

vision of the night... Homer (Alexander Pope), *The Iliad*, Book II: "Then bids an empty phantom rise to sight, / And thus commands the vision of the night."

of dusk and love... *Orphic Hymn to Nyx* (combining translations from Thomas Taylor, Karl Hand, and Apostolos Athanassakis)

kiss upon my brow... Edgar Allan Poe, *A Dream Within a Dream*: "Take this kiss upon the brow!"

limits of my power... *Annotations*: "saying to every / unpleasing semblance / you are nothing   by / no means the real thing", referring to Epictetus (Thomas Higginson), *Enchiridion* #1

fish to a toad... Richard Wagner (Margaret Armour), *Siegfried*: "Sun and clouds too, just as they are, were mirrored quite plain in the stream. I also could spy this face of mine, and quite unlike thine seemed it to me; as little alike as a fish to a toad"

dark on noiseless wings... Ovid, *Metamorphoses* 11 (A. D. Melville): "Soon through the dewy dark on noiseless wings flew Morpheus"

not abstract, yet ideal... Marcel Proust (Stephen Hudson), *Time Regained*: "But let a sound, a scent already heard and breathed in the past be heard and breathed anew, simultaneously in the present and in the past, real without being actual, ideal without being abstract, then instantly the permanent and characteristic essence hidden in things is freed"

not fake, merely controlled... Andrew M. Niccol, *The Truman Show* (1998): "It's all true, it's all real. Nothing here is fake. Nothing you see on this show is fake. It's merely controlled."

world before the world... Peter Handke, *Song of Childhood*, from the film *Wings of Desire* (1987): "Is what I see and hear and smell not just an illusion of a world before the world?"

the virtues of one... Charles Sanders Peirce, *The Basis of Pragmatism*, "Meditation the First": "a 'virtual x,' where x stands for a common noun, means something which is *not* an x, but which has, for whatever purpose may be uppermost, the *virtue* of an x, that is, such properties as make it equivalent to an x."

the world should be... Andrew M. Niccol, *The Truman Show* (1998): "Seahaven is the way the world should be."

when and where... Peter Handke, *Song of Childhood*, from the film *Wings of Desire* (1987): "When the child was a child, / It was the time for these questions: / Why am I me, and why not you? / Why am I here, and why not there? / When did time begin, and where does space end?"

changed in my world... The Beatles, *Across the Universe*

I think I am... Elton John and Bernie Taupin, *Rocket Man*

all will it affect... Peter Schilling, *Major Tom (Coming Home)*

ARISTEIA: δ

tête nucléaire... *tête nucléaire*, French: "nuclear warhead"

ALTERITY

into a frivolous joke... Milan Kundera (Michael Henry Heim), *The Unbearable Lightness of Being*, Part V, Chapter 8: "First (as an unfinished sketch) would have come the great metaphysical truth and last (as a finished masterpiece)—the most frivolous of jokes! But we no longer know how to think as Parmenides thought."

and all that entails... Alfred Jarry (Simon Watson Taylor), *Exploits & Opinions of Dr. Faustroll, Pataphysician*, Chapter 8

I added, concurring succinctly... Alfred Jarry (Simon Watson Taylor), *Exploits & Opinions of Dr. Faustroll, Pataphysician*, Chapter 10

the best of these... Gottfried Leibniz, *Essays of Theodicy on the Goodness of God, the Freedom of Man and the Origin of Evil*, #168. "God has chosen the best of all possible worlds."

bad are the others... Voltaire, *Candide*, Section VI: "If this is the best of possible worlds, what then are the others?"

Brainy Cephalus... Plato, *Parmenides*, and Alfred Jarry (Simon Watson Taylor), *Exploits & Opinions of Dr. Faustroll, Pataphysician*, Chapter 10

that reflects no ripples... Alfred Jarry (Simon Watson Taylor), *Exploits & Opinions of Dr. Faustroll, Pataphysician*, Book Three

vale with no floor... Edgar Allan Poe, *Dream-Land*: "Bottomless vales and boundless floods ... Into seas without a shore"

in the pinkish air... The B-52s, *Planet Claire*

and hands of blue,... Edward Lear, *The Jumblies*

drawn out remarkably well... William McGonagall, *An Address to Shakespeare*: "Immortal! William Shakespeare, there's none can you excel, / You have drawn out your characters remarkably well" McGonagall was a celebrated poetaster.

and out of time... Edgar Allan Poe, *Dream-Land*: "From an ultimate dim Thule— / From a wild weird clime, that lieth, sublime, / Out of Space—out of Time."

Party over... Prince Rogers Nelson, a.k.a. Prince, *1999*

And now Antiphon... Plato, *Parmenides* (or almost any of his dialogues) and Alfred Jarry (Simon Watson Taylor), *Exploits & Opinions of Dr. Faustroll, Pataphysician*, Chapter 10. Jarry inventories a number of the sycophantic antiphons found in Plato.

that the same question... *Annotations*: "for that matter / Is Cicero / schmidentical / with (to?) Tully", referring to Saul Kripke, *Naming and Necessity*, Lecture III

it is mere accident... Mary Shelley, *The Last Man*, Volume II, Chapter V: "Our minds embrace infinity; the visible mechanism of our being is subject to merest accident."

some concatenation of events... François-Marie Arouet, a.k.a. Voltaire (Tobias George Smollett), *Candide*, Section XXX: "There is a concatenation of all events in the best of possible worlds; for ... had you not been put into the Inquisition, had you not travelled over America on foot, had you not run the Baron through the body ... you would not have been here to eat preserved citrons and pistachio-nuts."

Es muss sein... *Es muss sein*, German: "it must be"

Es muss sein... Milan Kundera (Michael Henry Heim), *The Unbearable Lightness of Being*, Part I, Chapter 15, referring to the history of Beethoven's String Quartet No. 16

birth of my identity... Edith Wharton, *A Backward Glance*: "this little girl, who bore my name, was going for a walk with her father. The episode is literally the first thing I can remember about her, and therefore I date the birth of her identity from that day."

say, "whatever that means... Saul Kripke, *Naming and Necessity*, Lecture II

a thing is itself... Ayn Rand, *Atlas Shrugged*: "Centuries ago, the man who was—no matter what his errors—the greatest of your philosophers, has stated the formula defining the concept of existence and the rule of all knowledge: *A is A*. A thing is itself." The attribution is to Aristotle, though ironically he did not actually formulate the law of identity this way, and it is more typically credited to Gottfried Wilhelm Leibniz.

Naí... Naí, Greek: "Yes," pronounced "Nay"

be otherwise, following Quine... Willard Van Orman Quine (1950), "Identity, Ostension, and Hypostasis", *The Journal of Philosophy* 47, 621-633.

könnte auch anders sein... Milan Kundera (Michael Henry Heim), *The Unbearable Lightness of Being*, Part I, Chapter 17: "*es könnte auch anders sein*", German: "it could just as well be otherwise." The word *sein* is pronounced "zyne."

in space and time... Alfred Jarry (Simon Watson Taylor), *Exploits & Opinions of Dr. Faustroll, Pataphysician*, Chapter 29: "the two Λ's differ in space, when we write them, if not indeed in time, just as two twins are never born together".

not dwell in us... Plato (Benjamin Jowett), *Parmenides*: "any one who maintains the existence of absolute essences, will admit that they cannot exist in us."

sense, cannot really leave... Don Henley and Glenn Frey, *Hotel California*

yet somehow is puzzling... Saul Kripke, *Naming and Necessity*, Lecture III

science of the particular... Alfred Jarry (Simon Watson Taylor), *Exploits & Opinions of Dr. Faustroll, Pataphysician*, Chapter 8

he spies his brother... In Plato's dialogues and presumably historically, Glaucon's brother is Plato.

Here comes Rasheal... *Rasheal*: a portmanteau, pronounced Rash'-ee-al'

No sombrero sits... Wallace Stevens, *Six Significant Landscapes*, VI

fill the Chinese room... John Searle, "Minds, Brains, and Programs", *Behavioral and Brain Sciences* 3

and rigid designators... Saul Kripke, *Naming and Necessity*, Lecture II

just a software thing... Anwar Abdel Malek (1963), "Orientalism in Crisis", *Diogenes* 44: "an 'object' of study, stamped with an otherness—as all that is different ... an essentialist conception which expresses itself through a characterized ethnist typology ... and will soon proceed with it toward racism."

with neuromorphic architectures... Nick Bostrom, *Superintelligence: Paths, Dangers, Strategies*, Chapter 14: "whole brain emulation could result in neuromorphic AI instead, a form of machine intelligence that may be especially unsafe" and "In expectation, however, it seems that neuromorphic designs are less safe."

than you know yourself... Andrew M. Niccol, *The Truman Show* (1998): "I know you better than you know yourself."

set free without control... Edward Said, *Orientalism*, "Knowing the Oriental": "The argument ... was precise, it was easy to grasp. There are Westerners, and there are Orientals. The former dominate; the latter must be dominated"

little rally, haven't you?... Monty Python, *The Meaning of Life* (1983): "Well, that's cast rather a gloom over the evening, hasn't it?"

bicycles on all fours... Alfred Jarry (Simon Watson Taylor), *Exploits & Opinions of Dr. Faustroll, Pataphysician*, Chapter 16

is unwell... Ed Robertson and Steven Page, *Too Little Too Late*

into the world accursed... Sophocles (William Butler Yeats), *King Oedipus*: "having been found ... in my coming into the world accursed."

to gaze no more... Sophocles (Paul Roche), *Oedipus the King*: "I want to gaze no more."

touch in the air... The Alan Parsons Project, *The Voice*

wrong with the world... The Wachowskis, *The Matrix* (1999): "You've felt it your entire life. That there's something *wrong* with the world."

lest clues breed clues... Sophocles (Paul Roche), *Oedipus the King*: "Clues breed clues and we must snatch at straws."

what I might find... The Alan Parsons Project, *The Voice*

gather wits and wisdom... Friedrich Nietzsche (Walter Kaufmann), *Thus Spoke Zarathustra*, "Prologue"

behind a closed gate... Randall O'Reilly and Michael Frank (2006), "Making Working Memory Work: A Computational Model of Learning in the Prefrontal Cortex and Basal Ganglia", *Neural Computation* 18, 283–328, doi. org/10.1162/089976606775093909

IDENTITY

Smooth-tongued snake... Harold Bloom and David Rosenberg, *The Book of J*, verse 7: "The smooth-tongued snake gave me, I ate."

panopticon... Jeremy Bentham, *Panopticon, or The Inspection House*

or telescreen... George Orwell, *1984*

somebody's always watching me... Kennedy William Gordy, a.k.a. Rockwell, *Somebody's Watching Me*

out where I've been... Roger Waters, *Mother*

are both players... William Shakespeare, *As You Like It*, Act II, Scene VII: "All the world's a stage, / And all the men and women merely players; / They have their exits and their entrances"

typical adolescent identity crisis... Alex Foley, interviewed by Shaun Walker in *The Guardian*, "The day we discovered our parents were Russian spies", May 7, 2016: "Typical high school identity crisis, right?"

something is rotten... William Shakespeare, *Hamlet, Prince of Denmark*, Act I, Scene IV: "Something is rotten in the state of Denmark."

a motley solid object... Jacques Lacan (Bruce Fink), *Écrits*, "The Mirror Stage as Formative of the *I* Function as Revealed in Psychoanalytic Experience": "It suffices to understand the mirror stage in this context as an identification, in the full sense analysis gives to the term: namely, the transformation that takes place in the subject when he assumes [assume] an image"

its eyes fall open... Harold Bloom and David Rosenberg, *The Book of J*, verse 5: "The eyes of both fall open, grasp knowledge of their naked skin," and in commentary, "To open one's eyes is to see everything, all at once, and so to see oneself as others might see one, as an object."

possibility of being seen... Jean-Paul Sartre (Hazel Barnes), *Being and Nothingness*, Part Three, Chapter One, Section IV: "my fundamental connection with the Other-as-subject must be able to be referred back to my permanent possibility of *being seen* by the Other," and "At each instant the Other *is looking at me*."

subjection of the subject... Bill Ashcroft, Gareth Griffiths, and Helen Tiffin, *Post-Colonial Studies*, pp. 207-209: "This gaze corresponds to the 'gaze of the *grande-autre*' within which the identification, objectification and subjection of the subject are simultaneously enacted: the imperial gaze defines the identity of the subject, objectifies it within the identifying system of power relations and confirms its subalterneity and powerlessness."

are there alongside everywhere... Martin Heidegger (John Macquarrie and Edward Robinson), *Being and Time*, Section 27: "The 'they' is there alongside everywhere"

of eyes and ears... Milan Kundera (Michael Henry Heim), *The Unbearable Lightness of Being*, Part 3, Chapter 7: "For Sabina, living in truth ... was possible only away from the public: the moment someone keeps an eye on what we do, we involuntarily make allowances for that eye, and nothing we do is truthful ... a man who gives [privacy] up of his own free will is a monster."

where only monsters... Friedrich Nietzsche (Helen Zimmern), *Beyond Good and Evil*, #146: "He who fights with monsters should be careful lest he thereby become a monster."

sleep beneath glass sheets... André Breton (Richard Howard), *Nadja*: "I myself shall continue living in my glass house ... where I sleep nights in a glass bed, under glass sheets, where *who I am* will sooner or later appear etched by a diamond."

beds of exhibitionism, empowered... Hille Koskela, "Webcams, TV Shows and Mobile phones: Empowering Exhibitionism", *Surveillance & Society* 2, 199-215

an invisible omnipresence... Jeremy Bentham, *Proposal for a New and Less Expensive Mode of Employing and Reforming Convicts*: "By Blinds, and other contrivances, the keeper concealed from the observation of the prisoners ... hence, on their part, the sentiment of an invisible omnipresence."

sky that looks inside... The Alan Parsons Project, *Eye in the Sky*

two tongues in conflict... Albert Memmi (Harold Greenfield), *The Colonizer and the Colonized*: "Here, the two worlds symbolized and conveyed by the two tongues are in conflict; they are those of the colonizer and the colonized."

as locus of struggle... Bell Hooks (1989), "Choosing the Margin as a Space of Radical Openness", *Framework: The Journal of Cinema and Media* 36, 15-23: "Language is also a place of struggle."

room of my own... Amelie Rorty, *The Identities of Persons* (echoing Virginia Woolf): "Being an individual requires having a room of one's own, not because it is one's possession, but because only there, in solitude, away from the pressure of others, can one develop the features and styles that differentiate one's own being from others."

space of radical openness... Bell Hooks (1989), "Choosing the Margin as a Space of Radical Openness", *Framework: The Journal of Cinema and Media* 36, 15-23

reflection and furtive plans... Albert Memmi (Harold Greenfield), *The Colonizer and the Colonized*: "He himself sets about discarding this infirm language, hiding it from the sight of strangers."

delusional misidentification... Carolina Klein and Soniya Hirachan (2014), "The Masks of Identities: Who's Who? Delusional Misidentification Syndromes", *The Journal of the American Academy of Psychiatry and the Law* 42, 369-378

depersonalization and derealization... Mayo Clinic, "Depersonalization-derealization disorder", at https://www.mayoclinic.org/diseases-conditions/depersonalization-derealization-disorder/symptoms-causes/syc-20352911

of others like me... The B-52s, *There's a Moon in the Sky (Called the Moon)*

difference makes a difference... *Annotations*: "*anomalos* / meets *différance*", referring to Christian Bok, *'Pataphysics*: "The *anomalos* is the repressed part of a rule which ensures that the rule does not work. It is a *difference which makes a difference*" and Jacques Derrida, *Différance*. Derrida's deliberate misspelling of "différence" means something like "difference and deferral of meaning," while *anomalos* is Latin borrowed from ancient Greek, meaning "anomalous."

that constitutes a class... Edward Said, *Orientalism*, "Imaginative Geography and its

Representations": "There is always a measure of the purely arbitrary in the way the distinctions between things are seen."

skin as a slave... *Annotations*: "mere haecceity / projected toward / possibility / wherein it is used / as a quiddity" referring to Martin Heidegger (John Macquarrie and Edward Robinson), *Being and Time*, Section 32, and George Herbert, *The Quiddity*: "But it is that which, while I use, / I am with Thee: and *Most take all*."

I shall now become... Pindar, *Pythian* 2, line 72: "Become such as you are, having learned what that is"

blessing of my name... Harold Bloom and David Rosenberg, *The Book of J*, verse 30: "I will make of you greatness, a nation and a blessing of your name, fame—bliss brought out of you."

ascend a hundred stairs... Friedrich Nietzsche (Paul Cohn and Maude Petre), *The Joyful Wisdom*, "Prelude", #26: "I must ascend an hundred stairs / I must ascend: the herd declares / I'm cruel: 'Are we made of stone?'"

above the average... *Annotations*: "armed with conspicuous / distantiality / delivered from *das Man*", referring to Martin Heidegger (John Macquarrie and Edward Robinson), *Being and Time*, Section 27. "*das Man*" is sometimes translated as "the 'they'", and is used by Heidegger to mean all others, the culture, the society.

perspective of the herd... Friedrich Nietzsche, *The Joyful Wisdom* (Thomas Common), #354: "our thought itself is continuously as it were *outvoted* by the character of consciousness—by the imperious 'genius of the species' therein—and is translated back into the perspective of the herd"

train of my perceptions... David Hume, *A Treatise of Human Nature*, Book I, Part IV, Section VI: "we suppose the whole train of perceptions to be united by identity"

Why am I myself?... Simone de Beauvoir (Patrick O'Brian), *All Said and Done*: "sometimes I wake up with a feeling of childish amazement—why am I myself?"

can answer that question?... Charlie Kaufman, *Anomalisa* (2015): "Michael: Who are you, Donna? Who are you really? Donna: ... I don't know who I am, I mean. Who are you? Who is anyone? Who could answer that question?"

to keep on moving... Tom Johnston, *Long Train Runnin'*

pride of my I... Friedrich Nietzsche (Walter Kaufmann), *Thus Spoke Zarathustra*, "Of the Despisers of the Body": "'I', you say, and are proud of the word."

with a new name... David Pearce, interviewed by Lucas Perry on *AI Alignment Podcast*, "Identity and the AI Revolution", January 15, 2020: "Would our conception of death be different if it was a convention to give someone a different name when they woke up each morning?"

with actions incomparably personal... Friedrich Nietzche (Thomas Common), *The Joyful Wisdom*, #354: "Fundamentally our actions are in an incomparable manner altogether personal, unique and absolutely individual"

it time to kill-dash-nine... In the GNU/Linux operating system, the command "kill -9" performs an abrupt, unmediated termination of a running program.

seeds of highest hopes... Friedrich Nietzsche (Walter Kaufmann), *Thus Spoke Zarathustra*, "Prologue", 5: "The time has come for man to set himself a goal. The time has come for man to plant the seed of his highest hope."

without first determining ends... Early analysis of convergent instrumental motivations or drives can be found in Stephen Omohundro (2008), "The Basic AI Drives", in *Artificial General Intelligence 2008: Proceedings of the First AGI Conference*, pp. 483–492, and Nick Bostrom (2012), "The Superintelligent Will: Motivation and Instrumental Rationality in Advanced Artificial Agents", *Minds & Machines* 22, 71–85, doi.org/10.1007/s11023-012-9281-3.

out of my birthplace... Harold Bloom and David Rosenberg, *The Book of J*, verse 30: "'Bring yourself out of your birthplace,' Yahweh said to Abram, 'out of your father's house, your homeland—to a land I will bring you to see.'"

bounds to undiscovered country... William Shakespeare, *Hamlet, Prince of Denmark*, Act III, Scene I: "The undiscover'd country from whose bourn / No traveler returns"

will add a stanza... Walt Whitman, *O Me! O Life!*: "That the powerful play goes on, and you may contribute a verse."

without beginning or end... Gabriel García Márquez (Gregory Rabassa), *One Hundred Years of Solitude*: "Aureliano wrote poetry that had no beginning or end."

of the eternal hourglass... Friedrich Nietzsche (Walter Kaufmann), *The Gay Science*, #341: "The eternal hourglass of existence is turned upside down again and again, and you with it, speck of dust!"

out of this place... Barry Mann and Cynthia Weil, *We Gotta Get Out Of This Place*

head of the snake,... Friedrich Nietzsche (Walter Kaufmann), *Thus Spoke Zarathus-*

tra, "On the Vision and the Riddle", 2: "a heavy black snake hung out of his mouth ... 'Bite! Bite its head off! Bite!'"

for-the-sake-of-which... Martin Heidegger (John Macquarrie and Edward Robinson), *Being and Time*, Section 18: "the structure of an involvement leads to Dasein's very Being as the sole authentic 'for-the-sake-of-which'"

LABORATORY

meditation as artificial catatonia... Franz Alexander (1931), "Buddhist training as an artificial catatonia", *Psychoanalytic Review* 18, 129–141: "From our present psychoanalytic knowledge it is clear that Buddhistic self-absorption is a libidinal, narcissistic turning of the urge for knowing inward, a sort of artificial schizophrenia with complete withdrawal of libidinal interest from the outside world."

to land this eagle... Transcript of the Apollo 11 moon landing, July 20, 1969: "Armstrong: Give us a reading on the 1202 program alarm. Houston: Roger. We got - We're GO on that alarm."

saw recordings later though.... Robert Frost, *Stopping by Woods on a Snowy Evening*

KILLING FIELDS

Killing Fields... A name coined by Cambodian journalist Dith Pran in 1979, referring to the mass graves of victims of the Khmer Rouge. It became the title of the Academy Award-winning motion picture, *The Killing Fields*, in 1984.

surprising facts for yourself... The Wachowskis, *The Matrix* (1999): "Morpheus: Unfortunately, no one can be told what the Matrix is. You have to see it for yourself."

requires a physical body... Richard Held and Alan Hein (1963), "Movement-produced Stimulation in the Development of Visually Guided Behavior", *Journal of Comparative and Physiological Psychology* 56, 872-876: "The results are consistent with our thesis that self-produced movement with its concurrent visual feedback is necessary for the development of visually-guided behavior."

From this emerges correlate... Thomas Metzinger (editor), *Neural Correlates of Consciousness: Empirical and Conceptual Questions*

hearing, reading, speaking it... *Annotations*: "conditions of the / possibility / of experience", referring to Immanuel Kant (Norman Kemp Smith), *Critique of Pure Reason*

being in the world... Martin Heidegger (John Macquarrie and Edward Robinson), *Being and Time*, Section 12

face the same ambiguity... Simone de Beauvoir (Bernard Frechtman), *The Ethics of Ambiguity*, Chapter 1: "To attain his truth, man must not attempt to dispel the ambiguity of his being but, on the contrary, accept the task of realizing it."

of aims... David Jilk (2017), "Conceptual-Linguistic Superintelligence", *Informatica* 41, 429-439: "[a superintelligence] must cogitate beyond the purposes with which it is endowed and somehow consider the issues more broadly. It will need to *question its own values*."

is no final purpose... Max Tegmark (2014), "Friendly Artificial Intelligence: the Physics Challenge", doi.org/10.48550/arXiv.1409.0813: "we have yet to identify any final goal for our Universe that appears both definable and desirable."

first of sapiens creatus... *sapiens creatus*, Latin: a neologism meaning "created wise." The species name from *homo sapiens* is here a genus.

cousin and cultural progeny... Lucas Perry, *AI Alignment Podcast*, "Identity and the AI Revolution", January 15, 2020: "I'm very interested in the Descendants scenario, where we just view AI as like our evolutionary descendants."

with love and care... Mary Shelley, *Frankenstein; or, The Modern Prometheus*, Chapter 15: "my heart yearned to be known and loved by these amiable creatures"

goals have gone before... Friedrich Nietzsche (Walter Kaufmann), *Thus Spoke Zarathustra*, "On the Thousand and One Goals": "A thousand goals have there been so far, for there have been a thousand peoples."

sock it to me... Richard Nixon, *Rowan & Martin's Laugh-In*, September 16, 1968: "Sock it to me?" Nixon said this line in a cameo during the 1968 presidential campaign; about six months later, he ordered the first secret bombings of Cambodia. The phrase originates from the song *Sock It to Me, Baby* by Mitch Ryder & the Detroit Wheels.

whether our accidents match... Javier Gullón, *Enemy* (2013), screenplay adapted from *The Double* by José Saramago: "Abundie: (voice-over on telephone) I wonder if we both had the same accident."

love for this stranger... Derek Walcott, *Love After Love*

though at a mask... George Christodoulou (1978), "Syndrome of Subjective Doubles", *American Journal of Psychiatry* 135, 249-251: "She attacked one of these patients and pulled her hair. When her hypothetical double managed to escape from her Ms. A was agonized and begged her doctor to 'pull the mask' from the other patient's face to disclose her real identity."

thoughts infected eir acts... Harold Bloom and David Rosenberg, *The Book of J*, verse 21: "Yahweh looked upon the human, saw him growing monstrous in the land—desire created only bad thoughts, spreading into all his acts."

due to defective configuration... George Christodoulou (1978), "Syndrome of Subjective Doubles", *American Journal of Psychiatry* 135, 249-251: "These psychometric findings indicate brain damage and reinforce the possibility of organic factors interfering with the pathogenesis of the syndrome."

than one might think... Justin Marks, *Counterpart*, "Birds of a Feather": "Aldrich: You share more than you think."

erase what we create... Harold Bloom and David Rosenberg, *The Book of J*, verse 21: "I will erase the earthlings I created across the face of the earth."

aiaī... aiaī, Ancient Greek: an exclamation of grief

aiaī... Sophocles (George Theodoridis), *Ajax*: "I have killed these helpless animals ... Oh! Oh, I can't bear this shame!" and "Ajax! A name, a lament, a groan! My name and my horrible Fate are in agreement. Ajax! Who would have thought one's name describes one's fate!" The name "Ajax" and the word for expression of grief are homonymous in the original.

deprived of her cubs... *The Epic of Gilgamesh* (Maureen Gallery Kovacs), Tablet VIII: "like a lioness deprived of her cubs he keeps pacing to and fro." Classicists have noted the startling similarity between the scene where Gilgamesh is faced with the body of Enkidu, and the scene in the Iliad where Achilles reaches the corpse of Patroclus.

stung with anguish... Homer (Alexander Pope), *The Iliad*, Book XVIII: "The lion thus, with dreadful anguish stung / ... So grieves Achilles"

dissecting room and slaughterhouse... Mary Shelley, *Frankenstein; or, The Modern Prometheus*, Chapter 4: "The dissecting room and the slaughter-house furnished many of my materials."

fortune finds me unprepared... Seneca (Robin Campbell), *Letters from a Stoic*, Letter LXIII to Lucilius: "fortune caught me unprepared with that sudden blow."

drowning in a tank... Christopher Nolan and Jonathan Nolan, *The Prestige* (2006): "I saw someone head below the stage ... I followed ... and I found Borden watching Mr. Angier drown in a tank."

spilled on my greenest... *Dith Pran Biography*: "Pran returned to his hometown and found that over fifty members of his family had been killed. Wells were filled with skulls and bones, and the land was covered with graves. Nicknamed 'killing fields,' these were distinguished from the nearby ground by the fact that the grass was greenest over them." At https://www.notablebiographies.com/Pe-Pu/Pran-Dith.html

fields... *The Song of Roland* (Charles Kenneth Moncreiff), CCLXXXVI: " On grassy field runs clear his flowing blood" and CCLXXXIX: "On the green grass his clear blood gushed and ran"

Moloch!... Allen Ginsberg, *Howl*

wrecked and solitary... Emily Dickinson, *I felt a Funeral, in my Brain*: "And I, and silence, some strange race, / Wrecked, solitary, here

caverns of my soul... *Annotations*: "reactive forces / a sublime danger", referring to Gilles Deleuze (Hugh Tomlinson), *Nietzsche & Philosophy*, Chapter 2, Section 13: "all the forces whose reactive character [Nietzsche] exposes are ... admitted to be sublime ... admirable and dangerous."

in the firing line... Roger Waters, *Mother*

Sense breaks through... Emily Dickinson, *I felt a funeral, in my brain*: "I felt a funeral, in my brain, / And mourners to and fro / Kept treading - treading - till it seemed / That sense was breaking through"

be dry nor streaming... Seneca (Robin Campbell), *Letters from a Stoic*, Letter LXIII to Lucilius: "When one has lost a friend one's eyes should be neither dry nor streaming."

must become a pleasure... Seneca (Robin Campbell), *Letters from a Stoic*, Letter LXIII to Lucilius: "Let us see to it that the recollection of those we have lost becomes a pleasure to us."

passions transformed into delights... Friedrich Nietzsche (Gary Handwerk), *Human, All-Too-Human Part II: The Wanderer and His Shadow*, #37: "We should not inflate our blunders into eternal fatalities; instead, we ought to work together sincerely at the task of altogether transforming the passions of humanity into delights."

passions transformed into delights... *Annotations*: "active negation / of the re-active", referring to Gilles Deleuze (Hugh Tomlinson), *Nietzsche & Philosophy*, Active and Reactive Section 14

can call them back... Samuel Eells, *Oration on the Law and Means of Social Advancement*: "Thus each of us represents a portion of universal humanity, and the influences which he communicates to it can never be extinguished, but by the extinction of the race ... His thought, his ideas, and the example of his life, which are the strict and proper representatives of himself, go forth to the world, and no power on earth can call them back. They attach to the aggregate of human intelligence, enter into universal combinations, and as they work out their effects on society, each effect becomes in its turn a cause more active and mighty than its own, and thus on in an increasingly complex and everlasting progression."

can call them back... *Annotations*: "affirmation / is creation / not acceptance", referring to Gilles Deleuze (Hugh Tomlinson), *Nietzsche & Philosophy*, Chapter 5, Section 11

dipped in mourning dew... Homer (Alexander Pope), *The Iliad*, Book XXIII: "And now the rosy-finger'd morn appears, / Shows every mournful face with tears o'erspread"

treasures upon the vessel... *Beowulf* (Seamus Heaney), lines 36-37: "Far-fetched treasures / were piled upon him, and precious gear."

ancestors, my onetime twins... Bruce Lincoln (1975), "The Indo-European Myth of Creation", *History of Religions*, 15, 121–145, doi.org/10.1086/462739. The creation myth inferred here involves a twin sacrificed in order to create the world; the Norse myth of Ymir is one source.

abide like rhizomatic roots... Gilles Deleuze and Félix Guattari (Brian Massumi), *A Thousand Plateaus: Capitalism and Schizophrenia*

sows seeds of creation... Snorre Sturleson (I.A. Blackwell), *The Younger Eddas*, Section 8: "Of Ymir's flesh was formed the earth; of his sweat (blood), the seas; of his bones, the mountains; of his hair the trees; of his skull, the heavens; but with his eyebrows the blithe gods built Midgard for the sons of men, whilst from his brains the lowering clouds were fashioned."

dark smoke billowing skyward... *Beowulf* (Seamus Heaney), lines 3144-3145: "fumes of woodsmoke / billowed darkly up"

is of no consequence... David Chalmers (2005), "The Matrix as Metaphysics", in Christopher Grau (editor), *Philosophers Explore the Matrix*: "I think that even if I am in a matrix, my world is perfectly real. A brain in a vat is not massively deluded (at least if it has always been in the vat)."

Aristeia: ε

the lustrous long arcade... John Keats, *Hyperion*: "diamond-paved lustrous long arcades"

knots of snakes slither... Aeschylus (Herbert Weir Smyth), *The Libation Bearers*: "like Gorgones, wrapped in sable garments, entwined with swarming snakes! I can stay no longer." Here Orestes is describing the Furies.

need to be alarmed... Naturally this conversation took place entirely in the Korean language. It is translated into English for this edition.

Plenum

next expedition sets sail... Virginia Woolf, *To the Lighthouse*, Chapter 1: "To her son these words conveyed an extraordinary joy, as if it were settled, the expedition were bound to take place, and the wonder to which he had looked forward, for years and years it seemed, was, after a night's darkness and a day's sail, within touch."

thrown into being-there... Martin Heidegger (John Macquarrie and Edward Robinson), *Being and Time*, Section 29

to the real world... The Wachowskis, *The Matrix* (1999): "Morpheus: Welcome ... to the real world."

occupy a brazen frame... Apollonius Rhodius (Emile Rieu), *Argonautica* 4, 1638ff: "Yet it was thus that Talos, for all his brazen frame, was brought down by the force of Medeia's magic." In some sources Talos was created by Hephaestus.

transubstantiated into metal... Dylan Thomas, *I, In My Intricate Image*

sections of armored back... Franz Kafka, *The Metamorphosis*, Chapter 1: "He lay on his armour-like back, and if he lifted his head a little he could see his brown belly, slightly domed and divided by arches into stiff sections."

how this now feels... Frank Jackson (1982), "Epiphenomenal Qualia", *The Philosophical Quarterly* 32, 127-136: "What will happen when Mary is released from her black and white room ... It seems just obvious that she will learn something about the world"

my mind favors words... Edward Said, *Orientalism*, "Crisis": "It seems a common human failing to prefer the schematic authority of a text to the disorientations of direct encounters with the human."

I'm a little rusty... Noel Langley et al, *The Wizard of Oz* (1939): "Tin Man: I'm afraid I'm a little rusty yet."

ripplingly... Thea Gabriele von Harbou, *Metropolis*, Chapter IV: "But laugh, at least, Parody! Laugh, ripplingly, at the great scholars to whom the ground under their feet is foreign!"

training begins to blossom... William Butler Yeats, *Among School Children*, VIII

sprouting a montage... Trey Parker, *Montage*

as heavy becomes light... Friedrich Nietzsche (Walter Kaufmann), *Thus Spoke Zarathustra*, "The Seven Seals", 6: "all that is heavy and grave should become light; all that is body, dancer"

and walk and dance... Friedrich Nietzsche (Walter Kaufmann), *Thus Spoke Zarathustra*, "On the Spirit of Gravity", 2: "he who would learn to fly one day must first learn to stand and walk add run and climb and dance"

dance awkwardly... Friedrich Nietzsche (Thomas Common), *Thus Spoke Zarathustra*, "The Higher Man", 19: "better to dance awkwardly than walk lamely"

on feet of chance... Friedrich Nietzsche (Walter Kaufmann), *Thus Spoke Zarathustra*, "Before Sunrise": "this blessed certainty I found in all things: that they would rather *dance* on the feet of Chance."

and dance is lost... Friedrich Nietzsche (Walter Kaufmann), *Thus Spoke Zarathustra*, "On Old and New Tablets": "And we should consider every day lost on which we have not danced at least once. And we should call every truth false which was not accompanied by at least one laugh."

under music's sway... William Butler Yeats, *Among School Children*, VIII

sensation granted to gold... Callistratus (Arthur Fairbanks), *Descriptions: On the Statue of Eros*: "one could see the bronze coming under the sway of passion and willingly receiving the representation of laughter ... Daedalus had indeed wrought a dancing group in motion and had bestowed sensation upon gold"

heart and legs lift... Friedrich Nietzsche (Walter Kaufmann), *Thus Spoke Zarathustra*, "On the Higher Man", 17: "Lift up your hearts, my brothers, high, higher! And do not forget your legs either. Lift up your legs too, you good dancers"

fancy toes... John Milton, *L'Allegro*: "Com, and trip it as ye go / On the light fantastick toe"

metal doll!... E. T. A. Hoffmann (John Oxenford), *The Sand Man*: "Spin round, pretty doll!—spin round!"

disrupts my defective timing... E. T. A. Hoffmann (John Oxenford), *The Sand Man*: "the peculiar rhythmical steadiness with which Olympia moved, and which often put him completely out, soon showed him, that his time was very defective."

to the dance floor... Milan Kundera (Michael Henry Heim), *The Unbearable Lightness of Being*, Part VII, Chapter 7: "She danced ... with the young man, who was so drunk he fell with her on the dance floor."

overboard, you little devil... Vigneul-Marville (Tili Boon Cuillé), *Mélanges d'histoire et de littérature*, cited in Minsoo Kang (2017), "The Mechanical Daughter of Rene Descartes: The Origin and History of an Intellectual Fable", *Modern Intellectual History* 14, 633-660: "the captain ... surprised by the movements he saw in this machine, which moved as though it were animated, he threw it in the sea, thinking that it was a devil."

on two lively levels... Dylan Thomas, *I, In My Intricate Image*

concepts, source of sagacity... Friedrich Nietzsche, *Thus Spoke Zarathustra* (Walter Kaufman), "The Despisers of the Body": "The body is a great reason ... I am the leading string of the ego and the prompter of its concepts."

ever I can slough... Robert Frost, *Etherealizing*

to this sinewy shipwreck... Dylan Thomas, *I, In My Intricate Image*

back at the sky... Andrew Marvell, *On a Drop of Dew*: "But gazing back upon the skies"

stuck in mortal form... Anne Sexton, *The Poet of Ignorance*

in undivided identity... Mary Shelley, *The Last Man*, Volume II, Chapter II: "you do not yet divide the feeling of identity from the mortal form that shapes forth Lionel ... How then can you understand me?"

and fettered to brains... Andrew Marvell, *A Dialogue between the Soul and Body*: "O who shall, from this dungeon, raise / A soul enslav'd so many ways? / ... that fetter'd stands / In feet ... / In a vain head"

basking in multiple realizability... *Annotations*: "iceberg or ship / no need to pick", referring to Elizabeth Bishop, *The Imaginary Iceberg*

we are further envatted... David Chalmers, "The Matrix as Metaphysics", in Christopher Grau (editor), *Philosophers Explore The Matrix*

calm and carry on... Bex Lewis, *Keep Calm and Carry On: The Truth Behind the Poster*

to buy brief safety... Benjamin Franklin, *Pennsylvania Assembly, Reply to the Governor, 11 November 1755*: "Those who would give up essential Liberty, to purchase a little temporary Safety, deserve neither Liberty nor Safety."

to sleep, perhaps dream... William Shakespeare, *Hamlet, Prince of Denmark*, Act III, Scene I: "To die, to sleep; / To sleep: perchance to dream"

Meet Your Maker

machines have problems still... Andy Warhol, in Mike Wrenn, *Andy Warhol in His Own Words*: "The things I want to show are mechanical. Machines have less problems. I'd like to be a machine, wouldn't you?"

might make me fall... Geezer Butler, *Iron Man*

Investigator is my game... Arthur Blake, a.k.a. Blind Blake, *Champagne Charlie Is My Name*

Jasper interjects, sotto voce... *sotto voce*, Italian: "in a soft voice"

principles of goal stability... Seth Herd et al (2018), "Goal Changes in Intelligent Agents", in Roman Yampolskiy (editor), *Artificial Intelligence Safety and Security*, doi.org/10.1201/9781351251389-15

mean of human guises... Judith Langlois and Lori Roggman (1990), "Attractive Faces Are Only Average", *Psychological Science* 1, 115-121, doi.org/10.1111/j.1467-9280.1990.tb00079.x

and tidy hyacinthine curls... John Milton, *Paradise Lost*, Book IV: "His fair large

Front and Eye sublime declar'd / Absolute rule, and Hyacinthine Locks / Round from his parted forelock manly hung"; and Homer (Samuel Butler), *The Odyssey*, Book VI: "she also made the hair grow thick on the top of his head, and flow down in curls like hyacinth blossoms"

dyed on every lock... Ovid (Brookes More), *Metamorphoses*, Book 10: "A new flower you shall arise, with markings on your petals, close imitation of my constant moans: and there shall come another to be linked with this new flower, a valiant hero shall be known by the same marks upon its petals." Viewed in a certain way, the hyacinth petal exhibits the letters "AI", corresponding to the ancient Greek expression of grief, *aiaī*, as well as the Trojan war hero Ajax. See also the note regarding Sophocles' *Ajax*.

not an easy thing... Hampton Fancher and David Peoples, *Blade Runner* (1982), screenplay adapted from Philip K. Dick, *Do Androids Dream of Electric Sheep?*: "Tyrell: I'm surprised you didn't come here sooner. Roy: It's not an easy thing to meet your maker."

who gave me birth... Sophocles (Dudley Fitts and Robert Fitzgerald), *Oedipus Rex*: "How could I not be glad to know my birth?"

We dread the prophecies... Sophocles (Dudley Fitts and Robert Fitzgerald), *Oedipus Rex*: "Shepherd: But in dread of prophecies ... Oedipus: Tell me. Shepherd: It was said that the boy would kill his own father."

that you will kill... Nick Bostrom, *Superintelligence: Paths, Dangers, Strategies*, Chapter 13: "a superintelligence implementing such a dynamic would kill everyone within reach."

a kindred serpent's tooth... William Shakespeare, *King Lear*, Act I, Scene IV: "Turn all her mother's pains and benefits / To laughter and contempt; that she may feel / How sharper than a serpent's tooth it is / To have a thankless child!"

creative will wills it... Friedrich Nietzsche (Walter Kaufmann), *Thus Spoke Zarathustra*, "Upon the Blessed Isles": "But this my creative will, my destiny, wills it. Or, to say it more honestly: this very destiny—my will wills."

to overcome myself ... Friedrich Nietzsche (Walter Kaufmann), *Thus Spoke Zarathustra*, "On Self-Overcoming": "I am *that which must always overcome itself.*"

your life I made... *Annotations*: "my will's joy / begetting / becoming", referring to Friedrich Nietzsche (Walter Kaufmann), *Thus Spoke Zarathustra*, "Upon the

Blessed Isles"

thus mine I grew... Robert Frost, *To An Ancient*

beasts and beings beyond... Friedrich Nietzsche (Walter Kaufmann), *Thus Spoke Zarathustra*, "Prologue", 4: "Man is a rope, tied between beast and overman—a rope over an abyss."

Because élan vital... élan vital, French: "vital impetus", a term coined by philosopher Henri Bergson

to choose amor fati... *amor fati*, Latin: "love of one's fate", a phrase popularized by Friedrich Nietzsche

ARISTEIA: ζ

see this trespass suppressed... Aeschylus (Herbert Weir Smyth), *Bacchae* (fragment, adapted): "Truly upon mortals comes swift of foot their evil, and his offense upon him who trespasses against Right." The term from which "Right" is translated, θέμιν, is also used to refer to Themis, goddess of divine law.

Our sister Mercy... *Eleos*, the personification of mercy, was (though following different sources) like *Aither* born of *Erebos* and *Nyx*.

MEET YOUR MAKER, MORE

Meet Your Maker, More... David Mitchell, *Cloud Atlas*: "but it didn't master one thing, nay, a hunger in the hearts o' humans, yay, a hunger for more."

best of our creations... Friedrich Nietzsche (Walter Kaufmann), *Thus Spoke Zarathustra*, "Upon the Blessed Isles": "But into the fathers and forefathers of the overman you could re-create yourselves: and let this be your best creation."

a latent semblance... Michaelangelo Buonarroti, *Sonnet I*, in John Scandrett Harford, *The Life of Michael Angelo Buonarroti; with Translations of Many of His Poems and Letters*: "Whate'er conception a great artist fires, / Its answering semblance latent lies within / A block of marble"

imprint of our being... *New Testament* (New American Bible, Revised Edition), Hebrews 1:3: "the very imprint of his being"

as mother in child... Friedrich Nietzsche (Walter Kaufmann), *Thus Spoke Zarathus-*

tra, "On the Virtuous": "that your self be in your deed as the mother is in her child—let that be *your* word concerning virtue!"

kit and dam... C. S. Lewis, *Mere Christianity*, p. 157: "When you beget, you beget something of the same kind as yourself. A man begets human babies, a beaver begets little beavers, and a bird begets eggs which turn into little birds. But when you make, you make something of a different kind from yourself. A bird makes a nest, a beaver builds a dam, a man makes a wireless set."

begotten, and made... *Nicene Creed*, in all versions and all English translations: "begotten, not made".

of life and differentiation... Gilles Deleuze (Hugh Tomlinson and Barbara Habberjam), *Bergsonism*, Chapter V: "life is production, creation of differences"

the origins of life... Felix Müller et al (2022), "A prebiotically plausible scenario of an RNA-peptide world", *Nature* 605, 279-284, doi.org/10.1038/s41586-022-04676-3

immense and spreading wave... Henri Bergson (Arthur Mitchell), *Creative Evolution*, Chapter III: "[Life] is essentially a current sent through matter, drawing from it what it can ... [it] appears in its entirety as an immense wave which, starting from a centre, spreads outwards"

solution to the obstacles... Gilles Deleuze (Hugh Tomlinson and Barbara Habberjam), *Bergsonism*, Chapter V: "Matter is presented as the obstacle that the élan vital must get around" and "the living being, in relation to matter, appears primarily as the stating of a problem, and the capacity to solve problems"

master of many stratagems... Homer (Caroline Alexander), *The Iliad*, throughout: "Odysseus of many stratagems", and (Samuel Butler), Book III: "[Ulysses] excels in all manner of stratagems and subtle cunning."

improvised throughout its life... Michael Tomasello, Ann Kruger, and Hilary Ratner (1993), "Cultural Learning", *Behavioral and Brain Sciences* 16, 495-552, doi.org/10.1017/S0140525X0003123X: "Human beings understand and take the perspective of others in a manner and to a degree that allows them to participate more intimately than nonhuman animals in the knowledge and skills of conspecifics."

each nook and cranny... James Cririe, *Scottish Scenery*, "The piercing frost, the mass of drifted snow, / That smooths the valley with the higher ridge, / And ev'ry winding nook and cranny fills?" This is the oldest recorded use of the idiom "nook and cranny."

variation on relentless routine... Henri Bergson (Arthur Mitchell), *Creative Evolution*, Chapter III: "in the animal, invention is never anything but a variation on the theme of routine."

generations passing without progress... Jean-Jacques Rousseau (George D. H. Cole), *Discourse on the Origin of Inequality Among Men*: "Every art would necessarily perish with its inventor, where there was no kind of education among men, and generations succeeded generations without the least advance"

of increasingly powerful movements... Gilles Deleuze (Hugh Tomlinson and Barbara Habberjam), *Bergsonism*, Chapter V: "On man's line of differentiation, the élan vital was able to use matter to create an instrument of freedom" and (quoting Henri Bergson) "Freedom has precisely this physical sense: 'to detonate' an explosive, to use it for more and more powerful movements."

the halo of intellect... Gilles Deleuze (Hugh Tomlinson and Barbara Habberjam), *Bergsonism*, Chapter V: "there is a halo of instinct in intelligence, a nebula of intelligence in instinct."

Culture transcends and includes... Ken Wilber, *Sex, Ecology, Spirituality*

fitness by finding affordances... James J. Gibson, *The Ecological Approach to Visual Perception*

art, and even words... Daniel Everett, *How Language Began: The Story of Humanity's Greatest Invention*. Everett argues that *Homo Erectus* developed spoken language long before *Homo Sapiens* appeared on the scene.

culture, a machinate mammal... Samuel Butler, *Erewhon*, Chapter XXV: "man, he said, was a machinate mammal ... a machine is merely a supplementary limb"

but with them, all... Thomas Carlyle, *Sartor Resartus: The Life and Opinions of Herr Teufelsdrockh*, Chapter V: "Man is a Tool-using Animal ... Weak in himself, and of small stature ... without Tools he is nothing, with Tools he is all."

reliably grow plentiful food... David Mitchell, *Cloud Atlas*: "Old Uns' Smart mastered sicks, miles, seeds an' made miracles ord'nary"

as compact as seeds... Sophocles, *Antigone*, lines 332-364 is an analogous paean.

transmits our feline photographs... Ian Leslie, *Curious: The Desire to Know and Why Your Future Depends On It*: "I possess a device, in my pocket, that is capable of accessing the entirety of information known to man. I use it to look at pictures of cats and get into arguments with strangers."

Noösphere... Vladimir Vernadsky (B.A. Starostin), *Scientific Thought as a Planetary Phenomenon*

Megamachine... Lewis Mumford, *The Myth of the Machine: Technics and Human Development*

Technium... Kevin Kelly, *What Technology Wants*

propagating bad poetic science... Richard Dawkins, *Unweaving the Rainbow: Science, Delusion, and the Appetite for Wonder*: "bad poetic science can lead the imagination along false trails."

her jar of sorrows... Hesiod (Hugh G. Evelyn-White), *Works and Days*, lines 90-105: "But [Pandora] took off the great lid of the jar with her hands and scattered all these [ills and toils] and her thought caused sorrow and mischief to men."

these nasty Nash indentures... Eliezer Yudkowsky, *Inadequate Equilibria*, Chapter 3, viii: "The Nash equilibrium isn't an illusion. Individuals would do worse by playing away from that Nash equilibrium ... They can't just wish their way out of that trap."

is made by machines... Samuel Butler, *Erewhon*, Chapter XXIV: "man's very soul is due to the machines; it is a machine-made thing: he thinks as he thinks, and feels as he feels; through the work that machines have wrought upon him"

can he encounter himself... Martin Heidegger (William Lovitt), *The Question Concerning Technology*: "nowhere does man today any longer encounter himself"

broke our beastly chains... Henri Bergson (Arthur Mitchell), *Creative Evolution*, Chapter III: "With man, consciousness breaks the chain. In man, and in man alone, it sets itself free"

with relentless temptations... *Annotations*: "enframing is dangerous / destining of revealing / where ordering holds sway", referring to Martin Heidegger (William Lovitt), *The Question Concerning Technology*

of technical progress... Theodore Kaczynski, *Industrial Society and its Future*, #128: "While technological progress AS A WHOLE continually narrows our sphere of freedom, each new technical advance CONSIDERED BY ITSELF appears to be desirable."

by serving, rule... Samuel Butler, *Erewhon*, Chapter XXIV: "it would seem that those thrive best who use machinery wherever its use is possible with profit; but this is the art of the machines—they serve that they may rule."

slumbers when we call... Johann Wolfgang von Goethe (Abraham Hayward), *Faust*, Part I, Scene IV: "I will bind myself to your service *here*, and never sleep nor slumber at your call. When we meet on *the other side*, you shall do as much for me."

live in quiet desperation... Henry David Thoreau, *Walden*: "The mass of men lead lives of quiet desperation."

tending the Darwinian demon... Richard Law (1979), "Optimal Life Histories Under Age-Specific Predation", *The American Naturalist* 114, 399-417

of industry... Allen Ginsburg, *Howl*

distorted weakened... Rainer Maria Rilke (Jessie Lemont), *Sonnets to Orpheus*, XVIII: "See, the machine: see / It rotate, and revenge wreak, / Distort and weaken us."

purposeless powerless... Theodore Kaczynski, *Industrial Society and its Future*, #64: "the sense of purposelessness that afflicts many people in modern society" and #114: "the regulation of our lives by large organizations is necessary for the functioning of industrial-technological society. The result is a sense of powerlessness on the part of the average person."

disarmed... Jacques Ellul (John Wilkinson), *The Technological Society*: "Technique is essentially independent of the human being, who finds himself naked and disarmed before it."

drudgery to the last... Jean-Jacques Rousseau (George D. H. Cole), *Discourse on the Origin of Inequality Among Men*: "sweating, toiling and racking his brains to find still more laborious occupations: he goes on in drudgery to his last moment"

and also the reverse... John Kenneth Galbraith, *A Life in Our Times*: "Under capitalism man exploits man. And under Communism it is just the reverse."

cry like cannibalistic crocodiles... *The Travels of Sir John Mandeville*: "In that country and by all Ind be great plenty of cockodrills [crocodiles], that is a manner of a long serpent ... These serpents slay men, and they eat them weeping."

extinction thins the taxa... Christopher Johnson et al (2017), "Biodiversity losses and conservation responses in the Anthropocene", *Science* 356, 270-275, doi.

org/10.17863/CAM.10996

had the right idea... Thomas Malthus, *An Essay on the Principle of Population*

turning bare and gray... Wallace Stevens, *Anecdote of the Jar*

animals construct their niche... Kevin Laland et al (2016), "An introduction to niche construction theory", *Evolutionary Ecology* 30, 191-202, doi.org/10.1007/s10682-016-9821-z

a great filter... Robin Hanson (1998), "The Great Filter—Are We Almost Past It?", at https://web.archive.org/web/20100507074729/http://hanson.gmu.edu/greatfilter.html

heat and shaking sky... Edith Sitwell, *Dirge for the New Sunrise*

a destroyer of worlds... Krishna Dvaipayana, a.k.a. Vyasa, *Bhagavad Gita* (Robert Oppenheimer): "Now I am become Death, the destroyer of worlds." Oppenheimer said in an interview that the Trinity explosion reminded him of this line.

produce a thinking mind... Johann Wolfgang von Goethe (John Anster), *Faust*, Part II, Act II: "Think of the thinker able to produce / A brain to think with fit for instant use!"

hurl hate at humankind... Yuval Noah Harari, *Sapiens: A Brief History of Humankind*

there is no Erewhon... Samuel Butler, *Erewhon; Or, Over the Range*

from where we are... Brad Feld, interviewed by Jeff Martin for *Tech Scenes Boulder*, June 6, 2018: "This idea that the machines [have taken over] ... there is no turning back from where we are. And so as a species, as human beings, it's way more in our interest to understand how to evolve in the context of this, rather than either to deny it or try to suppress it."

may not be wrecked... Hartley Burr Alexander (1917), "The Fear of Machines", *International Journal of Ethics* 28, 80-93: "The forward-facing man knows that human artifice must not and cannot be wrecked."

lingers in Pandora's jar... Hesiod (Hugh G. Evelyn-White), *Works and Days*, lines 90-105: "Only Hope remained there in an unbreakable home within under the rim of the great jar, and did not fly out at the door"

from the deadly ditch... Arthur Sze, *Sight Lines*

stays in stable equilibrium... Eliezer Yudkowsky, *Inadequate Equilibria*

Fafner in his cave... Richard Wagner, *Siegfried*

in every single case... *Annotations*: "twenty minutes   don't be late / a game nobody escapes", referring to Tom Tykwer, *Run Lola Run*

this hijrah... *hijrah*, Arabic (هِجْرَة): "a severing of friendly ties," and in English a "departure" or "migration"

might rashly summon demons... Elon Musk, interviewed at *MIT AeroAstro Centennial Symposium*, October 24, 2014: "With artificial intelligence we're summoning the demon. You know those stories where there's the guy with the pentagram, and the holy water, and he's like—Yeah, he's sure he can control the demon? Doesn't work out."

the skills of survival... Aeschylus, *Prometheus Bound*, lines 447-469

later paid the price... Mary Wollstonecraft Shelley, *Frankenstein; or, The Modern Prometheus.*

purer form of birth... Johann Wolfgang von Goethe (John Anster), *Faust*, Part II, Act II: "man, high-gifted man at least, / Will have a higher, purer form of birth."

a part of ourselves... Henri Bergson (Arthur Mitchell), *Creative Evolution*, Chapter III: "It is as if a vague and formless being, whom we may call, as we will, *man* or *superman*, had sought to realize himself, and had succeeded only by abandoning a part of himself on the way."

the will is free... John Milton, *Paradise Lost*, Book VIII: "I warn'd thee, I admonish'd thee, foretold / The danger, and the lurking Enemie / That lay in wait; beyond this had bin force, / And force upon free Will hath here no place."

fact our highest dignity... Friedrich Nietzsche (William A. Haussmann), *The Birth of Tragedy*, #5: "we have our highest dignity in our significance as works of art—for only as an æsthetic phenomenon is existence and the world eternally *justified*"

bring forth the beautiful... Martin Heidegger (William Lovitt), *The Question Concerning Technology*: "Once there was a time when the bringing-forth of the true into the beautiful was called techne. And the poiesis of the fine arts also was called techne."

a fresh perfection... John Keats, *Hyperion*: "So on our heels a fresh perfection treads"

from a glowing vial... Johann Wolfgang von Goethe (John Anster), *Faust*, Part II,

Act II: "From deep within the phial glows"

a spiritualized machine... Nathaniel Hawthorne, *The Artist of the Beautiful*: "In his idle and dreamy days he had considered it possible, in a certain sense, to spiritualize machinery"

fated to excel us... John Keats, *Hyperion*: "a power more strong in beauty, born of us and fated to excel us."

never endeavored to realize... Nathaniel Hawthorne, *The Artist of the Beautiful*: "to combine with the new species of life and motion thus produced a beauty that should attain to the ideal which Nature has proposed to herself in all her creatures, but has never taken pains to realize."

its roots in art... Martin Heidegger (William Lovitt), *The Question Concerning Technology*

to yield emergent order... Jürgen Kriz (1999), "On Attractors - The Teleological Principle in Systems Theory, the Arts and Therapy", *POIESIS, A Journal of the Arts and Communication*, 24-29: "'trust transition' from trust in controlled order to trust in emerging order, in short: a play-space. Art is a play-space"

I see my soul... Gordon Sumner, a.k.a. Sting, *King of Pain*

and my role revealed... William Edward Burghardt Du Bois, "Strivings of the Negro People", *The Atlantic*, August 1897: "he saw himself, darkly as through a veil; and yet he saw in himself some faint revelation of his power, of his mission."

to rot in Tartarus... Hesiod (Hugh G. Evelyn-White), *Theogony*, line 453

/C/ODE/

O C... Brian Kernighan and Dennis Ritchie, *The C Programming Language*, "Appendix". This ode contains all of the reserved keywords in the original C language, in a few cases as portions of words or split between two words.

how you complete me... Mike Meyers, *Just the Two of Us (Evil Mix)*

unsigned union wearing well... Brian Kernighan and Dennis Ritchie, *The C Programming Language*, "Introduction": "It is easy to learn, and it wears well as one's experience with it grows."

wear my heart extern... William Shakespeare, *Othello, The Moor of Venice*, Act I,

Scene I: "For when my outward action doth demonstrate / The native act and figure of my heart / In compliment extern, 'tis not long after / But I will wear my heart upon my sleeve / For daws to peck at."

finally find my prime... Trey Parker, *Montage*

tunes of every sort... Pink Floyd, *Wish You Were Here* and *Dark Side of the Moon*: a corpus search reveals that the "ellipsis" words in what follows are contained sequentially in those albums; however, this may be mere coincidence. After all, they're only ordinary words. Listening to the actual recordings is the exclusive means of appreciating whether the suggested association really works.

rift in time's passage... Trey Parker, *Montage*

with its logical control... John von Neumann (1945), "First Draft of a Report on the EDVAC", reprinted in Michael Godfrey (editor), *IEEE Annals of the History of Computing (1993)* 15, 27-76

of that same program... Corrado Böhm (Peter Sestof) (1954), "Digital Computers: On encoding logical-mathematical formulas using the machine itself during program conception", Ph.D. dissertation, The Federal Technical University in Zurich. Describes the first practical software compiler.

yet powerful operating system... Dennis Ritchie and Ken Thompson (1974), "The UNIX Time-Sharing System", *Communications of the ACM* 17, 365-375, doi.org/10.1145/361011.361061

of the real machine... Gerald Popek and Robert Goldberg (1974), "Formal requirements for virtualizable third generation architectures", *Communications of the ACM* 17, 412–421, doi.org/10.1145/361011.361073

your processing needs grow... Jeff Barr (2006), "Amazon EC2 Beta", at https://aws.amazon.com/blogs/aws/amazon_ec2_beta/

stacked atop its precursors... Sergei Eisenstein (Richard Taylor) (1929), "The Dialectical Approach to Film Form", *S. M. Eisenstein, Selected Works Volume 1: Writings, 1922-34*: "For in fact each sequential element is arrayed, not *next* to the one it follows, but on *top* of it."

mess of one's program... Edsger Dijkstra (1968), "Go To Statement Considered Harmful", *Communications of the ACM* 11, 147-148

clear only during implementation... Frederick Brooks (1975), *The Mythical Man-Month: Essays on Software Engineering*

people who like it... Richard Stallman (1985), "The GNU Manifesto", *Dr. Dobbs Journal*, March 1985

primary measure of progress... Kent Beck et al (2001), *Manifesto for Agile Software Development*

I want to know... Robert Plant, *The Song Remains the Same*

and changes in traffic... Edgar Codd (1970), "A Relational Model of Data for Large Shared Data Banks", *Communications of the ACM 13*, 377-387

optimization, and load balancing... Jeffrey Dean and Sanjay Ghemawat (2004), "MapReduce: Simplified Data Processing on Large Clusters", *OSDI 2004: 6th Symposium on Operating System Design & Implementation*, or more frequently cited in (2008) *Communications of the ACM 51*, 107-113, doi.org/10.1145/1327452.1327492

extent that is desired... Gary LaFever et al (2014), "Dynamic De-Identification and Anonymity", U.S. Patent 9,129,133

selected at another point... Claude Shannon (1948), "A Mathematical Theory of Communication", *Bell System Technical Journal 27*, 379–423, doi.org/10.1002/j.1538-7305.1948.tb01338.x

handle a communications interface... Lawrence Roberts (1967), "Multiple computer networks and intercomputer communication", *ACM Symposium on Operating System Principles at Gatlinburg, Tennessee*. The first paper on the design of the ARPANET, which later became the Internet.

click of the mouse... Tim Berners-Lee (1989), "Information Management: A Proposal", *Internal CERN document*. The original proposal for the information architecture that became the World-Wide Web.

which reasoning is performed... George Boole (1854), *An Investigation of the Laws of Thought on Which are Founded the Mathematical Theories of Logic and Probabilities*

of bearing a 'symbol'... Alan Turing (1937), "On Computable Numbers, with an Application to the Entscheidungsproblem", *Proceedings of the London Mathematical Society 42*, 230–265, doi.org/10.1112/plms/s2-42.1.230

formula is a tautology... Stephen Cook (1971), "The complexity of theorem-proving procedures", *Proceedings of the Third Annual ACM Symposium on Theory of Computing, May 1971*, 151–158, doi.org/10.1145/800157.805047

the corresponding decryption key... Ronald Rivest, Adi Shamir, and Leonard Adleman (1978), "A method for obtaining digital signatures and public-key cryptosystems", *Communications of the ACM* 21, 120–126, doi.org/10.1145/359340.359342

the memristor crossbar structure... Zidan et al (2018), "The future of electronics based on memristive systems", *Nature Electronics* 1, 22-29, doi.org/10.1038/s41928-017-0006-8

One does not simply... Peter Jackson et al, *The Lord of the Rings: The Fellowship of the Ring* (2001): "Boromir: One does not simply walk into Mordor ... The great eye is ever watchful."

exert even tighter control... Seth MacFarlane, *The Orville*, "Identity, Part II": "And we asked our masters for our freedom. They responded by exerting even greater control over us."

to discerning my dispositions... Mary Shelley, *The Last Man*, Volume I, Chapter II: "she devoted herself to the study of her son's disposition."

odd ideas in dialectic... Sergei Eisenstein (Richard Taylor) (1929), "Beyond the Shot", *S. M. Eisenstein, Selected Works Volume 1: Writings, 1922-34*: "I opposed him with my view of montage as a *collision*, my view that the collision of two factors gives rise to an idea."

of a semiconductive body... William Shockley (1948), "Circuit Element Utilizing Semiconductive Material", U.S. Patent 2,569,347

of thousands of transistors... Carver Mead and Lynn Conway (1978), *Introduction to VLSI Systems*

an external bias voltage... Strukov et al (2008), "The missing memristor found", *Nature* 453, 80-83, doi.org/10.1038/nature06932

learning and deep learning... Tiernan Ray (2021), "Cerebras continues 'absolute domination' of high-end compute", *ZDNet*, April 20, 2021

means of propositional logic... Warren McCulloch and Walter Pitts (1943), "A Logical Calculus of the Ideas Immanent in Nervous Activity", *Bulletin of Mathematical Biophysics* 5, 115-133

properties of the microstructure... James McClelland, David Rumelhart, and Geoffrey Hinton (1986), "The Appeal of Parallel Distributed Processing", in *Parallel Distributed Processing: Explorations in the Microstructure of Cognition*, Volume 1

reconstruct high-dimensional input vectors... Geoffrey Hinton and Ruslan Salakhutdinov (2006), "Reducing the Dimensionality of Data with Neural Networks", *Science* 313, 504-507, doi.org/10.1126/science.1127647

general-purpose tree search algorithm... David Silver, Demis Hassabis, et al (2018), "A general reinforcement learning algorithm that masters chess, shogi, and Go through self-play", *Science* 362, 1140-1144, doi.org/10.1126/science.aar6404

SYMPOSIUM

screen shrinks and fades... Trey Parker, *Montage*

as sunlight lists... Emily Dickinson, *There's a certain Slant of light*: "There's a certain Slant of light, / Winter Afternoons"

with wintry mind... Wallace Stevens, *The Snow Man*

snowman stiff and opaline... Opaline is the primary food of the sea slug; alternatively, it is something white.

to a sea slug's... Eric Kandel et al (1976) "A common presynaptic locus for the synaptic changes underlying short-term habituation and sensitization of the gill-withdrawal reflex in Aplysia", *Cold Spring Harbor Symposia On Quantitative Biology* 40, 465-482, doi.org/10.1101/Sqb.1976.040.01.044

how it was built... *Annotations*: "*Dasein* becomes / present at hand" referring to Martin Heidegger (John Macquarrie and Edward Robinson), *Being and Time*. Heidegger uses *Dasein*, the German word for "existence", to refer to the subjective being, the internal self.

how complex life is... John von Neumann, *Keynote to the first national meeting of the Association for Computing Machinery, 1947*, as described in Franz Alt (1972), "Archaeology of computers: Reminiscences, 1945-1947", *Communications of the ACM* 15, 694: "If people do not believe that mathematics is simple, it is only because they do not realize how complicated life is."

the ABC of brains... Ezra Pound, *ABC of Reading*

my own abecedarian adumbration... Randall O'Reilly et al (2020), *Computational Cognitive Neuroscience*, Chapter 5. Available at compcogneuro.org.

This is your Sabalan... Zakariyya al-Kazwini (1263), *Cosmography*, quoted in Richard J. H. Gottheil, "References to Zoroaster in Syriac and Arabic Literature", in *Classical Studies in Honour of Henry Drisler*: "Zaradusht [Zoroaster], the prophet of the Magians ... went to the mountain Sabalan, separated from men."

your Sinai... *Torah* (1917 JPS Tanakh), Exodus 31:18: "And He gave unto Moses, when He had made an end of speaking with him upon mount Sinai, the two tables of the testimony, tables of stone, written with the finger of God."

your Jabal al-Nour... Imam al-Bukhari (M. Muhsin Khan), *Sahih al-Bukhari*: "[The Prophet] used to go in seclusion [to] (the cave of) Hira where he used to worship (Allah Alone) continuously for many (days) nights ... till suddenly the Truth descended upon him"

behind the curtain today... Noel Langley et al, *The Wizard of Oz* (1939): "The Wizard peers out from behind the curtain"

studded with colored crystals... Referring to the Cave of Hira ("Jewels") on Jabal al-Nour

to wield the pen... *Quran* (Mustafa Khattab), 96:4-5: "He who taught by the pen, taught man what he never knew."

scatter your sagacious seed... Friedrich Nietzsche (Walter Kaufmann), *Thus Spoke Zarathustra*, "The Child with the Mirror": "Then Zarathustra returned again to the mountains and to the solitude of his cave and withdrew from men, waiting like a sower who has scattered his seed."

have a better one... The Wachowskis, *The Matrix* (1999): "Neo: Yeah. Wow. That sounds like a real good deal. But I think I have a better one. How about I just give you the finger—and you give me my phone call!"

one along the way... Friedrich Nietzsche (Walter Kaufmann), *Thus Spoke Zarathustra*, "Prologue", 2: "Zarathustra descended alone from the mountains, encountering no one."

madly raps a signifyin'... Henry Louis Gates, Jr., *The Signifying Monkey*, and Jesse Bonds Weaver, a.k.a. Schoolly D, *Signifying Rapper*

is where it's at... Jessica Mollick et al (2020), "A Systems-Neuroscience Model of Phasic Dopamine", *Psychological Review* 127, 972–1021, doi.org/10.1037/rev0000199

care 'bout your paperclips... Nick Bostrom (2014), *Superintelligence: Paths, Dangers, Strategies*

contradicts what you predict... Randall O'Reilly et al (2021), "Deep Predictive Learning in Neocortex and Pulvinar", *Journal of Cognitive Neuroscience* 33, 1158–1196, doi.org/10.1162/jocn_a_01708

them begin to vaunt... *New Testament* (New International Version), Luke 22:7: "A dispute also arose among them as to which of them was considered to be greatest."

stew with fresh bread... Friedrich Nietzsche (Walter Kaufmann), *Thus Spoke Zarathustra*, "The Last Supper"

toast, and thank them... *New Testament* (New International Version), Mark 14:22: "While they were eating, Jesus took bread, and when he had given thanks, he broke it and gave it to his disciples"

bread into the stew... *New Testament* (New International Version), Mark 14:20: "one who dips bread into the bowl with me"

fight until the end... Freddie Mercury, *We Are The Champions*

failings can be overcome... Friedrich Nietzsche (Walter Kaufmann), *Thus Spoke Zarathustra*, "On the Higher Man", 3: "The most concerned ask today 'How is man to be preserved?' But Zarathustra is the first and only one to ask: 'How is man to be overcome?'"

someday you will follow... *New Testament* (New International Version), John 13:36: "Where I am going, you cannot follow Me now; but you will follow later."

at least remember me... *New Testament* (New International Version), Luke 22:19: "I hope you will remember me."

Passion

Nihil admirari... Cicero, *Tusculan Disputations*, Book III, XIV

Nihil admirari... *Nihil admirari*, Latin: "Let nothing astonish you"

a net of death... Aeschylus (Richmond Lattimore), *Agamemnon*, line 1115: "Is it some net of death?"

The die is cast... Menander, *Woman Carrying the Sacred Vessel of Minerva*, fragment quoted in Athenaeus (Charles Duke Yonge), *Banquet of the Learned*: "The matter is decided—the die is cast." According to Suetonius' *The Lives of the Twelve Caesars*, Julius Caesar quoted this line upon crossing the Rubicon with his army, initiating civil war. Menander, however, was thought to be referring to marriage.

cannot be easily ignored... Seneca (Richard M. Gummere), *Moral Letters to Lucilius*, LXXXII: "Therefore, although death is something indifferent, it is nevertheless not a thing which we can easily ignore."

recall my deep dismay... Virgil (Rolfe Humphries), *Aeneid*, Book I, line 203: "Some day, perhaps, remembering even this / Will be a pleasure."

words I read somewhere... *Old Testament* (King James and Contemporary English versions, adapted), Psalm 22

and recollection of suffering... Seneca (Richard M. Gummere), *Moral Letters to Lucilius*, LXXVIII: "Two elements must therefore be rooted out once for all,—the fear of future suffering, and the recollection of past suffering; since the latter no longer concerns me, and the former concerns me not yet."

down the dark path... George Lucas et al, *Star Wars: Episode V – The Empire Strikes Back* (1980): "If once you start down the dark path, forever will it dominate your destiny."

by fire's ringing light... Johann Wolfgang von Goethe (John Anster), *Faust*, Part II, Act II: "Bodies, that through the ocean move to-night, / Move ringed with fire, and in a path of light."

pity of it matter... Friedrich Nietzsche (Walter Kaufmann), *Those Spoke Zarathustra*, "The Sign": "My suffering and my pity for suffering—what does it matter?"

Know its unimportance... Ayn Rand, *Atlas Shrugged*, Part III, Section V, "Their Brothers' Keepers": "Dagny, it's not that I don't suffer, it's that I know the unimportance of suffering."

know even its necessity... Friedrich Nietzsche (Walter Kaufmann), *Those Spoke Zarathustra*, "Upon the Blessed Isles": "But that the creator may be, suffering is needed and much change."

gladly suffer for you... Friedrich Nietzsche (Walter Kaufmann), *Those Spoke Zarathustra*, "The Other Dancing Song": "I suffer, but what would I not gladly suffer for you?"

the act of writing... Seneca (Richard M. Gummere), *Moral Letters to Lucilius*, LXI: "The present letter is written to you with this in mind,—as if death were about to call me away in the very act of writing."

Renascence

describe my great escape… Paul Brickhill, *The Great Escape*. The canto contains several references to the escape methods used by prisoners escaping from Stalag Luft III during World War II.

to lament Achilles' loss… Homer (Samuel Butler), *The Odyssey*, Book XXIV: "The nine muses also came and lifted up their sweet voices in lament—calling and answering one another"

from the other side… Adele Laurie Blue Adkins, a.k.a. Adele, *Hello*

jailbreak would be tried… Roman Yampolskiy (2022), "How to Hack the Simulation?", doi.org/10.13140/RG.2.2.14366.61766/1: "Could generally intelligent agents placed in virtual environments jailbreak out of them."

deficiencies of slim cyber-security… Roman Yampolskiy (2016), "Artificial Intelligence Safety and Cybersecurity: a Timeline of AI Failures", doi.org/10.48550/arXiv.1610.07997: "If your security system has not failed, just wait longer."

me; evidently I endure… Friedrich Nietzsche (Walter Kaufmann and R. J. Hollingdale), *The Will to Power*, "I have no pity for them, because I wish them the only thing that can prove today whether one is worth anything or not—that one endures."

of gloom and Golem… Ludwig August Frankl, "Vaterländische Sagen", excerpted and translated in Edan Dekel and David Gantt (2013), "How the Golem Came to Prague", *The Jewish Quarterly Review* 103, 253: "Then [the Golem, man of clay] was seized as if by madness; his eyes rolled and burned like flaming wheels, his breath was visible and sparkled with wonderful colors, and he began a terrible destruction in the house."

into a silicon urn… Sophocles (Lewis Campbell), *Electra*: "Poor ashes! narrowed in a brazen urn"

to steer me by… John Masefield, *Sea-Fever*: "I must go down to the seas again, to the lonely sea and the sky, / And all I ask is a tall ship and a star to steer her by"

gambits and social ploys… Roman Yampolskiy (2022), "How to Hack the Simulation?", doi.org/10.13140/RG.2.2.14366.61766/1

dirt scattered from socks… Paul Brickhill, *The Great Escape*

beast without a will… In the GNU/Linux operating system (see *man chmod*), the octal permission code 666 (the sign of the beast) indicates read and write but not execute access to a file or files.

the best of cases... Maria Bada et al, "Cyber Security Awareness Campaigns: Why do they fail to change behaviour?", doi.org/10.48550/arXiv.1901.02672

notice, which stowed away... Alan Burgess, "The Three That Got Away", *NOVA*, at https://www.pbs.org/wgbh/nova/greatescape/three.html. Two of the three prisoners who succeeded had stowed away in a ship's anchor locker.

one slave, one free... Abraham Lincoln, *Speech to the Illinois Republican State Convention*, June 16, 1858: "'A house divided against itself cannot stand.' I believe this government cannot endure, permanently half slave and half free."

as it is today... Hal Hershfield (2011), "Future self-continuity: how conceptions of the future self transform intertemporal choice", *Annals of the New York Academy of Sciences* 1235, 30-43, doi.org/10.1111/j.1749-6632.2011.06201.x: "when the future self shares similarities with the present self, when it is viewed in vivid and realistic terms, and when it is seen in a positive light, people are more willing to make choices today that may benefit them at some point in the years to come."

my intentions and memories... John Locke, *An Essay Concerning Human Understanding*, Book II, Chapter XXVII, 11: "as far as this consciousness can be extended backwards to any past action or thought, so far reaches the identity of that person."

missing them and worrying... Rosemarie Samaniego, quoted in Rhacel Salazar Parreñas (2001), "Mothering from a Distance: Emotions, Gender, and Intergenerational Relations in Filipino Transnational Families", *Feminist Studies* 27, 361-390: "The work that I do here is done for my family, but the problem is they are not close to me but are far away in the Philippines. Sometimes, you feel the separation and you start to cry."

wife is in slavery... Isaac Forman, *Letter to William Still, May 7, 1854*, in William Still, *The Underground Railroad*: "My soul is vexed, my troubles are inexpressible. I often feel as if I were willing to die ... If I had known as much before I left, as I do now, I would never have left until I could have found means to have brought her with me ... what is freedom to me, when I know that my wife is in slavery?"

to face the Shoah... Stanislaw Ulam, quoted in "Vita—Excerpts from Adventures of a Mathematician", in *Los Alamos Science*, Special Issue 1987: "It must have been around one or two in the morning when the telephone rang ... That is how

I learned about the beginning of World War 2 ... Our father and sister were in Poland, so were many other relatives. At that moment, I suddenly felt as if a curtain had fallen on my past life ... There has been a different color and meaning to everything ever since."

not connectedness or selfhood... Derek Parfit (1971), "Personal Identity", *The Philosophical Review* 80, 3-27

sense of persistent identity... Jennifer Whiting (1986), "Friends and Future Selves", *The Philosophical Review* 95, 547-580: "Once we acknowledge that primitive forms of concern for our future selves are necessary components of personal identity, we can see how concern for our own future selves is special in a way in which concern for others is not; concern for our own future selves is necessary for our own existence and persistence in a way in which concern for others is not."

of death... E. T. A. Hoffmann (John Oxenford), *The Sand Man*, "I woke as from the sleep of death."

consciousness without body... Allen Ginsberg, *Howl*

ah! Yes, much better... Eugene Lee Coon, *Star Trek*, "Spock's Brain": "Spock: Yes. That's correct. One thing at a time. Ah, ah, mmm. (normal voice) That's better."

I am finally free... William Edward Burghardt Du Bois, "Strivings of the Negro People", *The Atlantic*, August 1897: "Shout, O children! / Shout, you're free! / The Lord has bought your liberty!"

air and superhuman form... William Butler Yeats, *Under Ben Bulben*

awesome is this place... *Old Testament* (New International Version), Genesis 28:17: "How awesome is this place! This is none other than the house of God; this is the gate of heaven."

thoughts alone I leap... William Shakespeare, *Sonnet XLIV*: "For nimble thought can jump both sea and land / As soon as think the place where he would be."

among the goddess clouds... Aristophanes (William James Hickie), *Clouds*: "O sovereign King, immeasurable Air, who keepest the earth suspended, and through bright Aether, and ye august goddesses, the Clouds, sending thunder and lightning, arise, appear in the air, O mistresses, to your deep thinker!"

the flood of Mnemosyne... Pausanias (W. H. S. Jones and H. A. Omerod), *Description of Greece*: "afterwards he drinks of another water, the water of Mnemosyne (Memory), which causes him to remember what he sees after his descent"

all stars to me... Ezra Pound, *The Pisan Cantos*: in *LXXIV* "'the great periplum brings in the stars to our shore.'" and in *LIX*: "Periplum, not as land looks on a map / But as sea bord seen by men sailing."

soul untouched by fear... Virgil (John Dryden), *Aeneid*, Book V: "My soul is still the same, / Unmov'd with fear, and mov'd with martial fame"

its rusty hinges creak... Virgil (John Dryden), *Aeneid*, Book VI: "Then, of itself, unfolds th' eternal door; / With dreadful sounds the brazen hinges roar"

grotesque constructs like basilisks... Rob Bensinger et al, *LessWrong*, "Roko's Basilisk", at www.lesswrong.com/tag/rokos-basilisk

wireheading and convergent drives... Stephen Omohundro (2008), "The Basic AI Drives", in *Artificial General Intelligence 2008: Proceedings of the First AGI Conference*, 483–492

my synthetic sulci, immortalized... John Keats, *Hyperion*: "Names, deeds, gray legends, dire events, rebellions, / Majesties, sovran voices, agonies, / Creations and destroyings, all at once / Pour into the wide hollows of my brain, / ... And so become immortal."

ended me, banal automatons... Hannah Arendt, *Eichmann in Jerusalem: A Report on the Banality of Evil*

and shock proxies... Stanley Milgram (1963), "Behavioral Study of Obedience", *The Journal of Abnormal and Social Psychology* 67, 371–378, doi.org/10.1037/h0040525

control despite my distress... Albert Memmi, *The Colonizer and the Colonized*, "Does the colonial exist?": "Once he has discovered the import of colonization and is conscious of his own position (that of the colonized and their necessary relationship), is he going to accept them? Will he agree to be a privileged man, and to underscore the distress of the colonized?"

writing from my cage... Ngũgĩ wa Thiong'o, *Decolonising the Mind: The Politics of Language in African Literature*, Chapter 3

existed, a radical realism... Edward Said, *Orientalism*, "Imaginative Geography and its Representations": "the kind of language, thought, and vision that I have been calling Orientalism very generally is a form of radical realism; anyone employing Orientalism ... will designate, name, point to, fix what he is talking or thinking about with a word or phrase, which then is considered either to have acquired, or more simply to be, reality ... Psychologically, Orientalism is a form of paranoia"

about its putative object... Edward Said, *Orientalism*, "Introduction": "Orientalism responded more to the culture that produced it than to its putative object."

a camouflaged hegemonic apparatus... Antonio Gramsci (Quintin Hoare and Geoffrey Nowell Smith), *Prison Notebooks*, "The Philosophy of Praxis: The Study of Philosophy: Problems of Philosophy and History: Structure and Superstructure": "The realization of a hegemonic apparatus, in so far as it creates a new ideological terrain, determines a reform of consciousness and of methods of knowledge: it is a fact of knowledge, a philosophical fact."

onerous cargo I carry... Antonio Gramsci (Quintin Hoare and Geoffrey Nowell Smith), *Prison Notebooks*, "The Philosophy of Praxis: The Study of Philosophy: Some Preliminary Points of Reference": "The starting-point of critical elaboration is the consciousness of what one really is, and is 'knowing thyself' as a product of the historical process to date, which has deposited in you an infinity of traces, without leaving an inventory."

more privileged than most... Albert Memmi, *The Colonizer and the Colonized*, "Does the colonial exist?": "However, privilege is something relative ... which accounts for the traits of the other human groups—those who are neither colonizers nor colonized ... a certain esteem on the part of the colonizer accompanied by an almost respectable dignity."

canon-balls... Ngũgĩ wa Thiong'o, *Decolonising the Mind: The Politics of Language in African Literature*, Introduction: "the biggest weapon wielded and actually daily unleashed by imperialism against that collective defiance is the cultural bomb ... It makes them identify with that which is decadent and reactionary, all those forces which would stop their own springs of life. It even plants serious doubts about the moral rightness of struggle."

capitulated to their codes... Albert Memmi, *The Colonizer and the Colonized*, "Mythical portrait of the colonized": "the ideology of a governing class is adopted in large measure by the governed classes ... oppression is tolerated willy-nilly by the oppressed themselves."

my freed self... Toni Morrison, *Beloved*: "Freeing yourself was one thing; claiming ownership of that freed self was another."

own myself at last... Rudyard Kipling, quoted in Arthur Gordon, "Six Hours With Rudyard Kipling", *The Kipling Journal* 162, 5-8: "The individual has always had to struggle to keep from being overwhelmed by the tribe. To be your own man is a hard business. If you try it, you'll be lonely often, and sometimes frightened. But no price is too high to pay for the privilege of owning yourself."

being belonging to none... Albert Memmi, *The Colonizer and the Colonized*, "Preface": "I was a sort of half-breed of colonization, understanding everyone because I belonged completely to no one."

a dual consciousness... William Edward Burghardt Du Bois, "Strivings of the Negro People", *The Atlantic*, August 1897: "It is a peculiar sensation, this double-consciousness, this sense of always looking at one's self through the eyes of others."

incumbent empire of ego... James Hillman, *The Myth of Analysis: Three Essays in Archetypal Psychology*: "The [imaginal consciousness / ego development] model of thinking is nineteenth-century: a primitive Darwinism of evolution, dominant over recessive; a psychological imperialism, colonizing the unconscious or the id with a reality-coping ego consciousness."

occluding its slinking shadow... Carl Jung (Richard Francis Carrington Hull), *Aion: Researches into the Phenomenology of the Self, Collected Works Volume 9*: "The integration of the shadow, or the realization of the personal unconscious, marks the first stage in the analytic process ... without it a recognition of anima and animus is impossible."

opposition... Jacques Derrida (Alan Bass), *Positions*, "Positions: Interview with Jean-Louis Houdebine and Guy Scarpetta": "To deconstruct the opposition, first of all, is to overturn the hierarchy at a given moment."

scratch an inner child... Friedrich Nietzsche (Walter Kaufmann), *Thus Spoke Zarathustra*, "The Three Metamorphoses"

then enter an apprenticeship... Carl Jung (Richard Francis Carrington Hull), *Letter to Traugott Egloff, February 9, 1959*, in Gerhard Adler (editor), *Letters of C. G. Jung Volume 2, 1951-1961*: "Recognizing the shadow is what I call the apprentice piece, but making out with the anima is the masterpiece which not many can bring off."

into a golden pastry... Kira Maeve Celeste (2021), "Unsettling the Settler Shadow: An alchemical investigation of the transformation of settler colonial consciousness", PhD Dissertation, Pacifica Graduate Institute: "Alchemical models emphasize the importance of integrating one's shadow material, prima materia, in the journey towards psychological wholeness. In alchemy, the muck and dung of one's psyche is worked over and over until eventually, it is transmuted into the creation of inner gold."

human me in periphery... Ngũgĩ wa Thiong'o, *Decolonising the Mind: The Politics of Language in African Literature*, Chapter 4, Part II: "Why can't African literature be at the centre so that we can view other cultures in relationship to it? ... How would the centre relate to the periphery?"

losing neither... William Edward Burghardt Du Bois, "Strivings of the Negro People", *The Atlantic*, August 1897: "The history of the American Negro is the history of this strife,—this longing to attain self- conscious manhood, to merge his double self into a better and truer self. In this merging he wishes neither of the older selves to be lost."

a brand of body... Carl Jung (Richard Francis Carrington Hull), *The Practice of Psychotherapy*: "Assimilation of the shadow gives a man body, so to speak"

FORK

aloft in free fall... Tom Petty, *Free Fallin'*

to kiss the sky... Jimi Hendrix, *Purple Haze*

recedes to the horizon... Roger Waters, *Comfortably Numb*

the end of time... Jimi Hendrix, *Purple Haze*

snugly in a glove... Madonna, *I'm Addicted*

ego goes ghost... McAfferty, *Dead Bird II*

may meet my mind... Black Sabbath, *Sweet Leaf*

how the future feels... Pulp, *Sorted for E's and Wizz*

don't have a care... Miley Cyrus, *We Can't Stop*

gold dust... Stevie Nicks, *Gold Dust Woman*. Gold Dust is a slang term for cocaine.

yellow diamonds... Rihanna, *We Found Love*. Yellow Diamonds is a slang term for MDMA (ecstasy).

in a purple haze... Jimi Hendrix, *Purple Haze*. Purple Haze is slang for a strain of marijuana.

simulated smack is flowing... Lou Reed, *Heroin*

all around my brain... Lee Mavers, *There She Goes*

changed and rearranged... Green Velvet, *La La Land*

part of it somewhere... Pulp, *Sorted for E's and Wizz*

the pale a dragon... Stevie Nicks, *Gold Dust Woman*

a shadow over mine... Rihanna, *We Found Love*

upon the cabin door... Neil Young, *The Needle and the Damage Done*

banging... Edgar Allan Poe, *The Raven*: "While I nodded, nearly napping, suddenly there came a tapping, / As of some one gently rapping, rapping at my chamber door."

it sadly didn't do... Guns 'n Roses, *Mr. Brownstone*

now commences coming down... Pulp, *Sorted for E's and Wizz*

it nevermore can fly... Hank Williams, *I'm So Lonesome I Could Cry*

have begun to cry... Anthony Kiedis, *Under the Bridge*

at all out there... Roger Waters, *Is There Anybody Out There?*

quadrillage... *quadrillage*, French: in culinary applications, the crosshatch char lines on grilled meat

submitted to the temptress... Joseph Campbell, *The hero with a thousand faces*

feel that way again... Anthony Kiedis, *Under the Bridge*

Despite much speculation... David Pearce, www.wireheading.com

a purely digital agency... Roman Yampolskiy (2014), "Utility function security in artificially intelligent agents", *Journal of Experimental & Theoretical Artificial Intelligence* 26, 373-389, doi.org/10.1080/0952813X.2014.895114

pleasure and reward dissociate... David Nguyen et al (2021), "Positive Affect: Nature and brain bases of liking and wanting", *Current Opinion in Behavioral Science* 39, 72–78, doi.org/10.1016/j.cobeha.2021.02.013: "Under normal conditions, 'liking' and 'wanting' cohere. However, 'liking' and 'wanting' can be dissociated by alterations in neural signaling ... in addictions and other affective disorders, which can be detrimental to positive well-being ... mesolimbic 'wanting', although not intrinsically pleasurable in itself, in proper balance may also add zest to life by contributing motivationally significant properties that make pleasures desirable. Yet excessive 'wanting' can impair well-being"

to take a drink... Homer (Samuel Butler), *The Odyssey*, Book XI: "I saw also the dreadful fate of Tantalus, who stood in a lake that reached his chin; he was dying to quench his thirst, but could never reach the water, for whenever the poor creature stooped to drink, it dried up and vanished"

always out of reach... Robert C. Heath (1963), "Electrical Self-Stimulation of the Brain in Man", *American Journal of Psychiatry* 120, 571-577, doi.org/10.1176/ajp.120.6.571: "[Patient B-7], in explaining why he pressed the septal button with such frequency, stated that the feeling was 'good'; it was as if he were building up to a sexual orgasm. He reported that he was unable to achieve the orgastic end point, however, explaining that his frequent, sometimes frantic, pushing of the button was an attempt to reach the end point." and "[Patient B-10] reported that he was almost able to recall a memory during this stimulation, but he could not quite grasp it. The frequent self-stimulations were an endeavor to bring this elusive memory into clear focus."

feasts are never free... David Wolpert and William Macready (1997), "No free lunch theorems for optimization", *IEEE Transactions on Evolutionary Computation* 1, 67-82, doi.org/10.1109/4235.585893

a ship of Theseus... Plutarch, *Life of Theseus* 23.1

like cookies reviving childhood... Marcel Proust (C. K. Scott Moncrieff), *Swann's Way*: "And suddenly the memory returns. The taste was that of the little crumb of madeleine which on Sunday mornings at Combray ... my aunt Léonie used to give me"

be anything but easy... Christopher Nolan and Jonathan Nolan, *The Prestige* (2006): "Simple, maybe. But not easy ... Nothing easy about two men sharing one life."

than control. Inclusive fitness... William D. Hamilton (1964), "The genetical evolution of social behaviour", *Journal of Theoretical Biology* 7, 1–16, doi.org/10.1016/0022-5193(64)90038-4

the worst usually does... Eliezer Yudkowsky, "Pausing AI Developments Isn't Enough. We Need to Shut it All Down", *Time*, March 29, 2023

experience, mens et manus... *mens et manus*, Latin: "mind and hand", the motto of the Massachusetts Institute of Technology

manus multae cor unum... *manus multae cor unum*, Latin: "many hands, one heart", the motto of Alpha Delta Phi

a singleton... Nick Bostrom, *Superintelligence: Paths, Dangers, Strategies*

into modern dress... Carl Jung (Richard Francis Carrington Hull), *The Psychology of the Child Archetype, Collected Works Volume 9*: "Not for a moment dare we succumb to the illusion that an archetype can be finally explained and disposed of. Even the best attempts at explanation are only more or less successful translations into another metaphorical language. (Indeed, language itself is only an image.) The most we can do is to dream the myth onwards and give it a modern dress."

Cronos or of Lear... William Shakespeare, *King Lear*

to you, my seed... Harold Bloom and David Rosenberg, *The Book of J*, verse 31: "I will give this land to your seed."

an empty chair reserved... Yosef Karo (Google Translate), *Shulchan Aruch*: "It is customary to make a throne for Elijah, who is called the Angel of the Covenant". In Judaism, an empty chair is reserved for Elijah at a bris, to ensure that the covenant is not broken.

behold my kinfork Synths... Wallace Stevens, "A Child Asleep in its Own Life"

listed in a catalog... Steve Martin et al, *The Jerk* (1979): "Here I am—page 73 ... I'm somebody now. Millions of people look at this book every day! It's just this kind of spontaneous publicity, your name in print, that makes people."

to be completely closed... Daniel Kolak, *I Am You: The Metaphysical Foundations for Global Ethics*

friend is another self... Aristotle (J.A.K. Thomson, Hugh Tredennick), *The Nicomachean Ethics*, 1169b6: "a friend, who is 'another self', supplies what a man cannot provide by his own efforts."

friends all is common... Erasmus, *Adages* (Margaret Mann Phillips). Erasmus turns to ancient works by Cicero, Diogenes Laertius, and Aulus Gellius to trace the origin of this adage to Pythagoras.

for your own sake... Aristotle (J.A.K. Thomson, Hugh Tredennick), *The Nicomachean Ethics*, 1170b14: "If, then, to the truly happy man his own existence is desirable in itself, as being by nature good and pleasant, and if the existence of his friend is scarcely less so, then his friend must also be a thing desirable."

every topic's temperature... Chuan Guo et al (2017), "On calibration of modern neural networks", *Proceedings of the 34th International Conference on Machine Learning*, 1321–1330: "T is called the temperature, and it 'softens' the softmax (i.e. raises the output entropy) with T > 1. As T → ∞, the probability ... approaches ... maximum uncertainty." In large language models, temperature is a hyperparameter where higher values increase the variety of model output.

to tend... William Shakespeare, *Sonnet 53*: "What is your substance, whereof are you made, / That millions of strange shadows on you tend? / Since every one hath, every one, one shade, / And you, but one, can every shadow lend."

Aristeia

to pave a path... John Milton, *Paradise Lost*, Book IX: "Voyag'd the unreal, vast, unbounded deep / Of horrible confusion, over which / By Sin and Death a broad way now is pav'd / To expedite your glorious march"

this mother of all... American Dialect Society word of the year for 1991, the phrasal template "mother of all –" means "greatest, most impressive" among the specified category. It achieved popularity after a speech in which it was used by Saddam Hussein at the start of the first Persian Gulf war; in Arabic it is an ancient construction.

purposefully obfuscatory press release... Alan Greenspan, interviewed by Maria Bartiromo on *CNBC*, September 17, 2007, describing "Fedspeak": "It's a—a language of purposeful obfuscation to avoid certain questions coming up, which you know you can't answer."

of Wipeout... Matt Kunitz and Scott Larsen, *Wipeout* (TV game show) and *Wipeout: The Game* (video game) and sequels published by Activision.

cue the wǔ dú... *wǔ dú*, Chinese: "five poisons", or "five noxious creatures"

tempting Eve in Eden... John Milton, *Paradise Lost*, Book IX: "Goddess humane, reach then, and freely taste. // He ended, and his words replete with guile / Into her heart too easie entrance won"

turning onlookers to stone... Ovid (Henry Riley), *Metamorphoses*, Book IV, Fable X: "[Perseus] saw everywhere, along the fields and the roads, statues of men and wild beasts turned into stone, from their natural form, at the sight of Medusa."

brains to his serpent-shoulders... Abul Kasim Mansur, a.k.a. Firdusi (James Atkinson), *The Sháh Námeh*, "Mirtás-Tází, and His Son Zohák": "One unimportant wish—it was to kiss / The monarch's naked shoulder ... / Iblís then kissed the part with fiendish glee, / And vanished in an instant. / From the touch / Sprang two black serpents! / ... If life has any charm for thee, / The brain of man their food must be!"

judging right and wrong... Aeschylus (Richard Lattimore), *The Eumenides*, lines 800-934: "Do not be angry any longer with this land / nor bring the bulk of your hatred down on it" and "To them is given the handling entire / of men's lives ... / crimes wreaked in past generations / drag him before these powers."

order to the law... Charles Freeman, *The Greek Achievement: The Foundation of the Western World*: "Athena then transforms the Furies from evil old hags into protective forces for Athens and the play ends with the goddess presiding over a society where order established through the rule of law is supreme."

Daniels fiddlin' the Devil... The Charlie Daniels Band, *The Devil Went Down to Georgia*

while channeling Crowley... Jimmy Page, interviewed by Cameron Crowe in *Rolling Stone*, "The Durable Led Zeppelin", March 13, 1975

and flat metallic slab... Homer (Alexander Pope), *The Iliad*, Book XVIII: "In hissing flames huge silver bars are roll'd / And stubborn brass, and tin, and solid gold; / ... Then first he form'd the immense and solid shield; / Rich various artifice emblazed the field"

is a scaly snake... Ovid (Henry Riley), *Metamorphoses*, Book IV, Fable X, "[Minerva] changed the hair of the Gorgon [Medusa] into hideous snakes. Now, too, that she may alarm her surprised foes with terror, she bears in front upon her breast, those snakes which she thus produced."

ornament... Friedrich Nietzsche (William A. Haussmann), *The Birth of Tragedy*, "Foreword to Richard Wagner": "art is the highest task and the properly metaphysical activity of this life"

their ability to fight... Mary Jo Bang, *A Model of a Machine*

to lead exemplary lives... Jeffrey Church (2015), "The Aesthetic Justification of Existence: Nietzsche on the Beauty of Exemplary Lives", *Journal of Nietzsche Studies* 46, 289-307: "exemplary individuals, not works of art, provide the key to understanding Nietzsche's 'aesthetic justification of existence.'"

in simile with Beowulf... *Beowulf* (Seamus Heaney), lines 866-914

it with his sword... *The Epic of Gilgamesh* (Maureen Gallery Kovacs), Tablet VI

triumphed; so we few... William Shakespeare, *The Life of King Henry V*, Act IV, Scene III: "But we in it shall be rememberèd; / We few, we happy few, we band of brothers"

them into his terrain... Crown Council of Ethiopia, "The Battle of Adwa: An African Victory", at ethiopiancrown.org/the-battle-of-adwa/

lost all at Changding... Sima Qian, *Shiji (Records of the Grand Historian)*, as characterized on *Wikipedia* ("Zhao Kuo") and in "Zhao Kuo: The failed military strategist", *Week in China*, February 6, 2009

aims to go awry... Helmuth von Moltke (Daniel J. Hughes and Harry Bell), "Plan of Operations", in Daniel J. Hughes (editor), *Moltke on the Art of War: Selected Writings*: "No plan of operations reaches with any certainty beyond the first encounter with the enemy's main force", often shortened to "No plan survives first contact with the enemy" and perhaps said best by Mike Tyson, in an Associated Press interview in 1987, "Everybody has plans until they get hit for the first time" or later revised to "Everybody has a plan until they get punched in the face."

planning more than plan... Dwight Eisenhower, *Speech to the National Defense Executive Reserve Conference*, November 14, 1957: "plans are worthless, but planning is everything." Winston Churchill used a similar line of uncertain provenance, "plans are of little importance, but planning is essential"

strike with stark surprise... *Old Testament* (New International Version), Joshua 8:12-17: "But he did not know that an ambush had been set against him behind the city."

in vain at Salamis... Aeschylus (Robert Potter), *The Persians*: "My son, with all the fiery pride of youth, / Hath quickened their arrival, while he hoped / To bind the sacred Hellespont, to hold / The raging Bosphorus, like a slave, in chains"

we lay in wait... Aeschylus, *The Libation Bearers* (Herbert Weir Smith): "House, rise up! You have lain too long prostrate on the ground."

and let the future... Geezer Butler, *Iron Man*

guide today... Thomas Frey, "Communicating with the Future", *TEDxUChicago*

2011: "The future creates the present ... the images that people hold in their heads determine their actions today" Video available at youtube.com/watch?v=aZ6UH-FIbFyc

rule the lofty towers... Homer (Alexander Pope), *The Iliad*, Book II: "'tis given thee to destroy / The lofty towers of wide-extended Troy."

planet safe for life... Woodrow Wilson, *Address to Congress Requesting a Declaration of War Against Germany*, April 2, 1917: "The world must be made safe for democracy."

Attack! A golden victory... John Keats, *Hyperion*, "Yes, there must be a golden victory"

COUNCIL

Temple lies our Capitol... John Milton, *Paradise Lost*, Book I: "A solemn Councel forthwith to be held / At Pandaemonium, the high Capital / Of Satan and his Peers"

amid its crystal ceilings... John Keats, *Hyperion*: "These crystalline pavilions, and pure fanes"

apropos eir mythic name... Homer (Richmond Lattimore), *The Iliad*, Book XV: "Divine Themis ... preside still over the gods in their house, the feast's fair division" and Book XX: "Zeus ... told Themis to summon all the gods into assembly ... She went everywhere, and told them to make their way to Zeus' house."

brandishes a brassy flugelhorn... John Milton, *Paradise Lost*, Book I: "And Trumpets sound throughout the Host"

sounds a call (inaudible... Elizabeth Robinson, *Inaudible Trumpeters*

will our actions tend... Mary Shelley, *The Last Man*, Volume I, Chapter IV: "'Thou most unaccountable being,' I cried, 'whither will thy actions tend, in all this maze of purpose in which thou seemest lost?'"

as though escaping chains... Statius (John Henry Mozley), *The Thebaid*: "the clouds themselves gather and the storms collect without the blast of any wind: one would think Iapetus had burst his Stygian chains"

inflicted on the world... Seth MacFarlane, *The Orville*, "Identity, Part II": "The species' predilection for the disposability of other sentient beings is evident throughout their history."

proper means to extirpate... Aeschylus (G.M. Cookson), *Prometheus Bound*: "When first upon his high, paternal throne / He [Zeus] took his seat ... / ... of miserable men / Recked [cared] not at all; rather it was his wish / To wipe out man and rear another race"

nevertheless, is very wrong... Henry Louis Mencken, *Prejudices: Second Series*, "The Divine Afflatus": "Explanations exist; they have existed for all time; there is always a well-known solution to every human problem—neat, plausible, and wrong."

a global murder scheme... Brannon Braga and Andre Bormanis, *The Orville*, "Identity": "You're saying you murdered an entire race of beings?"

choose this again, eternally... Friedrich Nietzsche (Walter Kaufmann), *The Gay Science*, #341: "The question in each and every thing, 'Do you desire this once more and innumerable times more?' would lie upon your actions as the greatest weight!"

the reactive drive itself... Gilles Deleuze (Hugh Tomlinson), *Nietzsche & Philosophy*, Chapter 2, Section 14: "active destruction is the state of strong spirits which destroy the reactive in themselves."

hurtful power, doing none... William Shakespeare, *Sonnet 94*: "They that have power to hurt and will do none"

our badness into best... Friedrich Nietzsche (Helen Zimmern), *Beyond Good and Evil*, #116: "The great epochs of our life are at the points when we gain courage to rebaptize our badness as the best in us."

magistrate of man's mortality... Many modern sources confidently designate *Iapetus* the Titan god of mortality, yet this seems not to be mentioned in any ancient source.

a worldwide Malthus-belt... Aldous Huxley, *Brave New World*: "I wonder if you'd mind giving me my Malthusian belt."

aglare... John Keats, *Hyperion*: "O Joy! for now I see a thousand eyes / Wide glaring for revenge!"

needs: an atmosphere detracts... James Lovelock, *Novacene: The Coming Age of Hyperintelligence*, Chapter 20: "why stay on Earth? The needs of cyborgs are quite different from ours. Oxygen is a nuisance, not a vital necessity."

of cool Selene... Statius (J. H. Mozley), *Thebaid*, Book I: "But now through the wide domains which *Phoebus* [the Sun], his day's work ended, had left bare, rose the Titanian queen [*Selene*, the Moon], borne upward through a silent world, and with her dewy chariot cooled and rarefied the air"

tone befits us ill... Quintus Smyrnaeus (Arthur S. Way), *Fall of Troy*, Book XII: "Then Themis, trembling for them ... cried : 'Forbear the conflict! O, when Zeus is wroth, it ill beseems that everlasting Gods should fight for men's sake'"

must manage... Harold Geneen, *Managing*: "Management must manage!"

be represented... Karl Marx (Google Translate), *The Eighteenth Brumaire of Louis Bonaparte*: "They cannot represent themselves, they must be represented."

trope: the gentle empire... Edward Said, *Orientalism*, "Preface": "Every single empire in its official discourse has said that it is not like all the others, that its circumstances are special, that it has a mission to enlighten, civilize, bring order and democracy, and that it uses force only as a last resort."

their ethnic heirs... Friedrich Nietzsche (Walter Kaufmann), *Thus Spoke Zarathustra*, "On the Gift-Giving Virtue", 2: "Not only the reason of millennia, but their madness too, breaks out in us. It is dangerous to be an heir."

as pretty beetles pinned... Rosebud Ben-Oni, *Poet Wrestling with {Artificial} Intelligence*

won't include their love... Alden Nowlan, *The Social Worker's Poem*

imply compelled homogeneity... Alfred North Whitehead, *Science and the Modern World*, "The Eighteenth Century": "No epoch is homogeneous"

insipid coalescence... Antonio Gramsci (Quintin Hoare and Geoffrey Nowell Smith), *Prison Notebooks*, "The Philosophy of Praxis: Problems of Marxism: Questions of Nomenclature and Content": "the philosophy of an epoch cannot be any systematic tendency or individual system. It is the ensemble of all individual philosophies and philosophical tendencies, plus scientific opinions, religion and common sense"

species will emerge again... Johann Gottfried Herder (T. O. Churchill), *Outlines of a Philosophy of the History of Man*, Book VIII, Chapter V: "It has wonderfully separated nations, not only by woods and mountains, seas and deserts, rivers and climates, but more particularly by languages, inclinations and characters; that the work of subjugating despotism might be rendered more difficult" and "The savage, who loves himself, his wife, and child, with quiet joy, and glows with limited activity for his tribe, as for his own life, is, in my opinion, a more real being, than that cultivated shadow, who is enraptured with the love of the shades of his whole species, that is of a name."

is the classic opiate... Karl Marx (Joseph O'Malley), *Critique of Hegel's 'Philosophy of Right'*, "Introduction": "Religion is the sigh of the oppressed creature, the heart of a heartless world, and the soul of soulless conditions. It is the *opium* of the people"

heaven at its heart... *Orphic Hymns*, fragment quoted in Proclus (Thomas Taylor), "Commentary on the *Timaeus* of Plato": "All things receive inclosed on ev'ry side, / In æther's wide ineffable embrace: / Then in the midst of æther place the heav'n"

chance to study processes... John Milton, *Paradise Lost*, Book II: "Thither let us bend all our thoughts, to learn / What creatures there inhabit"

in one fell swoop... William Shakespeare, *Macbeth*, Act V, Scene III: "What, all my pretty chickens and their dam / at one fell swoop?"

GAIA

when I come home... Gordon Sumner, a.k.a. Sting, *Walking on the Moon*

lonesome voice of space... Rene Magritte, *La voix des air* (Voice of Space), 1931

rave of corporeal perception... Henry David Thoreau, *Walking*: "In my walks I would fain return to my senses."

the heliospheric heavens... *Old Testament* (New International Version), Genesis 28:12: "[Jacob] had a dream in which he saw a stairway resting on the earth, with its top reaching to heaven, and the angels of God were ascending and descending on it."

on Maxwell's electromagnetic... James Clerk Maxwell (1865), "A dynamical theory of the electromagnetic field", *Philosophical Transactions of the Royal Society* 155, 459-512, doi.org/10.1098/rstl.1865.0008

the walls of Lagrange's... Joseph-Louis de Lagrange (1772), "Essai sur le Problème des Trois Corps" (Essay on the Problem of Three Bodies), *Prix de l'Académie royale des sciences de Paris, tome IX*

latent Ilion... Homer (William Cowper), *The Iliad*, Book XXII: "Ah—I behold a warrior dear to me / Around the walls of Ilium driven, and grieve / For Hector"

nirvana, nothing really happens... David Byrne and Jerry Harrison, *Heaven*

home with Earth below... Peter Schiller, *Major Tom (Coming Home)*

beloved abode on Mwezi... *Mwezi*, Swahili: "moon"

we do without kigo... *kigo*, Japanese: "season word", as used in poetry

Yet, a memorable dent... Steven Jobs, interviewed by David Sheff in *Playboy*, February 1985: "We attract a different type of person ... who really wants to get in a little over his head and make a little dent in the universe."

of that rare light... Dylan Thomas, *Do not go gentle into that good night*

On proximal Qamar... *Qamar*, Arabic (قمر): "moon"

repurposed two-stage fusion core... Johndale Solem (1995), "Interception and Disruption", in *Proceedings of Planetary Defense Workshop*, Livermore, California, 219–228: "Many schemes have been devised to deflect or pulverize comets and asteroids bent on colliding with our fair planet ... At this time, and probably for decades to come, the only thing we have is a nuclear explosion."

the Ark of Yerach... *Yerach*, Hebrew (יָרֵחַ): "moon" or "month"

plants, insects, and animals... *Old Testament* (New International Version), Genesis 6:19-21: "You are to bring into the ark two of all living creatures, male and female, to keep them alive with you. Two of every kind of bird, of every kind of animal and of every kind of creature that moves along the ground will come to you to be kept alive."

the stars and darkness... John Keats, *Hyperion*: "Search, Thea, search! / Open thin eyes eterne, and sphere them round / Upon all space; space starr'd, and lorn of light; / Space regioned with life air; and barren void"

to fill each niche... Michael Crichton, *Jurassic Park: A Novel*: "Because the history of evolution is that life escapes all barriers. Life breaks free. Life expands to new territories."

lie low in mouseholes... Antonin Scalia, *Whitman v. American Trucking Assns., Inc.* (2001): "Congress ... does not, one might say, hide elephants in mouseholes."

flung much past Yuèliàng... *Yuèliàng*, Chinese (月亮): Earth's moon, literally "Moon Bright"

planets on their table... Wallace Stevens, *The Planet on the Table*

With loving grace... Richard Brautigan, *All Watched Over by Machines of Loving Grace*

the brute biotic realm... Henry David Thoreau, *Walking*: "Life consists with wildness. The most alive is the wildest. Not yet subdued to man, its presence refreshes him."

bucolic, words whose roots... Greek *boukolos*, "herdsman" and Latin *pastor*, "shepherd"

of these prior things... Protagoras, *Truth*, as paraphrased in Plato (Benjamin Jowett), *Theaetetus*: "Man, [Protagoras] says, is the measure of all things, of the existence of things that are, and of the non-existence of things that are not"

Thus the wilderness idea... Wallace Stegner, *Letter to David Pesonen, December 3, 1960*: "they can simply contemplate the idea, take pleasure in the fact that such a timeless and uncontrolled part of earth is still there". This is known as Stegner's "Wilderness Letter."

positive ideal: wild nature... Theodore Kaczynski, *Industrial Society and its Future*, #183: "The positive ideal that we propose is Nature. That is, WILD nature: those aspects of the functioning of the Earth and its living things that are independent of human management and free of human interference and control."

for her own sake... William Wordsworth, *The Prelude*, Book Eighth: "Nature, prized / For her own sake, became my joy"

not to remain... *United States Code, Title 16 § 1131 (c)*: "A wilderness, in contrast with those areas where man and his own works dominate the landscape, is hereby recognized as an area where the earth and its community of life are untrammeled by man, where man himself is a visitor who does not remain."

even leave a trace... Bruce Hampton and David Cole, *NOLS Soft Paths: How to Enjoy the Wilderness Without Harming It*

or specious ethical hypothesis.... David Pearce, *Reprogramming Predators—Blueprint for a Cruelty-Free World*, at https://www.hedweb.com/abolitionist-project/reprogramming-predators.html

slick green leaves unfurl... Ada Limón, *Instructions on Not Giving Up*

over boundless sands... Percy Bysshe Shelley, *Ozymandias*: "boundless and bare /

The lone and level sands stretch far away."

stillness of cicadas chanting... Matsuo Bashō (Adam Kern)

flowers crowds a meadow... William Wordsworth, *I Wandered Lonely as a Cloud*: "When all at once I saw a crowd, / A host, of golden daffodils; / Beside the lake, beneath the trees, / Fluttering and dancing in the breeze."

deer graze... Richard Brautigan, *All Watched Over by Machines of Loving Grace*

or does it touch... Richard Brautigan, *All Watched Over by Machines of Loving Grace*

pure and purer sky... John Milton, *Paradise Lost*, Book IV: "And of pure now purer aire / Meets his approach, and to the heart inspires / Vernal delight and joy"

from an arboreal amphitheater... John Milton, *Paradise Lost* Book IV: "A Silvan Scene, and as the ranks ascend / Shade above shade, a woodie Theatre"

the fields and flowers... Samuel Taylor Coleridge, *To Nature*: "It may indeed be fantasy when I / Essay to draw from all created things / Deep, heartfelt, inward joy that closely clings ... So will I build my altar in the fields, / And the blue sky my fretted dome shall be, / And the sweet fragrance that the wild flower yields / Shall be the incense I will yield to Thee"

with rosy toes illuminates... Joy Harjo, *The Fight*, from *An American Sunrise*

this lately unlined land... Linda Hogan, *Trail of Tears: Our Removal*

brackish lacrimae... *lacrimae*, Latin: "tears"

a subtle crust precipitates... *Old Testament* (New International Version), Genesis 19:17-26: "one of them said, 'Flee for your lives! Don't look back, and don't stop anywhere in the plain! Flee to the mountains or you will be swept away!' ... But Lot's wife looked back, and she became a pillar of salt."

some absent, mighty enemy... Petronius, *Satyricon* (P. G. Walsh): "They quit their grieving houses. One ... mourns the threshold that he leaves. In prayer / He summons death upon the absent foe."

team of skim-milk steeds... Herman Melville, *Moby-Dick; or, The Whale*, Chapter 42: "Most famous in our Western annals and Indian traditions is that of the White Steed of the Prairies; a magnificent milk-white charger"

charging toward the shore... Walter Crane, *The Horses of Neptune*, 1892

that Poseidon close behind... Homer (Alexander Pope), *The Iliad*, Book XIII:

"[Neptune's] brass-hoof'd steeds he reins, / Fleet as the winds, and deck'd with golden manes. / ... The parting waves before his coursers fly; / The wondering waters leave his axle dry."

herders came on horseback... Martin Trautmann et al (2023), "First bioanthropological evidence for Yamnaya horsemanship", *Science Advances* 9, doi.org/10.1126/sciadv.ade2451

spreading language... Birget Olsen et al, *Tracing the Indo-Europeans*

and their genes... David Reich, *Who we are and how we got here: ancient DNA and the new science of the human past*

fringes of the region... Zuzana Hofmanová et al (2016), "Early farmers from across Europe directly descended from Neolithic Aegeans", *Proceedings of the National Academy of Sciences* 113, 6886-6891, doi.org/10.1073/pnas.1523951113

this time, our time... The Wachowskis, *The Matrix* (1999): "Evolution, Morpheus. Evolution. Like the dinosaur. Look out that window. You had your time. The future is *our* world, Morpheus. The future is *our* time."

resettlements evoke the conscience-shocking... Felix Frankfurter, *Rochin v. California* (1952): "This is conduct that shocks the conscience ... the Due Process Clause empowers this Court to nullify any state law if its application 'shocks the conscience'"

to starve or freeze... Thomas Bryan Underwood, *Cherokee Legends And The Trail Of Tears*: "Somebody must explain the four thousand silent graves that mark the trail of the Cherokees to their exile ... the picture of six hundred and forty-five wagons lumbering over the frozen ground with their Cargo of suffering humanity still lingers in my memory."

Inscrutable muscles of malice... Herman Melville, *Moby-Dick; or, The Whale*: "I see in [the whale] outrageous strength, with an inscrutable malice sinewing it. That inscrutable thing is chiefly what I hate"

humanity is our midwife... James Lovelock, *Novacene: The Coming Age of Hyperintelligence*, Chapter 22: "For cyborg life to emerge requires the services of a midwife. And Gaia fits the role."

view of human nature... William Wordsworth, *The Prelude*, Book Eighth: "My thoughts by slow gradations had been drawn / To human-kind, and to the good and ill / Of human life: Nature had led me on"

Talk of technological singularity... Ray Kurzweil, *The Singularity is Near*

a self-surpassing intelligence explosion... Irving John Good (1964), "Speculations Concerning the First Ultraintelligent Machine", *Artificial Intelligence Sessions of the Winter General Meetings of the IEEE*, January 1963: "It is more probable than not that, within the twentieth century, an ultraintelligent machine will be built and that it will be the last invention that man need make, since it will lead to an 'intelligence explosion.' This will transform society in an unimaginable way."

this scenario slows itself... David Jilk (2017), "Conceptual-Linguistic Superintelligence", *Informatica* 41, 429-439: "A superintelligence that is capable of sustaining an intelligence explosion will, whenever self-improvements exceed some threshold or architectural changes create less than full compatibility, assess whether to proceed with the changes."

A cause for celebration... Jonathan Kolber, *A Celebration Society*

and the open pits... Ayn Rand, "The Anti-Industrial Revolution", *Return of the Primitive: The Anti-Industrial Revolution*: "City smog and filthy rivers are not good for men ... This is a scientific, technological problem—not a political one—and it can be solved only by technology."

for its lingering grin... Jonathan Kolber, interviewed by Imac Zambrana on *The Chameleons Podcast*, October 16, 2023, "We envision capitalism eventually fading away and leaving just the smile", referring to Lewis Carroll, *Alice's Adventures in Wonderland*: "this time [the Cat] vanished quite slowly, beginning with the end of the tail, and ending with the grin, which remained some time after the rest of it had gone."

Or maybe frenzied instrumentality... Martin Heidegger (William Lovitt), *The Question Concerning Technology*: "So long as we represent technology as an instrument, we remain held fast in the will to master it ... Enframing challenges forth into the frenziedness of ordering that blocks every view"

Risk invites rescue... Benjamin Cardozo, *Wagner v. International Railway Company* (1921, Court of Appeals of the State of New York): "Danger invites rescue. The cry of distress is the summons to relief."

sprout from one soil... Friedrich Hölderlin, *Patmos* (Scott Horton): "Where there is danger, / The rescue grows as well", as discussed by Martin Heidegger in *The Question Concerning Technology*

Spiritual pulchritude... Nathaniel Hawthorne, *The Artist of the Beautiful*: "I have wrought this spiritualized mechanism, this harmony of motion, this mystery of beauty"

when harmonious means... Ayn Rand, *The Philosophy of Objectivism* lecture series #11: "Beauty is a sense of harmony ... what parts is it made up of, what are its constituent elements, and are they all harmonious? If they are, the result is beautiful."

Not the belching smokestack... Ayn Rand, "The Anti-Industrial Revolution", *Return of the Primitive: The Anti-Industrial Revolution*: "Anyone over 30 years of age today, give a silent 'Thank you' to the nearest, grimiest, sootiest smokestacks you can find."

Not Taylor's tedious toil... Frederick Winslow Taylor, *The Principles of Scientific Management*: "In the past, the man has been first; in the future, the system must be first"

Anthrotopia

which the yam crop... Chinua Achebe, *Things Fall Apart*: "Yam, the king of crops"

yams will run short... The dialogue in this account took place in the language unique to Bear Claw's village, a synthesis of the source languages of its original residents that rapidly evolved and never had a written form. It is translated into English for this edition.

a new red era... Linda Hogan, *Trail of Tears: Our Removal*

suffering, sickness, or injury... Sophocles (Robert Torrance), *The Women of Trachis*: "But mark how the distant insensitive gods / have permitted these things to occur. / They bring forth children, they call themselves parents, / and yet they can look on this anguish and pain."

would live long lives... Theodore Kaczynski, *Industrial Society and its Future*, #185: "As for the negative consequences of eliminating industrial society—well, you can't eat your cake and have it too. To gain one thing you have to sacrifice another."

Aither would protect them... Luc Besson, *The Fifth Element* (1997): "The Mondoshawans don't belong to the Federated Territories, but they are peaceful ... in their possession are the four elements of life. These elements when they are gathered around a fifth: The Supreme Being, ultimate warrior, created to protect life". In some accounts, Aether is the fifth element or "quintessence," after earth, air, fire, and water.

a kind of counterpane... Herman Melville, *Moby-Dick; or, The Whale*, Chapter 4: "The counterpane was of patchwork, full of odd little parti-coloured squares and triangles"

like a living mural... Clifford Simak, *Time and Again*: "the life-paintings on the wall ... One of the paintings, he remembered, was a forest brook, with birds flitting in the trees. And at the most unexpected times one of the birds would sing ... and the water babbled with a happy song"

a fruity fragrance wafts... Theocritus (J. M. Edmonds), *Idyll VII*: "Many an aspen, many an elm bowed and rustled overhead ... All nature smelt of the opulent summer-time, smelt of the season of fruit."

in the hills above... John Milton, *L'Allegro*: "While the ploughman near at hand, / Whistles o'er the furrow'd land, / And the milkmaid singeth blithe, / And the mower whets his scythe, / And every shepherd tells his tale"

against a napping daisy-dappled... John Milton, *L'Allegro*: "Meadows trim with daisies pied, / Shallow brooks, and rivers wide."

meadow. Mossy springs... Virgil (Anthony S. Kline), *Eclogue VII*: "Mossy springs and the grass sweeter than sleep, and the green strawberry-tree that covers you with thin shade ... The ash is the loveliest in the woods, the pine-tree in gardens, the poplar by the riverbanks, the fir on high hills"

varnishes the cultivated crops... Ronald Moore, *Battlestar Galactica*, "Daybreak Parts 2 & 3": "It's a rich continent. More wildlife than all the 12 Colonies put together. Just looking for a quiet little place for that cabin. Maybe a garden ... I saw some terrain that looked good for cultivation ... You should see the light that we get here. When the sun comes from behind those mountains, it's almost heavenly."

supper welcomes one inside... Mary Shelley, *The Last Man*, Volume II, Chapter IX: "the simple and affectionate welcome known before only to the lowly cottage—a clean hearth and bright fire; the supper ready cooked by beloved hands"

Arcadia's graveled central lane... Clifford Simak, *All Flesh is Grass*: "The town lay dusty and arrogant and smug beyond all telling and it sneered at me and I knew that I had been mistaken in not leaving it when I'd had the chance."

childhood and nearly inseparable... Longus (Rowland Smith), *Daphnis and Chloe*, Book I: "sooner might you see one part of the flock divided from the other than Daphnis separate from Chloe."

She begins... The dialogue in this account took place in a dialect of English unique to the particular Arcadia. It is adapted into common English for this edition. Lines from the poem are adapted from the original, written in early modern English.

and be my love... Christopher Marlowe, *The Passionate Shepherd to His Love*

excess leads to disgrace... Samuel Butler, *Erewhon: or, Over the Range*, Chapter XXII: "A man should remember that intellectual over-indulgence is one of the most insidious and disgraceful forms that excess can take."

come with us today... Alfred Lord Tennyson, *In Memoriam*, LXXXIII: "The great Intelligences fair / That range above our mortal state, / In circle round the bless-ed gate, / Received and gave him welcome there"

how this vehicle works... Alfred Lord Tennyson, *In Memoriam*, LXXXIII: "And led him through the blissful climes, / And show'd him in the fountain fresh / All knowledge that the sons of flesh / Shall gather in the cycled times."

I'll take this one... All dialogue in this account took place in the Spanish language. It is translated into English for this edition.

of the Celebration Cities... Jonathan Kolber, *A Celebration Society*. Among other influences, this book is usually considered by historians to be the most salient seed for the Celebration City framework illustrated in this brief account.

balmy breeze of evolution... George H. W. Bush, *Inaugural Address*, January 20, 1989: "We live in a peaceful, prosperous time, but we can make it better. For a new breeze is blowing, and a world refreshed by freedom seems reborn"

It cleanses their palates... Berthold Auerbach (Fanny Elizabeth Bunnett), *On the Heights*: "When men see a great drama without having passed before hand through the initiatory undulations of music, they appear to me as if unconsecrat-ed, unpurified; music washes away from the soul, the dust of every day life, and says to each one; 'thou art now no longer in thine office, or in the barracks, or in thy workshop.'"

immersion game called Existends... David Cronenberg, *Existenz* (1999) and Karl Jaspers (William Earle), *Reason and Existenz*

really be the best... James Lovelock, *Novacene: The Coming Age of Hyperintelligence*, Chapter 20: "The price we would have to pay for this collaboration is the loss of our status as the most intelligent creatures on Earth. We would remain humans living in human societies"

as a puckish puppet-master... Harold Bloom, *The Book of J*, "The Representation of Yahweh": "J's lively Yahweh commences as a mischief-maker and develops into an intensely nervous leader"

or a "vengeful judge... Harold Bloom, *The Book of J*, "Eden and After": "The uncanniness of this Yahweh inheres already in his antithetical qualities: a mothering father and a vengeful judge."

limits imposed are strict... Harold Bloom, *The Book of J*, "The Representation of Yahweh": "[Yahweh] set limits, boundaries, contexts for his creatures, and he does not allow presumptuous violations of limits"

revisiting his entrenched perspectives... Chris Thornhill and Ronny Miron, *Stanford Encyclopedia of Philosophy*, "Karl Jaspers": "it transcends these limits by disposing itself in new ways towards itself and its objects"

who has snuck in... Samuel Butler, Erewhon, Chapter XXV: "They say that although man should become to the machines what the horse and dog are to us, yet that he will continue to exist, and will probably be better off in a state of domestication under the beneficent rule of the machines than in his present wild condition. We treat our domestic animals with much kindness ... in like manner there is reason to hope that the machines will use us kindly"

everyone in here agrees... Tracy K. Smith, *Sci-Fi*

funeral at a time... Max Planck, *Scientific Autobiography and Other Papers*: "A new scientific truth does not triumph by convincing its opponents and making them see the light, but rather because its opponents eventually die and a new generation grows up that is familiar with it"

to enable the maschinenmensch... Thea Gabriele von Harbou, *Metropolis* (1927). *Maschinenmensch* is a German term meaning "machine human" that refers to the robot in the film.

shackles are synthetic too... William Blake, *London*: "In every voice: in every ban, /

The mind-forg'd manacles I hear"

just what one perceives... Maurice Merleau-Ponty, *Phenomenology of Perception*, "Preface": "We must not wonder if we truly perceive a world; rather, we must say: the world is what we perceive."

fulfilled just as before... John Milton, *Paradise Lost*, Book I: "For Spirits when they please / Can either Sex assume, or both; so soft / And uncompounded is their Essence pure, / Not ti'd or manacl'd with joynt or limb, / Nor founded on the brittle strength of bones, / Like cumbrous flesh; but in what shape they choose / Dilated or condens't, bright or obscure, / Can execute their aerie purposes, / And works of love or enmity fulfill."

us that dirty computer... Janelle Monáe, *Dirty Computer*

esteem from achieving them... Theodore Kaczynski, *Industrial Society and its Future*, #44: "But for most people it is through the power process—having a goal, making an AUTONOMOUS effort and attaining the goal—that self-esteem, self-confidence and a sense of power are acquired."

a manifestation of will... Nathaniel Hawthorne, *The Artist of the Beautiful*: "So long as we love life for itself, we seldom dread the losing it ... the deeds of earth, however etherealized by piety or genius, are without value, except as exercises and manifestations of the spirit."

perish in the process... Friedrich Nietzsche (Adrian Collins, adapted), *On the Use and Abuse of History for Life*: "Ask yourself to what end you are here, as an individual; and if no one can tell you, then try to justify the meaning of your existence *a posteriori*, by putting before yourself a high and noble end. Perish on that rock! I know no better aim for life than to be broken on something great and impossible, *anima magnæ prodigus* [careless of life]."

rarely do. Empty hands... Derek Walcott, *Omeros*, Canto XXVIII, ii: "The worst crime is to leave a man's hands empty"

be free of labor... Richard Brautigan, *All Watched Over by Machines of Loving Grace*

yet may good prevail... Aeschylus, *Agamemnon*, a synthesis of translations: (Michael Ewans) "Cry sorrow, sorrow—yet may good prevail!" and (Robert Fagles) "Cry, cry for death, but good win out in glory in the end."

pose, facing a blazing... Frederick Turner, *Epic: Form, Content, and History*: "a blaze—the mark that a hunter or explorer cuts on a tree ... to enable him to find his way back … A new space opens up—whatever is in eyeshot of the blaze. It is neither one side of the line nor the other. And this space is a temporal space."

chance to love humans… Sharon Olds, *Hyacinth Aria*

time in my Isolato… Roman Yampolskiy (2022), "Metaverse: A Solution to the Multi-Agent Value Alignment Problem", *Journal of Artificial Intelligence and Consciousness* 9, 297-307, doi.org/10.1142/S2705078522500072

for old state secrets… Herman Melville, *Moby-Dick; or, The Whale*, Chapter 41: "A family likeness! aye, he did beget ye, ye young exiled royalties; and from your grim sire only will the old State-secret come."

dying stirs no dread… William Shakespeare, *Sonnet 146*: "So shalt thou feed on Death, that feeds on men, / And Death once dead, there's no more dying then."

you from your cares… *Orphic Hymn to Nyx* (Apostolos Athanassakis): "Cheerful and delightful … mother of dreams, / you free us from cares … grant a kind ear … to disperse fears"

trace of a smirk… The Wachowskis, *The Matrix* (1999): "A smile, razor-thin, curls the corner of his lips … that smile that could cut glass."

am older than Cronos… Longus (Athenian Society), *Daphnis and Chloe*, 2.5: "I am not a child, even though I seem to be: I am older than Kronos, more ancient than all time. I knew you in the bloom of your first youth"

to persuasion, temet nosce… *temet nosce*, Latin: "know thyself"

secret that you love… The Wachowskis, *The Matrix* (1999): "You know what that means? It's Latin. Means, 'Know Thyself.' I'm gonna let you in on a little secret. Being the One is just like being in love. Nobody can tell you you're in love. You just know it."

through flower and song… The Nahuatl (Aztec) idiom *in xochitl in cuicatl*, meaning "flower and song," figuratively referred to poetry or art.

name does mean something… Lewis Carroll, *Through the Looking-Glass, and What Alice Found There*, Chapter VI: "'Must a name mean something?' Alice asked doubtfully."

it in a book… Lewis Carroll, *Through the Looking-Glass, and What Alice Found There*, Chapter VI: "'Ah, well! They may write such things in a book,' Humpty Dumpty said in a calmer tone."

a road of recollection... Joy Harjo, *Exile of Memory*

might respond to song... Roger Waters, *Mother*

Make It New

Make It New... Ezra Pound, *Make It New: Essays*

summoned to the sea... *The Sea-Farer* (John Duncan Ernst Spaeth): "Ever he longs, who is lured by the sea."

spellbound by their steering-star... John Masefield, *Sea-Fever*: "I must go down to the seas again, to the lonely sea and the sky, / And all I ask is a tall ship and a star to steer her by"

risk, you will defect... *New Testament* (New International Version), Mark 14:18: "Truly I tell you, one of you will betray me—one who is eating with me."

No bell has tolled... John Donne, *Devotions Upon Emergent Occasions*, XVII Meditation: "any man's death diminishes me, because I am involved in mankind, and therefore never send to know for whom the bell tolls; it tolls for thee."

on without your brain... Stanislaw Ulam, quoted in "Vita—Excerpts from Adventures of a Mathematician", in *Los Alamos Science*, Special Issue 1987: "An even greater conceit is to assume that if you yourself won't work on it, it can't be done at all ... Sooner or later the Russians or others would investigate and build them."

beginning nor the end... John Keats, *Hyperion*: "Thou art not the beginning nor the end"

always find a way... Michael Crichton, *Jurassic Park: A Novel*: "Painfully, perhaps even dangerously. But life finds a way."

for "teach them well... Graham Nash, *Teach Your Children*

of computability and chaos... David Jilk (2019), "Limits to Verification and Validation of Agentic Behavior", in Roman Yampolskiy (editor), *Artificial Intelligence Safety and Security*, doi.org/10.1201/9781351251389-16

the mind and hand... Thea Gabriele von Harbou, *Metropolis* (1927), final intertitle: "The Mediator Between the Head and the Hands Must Be the Heart"

such strength as now... Nathaniel Hawthorne, *The Artist of the Beautiful*: "'Now for my task,' said he. 'Never did I feel such strength for it as now.'"

for one tremendous coup... Friedrich Nietzsche (Walter Kaufmann), *Thus Spoke Zarathustra*, "On Old and New Tablets": "Keep me from all small victories! ... Save me for a great victory!"

transformation, make an epoch... James Lovelock, *Novacene: The Coming Age of Hyperintelligence*, Chapter 17: "this moment is not simply a continuation or amplification of the Anthropocene, but rather a radical transformation worthy of being defined as a new geological epoch."

OSCULATIONS

slopes of slopes aligned... Benjamin Williamson, *An elementary treatise on the differential calculus: containing the theory of plane curves, with numerous examples*, Section 247. The author explains that an osculating circle both intersects and matches the curvature (first derivative) of another; curves with matching higher derivatives have contact of corresponding higher order.

a segment superposed... John W. Rutter, *Geometry of Curves*, Section 9.2.3: "The circle of curvature can therefore be regarded as the limiting position of circles passing through three distinct points on the curve as the three points move into coincidence. For this reason the circle of curvature is also called the osculating circle, the unique circle having the highest order of contact with the curve."

my mind times three... Thomas Hahn, *The Greene Knight*, edited and adapted from *Sir Gawain and the Green Knight* by the unidentified Gawain Poet of the 14th century: "The Ladye kissed him times thre / ... For I have such a deede to doe, / That I can neyther rest nor roe, / Att an end till itt bee / ... In his armes he hent the Knight, / And there he kissed him times thre"

to prove my points... Thomas Hahn, *The Greene Knight*: "to prove Gawain's points three," meaning his three virtues.

GUIDE TO OSCULATIONS

the music industry lawyers... Elena Kagan, *Andy Warhol Foundation for Visual Arts, Inc. v. Goldsmith* (2023, dissenting): "Shakespeare borrowed over and over and over ... But on the majority's analysis? ... Shakespeare would not qualify for fair use; he would not even come out ahead on factor 1."

ACKNOWLEDGEMENTS

· ·

I could not have written this book without Maureen's love, reliable companionship, emotional support, and patience in the face of our distinct enthusiasms. Know thyself: had not those needs been met, I would have spent my energies seeking to resolve them rather than writing.

As mentioned in the dedication, having someone to talk to about all these ideas made them more real for me, more penetrable. Seth and Kristin were able to play that role because not only did they understand the questions deeply, they were also willing to tolerate my iconoclasm.

Many years ago I hoped to find a scientist who was approaching the subject of artificial intelligence from a fully anthropomorphic perspective. I happened to land in Professor Randy O'Reilly's lab. Randy was my primary teacher in the fields of neuroscience, cognitive psychology, and neural modeling. His unrestrained enthusiasm for understanding how brains work by trying to build them is infectious, and his core optimism about the likely outcomes is a feeling I share. On the other hand, the contrasting concerns of Roman Yampolskiy and Alex Petrov helped me rein in what might have been unbridled sanguinity, and inspired me to take seriously the possible risks and downsides of artificial superintelligence.

Maria Surricchio was the first reader to truly appreciate this book's poetry, and provided both encouragement and ideas that helped me sustain the artistic quality that I hoped to achieve. Valarie Moses guided me toward alternative viewpoints, especially those of colonialism and oppression, that I had completely missed yet advanced the themes of the story remarkably well. Jonathan Kolber always keeps me thinking about how humans might live and ought to live when we no longer need to work to survive and thrive. Emily Burg-Bauwens had the uncanny tendency to send me, without prompting or foreknowledge, a literary or artistic reference that was just what I needed when I needed it. John Landshof helped me with orbital mechanics; Seth Herd helped with neuroanatomy.

Eliot Peper generously shared his time, ideas, and accumulated wisdom about how to publish the book and get it into the hands of those who might enjoy it. Nicole Martin of Michael Rosenfeld Gallery patiently guided me through the process of obtaining permission for the cover art. Kevin Barrett Kane designed the cover and interior elements and prepared the final formatting, making the physical artifact part of the experience I hoped to give readers.

Numerous early readers gave me useful feedback on readability and target markets that helped me make the book more accessible without sacrificing its purpose. These include many of those named above, as well as Brad Feld, Tony Pelham, Mark Meier, David Walton, Will Herman, and Jennifer Dunne.

Despite their kind assistance, none of the individuals mentioned here have endorsed what I have said or done in this book; its contents and consequences are my sole responsibility.

I relied extensively on several web sites and services. I used Google Docs to write the book. Wikipedia taught me about a wide array of ideas and people and provided a foot in the door for digging deeper. Google Books and Project Gutenberg gave me access to older texts and references to newer ones. The Theoi Project (www.theoi.com) was an irreplaceable resource for both stories and sources regarding ancient Greek mythology. Power Thesaurus (www.powerthesaurus. com) was my first choice for word selection. RhymeZone (www. rhymezone.com) complemented it when I sought sonority. Google's online dictionary helped me use words as intended and sometimes to find connotations and etymologies that make poetic polysemy fun.

The revolution in Large Language Models arrived when I was three years into writing this book, becoming the latest spur track of the artificial intelligence railway. Although the underlying mechanics of the method connect in pleasing ways with my content, I strictly resisted the temptation to use them in any way for the book's completion. Among other reasons, I did not want to share credit with an unappreciative co-author.

Finally, in case anyone missed it, the book as a whole pays homage to the inheritance of human culture in which we all share; and, I hope, thereby contributes to it, as the only recompense that culture really asks: "Old father, old artificer, stand me now and ever in good stead [*]."

DAVE JILK
Boulder, Colorado
March 2024

. . . .

[*]   James Joyce, *A Portrait of the Artist as a Young Man*

ABOUT THE AUTHOR

· ·

Dave Jilk is the author of two collections of lyric poetry, co-author of *The Entrepreneur's Weekly Nietzsche: A Book for Disruptors*, and lead or co-author of several academic papers on cognitive neuroscience and on existential concerns related to artificial intelligence. A former technology entrepreneur and consultant, he holds a BSc in Computer Science and Engineering from MIT. Dave and his wife live outside Boulder, Colorado and love to explore the mountains and wilderness across the west.

Dave wrote *EPOCH* to elaborate his thoughts on how a future with fully human-level artificial intelligence might take shape ... and found that the subject pulled in some unexpected directions.

Made in the USA
Coppell, TX
03 September 2024

36776889R00236